A Fatal Fleece

A Fatal Fleece

A SEASIDE KNITTERS MYSTERY

Sally Goldenbaum

AN OBSIDIAN MYSTERY

OBSIDIAN
Published by New American Library,
a division of Penguin Group (USA) Inc.,
375 Hudson Street, New York, New York 10014, USA
Penguin Group (Canada), 90 Eglinton Avenue East, Suite 700, Toronto,
Ontario M4P 2Y3, Canada (a division of Pearson Penguin Canada Inc.)
Penguin Books Ltd., 80 Strand, London WC2R 0RL, England
Penguin Ireland, 25 St. Stephen's Green, Dublin 2,
Ireland (a division of Penguin Books Ltd.)
Penguin Group (Australia), 250 Camberwell Road, Camberwell,
Victoria 3124, Australia (a division of Pearson Australia Group Pty. Ltd.)
Penguin Books India Pvt. Ltd., 11 Community Centre,
Panchsheel Park, New Delhi - 110 017, India
Penguin Group (NZ), 67 Apollo Drive, Rosedale, Auckland 0632,
New Zealand (a division of Pearson New Zealand Ltd.)
Penguin Books (South Africa) (Pty.) Ltd., 24 Sturdee Avenue,
Rosebank, Johannesburg 2196, South Africa

Penguin Books Ltd., Registered Offices:
80 Strand, London WC2R 0RL, England

First published by Obsidian, an imprint of New American Library,
a division of Penguin Group (USA) Inc.

First Printing, May 2012
1   3   5   7   9   10   8   6   4   2

LIBRARY OF CONGRESS CATALOGING-IN-PUBLICATION DATA:
Goldenbaum, Sally.
A fatal fleece: a seaside knitters mystery/Sally Goldenbaum.
p. cm.
"An Obsidian mystery."
ISBN 978-0-451-23675-3
1. Knitters (Persons)—Fiction. 2. Recluses—Fiction. 3. Right of property—Fiction. 4. Murder—
Investigation—Fiction. 5. City and town life—Massachusetts—Fiction. I. Title.
PS3557.O35937F38 2012
813'.54—dc22   2011049867

Set in Palatino   ·   Designed by Elke Sigal

Printed in the United States of America

To Luke, Atti, Ruby, and Jules—
the dazzling lights in my life

Acknowledgments

First, grateful thanks to Cheryl Erlandson, a talented designer and owner of In the Loop yarn shop in Norfolk, Massachusetts, who designed Gabby's purple sweater in *A Fatal Fleece*. Along with Gabby (and Birdie, Nell, Izzy, and Cass), I thank her for sharing her artistry with all of us. Visit the In the Loop shop Web site: keepyourneedles happy.com/shop/. A special thanks to Mary Bednarowski, Nancy Pickard, and Sr. Rosemary Flanigan, who spent lots of time with me and with Finnegan, the old fisherman in *A Fatal Fleece*, exploring his life and his relationships and helping me figure out what he was all about. As always, thanks to my supportive, wise, and intuitive anchors—Andrea Cirillo and Christina Hogrebe—and to the wonderful Sandy Harding, whose magical spin brings the best out of my words. Thanks to my friends and to my family—Todd and Laila, Aria and John, Danny and Claud—and always, always, to Don. They truly make this whole business a family affair.

Cast of Characters

THE SEASIDE KNITTERS

Nell Endicott: Former Boston nonprofit director, semiretired and living in Sea Harbor with her husband

Izzy (Isabel Chambers Perry): Boston attorney, now owner of the Seaside Knitting Studio; Nell and Ben Endicott's niece; recently married to Sam Perry

Cass (Catherine Mary Elizabeth Halloran): A lobster fisherwoman, born and raised in Sea Harbor

Birdie (Bernadette Favazza): Sea Harbor's wealthy, wise, and generous silver-haired grande dame

THE MEN IN THEIR LIVES

Ben Endicott: Nell's husband

Sam Perry: Award-winning photojournalist married to Izzy

Danny Brandley: Mystery novelist and son of bookstore owners

Sonny Favazza and Joseph Marietti: Two of Birdie's deceased husbands

SUPPORTING CAST

Alphonso Santos: Wealthy construction company owner; once married to Sophia Santos, then Liz Palazola; Gracie Santos' uncle

Andy Risso: Drummer in Pete Halloran's band; son of Jake Risso

Annabelle Palazola: Owner of the Sweet Petunia restaurant; Liz and Sheila Palazola's mother

Angus McPherran: Enigmatic old man called the Old Man of the Sea by the locals

Archie and Harriet Brandley: Owners of the Sea Harbor Bookstore

August (Gus) McClucken: Owner of McClucken's Hardware on Harbor Road

Beatrice and Sal Scaglia: Councilwoman and her husband, manager of the town's deeds annex

Beverly Walden: Artist; Moira Finnegan's daughter

D. J. Delaney: Owner of Delaney & Sons Construction; wife, Maeve; son, Davey

Ella and Harold Sampson: Birdie's longtime housekeeper and groundsman

Esther Gibson: Police dispatcher (and Mrs. Santa Claus during holiday season)

Father Lawrence Northcutt: Pastor of Our Lady of Safe Seas Church

Finnegan: An old fisherman and longtime resident

Gabrielle Marietti: Birdie's ten-year-old granddaughter

Harry and Margaret Garozzo: Owners of Garozzo's Deli

Jane and Ham Brewster: Former Berkeley hippies, artists, and cofounders of the Canary Cove Art Colony

Jake Risso: Owner of the Gull Tavern

Jerry Thompson: Police chief

Laura Danvers: Young socialite and philanthropist, mother of three, married to banker Elliot Danvers

Mae Anderson: Izzy's shop manager; twin teenage nieces, Jillian and Rose

Mary Pisano: Middle-aged newspaper columnist; owner of the Ravenswood B and B

Mary Halloran: Pete and Cass' mother; secretary of Our Lady of Safe Seas Church

Merry Jackson: Owner of the Artist's Palate Bar & Grill

M. J. Arcado: Owner of M.J.'s Salon

Nick Marietti: Birdie's brother-in-law

Pete Halloran: Cass' younger brother and lead guitarist in the Fractured Fish band

Rebecca (Marks) Early: Lampwork artist in Canary Cove

Tommy Porter: Young policeman

Willow Adams: Fiber artist and owner of the Fishtail Gallery

A Fatal Fleece

Chapter 1

In Birdie Favazza's mind, city council meetings were about as bland as white bread. But tonight's meeting, from which she was mysteriously absent, would surely make her eat her words.

"He's gone loony tunes, that's what. The old codger has a screw loose." D. J. Delaney's booming voice echoed off the walls of the city hall meeting room.

Finnegan's land was the last item on the night's short docket, and most people had stayed to hear what the council would decide to do about it. Or perhaps that's why they'd come in the first place.

"It's such a small stretch of land," Nell Endicott had said to her husband as they drove the short distance from their house to city hall.

"But positioned perfectly between Canary Cove Road and the sea," Ben replied. "A diamond in the rough. Everyone wants a piece of it."

The energetic crowd of Sea Harbor residents had concurred as they sat shoulder to shoulder in the heated room, many with their own imagined plans for how it would be used—once they wrested it away from the crazy old man who lived there, that was.

A developer's dream.

Revenue for the town.

A fancy strip of shops? A small inn, perhaps?

Expensive summer condos.

Or a park with play equipment, a wading pool, and a skating rink in winter.

"I've offered the guy everything but my firstborn," D.J. continued, his eyes blazing. The developer sat near the front of the crowd, his wife, Maeve, at his side. "He won't listen to reason. People would kill for that land."

"Well, let's hope not," Ben Endicott said. His voice was a fan cooling the room's heated air. The voice of reason in the tempest the land debate had churned up.

"I say we concentrate on the new community garden," Ben continued. "Get everyone involved. Make it spectacular. It will butt right up to Finnegan's place, and once he sees those juicy Big Boys bending the vines, he'll come around and clean up his place—I'll bet on it. After all, that's what we all really want. Right?"

Nell held back a smile. No, that wasn't what they really wanted, and Ben knew it as well as anyone. No one would object to the unsightly acres being cleaned up, true. But what many really wanted was what they saw when they looked at the land: dollar signs. Lots of them.

"Maybe Finnegan would help with the garden," Willow Adams said hopefully. The young fiber artist liked the old man, and the complaints against him offended her. But even Willow had to admit that the land was an eyesore.

Next to her, Beverly Walden was still. Although the artist kept her opinions to herself, her face was as graphic as her contemporary paintings: bright, bold, and expressive. And from what Nell Endicott could tell from across the room, her expression confirmed the rumors that rumbled up and down the winding, narrow streets of Canary Cove: Beverly Walden didn't like Finnegan. And from all reports, the feeling was mutual.

A possible Greek tragedy in the making, because Beverly Walden was Finnegan and his late wife, Moira's, only child.

"I know the land's a problem," the police chief, Jerry Thompson, said from his chair near the front of the room. His calm voice brought everyone to attention. "It's not looking so great, sure, but Finn will come around."

"That land used to be so fine, just like the other places down there—neat little offices with flower boxes in front," Archie Brandley, the Sea Harbor Bookstore owner, said, rising from his chair. His head nodded with each word, and he looked down at his wife, Harriet. "Remember? Finn had that little bait shop, and Moira handed out hot dogs to fishermen, right along with the worms. She never took a dime for the dogs, only the bait."

Murmurs of agreement mixed with some chuckles rippled through the crowd from those who remembered the days when life moved a little slower—and later ones, too, when it was cheaper to buy bait from the bigger places in town and Finnegan finally closed the shop and decided to fish full-time. But Moira declared that very spot her favorite place on God's earth. So Finnegan renovated the building. He fixed up the first floor with a couple of offices for rent, and moved Moira from a small cottage above the Canary Cove Art Colony to the spacious top floor with the million-dollar view. Nothing but miles of blue and squabbles of gulls overhead. Fishing boats moving back and forth. And around the building, lots of green space and rosebushes, which Moira tended.

"It was after his Moira died that things got bad," Harry Garozzo, owner of the deli on Harbor Road, said. "Damn cancer took her and might as well have taken Finn, too—for a while, anyway."

Nell remembered hearing the stories. Moira's death was the beginning. And soon the land became a jungle of sea grass and broken bottles—a place for kids to hide a six-pack late at night or drifters to seek shelter, until driven away by Finnegan's BB gun. Eventually ocean winds ripped the paint from the cottage by the sea, and it decayed into a shack where drifters sometimes slept when the ocean's freezing gusts drove them inside and the owner was absent.

And old man Finnegan refused to clean it up.

He also refused to give it up, though the offers to buy the land would have made him a rich man.

Instead, he put up a wire fence that held in the weeds, trash trees, and tall, wavy grass. At the gate he fastened a NO TRESPASSING sign. Outside the fence, passersby—joggers and strollers, vacationers headed toward the Canary Cove art galleries—caught glimpses of Finnegan fiddling with rusted boat parts and lobster pots and bales of old fishing rope. Sometimes he'd be whistling, sometimes muttering to himself.

But no one ever saw him mowing the waist-high grass that offered him the privacy he coveted.

Sometimes at night, folks dining at the Ocean's Edge harbor restaurant would look out over the water and see him silhouetted against the lights, a bent black shape sitting on the end of his weather-beaten dock, scanning the sky with an old pair of binoculars, searching the sky for new planets.

Or maybe for his Moira.

"Finnegan can be downright nasty," Beatrice Scaglia said, not buying the love story that may have informed his land. She sat at the curved table in the front of the room, her red fingernails tapping on the wooden surface near the microphone. The councilwoman was impeccably dressed in a white linen suit, though the other council members sported knit shirts and khakis or cotton skirts and blouses. "We've had dozens of complaints and so have the police. And when Sergeant Tommy Porter, dressed in full uniform, stopped by to discuss them politely with him, he practically forced Tommy off his land." Her hand flapped through the air in the direction of the young policeman.

"I wonda what he's hiding out there." This came from the owner of a pizzeria on the edge of town, who'd been trying to get a place near the water for years. "Maybe he's, well, you know, growing somethin'. Maybe those weeds are hiding more than old lobsta traps. . . ." His words hung suggestively over the crowd.

What nonsense, Nell thought. She removed a nearly finished lace scarf from the bag at her feet. Knitting brought a calmness to her spirit, and all this negative talk about a decent man who liked his privacy was beginning to rile her up.

Beatrice Scaglia pulled the microphone closer but waited for a few moments, allowing the pizzeria owner's words to settle on anyone who might need further convincing that someone, somehow, needed to persuade Finnegan to vacate his land and allow it to be used sensibly. Finally she said, "I think we may need to impose serious fines on Finnegan, ones that will convince him to sell the property and move on with his life."

In the front row, an old man pushed himself up to a standing position, his white beard creating the illusion of Santa Claus himself. He leaned on a carved walking stick to keep his balance. Angus McPherran rarely showed up at public functions, and his presence caused a hush to fall over the room.

"Finn's mad because the police took away his driver's license," Angus said. "Had to be done, but it made him wicked mad. So he doesn't want any patrolman knocking on his door. He wonders what you're gonna take away next.

"And then there's the rest of you, pushing your way onto his property, trying to buy it out from under him to make yourselves rich. Shame on you." He threw a pointed look at D. J. Delaney, the developer, then went on. "So he doesn't want to pretty up the place. So what? That's his God-given right. It's his land, for chrissake."

Those gathered in the council meeting room nodded at the mention of Finnegan's driver's license. Everyone had heard about the day Chief Jerry Thompson said, "That's it, Finn," and took his license away forever. The bent lamppost in front of Harry Garozzo's deli was just a small reminder of Finnegan's slow responses and careless driving, not to mention the fear that rippled up and down Harbor Road when he'd come around the corner in his beat-up Chevy pickup. The chief had bought him a ten-speed bicycle with his own money to soften the blow, but Finn would often sit up in the cab of his truck, now a fixture on the weed-encrusted land, as if it somehow gave him back his freedom.

"Just leave the old coot be," Angus said. He gave another withering look toward D.J., then lowered his body back down onto the chair.

Subdued chuckles passed through the crowd when Angus called Finnegan old. Angus himself—the Old Man of the Sea, as the kids called him—was old enough that no one even tried to remember the exact year he was born. Angus had been around forever, was the way people looked at it. And his generosity to the city made people not ask his age but defer to him instead.

"No disrespect to you, Angus," Beatrice Scaglia said, "but the place has become an eyesore, plain and simple—and that *is* our business." One long red fingernail tapped on the table.

"I suppose it's not the best thing for Colony Cove," Ham Brewster admitted. Ham spoke with reluctance. He liked Finn well enough, just as most of the Canary Cove artists did. Finnegan was their self-appointed watchdog and street cleaner, fixing shutters and cleaning up the paper cups and lobster roll wrappings that tourists sometimes tossed in the narrow streets of the art colony. Finnegan's wife, Moira, had been an artist, he often told them—and it's what she'd have wanted him to do.

Nell watched Jane Brewster, a dear friend, cast her eyes to the floor. Jane agreed with what her husband said, but she didn't like herself for it. She and Ham headed the Canary Cove Arts Association—housed in a very neat building on the other side of Finn's land—and had worked hard to make the colony successful, safe, and beautiful. Finnegan's land was becoming a deterrent to business and an eyesore to all of them.

"And it's a hotbed for riffraff," Jake Risso, owner of the Gull Tavern, spoke up. Again, with some reluctance. "Not Finn's fault, but when I'm out in the boat I can see 'em, bums trying to hunker down over there. They think it's abandoned—"

"And, therefore, theirs," Beatrice said. "And it's not good for Finn himself. Just two weeks ago someone showed up in that rotted building and Finn caused an awful ruckus."

The crowd turned to look at Tommy Porter, the young policeman who had stopped the fight. If he hadn't, he'd told the reporter who dutifully wrote it up for the newspaper, the guy might not have seen the light of a new day. Finn was fuming mad, and the bum had a broken nose to show for it.

Tommy nodded at the attention, but declined from adding to the discussion.

Nell settled back in the chair, lulled by the buzz of conversation around her. She didn't often come to council meetings, agreeing with Birdie's evaluation, but Ben was chairing the new Parks and Open Spaces Committee, and his community garden idea was a brilliant one. She had come to support his plans, hoping it would overshadow the debate over Finnegan's run-down property.

But it hadn't, and now the comments in the room were less about assigning garden plots, building pathways, and bringing in mulch, and far more about ousting an old man from his rightful property.

Nell often jogged along the path that bordered the land in question. She understood clearly why people were upset. The whole area was seedy and unkempt. Beatrice Scaglia had hired teenagers to go in and mow the grass—a favor, Nell supposed, to townspeople who took their complaints to the councilwoman. Beatrice knew well that favors encouraged people to vote her way when election time came around.

But then, a while back, the fence went up and Beatrice's mowing stopped.

Directly across the room from Nell, Cass Halloran stood with her back against the wall, next to Danny Brandley. She looked distant, as if she were there in body but not much else. Every now and then Danny would glance down at her as if her mood were passing from her body into his own. His expression carried worry. Worry for Cass, Nell suspected. The mystery writer's affection for Nell's favorite lobsterwoman had ripened right along with his own successful career, and what Cass worried about, he probably did, too.

The burden of keeping the Hallorans' lobster business alive and thriving was a heavy one. Not an easy task in today's world.

Izzy Perry, owner of the Seaside Knitting Studio, wasn't at the meeting because her shop was still open and busy with vacationers getting started on knitting projects, but she'd promised to meet Nell and Cass and other friends for dinner. She sent her husband, Sam, to the meeting in her stead. Sam, as was his way, stood in the back, a camera hanging from a strap around his neck, just in case. Tonight Sam's camera went unattended as he listened intently to the conversation.

Birdie was absent, too, though she said she was coming. But when Nell had called earlier to offer her a ride, Ella, the housekeeper, said Birdie had received a phone call that sent her upstairs to shower, and then she was gone. Off without a word of explanation.

And Miss Birdie rarely showered in the middle of the day, Ella had shared.

Nell smiled as she recalled the tone in Ella's voice. Crisp and disapproving. Ella usually knew exactly where Birdie was, and that's the way she—and her husband and groundskeeper, Harold—liked it.

But Birdie and Izzy were among the minority missing the meeting. Many of the Canary Cove artists were there, and one whole row was filled with longtime residents who lived in the neighborhood above Canary Cove—the old captains' homes that had been redone and refurbished into coveted family homes—and a newer neighborhood just across the cove.

At the end of the row was Sal Scaglia, who with his wife had recently renovated one of those homes and turned it into a Sea Harbor showplace. He sat with a notebook on his lap, his dark-rimmed glasses in place, and his attention focused on his wife, Beatrice. He reminded Nell of a faithful pup, although she knew Sal wouldn't find that flattering. But he was exactly that: always there at the meetings, always at Beatrice's side during her campaigns and civic commitments. Appearing at cocktail parties and ribbon cuttings and store openings—the quiet, loyal man behind the successful and ambitious woman.

Beatrice was still tapping her fingernail, waiting for some overt agreement that the group as a whole needed to take immediate action. Silence stretched across the room like a taut rubber band ready to snap.

Finally, the awkward moment was broken by sounds coming from the back of the room.

Nell welcomed the distraction. She looked toward the noise.

Beatrice Scaglia peered over her microphone, straining to see into the shadows at the back of the room. Finally, she stood.

Bodies shifted on the benches and chairs, eyes moving toward the commotion.

Davey Delaney, the construction company owner's son, was standing just behind the last row of chairs. He was alone, as he usually was, leaving his wife, Kristen, home with their three children. Davey was the image of his father as a younger man—ruggedly built with a barroom-handsome face, muscular body with just the faintest beginning of a beer bulge. His thinning auburn hair had been bleached by the sun and was more red than brown. His piercing blue eyes were staring, but not at the council table in the front of the room. Instead, he had turned his broad shoulders sideways, his stance that of a tiger ready to pounce. He was staring into the shadows near the back door.

Nell followed his look.

A dozen feet away, just inside the wide council room doors, stood a slender man with a prominent nose and shadowed jaw. He stood apart from the others crowding the room. A Sox cap was pulled low on his forehead, partially covering a white bandage across his cheek, and an old denim shirt hung loose from his bony shoulders.

The man was conscious of Davey's glare and met it head-on. He scratched an unshaven chin, his expression unreadable.

Except for the microphone picking up the tapping of Beatrice Scaglia's fingernails, the room was quiet.

"I never liked you much, Delaney," the man finally said, breaking the silence. His robust voice was a contrast to the deep furrows of age that defined his face. "But I give you your space. Now, don't I do that? Your old man, too. Sure, I do. I always done that, even when you were a young upstart raidin' our traps out near the island, tangling lines, creating trouble. So now it's time you give me my space, Davey Delaney. You know what I'm saying here?"

The older man pushed his body away from the wall, standing tall now, his fingers curling into a fist at his side.

Although the man weighed half that of the hefty Delaney son and would likely have done little harm, Ben spotted the clenched fist and began moving toward the back of the room. Across the room, Ben's friend Ham Brewster did the same.

But when the man's arm rose, his fingers relaxed and went to his own head, not to Davey Delaney's. Slowly, he clasped the bill of his cap with gnarled fingers and removed it, inclining his head slightly to the dozens of people looking at him. He scanned the crowd, surprised at the attention coming his way.

"I just stopped by to be sure no one was robbing the place, maybe to see what all the hullabaloo was about, that's all," he said. He managed a lopsided smile. "Damned if it wasn't about me."

Davey Delaney ignored the man's words and his smile and took a step closer, his eyes flashing and a fire-engine blush crawling up his thick neck. His legs apart, his hands clenched, he leaned forward. "You hear this, old man. Mark my words. That land'll be ours someday and we'll treat it a damn sight better than you do. We've got some respect for the people living around it." Davey tried to keep his voice low, but it refused to whisper and the words passed across the hushed room.

The old man turned toward him again, his smile disappearing in a flash. One bent finger pointed at the younger man.

"My land?" he said. The words hung in the air, held up by incredulity. His finger shook and his voice rose, bringing the room to rapt attention.

"You . . . get . . . my . . . land?" He paused for just one moment, then held Davey Delaney immobile in his stare. His words shot out like bullets. "Over my dead body, you will."

The age-spotted hand dropped to his side, and after another slight nod to the crowd, Finnegan the fisherman put his cap back on his balding head, turned slowly, and with an arthritic limp, walked out of the Sea Harbor City Hall and into the approaching night.

Chapter 2

"**B**oth Davey Delaney and old Finnegan are full of hot air," Ben said, motioning to the hostess that they'd probably need a table for six or eight. Izzy and Sam had followed them to the yacht club in their own car. Cass and Dan Brandley weren't far behind, and there was no telling who else might show up. The heated discussion had heightened appetites, and the club's Monday-night seafood buffet was the perfect way to satisfy it.

"It was a surprise to have Finn show up like that," Sam Perry said. "The guy's a wanderer, though. I see him walking the beach, wandering around the harbor, offering advice to any fisherman who'll listen. I've gotten some great shots of him around town."

"He must miss the days of being out on the water," Nell said.

Liz Santos, the club manager, caught Nell's eye and waved her over to the lounge area. "I don't mean to be nosy, Nell. I'm very careful to give club members privacy."

Nell frowned. "Of course. I know that, Liz. You're always discreet."

"Well, usually, anyway." She smiled. "It's just that Birdie looks so happy, that's all. And it made me wonder who the distinguished-looking guy is. I've not seen him around here before. Let me know. They need me in the kitchen."

Cass and Izzy walked over.

"Did you see her?" Izzy asked.

"Who?" Nell asked. "Where?"

"There," Izzy said.

She pointed to a secluded area beyond the curved granite-topped bar.

Nell peered around several large ficus trees with tiny white lights wound around the branches.

It was Birdie. And a distinguished-looking man they'd never seen before. Her face was lit with pleasure.

"So this is why she wasn't at the meeting," Nell murmured.

"Who is he?" Izzy asked.

A partial profile revealed a prominent nose and strong chin. His graying hair was slightly long, curling over the collar of his knit shirt. A handsome sports jacket hung over the back of his chair. He leaned in toward Birdie, said something, and then reached out across the table and touched her hand. His laughter carried back to them, rich and full.

"She blushed!" Cass said.

The couple at the table next to the ficus trees looked up. Cass mumbled an apology.

"We're acting like kids," Nell said. "And I'm starving. Come." She motioned toward the table where Ben was already settled, along with Izzy's husband, Sam, Danny Brandley, and Cass' brother, Pete.

She looked back at Birdie. "It's probably one of her lawyers or trust managers. Birdie says they use these meetings with her as an excuse to escape the city."

She started to walk away, urging the others to follow, but was one second too late.

Birdie looked up and saw the women huddling behind the trees, pretending to be invisible, their eyes focused on her dining companion. A burst of laughter escaped the white-haired octogenarian's lips, causing several people sitting at the bar to look up and smile. Her eyes lit up like the lights on the trees that separated her from her friends.

Before anyone could react, she stood and waved her arms, beckoning them over to the table.

"Go," Cass said, giving Izzy a gentle nudge toward the table. "Birdie's calling."

Nell walked up behind them. By the time they reached the table, Birdie's dining companion was standing up. He was medium height, but as she looked into the lined, handsome face, it wasn't his height that made the difference. It was the deep-set blue eyes that smiled at them.

"Nicholas, these are my dear friends, Nell, Cass, and Izzy." Birdie waved her hand, encompassing the group.

Nicholas gently lifted each of their hands and warmed it with a brush of his lips. "Such a pleasure," he said.

Birdie continued, "And they are beside themselves with curiosity, wondering who in heaven's name *you* are and what delicious fortune brought you to Sea Harbor."

"That's it in a nutshell," Cass said.

Nicholas' laughter joined with Birdie's.

"A disappointment, I fear," Birdie said. "I'm sure your imaginations have conjured up something far more elaborate than the truth. Nicholas Marietti is my brother-in-law."

"Brother-in-law?"

"Brother-in-law?"

"Brother-in-law?"

The women's words collided in the air.

Brother-in-law. Nell hadn't known any of Birdie's three husbands. That had all been before her time as a permanent Sea Harbor resident, but her in-laws had known them all. And so had friends and neighbors who had lived in Sea Harbor their whole lives. So Nell had heard stories about the handsome men who had fallen beneath Birdie's spell. Her mind worked to fit names in slots. *Marietti.* Joseph Marietti. Birdie's last husband? An Italian businessman who came to New York on family business, vacationed in Sea Harbor one summer, and fell in love with Birdie Favazza. That sounded right.

A massive heart attack took him from Sea Harbor, from Birdie, and from life just three years into their marriage.

Birdie looked around at her friends. "I can read your thoughts, you know. You're all remembering that Joseph Marietti's family in Italy was certain he'd married a woman of questionable mores—

anyone named *Birdie*, of course, would be such a hussy. And they had nothing to do with me for the rest of Joseph's life."

"Shameful," Nicholas said beside her. "They were so far away, so stupid. They didn't understand that Joseph had found himself a dazzling diamond."

Birdie patted his arm. "Hush with the dramatics, Nicky." She looked at the others. "But, yes, except for Joseph's baby brother sitting here, the Marietti family didn't have much to do with me. But sweet Nick came to our wedding and kept in touch with us. We even went out to California to visit him once. When Joseph died, he was the one who came back to help me bury his brother."

Nick had lowered his head as Birdie talked, and Nell could feel the memories passing between them.

"A long time ago, Birdie," he said finally. "A long time."

"Not so long, dear." Her smile was met with the faint ring of a cell phone.

Nicholas pulled a phone from his pocket, glanced at the screen, then excused himself with an apology. "It's family," he explained, and quickly walked over to a corner in the lounge.

"What a lovely man. Where did he come from? Why is he here?"

"I was just finding that out when I saw the three of you spying on me. He showed up unexpectedly—a whim, he said. He's on a vacation trip, headed north to see beautiful things. And it struck him suddenly that Sea Harbor needed to be on the list. He's with someone—a woman friend, I suspect, though he's been secretive—and wants me to meet her. Nicholas has always been quite the ladies' man."

"Where is she?" Cass asked. "He left her in the car? That doesn't bode well."

They laughed, and Nell looked over at Nick. His hand covered one ear to block out the din of conversation in the lounge. The other gripped a cell phone and pressed it tightly to his ear. His face was intent, the charming smile dissolved by the rigid set of his jaw and deeply furrowed forehead.

"Of course not, Cass. She's at Mary Pisano's bed-and-breakfast.

They're spending the night at Ravenswood-by-the-Sea—though I told him how silly that was. I have more bedrooms in my home than the inn does, but he said they were already settled. Perhaps they wanted more privacy—who knows? And you know how charming Mary's place is. They'll love it. His companion had a bit of carsickness, Nick said. I don't suppose that bodes well for a romantic car trip up the coast. But hopefully she'll feel better tomorrow. I shall meet her for breakfast, and then they'll be off again on—"

Nick's reappearance and the somber expression on his face cut off Birdie's words. "Nicky?" she said, looking up.

"I am so terribly sorry." He bowed his head slightly as he spoke. He lifted Birdie's shawl from the chair back and wrapped it around her shoulders. "We need to leave right away, Birdie. It's an emergency. I need to talk to you about some things. I will explain on the way—" He looked at Nell, Cass, and Izzy and bowed his head again. "Please forgive my abruptness, ladies."

Birdie was out of the chair immediately. And after a quick, curious lift of her eyebrows to her friends, she followed Nicholas Marietti through the yacht club lounge and into the June night.

Chapter 3

The smell of loamy, composted soil rose from the tilled land, its odor heightened by the overnight rain and early-morning sunlight. Dew caught the day's new light and blinked like diamonds on the nearby sea grasses.

"Clearly you have a future as a rototiller, Ham. Who knew?" Nell leaned against a signpost that announced the new Canary Cove Community Garden in bold, hand-fashioned letters. A red bandana held back her wavy, streaked hair, and with another she wiped the perspiration from her forehead.

"The view from behind him was something to behold," Jane said, patting her husband on the behind. "Cute butt." She handed him a cold drink. The property adjacent to Finnegan's land on the east side was a decent-sized rectangle, running from the road back to the sea. A perfect size for the proposed garden. The city owned it and allowed the use, hoping that it would somehow convince Finnegan he didn't want his property to stick out like the awful eyesore it was. In addition, the garden traffic just might be more than the reclusive landowner could tolerate.

Maybe he'd just pack up and move away, some thought.

Ham took off his cap and wiped the sweat from his forehead with the back of his hand. "I'm sure I lost two pants sizes controlling this little beast."

"Well worth it," Cass said. "We'll turn you into a sex symbol yet."

Ham stroked his white beard and grinned.

"You've done a great job," Willow Adams said.

Several other artists joined in with effusive approval. They'd come over early, before the boutiques and galleries opened, to help where needed.

"We're planting sunflowers along Finnegan's fence over there," Jane Brewster said. "Beatrice Scaglia donated a pound of seeds and volunteered her husband, Sal, to plant them."

"Plant something beautiful," Councilwoman Scaglia had urged. "And tall. Very tall. Thick. Anything to block out the quack grass and junkyard lurking behind that ugly fence."

Jane waved at Sal, dutifully obeying his wife's orders in front of Finnegan's fence. Beverly Walden and Rebecca Early were tilling the soil beside him, taking pity on the quiet man.

Nell laughed at the familiar story. Beatrice had her fingers in everything in town—anything that endeared her to voters—but it was often Sal Scaglia's fingers that ended up doing the work.

"Beatrice is so hard on Finnegan," Willow said. She pushed a strand of thick dark hair from her eyes.

"Because people take their complaints to her, I think. She tries to solve their problems."

"I s'pose." Willow looked over at the fence.

Suddenly a head popped out between two clumps of tall grass.

"Gotcha," the gravelly voice said.

Willow jumped.

Finnegan was dressed in his usual attire—jeans and a torn T-shirt with a lobster on it, his denim shirt unbuttoned. The Sox hat was slightly crooked, shading a face darkened and fissured from years on the sea. He leaned on the fence. "Looks good, what you're doing here." A crooked finger pointed at the garden.

Ham's square hands leaned on the tiller handle. "Okay, then, Finn. Get your butt over here. We could use your expertise."

Finnegan's laugh matched his voice, husky from a smoking habit he'd tossed aside in an instant when his wife got cancer. "And then you'd come help *me*, right? Help me mow all this here down. I got your number, Ham Brewsta. Weren't born yesterday, you know."

They all laughed, relieved by the friendly teasing that had been lacking in the city hall discussion the night before.

"Heck, it's not a bad idea, Finn," Cass said. She flapped one hand at the tangled overgrown grass. "Place is a mess."

Of all of them, Cass was one of the few who easily passed back and forth through Finnegan's gate and whose friendship allowed easy teasing. But all her comment brought today was a slight grin.

"Don't think so, Cassoulet," the old man said, using the nickname he'd pinned on Cass when she was a youngster playing on her dad's lobster boat. "You know betta. I handle things my way. Wicked stubborn, that's what my Moira always said."

"An understatement. What if I helped?"

At that the old man allowed a gruff laugh. He shook his head. "But here's something I wouldn't turn away from, you know. I wouldn't turn away some of your ma's soda bread. That and a smile from you, missy, would make this old codger a happy man."

A wave of emotion passed through Nell as she listened. There stood the fisherman, seaworn and bent. And the dark-haired lobsterwoman, taking on the same challenges, the same monstrous sea, just as her father and Finnegan had once done. Cass spent long days checking traps, repairing equipment, untangling warp on troublesome buoys. And then there was the constant competition, the barrage of fishing regulations, dealing with buyers. Not an easy life.

"He knows the way of the sea, can read it like the palm of his hand," Cass had told her once about Finnegan. "He's a decent man, no matter what his place looks like. No matter how he acts sometimes. No matter what they say."

Finnegan leaned farther across the fence. "You keep your chin up, Cassoulet," he said. His face grew serious. "Things'll get better for you. That's a promise from me to you."

His words were intended to be private, softly spoken, but the wind whipped them up and passed them along to those standing nearby.

Cass hesitated for a moment, then reached through the fence and touched his arm. "Back at ya, Finn."

He nodded gravely. And then with a nod to the others, he turned, and using his arms like a swimmer's, parted the thick underbrush until he disappeared, swallowed up by waving grass.

Across Canary Cove Road, leaning against a shiny red Toyota truck with neatly painted letters on the side spelling out DELANEY & SONS, the son stood by himself, a baseball hat on his head, legs crossed at the ankles, and a slow smile creasing his suntanned face. He nodded a greeting to the gardeners patting the soil back in place around the bulbs they'd planted. Sal, Beverly Walden, and Rebecca Early sat back on their heels, surprised they were being watched, and nodded a hello.

But Davey's eyes didn't stay focused on the plants or on the gardeners mulching the flowers or on Ham, standing nearby, his fingers around the rototiller handle. Instead he focused on the slow-moving weeds that were swallowing up the fisherman, almost as if his look alone would make the old man disappear forever.

Izzy hugged her aunt Nell and relieved her of one of the white bags that held the knitters' dinner. She breathed in the familiar odor of garlic and lemon. It was the Thursday-night ritual that Izzy cherished as much as a shipment of vicuña yarn.

"Am I the first one? I called Birdie to see if she needed a ride but didn't get an answer. Have you heard from her?"

"Not a word, and it's killing me." Izzy pulled the top of the bag apart and looked inside. "Clams? Lobster?"

The banging of the front door interrupted, and Cass breezed in. She was across the room in seconds, taking the second bag from Nell. "I could smell it all the way down the street. It's shrimp. Shrimp with wine, lemon, and garlic sauce."

Nell laughed. "For someone whose primary cooking skill is heating up a can of beans, you have a remarkable ability to discern odors."

"Thank you. And I'm right, right?"

"Of course you are," Nell said, and turned toward the back-room steps.

Another banging of the door stopped her at the top step. Birdie. At last.

"Birdie, what . . ." But it wasn't Birdie who stood in a patch of late-day sunlight crisscrossing the hardwood floor.

It was a young girl with the most amazing head of hair Nell had ever seen.

Izzy and Cass glanced at Nell. Who was she? Clearly they didn't know her, either, which meant she was probably a part of that first wave of vacationing families, those who came to Cape Ann when ocean waters were still too chilly for most, but the choices of cottages were greater and the beaches quieter.

"Hi," Izzy said. "May I help you?"

The girl looked to be about nine or ten, with clear blue eyes and a broad smile. Her hair was blue-black, like a raven's feathers, shoulder length, and wildly curly, blowing in a dozen directions. It was held in place—barely—by a crocheted green beanie with an enormous orange flower in the center of the brim. Long, skinny legs bore bruises of various colors and sizes, and hanging over one shoulder, held in place by a wide canvas strap, was the likely source of the injuries: a battered skateboard.

"This is the yarn shop, right?" she asked. She looked over at a basket piled high with yarn.

On top of it sat Purl, the shop's calico cat. She looked at the young girl and purred a hello, then jumped from the pile to the floor and rubbed against her leg.

The youngster giggled, then leaned down and scooped Purl up into her arms, hugging the cat to her chest. She stood back up.

Izzy nodded. "Yes. This is the yarn shop. One of them, anyway."

"But the only one in this town?"

"That would be true."

Purl rubbed her head against the girl's cheek.

"Whew. That's good. I was supposed to meet her here and I promised I'd be on time." She shifted Purl slightly and looked down at a large watch that was as big as her narrow wrist. "I'm early. That's a first."

The laugh that followed was childlike and infectious, big and generous and spontaneous. Her face lit up, showing off a sprinkling of freckles across her nose. "I'm never early, not usually. I'm not very dependable, Heather says. That's my current stepmother. But my uncle says being dependable isn't always all it's cracked up to be. Sometimes you have to just be spontaneous." She stroked Purl's back with two fingers. "Do any of you guys work here?"

Her eyes went from one woman to the next, her look connecting with each of them. When she reached Cass, she paused, brows pulling together for a moment. Then she grinned again. "I know you. Oh, not really. Like, we haven't met, but I saw you a little while ago when I was at the harbor, watching the boats come in. This man I know said you catch lobsters. Right? That's so cool. He said he helped you paint your buoys and your boat."

Cass frowned. Besides her brother, Pete—and he'd been with her all afternoon—there was only one person who had helped paint her boat. "You know Finnegan?" Cass asked. Her brows lifted in genuine surprise.

"*Finnegan,* yes. He said I can call him Finn if I want to. He knows everything about the harbor and the boats and the kind of fish around here. We watched you bring your boat in. Finn said maybe you'd take me out with you sometime. I've never in my whole life been on a lobster boat. Central Park doesn't have lobsters." Another laugh, then she shoved her hands into the pockets of cutoff jeans. "My name's Gabby. Well, it's actually Gabrielle, but you can call me Gabby. What're your names?"

Nell looked at Cass who looked at Izzy, then back again, confused.

"Are you . . . are you a relative of Finn's?" Nell asked. Her thoughts stumbled over the few facts she knew about Finnegan's life. The daughter, Beverly. Could this beautiful child be Beverly's daughter? Finn's granddaughter? Something in her said no.

Gabby's laughter came often and easily. She let the leather strap slip from her shoulder and the skateboard fell to the floor with a thud. "Nope. We're not related. I guess you'd say I ran into him. He was leaning on the railing, his face all wrinkled up like the world was crashing down on him, and then it did. Or me, anyway. I crashed right into him on my board. And he didn't cuss, not once. He just picked me up and wondered if I was okay." She pointed to a Band-Aid on her knee.

"Ouch," Izzy said.

"It's not so bad. I've had a lot worse. Honest. So, is one of you Izzy? Finn said Izzy owns this shop. He even walked me down here to be sure I didn't end up in a hardware or bookstore, but I told him I could probably tell yarn from nails and books."

Izzy laughed. "I imagine you could. And I'm Izzy. These are my friends, Nell and Cass, but you already know Cass—at least by reputation."

"It's nice to meet you." She held Purl in the crook of her arm and shook their hands, then looked at Cass. "Finn calls you Cassoulet."

Cass laughed. "He's telling you all his secrets. He must like you."

"Sophie—that's our cook—taught me how to make cassoulet. I'm going to make Finn some if Nonna says it's okay. I don't think he eats enough. He's pretty skinny. Don't you think?" She looked around the shop for the first time. "Sophie taught me how to knit, too. And crochet." She lifted her eyes as if looking to the top of her head, then pulled off the beanie. Hair flew.

"I made this."

Izzy reached over and ran her fingers over the light cotton hat while Cass and Nell leaned in for a look. The weave was loose and carefree, the look quirky, matching their visitor perfectly.

"You did a great job. I love this hat. My younger customers would, too. Would you share your pattern with me?"

The girl tapped her head. "It's all up here. But I'll write it down for you. Sophie helped me with it. Sophie'd love it here so much. Look at all this yarn. I can tell the kitty loves it, too."

"Thanks. That's Purl. She lives here. Did you want to buy some yarn? Is that why you're meeting your friend here?"

Gabby caught her bottom lip between straight white teeth, thinking, her eyes moving over the tables of soft yarn, the neat white cubbies packed full. "Actually, I don't have money right now. But

I'll come back with money and my pattern. Or maybe when Nonna comes . . ." She frowned and the freckles across her cheeks danced. When she checked her watch again, Purl jumped to the floor but stayed close, rubbing again against her legs.

Nonna . . . Nana? Nell asked, "So you're vacationing here with your grandmother?" Esther Gibson's granddaughter, perhaps. She had so many that Nell never recognized them from one summer to the next.

"Yes. No. Well, sort of, I guess." Another grin, followed by a shrug. "It's very confusing, isn't it?"

Izzy laughed. "So your grandmother is picking you up here?"

"Yes. At six thirty sharp. She wouldn't let me leave the house unless I promised I'd be here, and she gave me exact instructions how to get here, but I told her I'm very good at directions." She pulled a phone out of her pocket and beamed. "It has a GPS app. But anyway, I was given strict orders. Two hours to explore and I couldn't leave Harbor Road. I had to be at this shop, in this very spot," she looked down at her feet, "at six thirty."

Gabby looked around the room again, then through the shop window that framed Harbor Road. A parade of cars and bikes. People strolling along the village street.

Her face lit up. "There she is. She's here. I knew she wouldn't forget me. Is that the hugest old car you've ever seen in your whole life?"

Nell, Cass, and Izzy stepped closer and followed her gaze. Gabby was absolutely right. It *was* the hugest old car they had ever seen. And one they knew well.

Birdie Favazza climbed out of the front seat of her Lincoln Town Car, spoke briefly to her driver, Harold, and then hurried toward the yarn studio's front door as if it were dependent on her to put out the fire inside.

Chapter 4

"So you've all met," Birdie said, closing the shop door softly. "I'm sorry to surprise all of you like this. It's been a crazy day. I didn't have a second to call, but I thought I'd get here before Gabrielle to explain . . ." She smiled at the young girl.

"Gabby. You can call me Gabby. Almost everyone does. Except for Heather. She thinks it's too . . . too something. Too common, maybe?"

"Gabby. All right, then," Birdie said. She looked around at the others. They were standing side by side, patiently silent, but their eyes lit with curiosity.

"Gabby came up to Sea Harbor with her great-uncle Nick to meet me."

The woman who got carsick, Nell thought. *Oh, my, what a surprise.*

"We're on a road trip to Maine—to see beautiful things and hike, eat lobster, and do whatever we want. We might even see Stephen King. We're free spirits, Uncle Nick says." She grinned.

Birdie nodded. "And you still will do all those things, sweetie. But after a short break. In the meantime, you'll be a lovely free spirit right here in Sea Harbor."

Gabby nodded, seemingly undeterred by the change in plans. "It's okay, Nonna. This is a great place. It has lobster boats. And you."

Nonna. Nell watched a look of surprise fill Birdie's face, followed by a look of confusion. She patted Gabby's hand as she explained to her friends, "Nicholas got a call that his mother is very ill—"

Nell gathered the words, sorting through them and putting them in some kind of sensible order. *Nicholas' mother. Joseph Marietti's mother. Birdie's mother-in-law.*

"She's dying," Gabby said softly, easing away Birdie's attempt at subtlety. "She's old. Older than sin—that's what Sophie, our cook, would say. And she has more money than Donald Trump, Sophie said. She lives in Italy. Our families don't talk to each other—my dad never even met his own nonna. Can you imagine that?" She wrinkled her forehead, as if remembering something, and then looked at Birdie with bright, excited eyes. "Me, either, but now I have."

"That's right, you have," Birdie said, finding a brief lull in Gabby's explanation. "So that's where Nick is. Gabby's uncle went to be with his mother."

"But my passport is locked away somewhere, and we didn't know where," Gabby filled in, her hands moving along with her words. "So he couldn't take me with him. But that's okay. It's a dysfunctional-family situation. I might not have been very welcome."

Gabby was clearly pleased with her analysis of the situation.

Nell looked over at Birdie, who nodded. The young girl had analyzed the situation perfectly.

"Gabby is going to stay with me until Nick comes back. Ella and Harold are thrilled to have someone to spoil, but I'm the lucky one." She looked at Gabby. "I get a granddaughter."

There was only a slight difference in their heights, and Gabby's clear blue eyes smiled into Birdie's easily. "I never knew you, did I? I didn't know you even existed. It's exciting. Like a mystery that we're solving together. We're pulling the skeletons out of the closet, Uncle Nick says. And the best part is that now I have a nonna for real. I've always wanted one."

"Nonna?"

"A granddaughter?"

"Birdie, what's going on?"

Their voices collided as Birdie rejoined them in the yarn studio's back room, after making sure Gabby was safely buckled in behind Harold. Ella was waiting at the big house on Ravenswood Road with a special pizza she'd made especially for Birdie's newly discovered granddaughter.

Birdie dropped her knitting bag on the table. She handed Izzy a bottle of chilled pinot gris. "I think we should open this right away, dear," she said.

Izzy laughed and gave her a quick hug. "*Nonna*. Imagine that."

"Start at the beginning and don't leave anything out." Nell stood at the old library table, tossing the lemony shrimp onto a bed of angel hair pasta. Izzy headed for the galley kitchen to get some glasses.

"Actually, Gabby's explanation was fairly accurate. She's quite precocious. And absolutely beguiling. You should see Ella and Harold. You'd think it was Christmas and Santa had brought them their sweetest desire."

"You never mentioned anyone named Gabby," Cass said. "Were you hiding her?"

"And her father, for that matter." Izzy passed around glasses of wine.

"That's because I never knew there was a Gabby—at least not one who was related to me. Nor that Joseph, my third husband, had a son before we met. It seems poor Joseph didn't know, either. I knew he was a hopeless romantic—everyone knew that. Those Italian eyes—oh, my." Birdie took a sip of wine.

"I never should have married Joseph," she went on. "I didn't need another man in my life. But there was something there. He was such a lovely, romantic man. And he loved to dance. That's what clinched it."

"Ben's parents used to talk about the parties up at your home. Gatsby-like, Ben's mother always said. Filled with music and laughter."

Birdie's cheeks pinked at the memories. "Yes, they were that. Joseph brought in elaborate bands. We had great fun. Too much, maybe. He never stopped long enough to find out that he had a heart not destined for such shenanigans."

"So he didn't know he had a child?" Cass prompted.

"Apparently not. He found out about Gabby's father shortly before he died. Some lawyer contacted him, apparently. When he knew it was for real, he told his brother, Nick, and asked him to do what was right. So Nick did, and I was never told."

Birdie paused as her past played out in front of her. Secrets from the dead. She collected her thoughts, and finally her lips lifted in a playful smile. "The child of Joseph's love child. Imagine that."

"So Nick knew, but not you."

Birdie nodded. "At the same time, he was becoming a well-known cancer researcher on the West Coast. He kept in touch with Joseph's son, Christopher, for whom he'd set up a trust, as per Joseph's instructions. Nick became Christopher's family, in a way, since his own father had died and the family in Italy would not have claimed a child born out of wedlock. When Christopher married and Gabby was born, Nick saw his new niece every time he was in New York. According to Nick, she needed a favorite uncle. Her dad is a decent man, but one with a weakness for women—and those women aren't always the best mothers to Gabrielle. Nick watches out for the little girl. He loves her dearly."

"So, that explains the summer road trip."

Birdie nodded. "Gabby's dad and latest wife are having problems and went off to some godforsaken place to have a shaman make their marriage perfect, or some such thing. He couldn't reach them last night or this morning."

"So you have a surprise house guest."

"Yes, I do, indeed. Until Nick comes back anyway. She's endearing, but, good lord, how am I going to keep a ten-year-old child busy?"

"Gabby seems pretty independent."

"No doubt about that. She begged me to let her explore this afternoon. What do I know about the limits of a child's world? So finally I gave her ninety minutes and had Harold patrolling, though she didn't know it. He followed her to the pier, sat in his car to be sure she was safe. I think Gabby's used to marching to her own drummer."

Cass picked up a pair of salad forks and piled generous helpings onto each plate. "My kind of girl. I like her already."

"Harold and Ella say she's a breath of fresh air."

"And this food is a breath of fresh air to me," Cass said. "I'm starving."

They all laughed, embracing the comfort brought about by things in their lives that never changed—like Cass' utter reliance on Nell's Thursday-night dinner.

Balancing plates and glasses, they moved from the knitting table to the circle of chairs near the fireplace. A ritual repeated nearly every Thursday evening, no matter the season. Food, knitting, and friendship. As sacred as the sunrise.

"We'll help you keep Gabby busy," Izzy said. "She can come to our kids' knitting class."

"Having met her, I'd say she'll be teaching it," Cass said.

"Ben and Sam can take her sailing," Nell said.

"I'd offer to take her out on the *Lady Lobster*," Cass said, "but the atmosphere these days isn't always pleasant."

"Which brings up another topic of discussion," Nell said. She looked over at Cass. "Are you all right, Cass?"

The smile slipped from Cass' face.

"Just the usual hassles of running a business. It's the old catch-twenty-two. We need to expand, hire, get another boat, new traps, all those things. All it takes is money." She managed a grin. "Pete got a lottery ticket this week. Who knows? Maybe we'll get lucky." She fingered her napkin, twisting it into a roll.

"Ben could help you get a loan."

"I'm ahead of you. Pete and I talked to him last week, bent his ear for advice."

Nell wasn't surprised. Ben's business and law background, coupled with a kind and generous personality, had served him well in his semiretirement. Sea Harbor's unofficial go-to man. He dished out sound advice to friends and neighbors with ease and grace—and a confidentiality that rivaled Father Northcutt's confessional.

"We'll figure it out. Ma has started another novena for us, so something good will happen. She promised." Cass smiled, but the worry lingered in her dark eyes.

"Mary Halloran has connections in all the right places," Nell said. "And we're here, too."

Nell felt the emptiness of her words. Being there for Cass and her brother, Pete, was a given. But it might not be enough. Expansion for the Hallorans' business was key. And that took money, of course. And though she, Ben, and Birdie would gladly help, Cass would never accept it, not in a million years.

After Patrick Halloran's death in a storm years before, his brother kept the small fishing business afloat until he retired. Unwilling to sell it, Cass and Pete had taken it on when they finished college. Cass loved the business passionately—although sometimes Nell wondered if it wasn't her father she loved, and hanging on to his business kept him close to her. But whatever the motivation, the last year had been difficult, as equipment began to deteriorate and competition forced the Halloran Lobster Company to grow—or perish, as so many others had done.

Birdie stood and refilled the wineglasses. "Patrick Halloran would burst wide open with Irish pride at what you and Peter have done, Cass. You'll pull through this. And we're all here to make sure you do."

"Oh, shush. Now you'll get me emotional." Cass held out one hand as if to ward off her friends' kindness. "I know you're here. You guys are always here, and I love you for it. But Pete and I need to figure this out. And we will."

"Danny's worried," Izzy said. She tossed the words into the conversation casually, but Nell knew there was more than that behind them.

Dan Brandley and Cass had become close in the past year, and it wasn't just Cass' mother, Mary, who was happy about it. But Nell had noticed the worried look on Danny's face at a recent gathering.

"Danny's got his own life to take care of. He doesn't need to worry about mine."

The words were spoken with an edge.

"That's what friends do, Cass," Izzy said.

Cass was silent for a moment, then said, "This is my pa's business that I'm trying to resuscitate. What does a mystery writer know about that? It needs Pete and me. And we'll make it work. Danny has his own things. He has all these book tours going on. He doesn't need to be worrying about me." She mopped up the remaining sauce with a hunk of bread.

"Why don't you go with him?" Izzy asked. She sat forward in her chair. "I've gone on out-of-town photo shoots with Sam and it's fun—I'm the pampered tagalong with no responsibility. Great food. Romantic hotels. You'd come back way less cranky—I guarantee it."

Cass responded with a flat laugh. She got up, brushed some bread crumbs from her T-shirt, and started clearing away plates, a clear sign that she was through with the discussion.

"It might be good for Danny, too," Nell said, not ready to give up. Cass worked harder than anyone she knew, and business woes or not, a getaway with dear Danny Brandley would do wonders for her. "I imagine book tours can be lonely."

Cass spoke with her back to them. "And leave Pete with this mess? No way. Anyway, the book tour is Brandley's thing, not mine. That's the last thing I want to do right now—tag along after a writer. He lives in a different world." She piled the plates on the counter and wiped her hands on a towel. "Besides, you all know perfectly well I couldn't survive for three days without Nell's cooking. End of story. But something I do need help with is this sweater."

She returned to her chair and pulled out a nearly finished bright yellow vest. "Now, here's something I have control of—and I'm proud of, if I do say so myself."

"You're almost finished with the fleece vest!" Izzy moved closer to get a better look. "Cass, this is amazing. I am so proud of you for sticking with it." She fingered the soft cotton yarn—a cotton fleece with just enough wool for resiliency.

Nell leaned in and touched the edge that would soon have a zipper running up its front. "It's a great color."

"Sunflower gold," Izzy said proudly, as if she had just found it in a pot at the end of a rainbow.

Cass laughed. "You're all acting as if you've never seen it before. Like Nell isn't putting in the zipper, and Birdie didn't pick the pattern, Izzy the yarn, the color. Not to mention the fact that she's nearly frogged it to death several times."

"Oh, phooey with that," Birdie said. "That's what it's all about— just like with relationships." She threw a pointed look at Cass over the top of her glasses. Then she reached for the vest and held it close. "Absolutely handsome, my dear."

Cass hadn't mentioned to any of them who would be wearing the vest, but she picked it up now and held it in the air. "It's for Finnegan. I love it, and I think he will, too."

"Finnegan?" Nell's brows lifted. She'd assumed it was for Danny, but now that she looked at it more closely, it wasn't really a Danny kind of sweater. But it'd be perfect for Finnegan to wear, sitting on his dock or out in his shiny boat, motoring around the coves. It was so bright, people would be able to spot him if he had an emergency and needed help.

"It was Ma's idea." Cass sat back on the couch and smoothed out a cable that ran up the front of the vest. "He's always helping us paint this or that or fix things on the *Lady Lobster*. Even tried to give me some money to fix the engine the other day. Crazy old coot. He needs his money more than I do."

"He hides it nicely, but Finnegan is a good soul," Birdie said.

Cass nodded. "Ma says this is probably the first new thing he's had to wear since Moira died. He's a raggedy fool, as she sweetly put it. Now he won't be."

Nell watched Cass' blunt fingers weaving in the stray yellow ends. Her eyes remained on the strands of sunshine gold, but her thoughts were clearly elsewhere. The dock? Her traps? Or on her accounting books and the equipment she needed to find money to buy?

Or with a very nice mystery writer who, in Nell's opinion, didn't deserve to be pushed aside as abruptly as Cass seemed to be doing.

The evening passed in a flash, as it did every Thursday evening when Izzy, Nell, Birdie, and Cass blocked out the world and surrounded themselves with the dreamy lusciousness of cotton, linen, bamboo, and soft skeins of cashmere.

A tangle of Izzy's thick multicolored hair fell across her face, and she brushed it back so she could see the pool of lavender spilling over her jeans. She was half finished with the hoodie—a soft alpaca yarn that begged to be touched.

"That will look wonderful on you, Iz," Nell said.

Izzy picked up a knit edge. As the light caught the strands of the plied yarn, different colors emerged from the lavender—a hint of blue and green, a touch of gold. "It makes me think of the sunset. The colors changing. I love it. Sam does, too. So, how's yours coming, Aunt Nell?"

Nell frowned for a moment, scanning the sheet of paper she'd set on the table. She looked at Izzy. "I know in the end I'll be happy that you talked me into designing something, but it's keeping me up at night right now. And I don't even know who this should be for."

"Gabby," the other three said in unison.

Gabby. Of course. A sweater was the perfect welcome for anyone new who happened into the knitters' lives—like Willow Adams or the Santos baby. Or Sam Perry and Danny Brandley, when they'd innocently come to Sea Harbor to teach a photo class and to write a book, and been caught up in the magic of the town and its people, never to leave. They'd all been welcomed, not just with lifelong friendships, but with sweaters or hats or wraps—not to mention Nell's amazing Friday-night dinners.

"Gabby?" Birdie said again, this time with a question at the end of it, as if exploring this sudden change in her life.

"You're a grandmother," Nell said. "And I will celebrate the amazing occasion by knitting your granddaughter a sweater. It's an honor. What fun."

"Instant nonna." Izzy leaned over and gave Birdie a quick hug. "And I know the exact yarn we'll use for this cardigan." She flew up the three steps to the cotton room—a cozy room with a rocking chair and colored photos of grazing sheep on the wall. In the next instant, she was back, her hands holding skeins of bright purple yarn, soft as clouds and as delicious-looking as a grape Popsicle. "We did a survey. Purple is the favorite color for ten-year-olds. And with her hair? It's perfect." She placed the armful of yarn in Nell's lap.

Instantly the skeins were passed around, fingers touching the strands of cotton.

"It's summery, light. Just perfect, Iz." Nell said. "Perfect for our first grandchild," she added.

Birdie sat quietly and soaked it all in. Then she said, "And each of you is now one of Gabby's newfound aunts. But names can't possibly say what you really are."

The phone rang, scattering the emotion of the moment, and hands immediately went into pockets and bags.

"We need to change our ring tones," Cass muttered, then looked at Birdie. "It's coming from your backpack."

Birdie fished out her phone, checked the name that appeared, and pressed Talk.

Ella talked loudly, probably because Harold refused to get the hearing aid he sorely needed. But her words were clear and reached each one of the knitters.

"It's the little one. She's gone."

Chapter 5

*I*t felt like déjà vu.

Nell, Izzy, Birdie, and Cass knew the routine well. Without a word, they folded up their knitting, locked up the shop, and piled into the Endicott CRV.

At least it wasn't raining, like the knitting night several years ago when they'd driven all over town looking for the gallery owner, Billy Sobel. Or the night, just one year ago, when Ella herself had disappeared, driving off in Birdie's Lincoln Town Car without a single driving lesson to her name. In the first instance, the missing person had ended up dead; in the second, Ella had ended up in the hospital, badly injured in a car accident.

Hopes for a better outcome silently filled the car as they drove at a snail's pace down Harbor Road, their eyes peeled for a slender-limbed girl with flying black hair.

Most of the retail shops were closed for the night, but all along the gaslit street, sounds of music and laughter floated through the open doors of cafés, restaurants, and bars. Nell idled the engine in front of Scoopers. The ice-cream shop was packed with people.

Cass ran in. Had anyone seen a young girl with wild black hair? Maybe on a skateboard?

No luck, her face told those waiting in the car.

Birdie was quiet. Nell glanced over and saw the worry filling her face. Gabby had been in her care less than a day. She barely knew the young girl.

And now she was gone.

Nell reached over and squeezed her friend's hand. "It'll be fine. She probably just needed some fresh air."

Birdie kept her eyes focused on the road straight ahead, as if looking away would make Gabby disappear forever. Her voice was strained and lacked the calming warmth they depended on from their oldest friend. "Ella said they'd had a good time at dinner," she said. "Gabby never stopped talking, and made Harold laugh so hard Ella was worried about his pacemaker. After dinner, he took her on a tour of the estate, showing off his gardens, the flagstone paths, and the rope hammock he'd just replaced. She was riding her skateboard around the driveway later when he went in to get a jacket. When he came out, she was gone. They searched the grounds, the woods between our house and Alphonso Santos' place. Alphonso said he saw her turning onto Ravenswood Road, headed toward town."

Nell pulled into the circle drive in front of the Ocean's Edge. The wide white porch that wrapped around the restaurant was filled with people. Surely someone would have seen the skateboarder.

Izzy hopped out and headed for the restaurant steps, but before she reached the entrance, Willow Adams and Pete came out, arms looped around each other. They nearly collided with Izzy's fast-moving body.

"Whoa." Pete reached out one hand to steady Izzy. "You must be awfully hungry, wild woman."

"We're looking for Gabby," she said breathlessly. "Have you seen her?"

"Who's Gabby?" Willow asked.

Izzy shook her head. "Silly. Of course you haven't met her yet. She's almost ten, dark hair. She might be lost."

"Was she skinny and about this tall?" Pete asked, lifting his hand to Izzy's shoulder.

Izzy nodded.

"With lotsa hair?" Willow asked. "And cruising like crazy on a skateboard?"

"That's her." Nell called from the car.

Beside her, Birdie released the air trapped in her lungs, her small body sinking back into the seat.

"I passed her riding along Canary Cove Road when I went to pick up Willow. She was hell on wheels speeding along that narrow strip. Not so safe with all the vacationers cruising the streets. I would have stopped, but I was late."

"But she was still there when we headed back that way. Remember?" Willow said.

"Where, exactly?" Izzy asked.

"Near the community garden. She was near the fence where we planted the sunflowers."

Birdie leaned through the passenger's window. "Finnegan's fence?"

Willow nodded. "She didn't act like she was lost. She didn't seem to be looking for help."

"But then she disappeared," Pete added.

"Disappeared?" Worry crept back into Birdie's voice.

Pete shrugged. "I checked in the mirror before we turned off Canary Cove Road—just to be sure she wasn't out in the road on that board. But she was gone."

"Maybe she went on toward the Canary Cove shops," Willow offered. "Jane and Ham's gallery was still open."

"No," Birdie said suddenly.

Nell looked over at her. "No?"

"No. I think I know where she is."

"Finnegan," Cass and Izzy said in unison.

"Her new friend," Nell said softly.

Willow frowned. "You mean she might have gone down to his place? Why would she do that?"

"That's a good question," Birdie said, more to herself than to anyone listening.

They waved good-bye and turned the CRV back down Harbor Road.

Nell drove slowly, careful of groups of vacationers who wandered back and forth across the main Sea Harbor street, seemingly unaware that the town had cars.

Once on Canary Cove Road, they peered into the shifting shadows that fell along the edges of the road. On either side of the winding strip, wavy sea grass turned ominous and the pounding of the surf filled their heads and hearts with impending danger.

Nell brought the car to a crawl as they approached the beginning of the rusty wire fence that surrounded Finnegan's property.

There were no streetlights here, but finally, just as the wind whipped up and threw an empty soda can beneath the wheels of the car, its bright beams caught two figures walking slowly along the side of the road toward Canary Cove.

"Thank the lord," Birdie murmured.

Finnegan turned around and shielded his eyes from the bright lights. He stepped to the easement, pulling the other figure along with him.

Gabby Marietti clutched a small blue-and-white cooler.

Nell pulled the car off the road and turned off the engine, leaving the lights on. They lit up the path of gravel and weeds, the rusty fence.

And Finnegan and Gabby—deer in the headlights. The large white bandage on Finnegan's face caught the light and bounced it back.

Finnegan began ranting before they were out of the car.

"If that damn . . ." he stopped short, looked down at Gabby, then started in again, choosing his words carefully. "If those dagnabbit cops had minded their own business, I'd be driving the kid home. Here, and she's skinned her knees nearly raw. Phone out of batteries. And I'm having to walk the girl to a phone in Canary Cove. Wicked stupid."

Gabby looked up at him. Her face was stern. "I told you, Finn, I'm fine."

"Fine, my foot. Look at you." He pointed one crooked finger toward Gabby's legs. Two awkward-looking bandages covered her knees—thick strips of gauze wrapped around her narrow leg several times and tied in a knot.

"Gabrielle," Birdie began, the lines across her forehead turning into fissures.

"It's nothing," Gabby said. Her black hair flew around her head as she talked. "My dad says I'll have scarred knees for the rest of my life. His wife says it's unattractive." She shrugged. "It's part of the package. I'm a kid. I fall."

"Where's your board?" Cass asked.

"I threw it out," Finnegan snapped. "Damn thing broke right in half."

Gabby frowned but kept her thoughts to herself.

At least it wasn't Gabby who broke in half, Nell thought. Finnegan may have unintentionally done them all a huge favor—skateboards and summer traffic didn't mix very well. The shopkeepers' association finally had banned them from Harbor Road during busy hours. She looked again at Gabby's skinned knees and Finn's attempt at bandaging. He'd tried to help her, tried to treat the superficial wounds. The man was a conundrum, but a kind one.

"It's okay, Finn. No problem. I've got another board back home," Gabby said.

Finnegan didn't look worried about the skateboard, but his concern over the young girl was written all over his wrinkled face. "So you'll be okay, kid? These ladies'll get you home safe. They're good folks."

Gabby nodded. She held up the small cooler and said to no one in particular, "We went fishing after I crashed. Three cod. Finn thought it'd make me feel better."

"In the dark?" Birdie placed one hand on Gabby's shoulder, as if to grab on tightly if she made any move to run. But it was Finnegan her eyes bore into. *What were you thinking, you crazy fool?* they said.

"Don't get your innards in an uproar, Birdie Favazza. It was her choice. The girl's never fished. Not once." He looked at Cass. "Patrick Halloran woulda done the same thing, and you damn well know it. Can't let a girl grow up without catching a cod. It ain't right."

"You're right, Finn," Cass said. "A right of passage, my dad called it." She placed a calming hand on his arm. "I remember fishing off your dock myself when I was a kid. Probably at night."

"We could see all the way across the harbor," Gabby said. "There were boats out there, and that one cool yacht with the bright blue stripe. Right, Finn?"

"I s'pose. Now, you sure you're okay, kid?" he said, looking down at her knees.

Gabby frowned, one hand on her hip. "Course I am. I'll have mine off sooner than yours." She wrinkled her nose at him.

Birdie looked at the bandage on the side of Finn's head. "I hope you're taking care of that wound, Finnegan."

Cass said, "The other guy looks a lot worse, I hear. Broken nose, no less."

"Damn right, Cassoulet." He managed a smile. "Bums have no right to take over my place."

He looked down at Gabby, then back at the women hovering around him. "Important thing is keeping kids like Gabby safe. I've no use for the riffraff that hangs around here."

Gabby looked at all of them, and for the first time seemed to sense the worry that had blanketed the group. Her dark brows pulled together and her voice softened when she looked at Birdie. "Were you guys worried, Nonna? It's not like Central Park or anything. I was okay. I know how to watch out for myself."

Nonna. The word was still startling. It was a new identity, one that was foreign to Birdie just days ago. Nell looked over at her friend.

Birdie took a deep breath. And then she wrapped Gabby in a tight hug. "You're freezing, child," she said. "It's time to go home."

"I told her as much. Said you'd be wicked worried." Finnegan shifted from one foot to the other. His worn black boots shuffled gravel as they moved. He looked down at the young girl at his side, and his craggy face softened. "I'll turn you into a fisherman yet, kid. You'll be as good as Cassoulet in no time."

He nodded as if affirming his own words, then turned around

and walked toward the gate that opened into his land. His head was low, his shoulders hunched.

In the distance, waving weeds were silhouetted against the lights of the art colony, and off to the right, the sea pounded a steady beat against the shore.

Birdie's eyes trailed the lone figure as he made his way into the night. She took a step to follow him, her small sneakers crunching on the gravel.

Then she stopped and stood still. Her words, carried on the night breeze, were spoken to the fisherman's retreating back.

"You're a good person, Finnegan," she said. "Thank you."

Finnegan didn't turn around or break his stride, but his head lifted slightly and his shoulders straightened.

And all of them knew he'd heard.

Chapter 6

It took Gabby Marietti one short week to wedge herself as tightly as a clam into the lives of Sea Harbor residents. With fresh bandages—colorful ones that Ella sent Harold out to buy—still crisscrossing her knees, the wild-haired girl tapped directly into the extraordinary empathy Sea Harbor residents were known for.

And she—along with Cass' fleece vest—gave Finnegan new life. The two were often seen strolling the harbor, the winsome young girl in the green beanie and the old fisherman in the bright yellow knit fleece. He'd brushed away moisture in his eye when Cass had given it to him—"Damn bug in my eye," he'd said—and slipped it on immediately, right over his old denim shirt.

And not a soul in town ever saw him without it again.

"Gabby looks good on that old pink Schwinn of yours," Cass said.

"Doesn't she, now? And she doesn't seem to mind that it only has three gears. She and Harold spent an hour scrubbing and shining it up." Birdie settled herself into a chair on the Artist's Palate deck and pulled a half-finished floppy hat from her backpack.

"The bruises don't seem to have held her back," Nell said.

"That's an understatement. I think Gabby knows more people in town than I do."

They all knew that to be a gross exaggeration. Birdie Favazza knew everyone in Sea Harbor. And if a few managed to briefly escape her acquaintance, they knew who the gracious lady in the magnificent house on the hill was—and they knew how integral she was to the town.

"Have you told Nick about Gabby's tumble?" she asked.

"Yes. He calls a couple times a day, wanting a complete report."

"So he calls you often?" Izzy said. Her brows lifted and a mischievous grin followed.

Birdie leaned over and patted her hand. "Sweet Izzy, I think your dear Sam and married life have turned you into a hopeless romantic. I'm an antique, sweetie."

Izzy held up both hands. "What? What did I say? It's nice he talks to you, that's all. Besides, what does age have to do with anything? And you're not an antique. You'll never be old."

Birdie laughed. "I like Nick. I always have. Joseph used to tease me about him, wondering if I had married the wrong brother."

"Did you?" Cass asked.

Birdie looked up, surprised at the abruptness of Cass' question. Then she laughed. "Of course not. I probably shouldn't have married anyone at that point in my life. It was full to the brim. But Joseph was convincing."

And he was very much in love with Birdie Favazza, according to all reports.

Everyone in town knew about Birdie's unexpected wedding to the dashing Italian businessman. He was absolutely smitten with her, people said. Devoted. And apparently didn't mind living in the shadow of Sonny Favazza, the man who had stolen Birdie's heart decades before and, even in death, still had possession of it.

"What did Joseph do for a living?" Izzy asked. "You never talk about him. Was he retired?"

Birdie waved one hand in the air. "Oh, it was such a long time ago."

"Not that long," Nell said.

"It seems like it sometimes. A lifetime. What did he do. . . . ?" Birdie wrinkled her forehead in thought. "Joseph and I had separate financial lives. It's easier that way when you marry at our age. We both had more money than we knew what to do with and decided not to mix it up. A prenuptial before it was in vogue, I guess you'd say. So we didn't bother each other about our investments and business dealings. His was a family business—antique imports. Lovely pieces, I remember from the pictures he showed me. There was a warehouse in New York and one in Italy. Joseph did the paperwork and record keeping and that sort of thing, so he could be anywhere. He had a little office down on the water, which was all he needed." She frowned, as if thinking back to that time, trying to clear her memory, to bring it back crisp and clear.

"Yes, that's right. After we married, Joseph suggested once, just once, that he might use my den—Sonny's den—for his business, but I rightly refused and he very nicely agreed, saying he'd probably be better in his own place anyway. So he found a nice little office down near the harbor." Birdie smiled at the memory. "He loved the smell of the sea and the sounds of fishermen picking up their bait and taking their boats out to sea. He said he never had that kind of feeling in New York or back in Florence. He always felt hemmed in."

"Is Nick his older brother?"

"No, younger," Birdie said, her fingers automatically wrapping the yarn around her needle. "Nick came to our wedding—a small affair—but his life was in California. He didn't seem to have any interest in the family business that Joseph was involved in. I don't think Nicky got along with his mother very well. He came to the States to go to medical school and went back to Italy rarely, as far as I know."

"Has he said when he'll be coming back for Gabby?" Nell asked.

"As soon as he can. He feels terrible about abandoning her, but I've assured him that Sea Harbor is truly the kind of village that helps raise children. I'm already wondering what Harold and Ella will do when she leaves. They adore her."

Emotion flitted across Birdie's face. Harold and Ella weren't the only ones who would miss Gabrielle Marietti.

"She's a good kid. As Finn would say, she's not half bad—the ultimate compliment." Cass lifted one leg across the bench to sit down, then frowned at the wet edges of her jeans. "Damn. Occupational hazard," she mumbled, a frown pulling her dark brows together.

"You've already been out on the *Lady Lobster*?" Nell asked. She looked down at the stain of seawater dampening the jeans' cuff. Cass was rarely completely dry.

"I went out early to check the traps in the cove. I like it early—no one bothers me. It's my time to meditate."

Cass had probably been up at dawn, meditation or not. There was always work to do. And she'd be going out later, too, baiting and checking traps, just like her father before her.

"Gabby brought me her pattern for that crazy beanie," Izzy said. She pulled a pink sock out of her bag and began turning a row. Socks were her travel projects, her half-finished hoodie left behind. "She's going to help teach a kids' class to make one. I think they'll love having someone their own age involved. She's also been scavenging through my bins of scrap yarn for a new project, she says. She won't tell me what she's making, though—says it will be the coolest surprise."

"From what I've gathered, Sophie the cook is her best friend. Gabby loves her," Birdie said.

"Finn is giving the cook serious competition. He's crazy about Gabby," Cass said. "I've never seen him so soft and mushy."

Nell laughed. They were an odd couple, for sure. She'd spotted them on Monday, sitting on a bench across the street from Izzy's shop, eating ice cream. The sparkle in Finnegan's eye was a welcome change from the defensive look he'd been wearing at the city council meeting not too many days before. Maybe Gabby was their secret weapon to get him to clean up his yard.

"She seems to have gotten through to him in a way few of us have," Birdie said. "Except maybe for you and your mom, Cass."

"Gabby doesn't want anything from him, that's why." Cass said. "Neither do we. Besides, he likes Ma's Irish stew."

That was true. So many people wanted a piece of Finnegan these days. They wanted him gone from a piece of land he loved. Maybe even gone from the town. Nell thought about the harsh tones the Delaneys and Beatrice Scaglia had used at the meeting.

All Gabby wanted from him was his company—and maybe the use of his fishing pole now and then.

"But even those of us who don't want anything from him aren't always made to feel welcome," Birdie reminded Cass. "I've often wondered what that's all about. It's a mystery to me. I've known Finnegan forever. We're friends, of a sort. But after Moira died, I'd try to take things over now and then—a pot roast, smoked salmon. He was getting so thin, it seemed to me. But I learned my lesson. I wasn't welcome. Might hurt myself on all the clutter, and there was poison ivy everywhere, he said, but that was an excuse, I always thought. And shortly after that he built a giant mailbox near the gate and told me that he'd sure welcome Ella's pot roast if I ever had a mind to give him some. I could just leave it in the box, he said."

Nell laughed. "A recluse who likes pot roast."

"It's strange, but, then, so is Finn," Cass said. "He lets me come to the house—if you can call it that—but that's about it. I've often wanted to prowl around and see what else is there. It's at least three acres. But I don't. I blindly obey. I've just gotten used to it, I guess. The man has earned his idiosyncrasies, is how I think about it."

"Ben's mother used to talk about how lovely that strip of land used to be. I think their dentist had an office there. It was neatly kept."

Cass nodded. "I remember it because my dad would pull up in his boat to buy bait. Moira would always have hot dogs ready for us. We loved it. Pete'd eat five dogs, and Finnegan would tease him something fierce. Told him he'd soon be barking."

Birdie picked up her knitting and began doing yarn overs on the rim, looping the yarn from front to back, then knitting the next stitch. The yarn lay across her lap like silky seaweed. "It was a lovely structure back then. A twin building was just on the other side of that little access path where the Arts Association is now. Both buildings had a couple of offices and an apartment above. Joseph rented one of the offices—I'm not sure which. Finnegan was different back then. Moira grounded him. He was always intolerant of things he thought were unjust, but Moira tempered it, let him keep his values without hurting people in the process."

Cass put her elbows on the table, her chin resting on her hands. "After my dad died, Finn was always there, helping us with the traps, painting buoys, fixing lines. He'd never take a penny. It's a mystery to me—just like it is to everyone else—why he won't clean up his yard, but it's his own business." Cass shifted over on the bench as Merry Jackson approached, balancing a round tray holding mugs and plates.

The bar owner squeezed her narrow hips between Cass and Izzy and set the tray on the table. "This is today's special," she said. "And probably tomorrow's, too. My homemade granola. You'll love it—I promise." She set down four giant beer mugs filled with fruit, nuts, and fat grains, all topped off with yogurt. Next came a basket of warm elderberry muffins and a pot of whipped butter.

Izzy scooped up a dollop of yogurt with her finger and licked it clean. "Fantastic."

"I especially like the beer mugs. Nice presentation, Merry."

"Oh, shush." Merry swatted Cass with a napkin. "I'm keeping my artists healthy," she said. "Whether they like it or not."

For as long as the Artist's Palate had anchored the north end of Canary Cove, the Palate's bill of fare had featured margaritas and thirty-plus kinds of beer served with fried everything—squid, clams, pickles, fish, asparagus. But once her ex-husband was no longer a part of the business, Merry changed things. In nice-weather months, she put out coffee pots and mugs and opened the gate to the deck early in the morning. Hot coffee and orange juice for the Canary Cove artists before they rolled back their awnings and opened their gallery doors. That was her goal. Until the day she saw Ham Brewster munching down potato chips with his hastily drunk coffee. The next morning she added whole-grain muffins and slapped Ham's hand hard when he reached for a bag of bar chips.

"It just grew," she said with a shrug when the *Sea Harbor Gazette* ran a feature article on her. Her homemade granola and fresh fruit were a hit. And the fact that it meant adding hours to her day didn't seem to bother the diminutive bar owner.

"So I heard you talking about Finnegan." Merry leaned in closer, her body as nimble as a ballet dancer's. A long blond braid fell over one shoulder. "His daughter's over there, so keep it low."

She nodded toward Beverly Walden, sitting near the railing with several other Canary Cove artists.

She seemed oblivious to the group around her, her eyes focused beyond the trees at the sea and a small island out past the point. She looked peaceful somehow, happy, as if she were spinning a perfect life for herself out on that little piece of land, or maybe off on one of the luxury boats that sailed out of the harbor and into the sea.

Beverly was thirty-eight, according to the bio they'd seen at her art show. Not beautiful by Hollywood standards, she was, neverthe-less, an interesting-looking woman with a curvy figure and a certain sensuousness about her. Streaked brown hair hung loose beyond her shoulders. She'd been back in Sea Harbor just a few months, but everyone knew who she was—Finnegan's prodigal daughter, though rumor had it she hadn't been as well received by her father as her biblical counterpart.

"See that look on her face?" Merry said. "I'm thinking she has a boyfriend. Man friend, I suppose you'd say. She's been wearing makeup, edgier clothes." Merry's mouth lifted in a mysterious smile. "I know the look."

"She's nice-looking," Birdie said, turning back to the table. "She looks like her mother, with that long nose and high cheekbones. Rather mysterious, I think. She certainly doesn't look like Finnegan."

She was standing now, leaning on the railing that overlooked the sea in one direction and the parking lot in the other. When she lifted her hand in a wave, Nell followed its direction. Davey Delaney stood below on the asphalt, next to a Delaney truck. His hands were on his hips, sunglasses cutting the glare, and he looked up at her, as if maybe he'd been there watching for a while, hoping she'd look down.

Merry moved in closer and Nell's view was gone.

"They're probably both pleased that she doesn't look like her dad," Merry was saying. "There isn't much love lost between those two."

"That's the rumor. But how do you know?" Izzy asked.

"Same way you know all the gossip at your end of Harbor Road, Iz. Your knitting customers talk, just like folks do out here on the deck and at the bar. You keep your eyes open and the world spills out its secrets right in front of you."

Cass leaned in. "So spill it, Merry. What do you know?"

Merry laughed. "I know everything, Cass. And mostly I know when there might be trouble. Like last night." She paused for effect, then continued.

"Beverly was in here alone, having a few beers. I worry a little when people are drinking alone, so I took her over a crab cake and sat with her for a minute, suggesting some of this great new tea I got in. She was nice enough and not offended. She assured me she was fine, she had a nice evening to look forward to and was not going to get sloshed and ruin it. *Very fine* were her exact words. She looked happy, instead of that ultraserious look she had when she moved here."

Mother Earth—that's who Merry Jackson is turning into, Nell thought. When she took the microphone from Pete at a Fractured Fish performance, she poured her soul into their songs like a seasoned performer, but here in her bar and grill, the tiny blond dynamo took care of the world, or at least this little corner of it.

"And?" Cass prompted.

"And then Finnegan came in. He hangs out here sometimes. He's like our own Canary Cove security guard—watches out for all of us and never takes a dime for it. So I give him coffee or food when he stops by. Payment, sort of."

"It's a wonder you make any money, dear," Birdie said.

Merry laughed. "Oh, don't you worry about me, Birdie. I'm doing fine. Anyway, Finnegan sat down over there at the bar and I could tell he was watching us. Soon as I left Beverly's table, he walked over and took my place."

Nell glanced over again at the object of their conversation, but Beverly was gone, a coffee cup left behind. She looked around the lot and toward the galleries, but the only thing she saw was the tail end of Davey Delaney's truck rounding the corner.

"Finn went over to her? That couldn't have been good," Cass was saying.

"Unless they're both swallowing old feelings and making up," Izzy suggested.

"Well, I was hoping for that, too. Lately I'd seen some signs that maybe she wanted to make up. But I don't know. There's bad blood there. It had something to do with her mother's death, I think."

"Moira Finnegan died of cancer," Birdie said.

"That's what I hear from the Brewsters. Ham and Jane liked Moira. They said Beverly never came to see her. No one even knew where she was. So I'm not sure what her gripe with her father is. Seems he might have the better reason to be upset. Don't you think?"

Birdie had told Nell the story of Finnegan's daughter one night while they sat on the Favazza veranda, Hudson's Bay point blankets covering their legs as they looked up at a star-filled sky. She and Birdie had gone to the art opening where Beverly Walden's paintings were on display for the first time. Later, under the spell of a full moon and Birdie's sherry, they'd hashed over the evening—who was there, conversations they'd had. The art they'd liked and not liked.

Beverly's paintings lent themselves readily to the conversation. Turbulent, rolling oils, bright and bold, filled her canvases as unpredictably as the sea itself.

Beverly had been a fifteen-year-old runaway, Birdie told her, long before Nell and Ben had settled into the sprawling Endicott home on Sandswept Lane. She'd been a troubled child and youth—a bad seed, some called her—and one summer she began stealing things from local stores, hiding bracelets and books and T-shirts beneath her loose clothing. But nothing was really hidden in Sea Harbor. Most people looked the other way because she was Moira and Finn's daughter.

But after a while, and with hopes that the girl might get some help, Archie Brandley had turned her in. It wasn't the books she'd taken from his store, he'd said. He didn't give a hoot about them. But he guessed Beverly was stealing for the thrill of it, grabbing obscure books on business planning, menopause, and physics. Pencils and bookmarks. Things he rightfully assumed she had no interest in. Stealing for thrills was a sickness, in Archie's opinion, and the girl needed some help.

But instead of facing the consequences, Beverly had run away. And taken a substantial amount of Finnegan's hard-earned money with her.

For Moira's sake, Finnegan hired an investigator to find her, but to no avail.

"I don't know why Beverly came back all these years later. Finn says it was to torment him," Cass said.

Merry shrugged. "She told me she'd changed. But I told her I was about three when she ran away, so what did I know?"

"Maybe she doesn't steal anymore, but she sure doesn't treat her father well," Cass said. She wiped some muffin crumbs onto the deck for the birds. "So, what happened last night?"

"Oh yeah, that. Well, Finnegan was huffing and puffing about something. He didn't sit down, really, just put his hands on the table and started talking at her. He kept his voice low, but his eyes about seared right through her head."

"So you didn't hear anything?" Cass asked.

"Oh, I heard enough. Not the close face-to-face stuff. But after he had his say, he started to walk away, then looked back again, like he'd forgotten something. I couldn't tell if Beverly was mad or sad. But I know she had tears in her eyes when he said the next thing."

Merry lifted her brows and paused for effect.

"Yes, dear?" Birdie said, urging her to continue.

"By then I was wiping off the table next to them and I could hear him plain and clear. He told her she'd ripped a piece right out of her mother's heart and killed it. And wasn't that enough for her? Hadn't she ruined enough lives without killing any more?

"Those two didn't like each other," Merry concluded. "Not so you'd notice, anyhow."

Chapter 7

$\mathcal{N}$ ell had twenty minutes to run into the Cheese Closet before getting home to help Ben. As usual, she wasn't sure who would show up for Friday-night dinner on the deck, but cheese, wine, and the cheese shop's spicy sausages were a staple, no matter who—or how many—came. And on the rare occasions when there was too much food, Father Northcutt's soup kitchen and sometimes Father Larry himself were grateful for any leftovers.

The Cheese Closet was on Oak Street, nestled between the library and the old three-story stone building that housed the city offices. It was one of Nell's favorite places in Sea Harbor, and she fervently hoped it would escape the plight of so many small shops that disappeared in the blink of an eye. But as Ben often said, if the Endicotts' purchases were typical, Peggy and Tim Arruda's Cheese Closet would be around for a long, long time.

She pulled into an empty parking place and walked into the welcoming shop, taking a basket from the stack just inside the entrance. Getting in and out was usually difficult for Nell—she nearly always ran into acquaintances. But today, much to her surprise, the shop had only a half dozen people savoring its cheeses, exotic olive oils, sausages, and spreads.

"A temporary lull," Peggy Arruda assured her from across a display case. "Friday is always a busy day." The owner handed Nell a toothpick holding a square of cheese. "Try this. It's Nisa—from

Portugal. Timmy and I honeymooned there. The cheese is to die for. Ben will be crazy about it."

Nell nibbled on the small square. "Very smooth and creamy. Goat's milk?"

"No. It's from sheep. Merino, just like Izzy's lovely fleece yarn." She handed Nell another piece. "We both appreciate that magnificent beast. Izzy uses its amazing coat, and I use the milk."

Peggy was right: Ben would love it. Nell added a round to her basket, then moved through the aisles, filling the rest of it with far more than she had come in for. *Enough*, she scolded herself, and stepped into the short line that had formed at the checkout counter.

At first she didn't recognize the woman standing in front of her. It was the beautiful bottle of wine in her basket that caught Nell's eye. A flock of painted butterflies circled the bottle, merging together almost like a Rorschach test. Surrounding it were cheese and crackers, a package of colorful napkins, and two plastic wineglasses.

Beverly Walden turned and smiled at Nell.

"I was admiring your choices," Nell said. "It looks like the makings for a lovely, romantic picnic. All you need are candlesticks."

Beverly glanced at her basket, then blushed slightly. "I'm splurging."

"It's difficult not to in here. Is it a special occasion?"

"Special? No, not really. Well, yes, maybe. I guess it is special." A slow blush colored her cheeks.

Nell smiled. "Good. We all need special now and then."

"It's for a picnic over on the island," she said suddenly, as if needing to share her happy evening.

Tim, Peggy's husband, motioned to Beverly that he was ready for her. She lifted her basket to the counter.

Her hair was loose today, and she brushed it back from her cheek absently as she chatted with Tim. She seemed more at ease in her body than Nell remembered from the few times they'd been together. More relaxed. No. She seemed happy; that was the difference. The frown on her face and the slight hunch to her shoulders had been replaced with something lighter and brighter, and it had transformed her into a lovely, sensual woman.

Maybe Merry Jackson was right. Beverly had someone special in her life. And that someone liked cheese and wine.

Perhaps a dose of happiness would allow her to see her father in a new light. Nell was all for happy endings.

The pot was simmering on the stove, nearly ready. Pitchers. Trays. Glasses. Knives. Everything they'd need.

Outside the kitchen window the sky was deepening and sounds of Ben preparing the grill drifted in. In the distance a band began to play. *The yacht club,* Nell thought, leaning toward the window, listening to the happy sounds. And later there'd be fireworks over the ocean, celebrating a June wedding or anniversary or birthday. Signs of summer.

She breathed in the magic of Sea Harbor. The joy of friends. And the deep satisfaction she felt getting ready to welcome them into the home she loved.

The kitchen was the home's soul, a major renovation project when she and Ben made his parents' vacation home their permanent residence. They planned it together, and that's what it meant to Nell: a piece of her, a piece of Ben—a shared dream. They had wanted an open space where friends would gather and chop and dice and drink in the pleasure of being together. And that's exactly what it had become.

At the other end of the open space, a smooth stone fireplace, flanked by a comfortable sofa and chairs, warmed them on winter nights. The room beckoned—and friends and family responded. Sisal rugs softened the cherry floors, and the light neutral palette of the furniture—tans and whites with hints of soft green—gave full play to the sky and pine trees, the sloping green lawn, and the ocean beyond the woods, a piece of it visible from every window along the back of the house.

A slice of heaven.

Sam Perry was the first to walk into Nell's reverie, the sound of his boat shoes on the wood floors pulling her from her thoughts.

"What's this? And early. Aren't you missing someone? Where's your bride?"

Sam dropped the bouquet on the kitchen island and wrapped Nell in a giant hug.

"My amazing wife got stuck at the yarn shop, handling some crisis. So I'm here to help Ben with his martini making." He found a vase on the shelf beneath the island and filled it with water, stopping only to breathe in the aromas of wine and basil and butter floating up from the pot.

"The flowers are beautiful. Izzy has domesticated you, Sam. First a flower garden. Now a plot over at the community garden. What's next?"

Sam laughed. "You're so subtle, Nell. But who knows? We have a house. A garden. A sailboat. Maybe we'll get a dog next."

Nell laughed.

"So how's the scamp doing?" Sam asked.

"You must mean Gabby."

Sam nodded. "Ben and I are taking her out on the sailboat soon. She's quite the personality. A charmer."

"You must be talking about my granddaughter." Birdie walked into the kitchen, carrying a bag of rolls from Garozzo's Deli. "Step-granddaughter, I suppose I should say, but that doesn't roll off my lips quite as easily. *Granddaughter*. Oh, my. I must admit, I'm beginning to like the taste of it. A week ago I was worried about her having to spend part of her summer with an old lady. What fun is that? But that doesn't seem to be an issue with Gabby."

Sam took a bottle of olives from the refrigerator. "Old is definitely not an issue—not with you, not with Gabby. I saw her riding that ancient bike of yours around Canary Cove today. Ham and Jane were standing outside their gallery, doubled over laughing. There she was, hair flying, some funny-looking little hat slapped on her head, and next to her, wobbling along and trying to keep up, was Finnegan in his new fleece vest."

"Finnegan? On a bike?" Nell laughed.

"If you can call it that. It looked like something he had as a kid."

"She's brought new life to him. I worried a bit about her bothering him—"

"No worry there. Finnegan doesn't stand on ceremony. If he didn't want her around, he'd chase her off."

"An understatement." Ben came in from the deck. The smell of charcoal trailed in behind him.

"We're talking about Gabby and Finn, I can tell," Izzy said, following Cass and Danny across the room.

"She's a great distraction for him," Cass said. "The best thing that could have happened, with things heating up at his place."

Nell frowned. "Heating up how?"

"Beatrice Scaglia is on his case something fierce. A lot of those homeowners on the hill above Canary Cove are up in arms over the continued mess of his property."

Ben added, "Folks are insisting she do something about it. Davey Delaney is fueling their fury. The Delaneys are drooling to get their hands on that land. It's the last waterfront property available near town."

Cass set a covered platter on the counter. "But it's not available. It's Finn's."

"Cass is right," Izzy said. "Congresswoman Scaglia is just looking for a cause."

"I don't know about that," Ben said. "Beatrice has pretty high aspirations, and it all begins here in Sea Harbor. State representative? Who knows? But that means pleasing voters. This is serious business for her."

"She's a tough nut," Danny said. He pushed his sunglasses up into his hair and took a beer from the refrigerator. "I was writing on the Palate's deck yesterday, and she was canvassing the place for support. Getting people's take on things. Stirring them up, it looked to me. She even had Finnegan's daughter agreeing with her."

"Beverly?"

"Yeah. She and Davey Delaney were there, talking over in the corner, and Beatrice wandered over and left a flyer behind."

"It wouldn't take much to convince Beverly," Cass said. She peeled the foil wrap off a tray of lobster rangoon.

Izzy leaned over her shoulder, eyeing the crisp appetizers. "Good grief, is this my old friend Cass? What's happened to you? Has Danny turned you into a domestic diva?"

Cass shoved Izzy's hand away from the plate. "Brandley made these. I catch lobsters. I don't cook them."

Cass didn't eat them, either, which they teased her mercilessly about—the lobster fisherwoman who shuns her catch. "I'm just too close to them," was her traditional response. But tonight she didn't joke back. Nell watched her brisk response. Cass was usually the first to laugh at herself, but Izzy's comment seemed to have struck a chord. Something was on Cass' mind, and Nell didn't think it was lobster rangoon.

"So you think Beatrice's political aspirations are pushing her efforts?" Birdie looked at Ben.

"Probably. She needs the voters on her side, and Finnegan is a thorn in her efforts."

"I saw the two get into it in Archie's bookstore the other night," Izzy said. "Beatrice looked like she'd like to kill him. Poor Sal stood quietly by, two steps behind her, just like in the royal family."

Sal was shy, but he was his wife's biggest supporter. Some thought it a perfect match. He was good-looking, in a subdued, Clark Kent kind of way. He cleaned up nicely, as Birdie would say. And he was content to live in the shadow of the ambitious Beatrice—and in the comfort of her family fortune.

The slamming of the front screen door, the slap of Birkenstocks on the floor, and swish of a long peasant skirt announced the arrival of Ham and Jane Brewster. "Where's our new friend Gabby?" Jane asked, checking out the group.

"She went to a movie at the mall with Harold and Ella. I don't think they've been to a movie in twenty years. Gabby talked them into it."

Nell checked her pasta, turned off the stove, and shooed them all outside, urging Ben to mix his martinis. "And take Danny's amazing appetizer with you, or I'll eat every single one."

Izzy put her iPod into the Bose sound dock, and in minutes laughter mingled with Giovanna Bersola's energetic voice belting out "The Rhythm of the Night." And by the time Pete and Willow arrived and Ben took the scallop kebabs off the grill, villagers' feuds, unkempt property, and a wild-haired ten-year-old taking hold of their hearts were put aside. Bodies moved as one to the long table beneath the spreading branches of the old maple tree. Candles were lit, wine and water poured, and baskets of warm rolls placed at either end.

"Friday night on the Endicott deck. Our refuge. Our haven," Birdie said, lifting her glass. Her white head nodded slightly to each of those gathered around the table, the anchors in her life. "To friends," she said in a hushed voice.

"To friends!" Voices collided in the delicious-smelling air as plates were passed, wineglasses refilled, and Ben's scallop kebabs greedily devoured. Nell passed around the bowl of fresh pasta and vegetables and reminded them all, as she did every Friday night, "MIK"—more in kitchen, and there always was.

At first no one heard the ringing of the front doorbell.

But when the laughter died down, the ringing found a lull in the conversation and made itself heard. Izzy suggested they ignore it.

"No one we know uses your doorbell," she said, passing the bowl of pasta to Sam. "It's probably UPS or someone selling tickets to the Fourth of July picnic."

"Probably," Ben said. "But I'm one of those guys who absolutely cannot let a ringing phone or doorbell go unanswered. Not like some of you." He lifted his thick brows at Izzy and Cass as he pushed back his chair and stood up.

Izzy laughed. And then she looked beyond Ben to a figure standing in the doorway. She looked up at Ben. "It looks like you won't have to answer it after all."

They all looked toward the doorway and the figure outlined against the family-room light.

But it was Birdie who pushed out her chair and stood, her napkin fluttering to the floor.

"Nicholas," she said, her voice lifting in surprise. "Where did you come from?"

Chapter 8

*N*ick Marietti smiled and stepped out onto the deck.

Birdie moved to his side and accepted his kiss on each cheek.

"I came from Logan. Before that, Florence. I got in town an hour ago. And I'm sorry to barge in like this. I leave all of you so suddenly, then appear again like a ghost. No warning, no call. What must you think of me?"

"That you need to come and sit with us," Birdie said. She took his arm and led him over to the table.

Ben pulled over another chair, and before Nick was completely settled, Sam had put a glass of Scotch in his hands. "You look like you could use this," he said.

Nick's laugh was more a sigh. "How did you know?"

There was a moment of silence as they all focused on Nick Marietti, wondering how many questions it was polite to ask before he'd had a chance to eat—or, at the least, had a drink of Scotch.

Finally, Birdie said, "Have you seen Gabby yet?" As the words registered, a sudden shadow fell across her face.

Izzy, Nell, and Cass read her expression. *If Nicholas is here, Gabby will be leaving.*

"No, there wasn't anyone at your house. I thought she'd be here with you."

Birdie checked her watch. "Harold and Ella took Gabby to the movies tonight. They probably aren't back yet. How did you think to come here?"

"The innkeeper, Mary Pisano. I checked into a room there, and she said you'd be here. She thought Gabby'd be with you." He rolled the drink glass between his palms, ice cubes clinking against the side.

"The benefits of small-town living," Ben said. "Everyone knows where we'll be on Friday nights."

Nick nodded. "Seems so."

"Well, she was right to send you over." Nell set a full plate in front of him. "You're just in time for Ben's amazing scallops. The tomato and dill relish is wonderful."

"You are wonderful people. I barge into your gathering, and I'm treated like a king."

Ham stroked his graying beard. "You'll drop that king idea when we lead you to the dishwasher later."

"Oh, shush," Jane said to her husband. "We'll excuse him for tonight." She looked at Nick. "But only once."

Nick finally allowed a laugh and his shoulders relaxed. He slipped out of his sports jacket and hung it over the back of the chair. "Birdie says you've all had a hand in making my niece comfortable here. Thank you."

"Gabby doesn't need help to fit in," Izzy said. "She's pretty self-reliant."

"An only child?" Jane asked.

Nick nodded. "In a fancy penthouse on the Upper East Side. She considers Central Park her backyard. A definite worry for overprotective uncles like me."

"What about her father?" Nell began, but she let the words drop off. It wasn't her business, not really.

"Christopher's a nice guy. He loves his daughter, even when she baffles him. But he's not very savvy when it comes to picking wives. Too much money, too young, maybe." He looked at Birdie as if he were going to say something, then thought better of it, turned away, and spoke to them all. "Gabby's mother died when she was born, and there've been a string of stepmothers in and out of her life."

They listened to Nick's story about Christopher Marietti's failed marriages—the most recent one resulting in a trip to India for marital counseling from his new wife's current shaman. As they listened, they tried unsuccessfully to fit Gabby Marietti into the picture he painted.

Birdie brought them back to reality. "I suppose you've come to continue your trip with Gabby. Your mother . . . she must be better?"

Nick seemed surprised at the question. And then his expression cleared and he shook his head. "No, she isn't better. But she rallied while I was there. That's how she is: a will of steel. If she wasn't ready to die last week, to hell with the grim reaper; she wouldn't die. One day she was an old woman, shriveled in a bed that was way to big for her body. Then suddenly, as if she'd been given a magic tonic, she perked up. Called for lawyers. Family members. It was the old Francesca Marietti, ruling the world as if she were seventy again, instead of nearly one hundred. She was that way for three days, talking to each of her children, extracting promises from us about everything from the flowers for her funeral to the distribution of her estate and messes to clean up. And then, just as suddenly, she said to leave her alone, that she was tired, and she shriveled up again. The doctors aren't sure what's next, but they don't think it'll be long."

Birdie looked at him, her eyes judgmental. "Shouldn't you have stayed there with your mother? Gabby is fine with us."

Nick took a slow drink of Scotch, then set the glass down on the table and sat back in his chair. His shoulders sagged. "No, dear Birdie, I shouldn't be with my mother." His smile was enigmatic—not happy or sad, but puzzling. Then he rested one arm on the back of Birdie's chair and his whole body seemed to relax. "I left under orders."

Chapter 9

*L*ater, when they looked back on that weekend, they couldn't be sure who had made the decision to stay longer, Gabby or Nicholas. Or Birdie herself, suggesting Gabby needed a few more days in Sea Harbor. After all, she had a class to teach for Izzy.

But as Birdie told them the next morning, however it happened, Nick and Gabrielle were going to spend a few more days in town before continuing their trip up the coast.

Birdie sat back on the garden bench and wiped the perspiration from her forehead. They had come together at the community garden to water and weed. But mostly they were there to find out what had happened when Nicholas and Birdie left the Endicott deck the night before.

Birdie took the glass of iced tea that Izzy handed her. "Gabby was still up when we got home, playing hearts with Ella and Harold on the veranda. She was thrilled to see her uncle. Clearly the child loves that man. But the hug was quickly replaced by a sad face."

"She didn't want to leave?" Nell said.

"It was more definite than that. She *couldn't* leave, she said. It was absolutely impossible."

Cass sat back on her bare legs and tossed some weeds in a bag. "Why's that?"

"Because she had a knitting class to teach, a game to teach Harold, a fishing date with Finnegan, and she and Willow were working on a project. These were serious promises, she told her uncle, that simply couldn't be broken."

Nell laughed.

"There was much talk, voices going every which way. Harold and Ella being quite vocal in having Gabby stay longer. Nick—who looked like he hadn't slept in a few days—seemed content to let it swirl around him, his hands folded across his chest. And then he said he needed some sleep. Sure, they could stay a few more days. He had some work to do, and he could do it from here."

"From your house?"

"He's staying at the Ravenswood B and B."

"With all the rooms you have in your house?" Cass asked.

"It's fine. I invited him, but his things were already over there and it's just across the street."

"Gabby?" Izzy asked.

"She'll stay put. Harold and Ella insisted, and Nick was fine with it. She loves that little corner bedroom in my house—the one with the window seat and view of the sea. Or maybe it's Sonny's den down the hall from it that she loves the most. I find her in there often, looking through the telescope, curling up in his big leather chair, reading a book." Birdie smiled. "It's nice seeing her there."

Sonny Favazza's den was Birdie's special haven, and the fact that she shared it so freely with Gabby spoke louder than words. "You wear your new role nicely."

"Life is full of unexpected turns," she said.

"Where is Gabby today?"

"At Willow's. She loves the Fishtail Gallery and all the wooden mermaids that Willow's father created. She's helping Willow out, she says. Some mysterious project that she wouldn't tell me about."

"And Nick?" Izzy got up from the ground, one fluid movement that defied gravity. She brushed the dirt from her knees.

"He seemed in better spirits this morning. The visit with his mother took a toll on him, I think. He's spending the morning working."

"Sam texted me that he ran into him at the courthouse. He was dressed too nicely for Sea Harbor, Sam said. He suggested you get him some shorts and T-shirts."

"Why was he at the courthouse?" Birdie asked.

Izzy laughed. "Now, if it'd been me—brash and bold as I am—I might have asked, but my sweet husband is more discreet. He snapped Nick's picture, though. He calls his summer project 'A Portrait of the Sea . . . and the People Who Come to It'—or something like that. Be careful to brush your hair if you go out."

Birdie laughed. "Sam's photos tell stories. He's an amazing man."

"Yes, he is." Izzy grinned. "But one who doesn't ask the right questions."

"I was curious—that's all. I thought he was working at the B and B. Mary had offered him that beautiful den to use while he's here."

"He's a doctor, right? So what kind of work can he do from here?" Cass wiped her hands on her jeans. "I don't much like doctors. If I could have one on the other side of the country and check in on e-mail, I might consider checkups."

Birdie chuckled. "He's on the research staff at Stanford. And gives lectures all over. Sometimes back here at Dana-Farber. I suppose he's working on a paper or computing data or whatever it is researchers do when not in their office. Computers make it easy to work anywhere."

While Izzy headed for the storage shed hidden behind a clump of rhododendron bushes, Nell turned on the faucet and pulled the hose to the edge of the raised bed to water a patch of new seeds.

She turned the nozzle to spray and looked around, her mind moving to last night's dinner, to a to-do list on her kitchen island, to the rich garden beds that now filled a once empty lot. Beautiful, healthy, smelling of rich, loamy earth.

Then her gaze shifted from beauty to the beast. There it was, as it always was. The rusted fence that guarded Finnegan's land. The garden that sidled up to it was a pleasant reprieve, and the climbing vines and sprouting flowers along the roadside would help deter the mess from Canary Cove Road. But never completely.

In the distance, she heard the crunch of gravel on the invisible drive. Nell peered through the weeds.

A figure—a shadow, really, from where she stood—was visible just inside the gate. A man, well dressed.

Unable to get a better view and feeling a bit like a spy, she turned away. It was probably one of the many developers dreaming of where he would build a small inn or condominium complex when Finnegan came to his senses and gave up his land.

She turned off the water and called to the others. "I'm off to the market. Want a ride, Birdie?" She glanced back at Finnegan's property, then shook off an uncomfortable feeling that chilled her, a sudden cold breeze, unexpected on a warm Cape Ann day. *Silly.*

Cass was already packed up and ready to leave, a backpack slung over one shoulder and her cell phone pressed to her ear. After a few words, she slipped it into her pocket, her smile gone. "Pete says the *Lady Lobster*'s winch is broken. One more thing to fix. Poor boat needs a trip to the spa." She forced a smile to her face as she waved good-bye and followed Izzy to their cars.

Nell and Birdie waved them off and picked up their things. "I wish she'd let me help, but she's as stubborn as her father was. It's the Irish in her," Birdie said.

Cass was indeed stubborn—and proud. But she was also a survivor. Somehow this would all work out, and the Halloran lobster business would climb back on its once-steady feet.

The two women climbed into the car and Nell backed out slowly, then turned the car toward Harbor Road.

"Wait," Birdie said suddenly. She leaned forward in the seat, her hands on the dashboard, and stared through the windshield at Finnegan's gate.

Nell slowed to a crawl, then stopped. They both looked across the road.

The yellow knit vest caught their eye first. And then his tall, skinny form. Finnegan's stance was familiar, too—and defiant. One hand clutched the gate, the other a large stick. In front of him, his face equally stern, stood the figure Nell had seen through the fence, his face visible now.

Finnegan's angry voice lifted and carried across the street and through Nell's open car window.

"You're just like the rest of them," he yelled. "There's nothin' for you here. I don't care who you are in your fancy duds. Out, now!"

The pause that followed was as loud as the voices that came before. A chasm grew between the two men until one finally spoke, his head held high, one hand in the pocket of his tailored slacks. Casual. In control.

"I thought we could handle this nicely, Mr. Finnegan. I see you think differently." The man spoke carefully, the voice of a man used to people listening to him. He started to walk away, then turned again toward Finnegan, his back to the car across the street, his words muffled. "What's . . . mine . . ." The words were carried on the breeze, but separated from the rest of the sentence.

And with that, Nicholas Marietti turned away and climbed into a blue rental car.

Without a sideways glance and oblivious of the women watching him, he sped on down Canary Cove Road, a blur of blue disappearing out of their sight.

Chapter 10

Parties at Sal and Beatrice Scaglia's home usually had a political edge, though it was always subtly disguised. Tonight's cocktail gathering was to celebrate their newly remodeled home—*cocktails with friends*, the colorful invitation had read—but no one ever doubted that the guest list included those who might offer a political assist, should one be needed down the road.

"Do you think she'd make a good mayor?" Nell asked. Then she looked away from her question and out the window toward the churning sea. She was talking without thinking, uttering words while her mind was elsewhere. Idle chat. Something she didn't often do with Ben.

Ben maneuvered the car along the winding drive toward the Scaglia home. It was a peculiar evening sky, strangely ominous, with threads of clouds floating in front of the emerging crescent moon. The air was heavy, and below the cliff a pounding surf sent frothy plumes into the night sky. Rain, the weatherman had predicted. But Ben and Nell had both agreed that it wouldn't rain yet, not until after Beatrice's cocktail party. She wouldn't allow it.

"Mayor? Sure, she'd be fine." Ben said. He took the turns in the road with ease. "Beatrice is bright, articulate. And she has her constituents' interests at heart." He glanced over at his wife. "What's on your mind, Nellie? I'd guess it isn't Beatrice Scaglia's political future."

"That's not fair. At the least, I should be able to hide my thoughts in the dark." Nell shifted on the seat and pulled a knit wrap around her shoulders. A soft cashmere shawl, the color of the sea, and knit with love, Izzy had said when she gave it to her.

Ben reached over and rested one hand on her knee, his eyes on the road. He rubbed the silk fabric of her dress lightly. "Night, day. It doesn't matter. You wear your heart—and your worry—on your metaphorical sleeve. At least the sleeve I have privy to."

That was true enough. She could rarely keep things from Ben. He sensed her moods, her thoughts, sometimes even before they surfaced in her own consciousness. Ben just knew.

"It's Birdie's guest," he said, continuing to mine her thoughts.

"He's not really her guest."

"Whatever he is, he's here because of Birdie. Frankly, I think it's great. He's brought Birdie together with this little girl and given her a chance to be a grandmother. Birdie is loving the whole thing, and one week wasn't long enough. But besides all that, I like the guy. And I think Birdie does, too. If you ask me, she did marry the wrong brother."

"Yes, but—" *But what?* But they saw Nick arguing with Finnegan when Birdie thought he was working on a lecture at the B and B? That Izzy saw him at the courthouse? So? Somewhere buried in it all was the instinct to protect. But whom? And, good Lord, from what? Nell shook her head at her own foolishness. If there was anyone in this whole world who didn't need protecting, it was Birdie Favazza, one of the strongest women she knew. She didn't need it, and she certainly wouldn't want it.

Ben's voice was thoughtful. "As for seeing Nick talking to Finnegan, it can easily be explained. He's protective of Gabby, and she was hanging around the old man. If she were my niece, I'd have been over there, too, checking him out."

She looked at Ben's silhouette against the darkening sky. The strong nose and square chin, graying sideburns and full brows. The warm brown eyes that still, after all these years, managed to stir sensations deep inside her. His expression was soft in the moonlight, but clear. It spoke to her, told her that he loved her.

And that she worried about things that were better off left alone.

Ben drove around another bend and onto Gull Drive. The neighborhood was built along an inlet that allowed easy boat access to beaches, Sunrise Island, Canary Cove, and the harbor beyond.

"Maybe Nick is interested in building a place up here on Cape Ann and went to city hall to get the lay of the land," Ben said. "What if he wants a place to bring Gabby? That would be great for Birdie. As for Finnegan, the more people who approach him about that place of his, the closer we come to some kind of resolution. I sometimes think he's holding out now just on principle. He doesn't even have electricity half the time. It's not a great place for an old man to live."

Nell fell silent for the rest of the drive, allowing Ben's words to settle and soothe. But it wasn't easy. Birdie was happy that Nick was staying around a bit longer, but she'd been puzzled, too, by his encounter with Finnegan. And she said that Nick seemed different somehow, remote, not the friendly, gracious man who had brought his grandniece to Sea Harbor a week before. The trip to Italy had changed him.

Birdie had answered her own concerns with a logical explanation: he was worried about his mother—certainly reason enough for a man to appear slightly distant.

"Is Nick coming tonight?" Ben asked.

"I'm not sure. Birdie didn't say."

"We'll find out soon enough."

In the distance, the bright lights of Beatrice and Sal's beautiful home lit up the tree-lined road like a fireworks display. The first party of the summer season—and the Scaglias would make it one to remember.

They parked and walked up the flagstone path, warmed by lights, laughter, and the sounds of Pete Halloran's band, the Fractured Fish, playing from a veranda that wrapped around two sides of the house. Through the front windows and open doors they spotted Izzy and Sam talking to Archie and Harriet Brandley in front of a white, floor-to-ceiling bookcase. Archie was probably evaluating the collection. He told Nell once that he had the bad habit of sizing up people by the books he found in their home. And a home without any books? He'd never go back. It was probably haunted, he said.

The Brandleys' son, Danny, stood a short distance away, a serious look on his face as he and Cass talked, their heads lowered. He'd just come back from a successful book signing, according to his parents. Lines out the door in New York City, Archie had said. Nell made a mental note to congratulate him, though it didn't look as if Cass was doing exactly that.

People drifted in and out of view as Beatrice's hired staff for the evening—college students home for the summer and eager for work—moved through the crowd, offering drinks and delicate seafood appetizers to guests.

Beatrice, in a pair of Jimmy Choo platform sandals that made the diminutive hostess nearly as tall as Nell, welcomed them effusively at the door, urging them toward the food and drink. Standing a step or two behind her, her husband, Sal, smiled a greeting, and Nell smiled back. *The man never gets in two words edgewise,* she thought. On the other hand, he seemed content to stand in the shelter of Beatrice's dominant shadow. An odd pairing that seemed to work.

Davey Delaney walked up beside her, a bottle of beer gripped in one hand. "Evening, Nell," he said.

His mother, Maeve, stood a few steps away with D.J. The family seemed to travel as a unit. A fortress. Nell smiled. "How's your wife? Is she here?"

"Nope."

Nell nodded, feeling at a sudden loss for words. And Davey wasn't helping. Standing there, a half smile on his face. Silent as a stone.

"It's too bad she couldn't come. It's hard to get babysitters, I suppose."

"Nah, two of mine are almost old enough to babysit. But we have a nanny who stays with us. Works fine, especially at times like this. Kristen's out of town—a weekend with girlfriends."

It was the most Davey Delaney had said to her at one time in a while. "That's great. Moms need that."

"Dads, too," Davey answered. He nursed his beer, his eyes watching Nell in a way that made her nervous.

She was about to excuse herself when he cleared his throat. "I know Ben didn't like that tiff I had with Finnegan the other night. You probably didn't, either, him being a friend of yours. I just want you to know it's no big deal. I just wish the guy would wise up. We could make him rich."

Nell nodded, unsure of where the conversation was going. "I think he feels rich already, Davey. Maybe it's not to everyone's liking, but he's happy."

Davey took a long swallow of beer, draining the bottle. "You think he's happy living in a hovel?" He shrugged, his muscular shoulders straining against the fabric of a silky shirt open one button too many. "Maybe, maybe not. But it'll get cleaned up one way or another." He set his bottle down on a table and took another one from a passing waitress. Then he nodded once and wandered back to where his parents were standing.

Nell watched him for a minute, then walked away herself. Such a strange man.

She saw Izzy and Sam standing near the veranda doors, listening to Merry Jackson and Pete sing a medley of old tunes. Relieved to have a destination far away from Davey Delaney, she headed their way.

Izzy looked magnificent, a shimmering ice blue dress with tiny straps hugging her long, lean body. Nell's breath caught in her throat as she watched the young woman whom she loved so fiercely it sometimes hurt. She would be grateful forever to her sister, Caroline, for sharing her only daughter so generously, without a trace of resentment. "She'll always be my daughter," Caroline had said to Nell the day of Izzy's wedding a year before. "But she's your soul daughter, and she's a richer, fuller woman for it." And then they had both shed copious tears and wrapped their arms around each other as Izzy walked down the garden path to her waiting bridegroom.

Tonight she was looking up at Sam as if he were the only person in the room. A year of marriage hadn't tarnished the glow one single bit.

"What? What's that look, Aunt Nell?" Izzy embraced her, then pulled away, rolling the edge of Nell's shawl between her fingers. "It looks gorgeous on you. Just like I knew it would."

"Yep, gorgeous." Sam hugged them both. "My two gorgeous women," he said. "How did I get so lucky? Every man in the room is looking at me right now with pure, unadulterated envy."

"True," Izzy said. "You're a lucky man, Perry. And don't ever forget it." Two fingers crawled up his chest.

"Can't you two keep your hands off each other?" Esther Gibson came up behind them and followed her words with a resounding chuckle.

"Not working today, Esther?" Nell asked the gray-haired police dispatcher.

"I told the chief I'd do the night shift tonight, so I'll go in late. It's such a lovely place to knit, and I sometimes get more sleep there than I do at home—my dear hubby's snoring has gotten pretty bad."

"Things are quiet at the police station? That's a good thing." Sam lifted several wineglasses off a passing tray and passed them around.

"That's what I told Chief Thompson. 'It's going to be a calm summer,' I told him. I feel it in my bones."

"I'll drink to that." Nell lifted her glass and touched it to Esther's. "Quiet is good."

"Except for Finnegan, of course. He hasn't been very quiet lately. Now he wants a restraining order."

"Finnegan? Against whom?" Ben walked up behind Nell.

Esther chuckled again, a delightful rolling sound that made all those around her smile, too. "Oh, everyone in general. Certain people in particular. Developers, council members—particularly our Beatrice—and even her poor husband, Sal. Can you imagine? Shy Sal. And his wife couldn't hurt a fly. I told Finnegan as much."

"He's just trying to make a point," Ben said. "Beatrice got his goat at the city council meeting. But I saw him help her into her car the other day. Not a bad bone in the man's body, though he likes to cause a stir."

"Of course you're right," Esther said, waving the air. "I just don't like to see him getting ornery. It's bad for his blood pressure. He doesn't look all that healthy to me." Then she added, almost as an afterthought, "He wants the police to keep his daughter away, too," she said. "And that does bother me a bit. It doesn't seem a good way to live, separated from family like that."

"No, it doesn't," Nell said. And it didn't sound like the Finnegan she knew. Whatever bad blood existed between him and his daughter, this was a drastic step.

Esther smiled warmly as Cass and Danny joined the group. She put one hand on Cass' arm. "But no matter how many people Finnegan shoos away, he specifically mentioned that Cass can come on his property anytime."

"Along with her mother's cooking," Izzy laughed.

Cass agreed. "And with a boatload of warnings. 'Walk here.' 'Don't walk there.' It's crazy what I have to go through to give him a pot of stew."

Danny stood on the outside of the group, quiet, his eyes on Cass.

Nell watched him watching her. And then, with a start, she touched her forehead, a light going on. *Why, he's in love with her. Danny Brandley loves Cass.* It was suddenly as clear as day. Although they'd been spending plenty of time together, Cass had insisted—especially in recent weeks—that they were good friends. *That's all,* she said in a voice that forbade argument.

But the look in Danny's eyes tonight spoke of something far deeper than friendship. Nell glanced at Cass as she took a sip of wine. Did she love him in return? Months ago Nell would have said yes. But tonight she wasn't sure. Cass was difficult to read these days.

She moved closer to him as the others discussed Finnegan's strange directives.

"You okay, Danny? I hear the tour was a success."

"Tour? Oh, the book." He shoved his fingers through his thick blond hair. "Yeah, it was fine."

"But?"

He looked over at Cass. She was talking to Ben, her face unreadable. "Sometimes I can't figure her out."

"She's very independent. But you know that, I suspect."

"I like that about her. But she has a loan coming due soon. It's killing her. It'd be so easy for me to help now that I have some extra money, but she insists she doesn't need my help. It'll work out, she says."

Nell had no answer for him. Sometimes she wanted to shake Cass, too, to tell her that accepting help didn't have a thing to do with being independent or less strong. But she suspected that when it came to accepting help from a man who clearly loved you, it added a new dimension to the situation, especially if you hadn't sorted through your own feelings yet.

"And the other love of that man's life these days seems to be little Gabby," Esther was saying to the group. She lifted a tiny crab cake from a tray and looked at it with great delight. "I suspect if she asked Finnegan for his whole raggedy piece of land, he'd give it to her, no questions asked. That sweet girl has brought a liveliness to the old man I haven't seen since his Moira died."

With a wave good-bye, the dispatcher shuffled off to the other side of the room to monitor the appetizers her husband was piling on a small paper plate.

Nell spotted Birdie talking with Ham and Jane Brewster just outside the veranda doors. She headed that way. Ben followed. "No Nick?" he asked to Nell's back.

Birdie heard the question. "No," she said, rising on tiptoe to kiss Ben's cheek. "He and Gabby had a date for dinner at Duckworth's in Gloucester. Gabby suggested they invite Ella and Harold, too. They were thrilled, of course. Ella went out and bought a new dress."

Birdie's face lit up as she talked, and the smile coming from her eyes told Nell that whatever concerns about Nick that she might have had earlier in the day, she'd put them to rest. At least for now.

They moved to the edge of the veranda, a reasonable distance from the beat of Andy's drums, Pete's guitar, and Merry's keyboard, and looked out over the sweep of green lawn that sloped to the water's edge.

Tiny solar lights lit the pathway, and at its end, Sal Scaglia stood alone on the dock, a drink in his hand, looking out across the water through his horn-rimmed glasses. Escaping, Nell suspected. He was a dutiful husband, but one more comfortable managing the dusty, solitary Registrar of Deeds' annex than hosting a cocktail party. He stood near his brand-new yacht, not large, but equipped with every gadget known to man, Beatrice had told her recently. And Nell knew, as they all did, that the yacht was a gift to Sal from his wife. A well-deserved gift, many thought to themselves, for his patience and loyalty and willingness to always take a backseat to the vivacious Beatrice.

Chief Jerry Thompson and his date sauntered down to the dock, and Sal turned toward them, adjusting his glasses as he shifted into his role as Beatrice's husband, smiling, welcoming, gracious. He motioned toward the new boat with the luminous blue sides, moored at the dock next to a small speedboat. And in the next frame, he was offering Sea Harbor's well-loved police chief a quick spin around the cove.

The sky was nearly dark now, and in the distance, just over a hill of granite and around a bend, the lights of Canary Cove Art Colony lit up the horizon. On the Scaglia veranda, the music picked up and the patio filled with moving bodies.

Beatrice was everywhere, encouraging tours of her home, engaging in conversations with the mayor and council members, embracing guests before they walked to their cars. When she took off her shoes and joined the crowd on the dance floor, Ben suggested it might be a perfect time to slip out.

"Need a ride?" he asked Birdie as they moved toward the foyer.

"I do," Birdie said, looking at Izzy and Sam out on the dance floor. "My chauffeurs are otherwise occupied."

Mary Pisano was standing near the door in the shadow of her husband, Max, a giant bear of a man who was digging into his pockets for car keys.

"A wonderful party," she said. "Have you ever seen a fisherman dance as well as my Max?"

"Never," Nell said.

"And I'd guess a party like this one provides you with at least a week's worth of 'About Town' columns," Ben said.

Big Max guffawed. "Make that a month's worth. Mary doesn't miss a thing."

Mary simply smiled and patted a giant purse that didn't quite hide her yellow pad. "But where's Nicholas? I thought you'd bring that handsome hunk along for everyone to admire. I might have gotten some juicy comments."

Birdie tsked away Mary's comment, then gave the columnist-turned-innkeeper a quick hug. "He had plans tonight, dear, but I do want to thank you. Nick thinks the Ravenswood B and B is the finest in the land. I suspect it was your hospitality as much as anything that helped us convince him to spend a few more days here."

Mary looked puzzled. Then she broke into laughter. "Talk him into it? No way."

"What do you mean?"

"I mean that no one talked Nick Marietti into anything. He called me on his way back from Italy to see if I would hold a room for him. He said he'd be staying a few days, maybe as long as a week. Business and pleasure, he said—rather cryptically, I thought. That handsome Italian is playing games with you, Birdie."

Chapter 11

Sundays were made for breakfasts at the Sweet Petunia, a tradition Ben Endicott held close to his heart. It was the one day Nell allowed whole eggs—and sometimes a sausage or two—to enter into her husband's diet. A minor heart attack some years before had provided the couple both an excuse to cut back on their work in Boston—Ben as an executive in the family-owned business, and Nell, a director of an arts nonprofit—and the impetus to make the Endicott Sea Harbor vacation home a permanent address. And so they had, along with adding changes in diet and a routine that included walks and slow runs and trips to the new gym that had recently opened in town.

But never on Sunday mornings. Sunday mornings were reserved for Annabelle Palazola's creamy egg dishes, spicy sausages or crisp slices of bacon, and fresh fruit compotes. Dark-roasted coffee with sweet cream curls on top. In good weather, it was served on the rustic deck overlooking the Canary Cove Art Colony and the ocean beyond.

Nell smiled her thanks as a waitress poured coffee and set glasses of freshly squeezed orange juice in front of them. They were early today—the usual Sunday-morning crowd was still in bed or perhaps crowded into the pews of Our Lady of Safe Seas Church, listening to Father Northcutt's homily.

"The quiet is nice," she murmured, pulling needles and a skein of soft purple yarn from her bag.

"The quiet after the storm."

The storm had waited, as Ben had predicted, until well after Beatrice's party had ended. It had rolled down the coast from New Hampshire, soaking Sea Harbor with a vengeance. Then moved out to sea just as quickly as it came, leaving gardens and lawns refreshed and the streets washed clean.

"Noisy . . . but nice." Nell allowed a smile, knowing Ben was thinking of those moments after they both awoke to the crashing sound of the storm meeting the sea, when he'd held her close, and then allowed his sure hands to gently convince her that the storm was merely a backdrop for far more magical things.

The moment was broken by Izzy's appearing at the table and pulling out a chair next to Nell. Sam was close behind.

"Wasn't that a great storm last night?" she greeted them. "Sam and I ran by the garden this morning—the rain turned it into a blanket of sprouts. It'll be in great shape for the garden party in a couple weeks. Even the flowers in front of Finnegan's fence have grown."

Sam leaned over Izzy, dropped a kiss on Nell's cheek, then sat down next to Ben. "Great run. Great storm. Nice party, too."

"Beatrice does it right." Izzy fingered the purple yarn in Nell's lap. "Gabby will love this sweater. You're the best, Aunt Nell." She gave her a quick hug.

"You're chipper today." Ben tilted his head to one side, scrutinizing his niece's expression.

"I am?" Izzy feigned surprise. Then she lifted one shoulder in a shrug and looked across the table at Sam. "It's him. That guy. I like living with him. I wake up every day to great coffee."

Sam just smiled, but the look in his eyes when he gazed at Izzy had nothing to do with his prowess as a barista.

"Where're Birdie and her newfound family?" Sam asked.

"Dining at the Ravenswood. Mary Pisano puts on a brunch spread for guests, and Nick invited Birdie and Gabby to join him. But Cass is coming after running a quick errand for her mother."

"I'm glad Nick is staying around for a while." Izzy took a still-warm miniature cinnamon roll from the basket.

"It looks like a few days, at least." Or so he'd told Mary Pisano. Birdie hadn't wanted to discuss Mary's comment on the ride home. If Nick had planned ahead of time to stay on a few days but wanted it to follow an invitation, perhaps that was simply a gallant gesture. Enough said.

"Good," Izzy said. "Because Gabby is helping me with a class tomorrow. A dozen kids have signed up to make that crazy crochet hat she wears—the one with the huge orange flower in front."

"A trendsetter at age ten. She reminds me of you at that age, Izzy, always doing your own thing." Nell slipped her yarn back into the bag as plates of frittata magically appeared in front of them—without a single order having been placed. She smiled up at the waitress. "This looks perfect."

"Annabelle said you'd love it. It's Tuscan something-or-other."

A puddle of tomato sauce and melted cheese and slivers of basil colored the perfectly browned center of Annabelle's masterpiece.

Ben sighed with happiness and picked up his fork.

"So, when is Cass coming?" Izzy said.

Nell checked her watch. She frowned. "She said she'd be ten minutes or less. But that was a while ago."

"Oh, you know Cass. Her concept of time isn't always the same as ours."

Not always. But when it came to food, Cass was rarely late. And she'd been quite adamant on the phone that she was starving and would be there soon. Danny might come, too. "Have the food waiting," she'd said.

The sound of sirens broke through the Sunday-morning quiet, and heads turned automatically toward the sound, looking over the treetops, down toward the water.

"An awful sound," Nell said. She shivered.

"Maybe it's an ambulance going to help someone," Izzy suggested around a mouthful of egg. "That would make it a good sound, right?"

Nell smiled and sipped her coffee. But she couldn't shake the anxious feeling she always got when the pleasant sounds of summer were broken by the unnatural screech of an alarm. A fishing accident. A car gone off the road. Sirens did not herald good things, no matter how Izzy tried to position it.

"It looks like it's over near Canary Cove Road," Ben said, lifting himself slightly from the chair seat and looking down over the trees. "That bend in the road needs a warning sign. There've been too many bike accidents down there."

That's what it must be. A cyclist gone off the road. On a quiet Sunday, that would be enough to bring out any emergency-vehicle drivers resting on their laurels. Hopefully the injury would be minor and not require a cast—a definite burden when vacationing at the beach.

When Nell's phone rang, she checked the name and relief flooded over her. It was Cass.

Only then did Nell realize the siren, as they always did, had caused her to take silent inventory of those closest to her. She knew where Birdie was, but Cass, who should have been sitting at the table, shoveling down eggs, was missing. But now she was in touch to tell Nell she was late but would be there in two seconds.

Nell pressed the phone to her ear, and a relieved smile lifted her lips as she said hello.

In the next instant, the smile dropped away.

"No." Nell's single word was firm, a command to change what was happening. To block it out. She slipped the phone back into her pocket and looked at the others.

"There's been an accident," she said. "We need to go."

Chapter 12

It wasn't Cass, Nell assured them as they abandoned their eggs and hurried from the restaurant. Cass was fine.

"Well, not fine, not really. I couldn't understand most of what she was saying, except that she needed us and there'd been a terrible accident."

A police car and ambulance had taken up much of the gravel easement along Finnegan's fence by the time they arrived, and Nell noticed vaguely that the sunflowers they'd planted were flattened beneath the wheels of the emergency medical van. Cass' truck was pulled over near the community garden, the door open, and folded up on the seat, weeping softly, was Cass. Next to the door, Danny Brandley stood, one palm flat against the side of the car, a helpless look in his eyes.

They were out of the car in an instant.

"It's Finnegan . . ." Danny began as Izzy and Sam drew close. Ben and Nell were a footstep behind.

Cass pulled herself up in the seat, her hands grasping the steering wheel. Her cheeks were stained with tears, and a lost look dulled her eyes. "Finnegan," she repeated, her voice a hoarse whisper.

Nell stepped up next to Izzy. She leaned down, her face close to Cass'. "Where is Finnegan, Cass?"

Cass could be tough as nails, a fisherman from her toes to the very top of her black hair, but this bright Sunday morning, with the sun soaking up last night's rain and the toll of church bells rolling down the hill and waking the sleepy town, she was a rag doll. Nell resisted the urge to wrap her tight in her arms, something Cass would not appreciate—not with the medical personnel so close.

Ben touched Nell's shoulder and nodded toward the police car.

Tommy Porter, a young patrolman who not too many years ago mowed the Endicott lawn, was putting the police monitor back into his squad car. He closed the door and walked toward Cass' truck, his head low.

"Tommy, what's going on?" Ben asked. "Cass mentioned an accident."

"Ch . . . Chief Thompson i-is o-on his way," Tommy answered, the tension bringing back, but only for few moments, the stuttering he'd been burdened with during younger years. He walked closer to the truck, talking to Ben, but his eyes were on Cass. "It's o-old man Finn-egan. Cass— She . . . He . . ."

Cass climbed out of the truck, and Tommy stopped talking. Danny steadied her, his hand on the small of her back, and this time she didn't pull away. She looked around at her circle of friends and then her eyes sought Tommy's.

Her face was drained of color and her eyes locked into Tommy's.

"He's dead, isn't he, Tommy? Finnegan is dead. . . ."

News of old Finnegan's death spread slowly through town, casting a pall over the sleepy summer Sunday.

At the same time, vacationers, oblivious of the news, moved happily through the streets. Colorful beach bags swung from tan shoulders, and the sweet fragrance of coconut oil filled Harbor Road and Archie's bookstore.

A normal Sunday in the beach town that was suddenly not normal at all to those who lived there.

After the ambulance had taken Finnegan away and Cass had talked to Chief Thompson, they retreated to Ben and Nell's, where Nell quickly tossed together a plate of eggs, thick pieces of French toast dusted with cinnamon sugar, and a bowl of fresh fruit. Not up to Annabelle's standards, she told them, but enough to fill empty stomachs.

As she carried the tray of food out to the deck, Nell's cell phone rang. She handed the tray to Izzy and stepped back inside the family room.

Before Nell could say hello, Birdie began talking. "Esther Gibson called me," she said. "She didn't know much, but she said there'd been an accident."

Nell filled her in on the scant details that she knew. "Last night's storm made it difficult to know exactly what happened. It was muddy, as you can imagine."

"And Cass? Esther said she was there. Poor Cass. Oh, Nell, we know how awful such a thing is. . . ."

Nell nodded, remembering the terrible nightmares that plagued her a couple of years before, when she and Birdie had come upon someone they knew lying motionless—and very dead—in a snowy bank. "Yes. She was on her way to meet us for breakfast but stopped to deliver some food to Finnegan. It was awful for her, but she's here now—and she insists she's fine."

Nell looked across the deck while she talked. Cass was sitting next to Ben, with Danny hovering close, while Izzy and Sam set out plates, mugs, and a carafe of coffee. When they had arrived home, Cass had gone upstairs to Ben and Nell's bathroom and thrown water on her face. Some color had crept back into her face, but her eyes still held the horror of what she'd seen.

"Fine, nonsense," Birdie was saying into her ear. "She just stumbled upon a dead body. How could she be fine?" She told Nell she'd be over as soon as she and Nick were finished talking with Gabby about the accident. "Finnegan was her friend," she reminded Nell.

When Birdie showed up a short while later, she wasn't alone.

A pale-faced Gabby walked in ahead of Birdie and Nick. She smiled and went readily into the hug Nell offered.

"She wanted to come," Birdie said as Gabby walked on ahead, passing through the family room and out to the deck. "She's sad, but children have a way of funneling grief to a place where they can deal with it." She shook her head slowly. "It's an amazing gift."

"She hangs on to people she's lost, so they're never really far from her," Nick said. "A favorite teacher died last year, and Gabby is always telling me about conversations the two of them have. Things she learns from Miss Leah. Advice she gives. Her dad says there's a whole litany of people who live in her spirit world."

"Perhaps there's something there to learn," Birdie said.

Nick was quiet, his eyes following Gabby as she walked over to Cass and sat down next to her, not saying a word but resting one hand on Cass' knee.

"It's as if she's known you all her life," he said.

"We love her. She reminds me of what Birdie must have been like at that age."

"If Gabby grows up to be half the woman her grandmother is, she'll be a great lady," Nick said.

"Birdie is embracing this new role. You've given her a gift, bringing Gabby here."

"As we were driving into town that day, I realized that Birdie could turn us away. Close the door in our faces. I hadn't seen her in a long time, and then to drop this bombshell on her—it was a risk. My brother was wrong, maybe, to keep the fact that he had a son from her. But he knew how weak his heart was by then, that the writing was on the wall. I think he didn't want her to have to deal with his mistakes."

"Gabby came from that mistake, so it ended up being a blessing. But maybe it was a good thing not to tell Birdie. What could she have done?"

"That's the crux of it. Nothing. Sometimes it is far better not to know some things that you can't do anything about, things that might hurt you needlessly." He spoke with unusual passion and looked at Nell as if wanting her to listen carefully and to take his words and stash them away.

Then his voice returned to normal and he continued, talking about his brother. "Joseph had me put money into a trust for his son—more than Christopher would ever spend in a lifetime. Too much, maybe. But, nevertheless, he was taken care of, and so is Gabby. My brother was a secretive guy—he had his problems—but he never shirked his responsibilities."

"And you arranged for the amazing gift that came out of all that history to meet her grandmother. All's right with the world."

His eyes lingered on his niece. "This place is about as different from her Manhattan penthouse life as it can be, but she can't stop talking about her friends, the town, the lobsters. She loves it all."

"Finnegan seemed to be one of her favorites. Did you have the chance to know him?"

"No." The answer came quickly, definitively. "Gabby talked about him. He was teaching her how to fish somewhere down near Canary Cove, she said."

Yes, somewhere down where you had an argument with that very man whom you don't know. Less than a day ago. Nell's brows pulled together. She took a deep breath, then released it, along with the uncomfortable image of Finnegan spewing his anger on Nick Marietti. She wanted the thoughts gone, out of her head. Nick Marietti had done a wonderful thing bringing Gabby here. He was gracious and kind. And there was something about him that elicited trust and welcomed friendship. She liked him.

And he had just lied to her.

She forced a smile to her face. It didn't matter now. Whatever they had argued about was a nonissue. Finnegan was no longer able to argue. *Let it go.*

"This deck is our safe haven," she said, motioning for him to follow her. "A place to be with friends no matter what the occasion—happy or sad."

Nick took in the group gathering together in the comfortable circle of chaises and lounge chairs. "I should be embarrassed to be intruding like this. But you don't seem to allow it."

"No, we don't. You're practically a relative. We're glad you're here—and I know Birdie is happy that you and Gabby will stay a few more days. I hope it all means your mother is doing better?"

"She's rallied. Sometimes I think she uses the drama of death to play us all, get us to do her bidding. I went to Italy thinking I might be attending a funeral, and instead I came back to one here in Sea Harbor. Life is full of twists and turns, *sei d'accordo*?"

"Yes, most certainly." She smiled. Her own life had had its shares of curves, for sure, and whether they added lines to her forehead or etched joyful memories in her heart, the curves were always enriching in one way or another.

Nick's head leaned to one side, as if pondering a serious thought. Then he asked, "Were you close to the man who died?"

Nell considered the question for a moment. "Not close like I am to these people." She looked around the deck. "But Finnegan was a fixture around Sea Harbor. A few, like Cass and her family, Angus McPherran, and Birdie, too, knew him better than others. It's difficult to imagine the town without him. He'll be missed."

"Does he have relatives?"

"A daughter. His wife died a while ago." *His daughter*. Nell had barely given a thought to Beverly Walden. Surely she knew by now. Chief Thompson would have gone to her immediately. Or Tommy Porter. Nell hoped there was someone there with her. Even though the relationship might not have been good, the death of a parent was not an easy thing to face.

Ben walked across the deck and shook Nick's hand. "The eggs are getting cold, Nick. How about I fix a plate for you?"

Nell left Nick in Ben's care, checked on Gabby, who had gone inside to watch a movie, and then walked around to the deck railing to where Cass was sitting. She noticed with some satisfaction that she was able to eat. A good sign. But then she remembered that the awful part of finding a dead body in such an unnatural way usually came in the middle of the night. She silently hoped Danny would be there to help her through it.

Nell ignored the myriad questions squeezed tight inside her chest and instead picked up the coffee carafe and walked slowly around the group, refilling cups. Cass would talk when she was ready.

Ready was sooner than Nell thought.

"It was that crazy yellow fleece. That's the only reason I noticed him," Cass said, setting her plate down on the teak table. "Otherwise, I'd just have left the soda bread on the step. Ma insisted he get it this morning while it was still fresh. *Finn is just like your dad,* she said. *He doesn't use the sense the good lord gave him. He needs to eat.* And then I saw that familiar puddle of sunshine—the golden fleece vest, matted down in mud. . . ."

"I don't think he's taken it off since you gave it to him," Izzy said softly.

Cass nodded. "Yeah. He liked it. He put it right on that day and said that it was there to stay. *Finest knit fleece I've ever had,* he said. Then he told me his Moira would have loved it, too; she loved to knit. Yellow was her favorite color. She used to knit him yellow socks." Cass managed a smile. "Finn was a weird guy sometimes, but he cared about us. He kept telling me not to worry about our lobster business. It'd end up all right." She shook her head. "I didn't know what he was talking about half the time. He rambled."

Finally Ben broached the subject they hadn't touched. "Do you think with all that rain we had, he slipped and fell on a rock? How did he die?"

"It was hard to tell. There was a lot of blood. The police said he might have fallen on one of those old tractor parts. It . . ."

"They'll figure it out," Danny said, trying to move Cass away from the vivid memory.

"I didn't see him until I was right up near the house. He warned me all the time not to wander around—too much junk. I could get hurt. *Always stay on the path.*"

Nell could imagine the old man swimming his way through the tall weeds, tripping, maybe, on the rusted trash that filled his land. Falling in the dark.

In the dark. Why was Finnegan prowling around in the dark on a stormy night?

"I think he was still alive when I found him," Cass said. "I thought I felt a pulse, just a thread. I put my ear near his mouth and

I swear he said something to me." She looked around, hoping for affirmation. "*Cassoulet* . . . I think he said that . . . and *you'll be fine,* maybe. But the ambulance guys weren't sure. They thought I imagined it."

A young voice came from the other side of the deck. "Finnegan wanted people to do what was right. He got real mad when they didn't."

They looked across the deck.

No one had noticed Gabby's return. She was curled up in the big wicker rocker beneath the overhanging tree branch, her feet curled up beneath her and Nell's old copy of *The Wizard of Oz* open in her lap.

"Gabrielle, we didn't know you were out here," Nick said.

Gabby closed the book and hugged it to her chest. "It's okay, Uncle Nick. I can handle things." She looked down at the old book and traced the figure of Dorothy, her finger moving around the blue-and-white-checked dress, the slippers, and the tiny dog at her feet.

Two strong little girls, Nell thought. One not unlike the other, exploring a new land. Meeting a wizard . . .

Izzy began passing around a tray of collaches that Birdie had picked up on the way over. She wrapped one in a napkin and took it over to Gabby. "I loved that book, too," she said. "I even had a dog named Toto when I was growing up."

Gabby looked up and smiled, but they could see that her thoughts had drifted away from the land of Oz.

"His real name was Francis," she said, looking up. "Francis Finnegan."

Chapter 13

Cass and Izzy picked up Nell on Monday morning an hour earlier than usual.

Nell rubbed the sleep from her eyes, pulled on a pair of jersey shorts and an old T-shirt, and found them in the kitchen, helping themselves to glasses of water.

"Why so early?" she asked, searching the kitchen counter for her cell phone. "You even beat the paper boy."

"Couldn't sleep," Izzy said. "Finally Sam nudged me out of bed and told me to go take a run. At least I think that's what he said. And then he put a pillow over his head and went back to sleep."

Cass leaned over and touched her toes, feigning a warm-up. "Renting Izzy's old house definitely has its drawbacks." She pushed away black strands of hair hanging over her face and looked up at Nell. "She thinks she still lives there sometimes; walks right in. No privacy. Can I fire my landlord?"

Having Cass move into Izzy's house was a stroke of genius. It saved Izzy and Sam from having to make a decision about it for a while, and got Cass out of her two-room apartment. And moans or not, Cass loved the extra space and patch of green lawn.

Izzy ignored Cass' comments. "This woman never sleeps. It's supposed to be her day off and she's already been out checking traps for Pete. Can you believe it?"

Nell could. Cass probably hadn't wanted to run into any of the other fishermen whose traps were anchored in the coves. Old-timers who would now know about Finnegan and want to talk about him. She suspected Cass needed to process his death in a more private way.

"Francis," Cass said, shifting attention away from her work habits. "Can you believe that? I wonder if his mother called him Frank. Frank Finnegan. I had no idea. And that little scamp found it out, something we've speculated about for years." She shook her head and laughed. "I wonder what other secrets he told her."

Nell filled a water bottle, wondering the same thing.

Cass looked up at the clock. "Well, what are we waiting for? If we're going to put our bodies through this excruciating torture, we might as well get it over with." She headed for the back door.

Nell tied a light hoodie around her shoulders and followed the two younger women down the back deck steps and through the Endicott woods that led to the beach.

"We have it all to ourselves," Izzy said, stretching her arms wide. She dropped her hands to the sand and stretched her calf muscles.

"Perfect running sand," Cass said as they started out. "Not a single sand castle in sight."

Only at that early hour would the sand be like glass, the receding tide stroking it with gentle laps, smoothing and caressing. They were silent for the first stretch, Nell concentrating on measured breaths and simply keeping up. She knew Cass and Izzy were slowing their pace for her, but even the slowdown was a challenge on some days. Today was one of them.

They ran along the edge of manicured yacht club beach, and then, without conscious thought, they circled back along the shoreline that bordered Canary Cove. Small paths led up from the sea to houses that dotted the rocky land. As they ran past one, Cass pointed up the slope. "That white one is the house Finn's daughter is staying in," she called out. "He and Moira lived there a long time ago and Finn never sold it."

Nell looked up at the cozy home with flower boxes at each window. A small dock with washed-out letters spelling FINNEGAN was attached to the shore. Rope, a bucket, and hose sat at the end next to shoes and a bottle of soap.

"Looks like a boat's been moored here," Cass said, curious, then continued on along the path. "A neighbor, maybe. They all share."

The path grew narrow as they rounded the curve of land. Trees hugged one side and the rocky shore on the other. Soon they ran single file, with Izzy taking the lead.

"Look up ahead," she said, slowing down and pointing.

Beverly Walden sat on the old dock beneath the Artist's Palate parking lot. Her feet dangled over the side, and a small boat was tied to the dock.

The dock itself was small and rickety. Although the topic of fixing it up was a frequent one at Canary Cove Art Association meetings, it never seemed to change. One of the problems, Ham Brewster said, was that no one knew who really owned it. So all the artists continued to use it when they needed a break, to sunbathe, or to tie their boats to.

Standing just at the dock's edge, leaning against one of the posts, was Davey Delaney. He was dressed for exercise, in shorts and a T-shirt, a pair of sunglasses pushed to the top of his head. His eyes were focused on Beverly.

Izzy slowed to a virtual stop. She turned around and said softly, "Should we go back?"

Then Beverly looked up. For a moment it appeared she might topple off the dock. Quickly, she steadied herself and managed a wave.

Nell waved back and they continued at a slower pace along the path.

Davey Delaney managed a clumsy hello. Then he muttered that he needed to get back up to the Palate's deck. His coffee was getting cold. He turned and hurried up the steps.

"I hope we're not intruding," Nell said. She watched Davey's back as it disappeared.

Beverly looked up at the joggers, her eyes adjusting. Her cheeks were flushed, her eyes bright. She pulled her tank top down over her bare abdomen, then bent her legs and wrapped her arms around them. "No. I was just . . ."

She looked down at the boat. "I was just . . . I was just sitting here, easing into the day. I live near here."

It was Finnegan's boat bobbing at the side of the dock. His pride and joy, the only thing he'd ever splurged on since his wife died, or so his fishermen buddies said. It was a small boat, by some standards, but neat and freshly painted with a small cabin and the single word MOIRA carefully painted in deep purple letters across the white hull.

"We're sorry about your father," Nell said. "It's difficult when someone in your life dies suddenly."

Beverly seemed to be sorting through Nell's words, analyzing them. She forked her fingers through her hair and looked up again. "He wasn't in my life. He was an odd man. Lived by his own set of rules, I suppose you'd say. And he wanted everyone else to live by the same rules. Rigid ones."

An awkward silence followed. Then Beverly said, "I moved back here thinking . . . well, I don't know what I was thinking. Maybe that we'd see each other differently than when I was a kid? But I'd been away more than half my life. What chance was there for that? Maybe I just came to shake him up. I never liked him. He only adopted me because he loved my mother so much. I was . . . what, how old? Hadn't even hit puberty. I didn't have any choice in the matter."

Adopted. Birdie hadn't mentioned that, and Cass would have been too young to care about such details. The thing the rumor mill picked up and perpetuated was that she'd run away. And that was the story Nell had always heard: Finnegan had a daughter but she didn't even come back for her own mother's funeral.

Beverly went on. "But I'm glad I came back. It's brought me some unexpected happiness, and it's about time. And all in spite of a man named Finnegan. I found I didn't need him to be happy. He's just a . . . just a man who lived with my mother."

"Who loved your mother," Nell added.

She shrugged.

Nell watched the expression that came across Beverly's face as she talked. It wasn't chitchat. Beverly Walden was happy, the kind that starts on the inside and takes over your being. Unabashedly happy.

The day after her father was found dead.

"He loved that boat," Cass said suddenly, looking down at it.

The edge to her voice was noticeable, and there was a question lurking there, as if she wanted to say, *And what are you doing with it, with something he loved?*

Beverly nodded.

"So, you've been to his place?" Cass went on, not accepting a nod for a response.

Beverly didn't answer. Then she skirted the question and said, "It will take a few days before it's officially mine. But Officer Porter was able to get the boat released for me. She was my mother, you know." She shielded her eyes from the morning sun and looked up at them again, defying them to disagree.

"Of course she was," Nell said.

The awkward silence returned.

"Well, if we can do anything . . ." Nell began.

"Thank you," Beverly said. "I'm fine. It's too bad we couldn't reconcile before he died. But we didn't. So that's that. We'll have a funeral. File the will."

"Have you seen the will?"

"No. But the police assure me they will have it soon. And then those who liked him will have a chance to mourn, and the rest of us will be able to put it all behind us and move on."

With nothing more to say, they left, Beverly's odd words following them up the uneven granite steps to the Artist's Palate parking lot.

"What's wrong with that woman?" Cass asked as they walked across the parking lot to Canary Cove Road. "She's awful. Finnegan loved that boat with his life. I wonder if she even knows that. Or if she cares."

"She has the look of someone who hasn't had it easy," Nell said, trying to soften Beverly's words.

"Sure. But some of that is a matter of choice," Izzy said. "Why couldn't they see beyond their differences?"

"It isn't that Finn didn't like kids. Look at his relationship with Gabby." Cass kicked at a stone and watched it fly over the pathway.

"Maybe they tried. I suppose there will always be things we don't know. Secrets Finnegan took with him."

They slowed down when they reached the community garden, then stood side by side for a minute, breathing in the fragrance of fresh herbs and newly rained-on greens. The garden was responding to Saturday night's rain, perking up and begging for admirers.

"Wait till you see our new window display at the shop," Izzy said. "Mae's nieces are doing it. It'll make you want to come sit in the middle of a magical garden and knit."

"Knitting in a comfortable chair with a glass of wine suits me fine," Cass said, and wrinkled her nose at Izzy as they neared the fence that separated the garden from Finnegan's land.

They moved along, slowing again as they came to Finnegan's gate. The deep ruts from car tires formed an intricate design in the soppy soil.

The muddy road was more open now from the recent traffic, the house visible beyond the trees at the far end. It was a view Finnegan didn't allow most of the public to see. But now it was open, exposed. Naked. *It's what happens at death,* Nell thought. Suddenly one's life was opened up for the curious to explore, to look into, to pick apart, and to judge.

Nell shivered as she looked down the curvy, weed-choked drive.

She hadn't known the property to be any other way, but Birdie talked about years past when Finn's property was neat and clean, with a gravel drive and parking places for the tenants who rented office space from him. And a solid dock in back to moor small fishing boats.

The sound of a car in the distance caused the women to step back, as if they'd been caught doing something wrong and

Finnegan himself would pop up in the middle of a bed of weeds to scold them.

Izzy checked her watch and suggested they pick up their speed. "The shop is going to begin its day without me," she said. With Nell bringing up the rear, they started down the street toward Harbor Road and their homes. "I'm going at my own speed," Nell called ahead. "You two go on."

With that, Cass and Izzy flew down the road, their long legs carrying them like young deer, graceful and sleek. Nell smiled at their backs and decided she'd had enough jostling of her body parts for one morning. She slowed to a walk and breathed in the crisp, salty air.

Just beyond the edge of Finnegan's land was a wide path to the water used by some old-timers to launch their motorboats for a day of fishing, or for kids to park their bikes and walk along the shore, dragging makeshift rafts or inner tubes. It separated Finnegan's property from the nicely landscaped property and modern office of the Canary Cove Arts Association building. The two properties had once been twins, with neat matching buildings, but Finn had changed that. They were now as different as day and night.

A few bikes were parked on the gravel path, huddled together near the fence, and in the distance Nell spotted several teenagers jostling one another as they made their way down the path.

She smiled at the Huck Finn scene, remembering when Izzy was a teenager and would join the Endicott family for a few weeks each summer. She and her friends walked this same path, down to the private rocky shore that most vacationers didn't know about. They'd make their way along the rocks to one of the small docks that jutted out into the water behind Finnegan's place or the rickety dock where Beverly Walden had parked Finn's boat. Privacy. Away from summer kids, was how the kids saw it.

Such wonderful summers. Nell took a drink from her water bottle, then slipped it back into the holder hanging from her waist. She glanced down toward the water once more.

It was then that she noticed the dark blue Altima. It was farther along the gravel road, beyond the bikes, parked under a low-hanging tree that nearly hid it from view.

Nell took a few steps toward it, then stopped when she spotted the rental sticker on the bumper. She looked around for the driver, but the only sound was that of the sea and the teenagers ahead, tossing teasing comments back and forth.

Making her way to Finnegan's fence, she leaned over and separated some weeds with her hands, peering off into the shadows. All was quiet.

She looked down the road toward town and saw that traffic was picking up, with tourists headed out to Canary Cove. Shopkeepers going to work. The day was beginning.

And so must hers. She glanced once more at the car, then walked back toward the road and headed home, using the time to convince herself there were plenty of blue Altimas in this world. And the fact that it was the make and color of the car Nicholas Marietti had rented at Logan Airport a couple of days before was surely a coincidence.

Chapter 14

In spite of the sadness surrounding Finnegan's death—or maybe because of it—Izzy made sure that Gabby's crocheted-hat class happened as scheduled. Gabby herself insisted on it. Finnegan loved her beanie, she'd added.

Izzy asked Birdie and Nell to sit in as backup, just in case. One never knew what could happen with a room filled with preteens. It was the way Izzy did things: prepare for the unexpected. Nell decided it was a leftover from her days as a lawyer, when she always tried to cover her bases so the courtroom would hold no surprises. She watched her niece now, tapping two glass needles together for attention.

Gabby came up to Nell and Birdie and dipped her head low so the top of it faced them, and showed off her hat. "I could make you each one. What do you think?" She lifted her head and waited expectantly.

"Well, that's a nice offer," Birdie said. "But I'm not sure I have enough hair to hold it on."

Gabby touched the top of Birdie's head lightly, a gentle pat, as one would give a kitten. "Of course you do, Nonna," she said.

They each put in an order for a beanie with a flower.

Then Nell asked, "How are you doing, sweetie?"

Gabby thought about the question, wrapping a strand of hair around one finger. "Finn, well, he's my friend. He treats me like a kid, sure, but a kid he trusts, like I like and trust him—like a best friend, you know?"

On the other side of the room, Izzy was urging the crowd to quiet down. She began handing out the hat pattern.

Gabby looked up. "Oops, gotta go," she said, planting a quick kiss on Birdie's wrinkled cheek.

She looked at Nell, as if she was sorry she hadn't really answered her question. Her forehead wrinkled slightly, her eyes holding Nell's. "Finn's fine," she said.

Then in a flash she was off to the front of the room, where Izzy held the girls in rapt attention.

"Present tense." Birdie said, her fingers touching the warm spot left on her cheek.

"I noticed. Finn is still with her."

They turned their attention to Izzy standing on a small wooden box, explaining the class structure to an attentive group. The girls, their faces bright, tan, and smiling, looked at her like a well-loved teacher.

And she is that, Nell thought—well loved, and a born teacher. Personality. Intelligence. A great communicator. All the traits that had merited her an offer from a prestigious firm after law school. A career that made her father inordinately proud of her. A decent career, if not totally satisfying.

Until that awful day that changed her life—the day she had won a difficult case, getting a young man off on a burglary charge. An ordinary-looking man with a playful smile who had hugged Izzy outside the courtroom, an image replayed endlessly on television the next day. The photo of a young man, free and innocent, who, on his way to the T that very day, held up a neighborhood grocery shop and shot the owner and his wife to death.

Nell watched the pleasure that spread across Izzy's face now as she worked with the young girls. She had found her niche, owning her own business, researching and working with amazing fibers, amazing people. And now married to an amazing man.

When Izzy introduced Gabby, the crowd cheered. She'd become a pied piper, riding through town on Birdie's pink bike, her beanie holding down that mass of hair. Young girls sought her out, inviting her to join them at the beach or Scoopers ice-cream shop. But mostly Gabby hung out with the adults, begging Cass for a ride on the *Lady Lobster*, sitting cross-legged in the knit shop with Purl on her lap, hanging out with Willow Adams at the Fishtail Gallery. And then there was Finn, *her best friend*.

Nell watched her move through the gathering of girls, sitting on the floor or crowded around the table. She wore torn shorts and a T-shirt proclaiming her love for New York, along with the famous beanie—the loopy green crochet hat that hugged the crown of her head. Below it, hair flew out in all directions like an ocean spray.

Finn is fine, she'd said. And with the kind of assurance that made Nell think Finn himself had told her so.

"She's captivating," Nell whispered to Birdie.

Birdie smiled in that way grandmothers did. *Yes, she's captivating. She's lovely. She's my granddaughter.*

Nell hadn't mentioned seeing the blue car to Birdie. By the time she had moved into her day, it seemed foolish. A blue car parked on a road. She'd seen cars there before. The fact that it bordered Finnegan's property would never occur to most people. Why should it? What did it matter?

So she'd gone about the day, running errands, giving a fund-raising talk at the Arts Association, a quick stop at Coffee's, where those who knew Finnegan spoke quietly of the old man who had died on his land that weekend.

Nell heard the undertones, of course. The daughter would sell it and the land would be cleaned up. A new business built, perhaps? But there was still a sincere sadness that they had lost one of their own. A man who had lived in Sea Harbor nearly his whole life. A fixture.

And they would mourn him appropriately in Our Lady of Safe Seas, the big church on the hill.

Nell felt the familiar rub against her leg and absently picked up Purl, settling her between her and Birdie on the window seat. The room hummed with crochet activity interspersed with spurts of girlish giggles as crochet hooks caught threads of yarn. Izzy and

Gabby moved through the group, demonstrating the foundation chain, checking the tension, fixing mishaps.

Izzy had suggested a light cotton blend in happy summer colors for the hats—bright greens and oranges, tomato reds, cobalt blue. Colors as alive as the youthful bodies filling the room.

Izzy stooped down to help a group of girls sitting on the floor, then walked over to Birdie and Nell. "You two must have better things to do, and I think Gabby has this under control."

"And she's much better at crochet than I am, dear," Birdie said, lifting herself from the window seat. "I completely agree—we are window dressing. You don't need us."

"But I'll see you later?"

"Later?"

"The Fractured Fish?" Izzy prompted.

"I nearly forgot. The summer series starts tonight."

"It's old-time favorites, Pete says. Seventies covers. You'll love it."

Birdie feigned displeasure. "I'll have you know I just down-loaded a Taylor Swift album."

They laughed and made their way toward the steps, carefully climbing over legs and feet. Purl trailed after them.

"Taylor Swift?" Nell said. "Download?"

Birdie looked smug. "Gabby likes her. She's teaching me about her music." Birdie fished around in her pocket and pulled out a small silver square. "She and Nick gave me this iPod and they've been filling it with all sorts of music. It'll certainly pep up the tap dancing class I teach at the retirement center."

"Sometimes you amaze me, Birdie Favazza," Nell said, waving to Mae Anderson, Izzy's shop manager, and holding open the front door for her friend.

Purl parted company with them at the door, jumping into the display window as if to wave good-bye.

Just outside the door, a small group of women were looking into the window of the yarn shop. "What do you suppose Purl has done now?" Nell asked, looking around the women's shoulders to the display window.

"It's amazing," one of the women murmured.

And it was.

"How did we miss this on our way in?" Birdie asked. "It's a masterpiece."

Purl was the one who had caught everyone's interest, but it was her garden paradise that held that attention. She rolled over on a soft garden bed of taupe-colored cashmere that covered the floor of the display. Rising out of the cashmere ground cover was a tall stalk, green yarn wound high in every texture and hue. Along the sides and at the top, poking through the husks of yarn, were bright yellow yarn cobs. On another twisted green vine, tightly wound balls of tomato-red wool were waiting to be plucked. Slender knit beans dripped from another vine, and all around, lined up neatly in rows, were carrot tops, lime-colored leafy plants, strawberries, and cucumbers.

It was a veritable garden of yarn—cotton and silk blends, summer wool, airy cashmere, and alpaca. In the corner was a small, neat sign: KNIT A GARDEN. PLANT A GARDEN. CELEBRATE A GARDEN.

And below, the date and time of the community gathering that would be held in a couple of weeks to celebrate the community garden and the first fruits of everyone's efforts. A great excuse for a party, Willow Adams had exclaimed, as she signed up all her friends for the planning committee.

"Mae's nieces are following in Willow's footsteps. These are works of art."

As if reading their lips and affirming the twins' artistry, Purl rubbed her small pink nose on the cashmere ground, back and forth. Then she nuzzled down in her luxurious bed and closed her eyes.

"I need to talk to you two," Beatrice Scaglia said, appearing beside them out of nowhere. Her voice was anxious. She touched Birdie on the arm, her red fingernails tapping it lightly.

"Have you seen Izzy's lovely window?" Birdie asked.

"Everything Izzy does is wonderful." Beatrice looked around, then nudged them down the sidewalk, away from the group admiring the yarn garden.

"Is something wrong?" Nell asked to the councilwoman's back as they followed her clicking heels along the sidewalk.

"No," she said, stopping at the alleyway that separated the yarn shop from Archie's bookstore. She turned around and faced them, one hand smoothing out an imaginary wrinkle in her dress. "We need to talk."

"About?"

"Finnegan. He didn't seem to hold you in obvious contempt like he did some of us."

"He didn't hold you in contempt, Beatrice. He simply didn't like other people trying to control his life—or his land."

Beatrice brushed off Birdie's comment with a wave of her hand. "Do you know if there are relatives other than Beverly who might be in his will? Now that he's dead, we need to take care of that land as quickly as possible. My constituents are demanding action, but no one seems to know what's next, when the property will be sold. Has Ben mentioned anything? Sometimes he seems to know things before the mayor does."

Nell's face mirrored the surprise that flitted across Birdie's. "That's not really our business, is it? The man isn't even buried yet."

Beatrice seemed deaf to anything that didn't satisfy her questions. She went on as if Nell hadn't spoken a word. "His will is the main question. I assume the beneficiary is his daughter, but I'd like it confirmed. I had Sal check the deed at his office and all he could come up with is that Finnegan owned the land." Displeasure in her husband's failure to help was evident. "There isn't anyone else named on the deed, Sal said. No one. Not even his wife."

"He owned that land long before he married Moira." Birdie said.

"That's the peculiar thing. Finnegan has lived here forever. But what do we know about him? I never realized what a mystery he was until he left us."

Beatrice said the words *left us* as if Finnegan had intentionally gone off to some lovely place, leaving them the burden of figuring out his life—and his property.

"We know a lot. We know he was a kind, generous man who

helped many people, who patrolled Canary Cove, who painted Cass' buoys when she needed help. Who let his daughter live in that sweet house he and Moira owned. Who . . ."

"The daughter. Yes. I talked to her."

"You talked to her?" Nell's brows lifted.

"I was in Canary Cove today, so I stopped into that co-op gallery where she works and paints, introduced myself, and told her how sorry I was about her father. She seemed very uncomfortable—I suppose not too many people have stopped in. She's not the friendliest person in town. I just mentioned the property in passing."

"In passing?" Birdie frowned at her.

"I wondered if she had thought about it, assuming it would be hers, that's all. I offered to help in any way I could. What does the poor girl know about developers and land value around Sea Harbor?

"She mentioned it might be a nice place for additional galleries, kind of like an annex to Canary Cove. I thought that was an interesting idea and suggested luxury condos above the shops."

"Beatrice, her father just died. It seems a bit premature," Nell said.

"I don't think so. She didn't seem offended by my question, just nervous. But it was clear she'd been thinking about the land, too. But in the end, it doesn't matter, because she's never seen her father's will. She knows she's the probable heir, but she can't do anything until the will is read."

Birdie and Nell exchanged looks, but Beatrice went on. "She did, however, indicate that she'd have a copy of the will soon."

"If Beverly is Finn's only relative, I suspect you're right. It will be hers." Birdie said.

"I hope so. So soon, hopefully, we can get a bulldozer out there and clean it up."

The creak of Archie Brandley's bookstore door silenced Beatrice. They looked up to see Father Northcutt walking toward them.

"A bulldozer, Beatrice?" he asked. Thin strands of gray hair fluttered in the breeze. "For what?"

Father Larry's face was generous and open and always held a

smile. But reading his eyes, Nell could see he had caught more of the conversation than he acknowledged.

"The Finnegan place, Father," Beatrice said, quickly managing a smile. "We were just wondering what will happen to it and when it will be up for sale."

"For sale?"

"It's what everyone wants—the city, the neighbors, the artists, the developers, even his daughter. It's what's good for everyone. That's all we want, Father—what's best for Sea Harbor. We can't afford another accident over there."

Nell held back a smile. Beatrice wasn't a bad person—in fact, she liked her most of the time. She managed to do good things for the city, and people thanked her by voting for her. She was good at the political banter. But she was also good at manipulating situations to her best interests and to posturing herself just right.

Father Northcutt broke into a broad smile, folding his hands together over his ample girth. "Ah, Beatrice Scaglia, you are a wonder now. And I'd be wrong to think you didn't want the best for Sea Harbor."

Then he looked at all three of the women, his Irish eyes smiling on each of them. "But first we need to bury our dear friend Finnegan, to mourn his loss, and to send his spirit off in peace."

He paused, his jowls still moving from his words. When he continued, his face had grown more serious and his voice held a note of premonition, something Nell thought odd. Elusive.

"And once the dear man has been put to rest, then we shall accept what happens with that land along the harbor. Finnegan's wishes, even if they hold some surprises, will prevail. Sometimes wisdom resides where we least expect it."

The smile returned, and with a friendly good-bye, the priest sauntered across the street to greet Gus McClucken, idling in front of his hardware store.

Chapter 15

"He knows something we don't," Nell told Ben later that evening. She sat beside him in the CRV, heading over to the Fractured Fish's summer concert. Sam and Izzy listened from the backseat.

Nell looked through the window as they neared Finnegan's land, to the path that led to the water. There were bicycles roped together and hooked to Finnegan's fence for safekeeping. A motorcycle farther down the alley. Probably concertgoers who didn't want to get stuck in the Artist's Palate parking lot after the performance.

But no blue Altima.

Foolish thoughts, she chided herself. Why was she seeing mysteries lurking everywhere?

"Father Larry is well connected," Ben was saying beside her. "Maybe he does. I don't think Finnegan was a big churchgoer, but I often saw him with the padre, sitting down at the dock, philosophizing about life. People trust him."

"So you don't think it's mysterious?" Nell turned away from the window.

"Well, I do," Izzy spoke up from the backseat. "I think he was telling you something without actually saying it."

"I think he was telling Beatrice in a nice way to mind her own business," Sam said.

Izzy tapped his knee and he caught her fingers, wrapping them tightly in his own.

Nell looked back and nodded to Sam. "There was definitely

some of that. Finnegan died less than two days ago. He was urging her to back off a bit. But there was something more, something he wasn't saying." Somehow Nell felt sure of that, but explaining it was another matter.

Ben slowed down as they passed by Finnegan's gate. "Are you folks up for a short walk? How about we park at the community garden and check out the plants? It'll give me a quick getaway, too. I've been trapped in that restaurant parking lot one too many times." He pulled off the road and angled the car along the easement that ran in front of Finnegan's property and the garden next to it.

"The walk may work out the kinks," Sam said. "I spent my day being a fly on the harbor pier, sitting in a cramped fold-up chair, snapping photos. People don't see me after a while, and it's amazing what the camera captures."

"A peeping Tom, that's what my Sam has become." Izzy climbed out of the car. "Who would have thought?"

Sam's long legs followed her. "Yep. I'll know everyone's secrets. Better behave yourself, Izzy." He dropped a kiss on the top of her head.

"It'll be a great series, Sam," Ben said. He clicked the lock button on his key chain and followed Nell over to the raised garden beds.

The perimeter of the garden area was lit with solar lights that Ham and Jane had donated, and in the dim light, they saw several other plot tenders walking the narrow paths, pinching off tomato suckers and checking the soil in their raised beds.

At the back edge of the garden, Nell spotted Beverly Walden, standing alone near the storage shed. The long skirt of her pale blue sundress blew slightly in the wind, and light from the harbor boats shone through it. She wore a wide sisal hat with an elegantly flowing brim, a ribbon tied around the band. It was a completely unexpected look, and in that moment, she reminded Nell of a painting she'd seen of a woman looking off to sea, yearning for the return of her sailor.

Nell waved, but Beverly's attention was somewhere else. In the next minute she slipped off into the tree shadows near the shoreline.

Nell watched for a moment longer, but she was gone. Somewhere. Perhaps walking along the narrow sea path that wound behind all the galleries, all the way to the Artist Palate dock and beyond. A quick walk to the deck where the band was already filling the air with music.

"It looks good," Izzy said, crouching down over a row of carrot tops. "Look at all those tiny plants peeking out of the soil. They look so happy."

Ben laughed as Sam crouched down beside her. "Happy plants, we're leaving you now," he said in a low, husky voice, then lifted Izzy back up with him.

"The Fractured Fish are calling us," Nell said.

The foursome walked down the street to the beat of Andy Risso's drums and joined the parade of concertgoers, some singing along with the music, the old gaslights of Canary Cove lighting the way. It was a happy vibe—just like Izzy's carrot tops—and filled with the hope of summer. As it should be.

Ben looped an arm across her shoulders and massaged lightly. "Let it go, Nellie," he whispered, and beneath his sure fingers, the tightness in her back loosened, her spirit lightened.

The deck at the Artist's Palate was crowded with villagers and vacationers, families and couples. Whole families filled picnic tables, and off toward one corner, Nell waved at the Delaney clan, kids and all, enjoying themselves. Maeve waved Nell and Izzy over to introduce her grandchildren. "Their first Fractured Fish concert," she laughed, showing off their T-shirts.

"Beautiful kids, Kristen," Izzy said to their mom. "You should send Sasha over to our kids' beanie class."

While Izzy gave class dates and times to Kristen, Nell noticed that Davey had escaped the table. She watched him move through the crowd, patting folks on the back, laughing at comments. Soon he was swallowed up by the crowd near the back steps.

"Davey isn't crazy about crowds—he needs his breathing room," D.J. said, following Nell's look.

"I understand. It can get crazy here."

They made more small talk, and as Nell followed Izzy through the crowd, she wondered why D.J. felt compelled to explain Davey's behavior to her. She glanced back at the table. Davey still hadn't returned.

The college-student staff Merry had hired raced to keep up with orders, piling trays with calamari and shrimp pizzas, burgers and fried clams, and plates of fish and chips, while their boss entertained from the outdoor stage. All across the deck, feet stomped and hands clapped as Andy beat on his drums, his long blond hair flying, and Merry and Pete filled the summer air with "Ain't No Mountain High Enough."

Cass and the Brewsters waved from a table near the deck railing. "I think it's the last table," Cass said. "Sit."

Birdie and Nick were already there, and in between them sat Gabby, her bright green hat in place and a smile lifting her whole face.

"Gabby promised Pete she'd come to hear the band. So here we are," Birdie said. "Ready to rock."

Nick was quiet and preoccupied. But when Ben asked about his day, he responded with the gallantry they'd come to expect. Soon, with genuine interest, he was talking to Sam and Ben about their sailboat.

"The whole town must be here." Izzy leaned in to be heard over the music. She pointed to the table next to them. "Even the city council."

Nell looked over. There was Beatrice, her makeup perfectly applied and wearing a skirt and jacket. The mayor and his wife sat across from her, along with a business owner the city was trying to lure to Sea Harbor. Laura and Elliott Danvers were there, too, and Nell couldn't help but feel sorry for the high-profile couple, knowing they'd rather be with Sam and Izzy and their other friends, relaxing, clapping, having fun. They were often called in to help extol the merits of Sea Harbor businesses, and Laura, like her mother before her, always complied. Beatrice sat next to Laura, looking slightly out of place in the halter-and-sandals crowd, but she proved herself a good sport, clapping and mouthing the song lyrics.

"Now, that's the part of Beatrice that's endearing," Nell said to Ben.

"And then there's Sal," Birdie said, nodding toward the quiet man as he slipped away from the table and headed for the bar. "The poor man can't escape Beatrice's political schmoozing even at a Fractured Fish concert. He'd probably rather be off in that fancy yacht Beatrice bought him."

"That's a beast," Sam said. "He was cutting some mighty waves the other day over near the island."

"You two should talk," Izzy said to Sam and Ben. "How many times have Aunt Nell and I played second fiddle to your sailboat?"

Nell laughed. The handsome Hinckley Sou'wester that Sam and Ben had invested in was truly a cherished possession. Sam's other wife, Izzy called it sometimes.

Beatrice looked over and lifted a glass of wine in greeting, a gracious smile in place. The earlier conversation was forgotten, a part of the day's business, was how Nell imagined she thought about it. If you don't know the answer to a question, you go to the source. And for some reason, Beatrice thought she and Birdie might be a source. At least once Beverly Walden failed to answer all her questions.

Nell thought of the quiet woman being subjected to Beatrice's storm of personal questions. Being nervous was probably an understatement.

A while later, after the second pitcher of beer was emptied, a basket of fried calamari devoured, and a medley of old Beatles tunes played to a rousing crowd, Ben announced that the Endicott shuttle would soon be shuttling along home.

Izzy and Sam were out on the dance floor, with Gabby between them, her body wild and whirling to Pete's rendition of "Twist and Shout."

"She's having the time of her life," Birdie said.

"She doesn't do much of this in New York," Nick said, his eyes following Gabby's gyrations.

"Then we shall stay longer," Birdie said. "You two go along. We'll make sure everyone has a ride."

Nell slid her arm through Ben's. "Does this mean we're old fuddy-duddies?" she asked as they walked slowly back down Canary Cove Road to the car. "Even Birdie is outlasting us."

"Nope. Not in a million years," Ben whispered into her hair. "It simply means there are lots of ways to liven up an evening . . ."

The easement along the garden site was now packed with cars, all the way down to Finnegan's fence. They walked to the end of the row and Ben unlocked the CRV.

Nell stopped, her hand on the door. And then she frowned and took a few steps toward Finnegan's fence, straining to hear.

"Nellie, you're dreaming up mysteries again," Ben said, watching his wife from behind the wheel. "Hop in."

He leaned across the front seat and pushed open the door.

"I thought I saw lights." She climbed into the car.

"Harbor lights, probably," Ben said. "Or moonlight, maybe, reflecting off a piece of metal."

Nell nodded, settling back into the seat. She slipped out of her heeled sandals.

But minutes later, when Ben backed out and turned the car toward home, it wasn't harbor lights they saw.

Chief Jerry Thompson's patrol car was parked at the drive leading to Finnegan's property. A spotlight affixed to the side lit up the entrance to the property. The chief stood beside the car, one hand directing the beam.

And lit up like an actor on a stage was Tommy Porter, attaching a band of yellow police tape to the fence and beyond, wrapping Finnegan's land in the awful sign of crime.

Ben pulled over to the side of the road. Chief Thompson looked up, saw them, and walked slowly across the street. His shoulders were stooped, an invisible burden weighing them down. He leaned into the driver's window, his forearms resting on the edge.

"Ben. Nell." He tipped his head slightly.

"What's up, Jerry? The autopsy is back?"

Jerry nodded. "It was like we thought: he fell on the metal spike from a rusty tractor. But he didn't fall because of the rain or the dark night or anything like that. He fell because someone slashed his face—and his carotid—with a knife. Someone wanted Finnegan dead."

Chapter 16

A lthough the news had come in late Monday night, the *Sea Harbor Gazette* managed to get enough of the facts down to write a headline that sent the town spinning.

MAN'S DEATH RULED A HOMICIDE.

A homicide. Jerry had told them Finnegan died quickly, maybe even before he was stabbed by a piece of his own trash. His face was a mess, the chief said. Cass probably didn't notice it because there was so much blood, and debris from the storm covered his face, masking it. It also made fingerprinting nearly impossible.

Those facts were kept from the reporter, so instead he detailed the city hall confrontation just days before Finnegan's death and the efforts all across the peaceful town to wrest Finnegan's property from him. And without naming names, the reporter made it clear that the list of those who wouldn't be sad to have the land finally free of Finnegan was very long, indeed.

A small box at the end of the article urged readers to call or e-mail anything that might lead to the arrest of the individual or individuals involved in the crime.

"Why did he bring up all that city hall gossip?" Mary Pisano stomped across Coffee's patio and pulled out a chair across from Nell. She sat down as hard as her four-foot-eleven-inch frame could manage, and slapped the morning paper down on the table. One of her short legs swung into the table leg and she winced, rubbing the injured spot. "And since when did being an old crank merit being murdered? I'm so mad, I could spit nails."

"Mad might be the easiest emotion right now." Nell had carried several coffees outside. She thought Izzy might run by before the store opened. Maybe Cass and Birdie, too. The news the night before had instigated a flurry of text messages, but that didn't replace seeing one another. The Seaside Knitters hugged easily when times were tough.

"This is nuts," Mary said. Her laptop was tucked away in the backpack she'd set down on the flagstone patio. Nell knew she'd pull it out shortly, move over to the table beneath the old maple tree in the corner and pound out her opinion about Finnegan's death, which would become tomorrow's "About Town" column. But right now Mary was agitated and needed to vent.

"How could this happen in Sea Harbor?" she asked rhetorically. Her small fingers tapped out her frustration on the tabletop.

Nell poured a tiny container of cream into her coffee and stirred it until the strong brew turned the color of alpaca yarn. The thought had plagued her for hours. It wasn't that Finnegan didn't stir up controversy, but murder was something else entirely. "Maybe it was an argument gone sour," she offered, but without conviction.

But that was unlikely. Someone had taken a knife to Finnegan's face. It might not have been planned, but it was what it was—a vicious act of violence against one of the most nonviolent men they knew.

"How could Finnegan make anyone angry enough to kill him? Beneath his crusty facade, he was a peaceful man. The man nursed birds with broken wings back to health, for heaven's sake."

Nell was still.

"Maybe it was someone who didn't know him. A drifter, maybe. Remember last winter when Finn didn't have heat and stayed with Angus McPherran for a while? Some vagrants moved in and tried to light a fire to stay warm. Maybe one came back and Finnegan surprised him. Or the one he fought with not long ago."

The vagrant theory was a favorite of Mary's. It meant someone they didn't know, would never know, and would never return to Sea Harbor, was responsible for the awful deed. It meant that everything would be okay, the bad person was far away and could no longer cause discomfort or fear in their fair town.

But Nell knew that was rarely the case. Whoever did this awful thing may well have been someone they knew. Someone who lived down the street or shopped at Shaw's or was sitting right here on Coffee's patio, listening to the buzz all around him about the awful thing that had happened to Finnegan.

"Finn came around the B and B sometimes just to see if I needed help with peeling paint or broken locks."

"Speaking of your bed-and-breakfast, I hear you're treating Nicholas Marietti well."

"How could anyone not be nice to that charming man? My big hunk of a husband is a tad jealous, I think. Nick is the perfect guest. Truth be told, I don't see much of him."

"I thought he was working in your den?"

"Sometimes. He likes those old history books my grandfather collected. But he's gone a lot. A man about town. Sherry—she does the night shift—says he takes a key so he can come and go and doesn't disturb her if he gets in late."

"He's out late?"

"Oh, you know. Mostly he gets up early and goes out, I think. Henrietta O'Neal down the street is like that. Grabs her walking stick and off she goes before the sun is up. Those two have probably run into each other."

They both smiled at the thought of the rotund eighty-year-old ambling through the predawn streets of Sea Harbor with Nick Marietti. But her smile faded when she remembered seeing Nick early one morning. And he hadn't been walking with Henrietta O'Neal.

A shadow fell over the table as Cass and Birdie appeared, greeting Mary and pulling out chairs.

Cass wrapped Nell in a hug that lasted longer than usual. "It just plain sucks," she murmured into Nell's ear.

She settled her backpack on the floor and sat down. "Having Finn gone was bad enough. But happening this way?" She shook her head.

"And it's so close to us," Mary said. "Canary Cove. How many times a week do each of us pass Finn's place?"

"Gabby hung around there nearly every day." Birdie's voice was quiet and held a tone none of them were used to hearing there: *fear.*

Nell pushed a cup of coffee in front of her. "Not in the middle of the night." But she knew her words didn't matter. Having a child in one's life brought worry one couldn't anticipate. And Birdie now had a child in her life.

"Did the chief give you any more details?" Cass asked.

"They know the knife was a rigging knife."

"That narrows it down to every boat owner in Sea Harbor, which is almost everyone, including me." Cass said. "You don't go out on a boat without a knife."

"I have a garage filled with those things," Mary said. "Max throws the old rusty ones in a box, then trots down to McClucken's to buy new ones."

Sam and Ben had them, too. "Ben said the police will go through the property carefully today. He was sure the case would be solved quickly."

"Jerry wants this town safe more than any of us," Mary said. "Or at least as much. He will turn over all stones."

"Where's Gabby today?" Cass asked.

"Sam took her sailing. I think it was spur-of-the-moment, and more than likely Ben has been recruited."

Nell glanced down and checked her messages. "You're right."

"Sam thought it'd be good to get out on the water. It's a great pacifier."

"And a great excuse," Nell said. "Nothing would please those two more than if Gabby wanted to go out every day."

"And Nick?" Cass asked.

"He went, too. We talked to Gabby this morning. It's not easy to tell a ten-year-old that someone she cared about was killed. Here she is, a New Yorker, and she comes to quiet Sea Harbor to meet murder face-to-face."

"Nick is great with that little girl," Mary said. "I watch them sometimes, wandering around the B and B's back trails. They have a lovely kinship. With you and Nick beside her, Birdie, she'll be fine."

Birdie forced a smile. "Well, it will be up to Nick to be beside her, I'm afraid. He thinks it's time to take her to Maine—their original destination. I suppose he wants to get her out of all this mess. Perhaps it's best."

Nell sat quietly, listening, wondering at Nick's sudden move. He was thinking he'd be there a week, he had told Mary.

Cass put down her coffee mug with such force, it sloshed across the table. With a swipe of her napkin, she soaked up the liquid. "No," she said. "It's not best she leave now." She looked at Birdie and Nell. "You know I'm right, both of you. I haven't taken her out on the *Lady Lobster* yet. And we haven't looked for mussels or had a clambake. There's another beanie class scheduled, and the garden party is coming up."

She looked from one to the other, seeking agreement.

But there was no argument, of course. Cass was right. They weren't ready for Gabby to walk out of their lives. But their world had changed.

Murder did that.

A while later, Nell stopped by the yarn shop, hoping to see Izzy, if just for a moment. Mae was at the counter, her glasses slipping down her nose, trying to deal with a return. Her nieces, Jillian and Rose, moved in and out of the Magic Room—Izzy's name for the children's playroom—calming preschoolers, answering customers' questions, and helping someone find the perfect lightweight cotton blend for a summer sweater.

Izzy? Nell mouthed to Mae over a customer's head.

"She took a break," Mae said loudly. Then motioned Nell to the desk. She continued to punch the computer keys while she talked, her glasses slipping perilously close to the end of her long nose. "Willow called. She thought someone should go out to see Angus McPherran and talk to him about Finn. I told her she was a gem and it was a good idea. Those two were buddies, Angus and Finnegan. I saw them often, drinking beer at the end of the pier and talking about the good old days. She was looking for you, too, wondering if maybe you would want to go along."

Leave it to Willow and Izzy to think of the Old Man of the Sea. He was the one who had stood up for Finnegan at the city council meeting. And who gave Finn a warm bed when the nor'easters came and Finn had forgotten to pay his light bill. If he hadn't already heard the latest news, it would be kinder to hear it from two friends and not from a newspaper report written by someone who might be more motivated by additional inches on the front page than by facts.

"She just left, not two minutes ago. You could catch up with her at Willow's gallery."

Nell checked her watch. She had a couple of hours before a board meeting at the Sea Harbor Historical Museum. Willow and Izzy didn't really need her, but she was very fond of Angus.

Besides, she wanted to see Izzy and Willow. Bad news did that. And good news. It brought them together for comfort or for celebration.

Angus was sitting on a stone wall above the rocky coast, looking out to sea. His cabin, a neat two-bedroom home that smelled of pine and fresh air, was a few yards away. Window boxes overflowed with marigolds and geraniums, neatly planted and well cared for. The small house was all that he'd asked of the city when he donated the acres of land to them, the land that had become Anja Angelina Park, named after his cherished wife and Angie Archer, a young girl he had befriended. They were both gone now, but the park was a reminder of the beauty and love each of them had brought into old Angus' life. And now it was there for the whole community to enjoy, complete with hiking trails and a community center that fit right into the woods, where Willow Adams and others taught art and music and cooking.

The old man looked up as the three women approached, his weathered skin wrinkling into a sad smile. The old floppy hat that covered a meager head of thin white hair came off and he stood and bowed slightly. He was stooped these days, his white beard seeming to pull his shoulders forward, his body bending toward the earth.

"It's a sad day," he said. He motioned for them to join him on the wall, and eased himself back down. Nell sat down beside him, while Willow and Izzy sat cross-legged on the ground.

For a while they sat in silence, the pounding of the waves against the rocks and the wind whistling through the towering pines providing background for their thoughts.

"There goes the Hinckley." Angus pointed to a white sail sloping toward the sea near Sunrise Island.

"Our Hinckley?" Nell said. She and Izzy squinted against the glare. But what they saw was a dot of a sailboat.

"Yep. I know 'em all. That's Sam and Ben. See the way she heels?"

He fell silent again, and the others did, as well. The boat disappeared and they watched the parade of new ones—lobster boats off to work, whale-watching boats looking for a show. Yachts and sailboats, speedboats and small fishing vessels. The world Finn had left behind.

Willow cupped one hand over her eyes against the sun's glare and looked up at Angus. "He was a good man."

"Yep. And a good friend," Angus said. "At least as much as he could be. He spent time with me in the winter when his heat went off. Crazy fool."

"I guess if he had sold the land, he could have had a decent place to live."

"I suppose." Angus looked like he wanted to say more, but instead he turned his body sideways and looked out at the sea. "Finnegan had reasons for the things he did. Good reasons, I suspect."

"Do you have any idea who did this to him, Angus?" Nell asked.

Angus was silent for so long that Nell thought she might have offended him, although she wasn't sure how.

Finally, he answered. "He made a lot of people mad. Especially when he got his righteous hackles up. Finnegan was a black-and-white fellow—though you'd never know it for the ruckus he made when they took his driver's license away." Angus shook his head and chuckled at the memory. "He was one furious fellow that day, even though he knew as well as anybody that it was the right thing to do. Elsewise, sure and he'd be killing someone with the way he drove that truck. The truck had stopped obeying him, he said. I guess it had.

"But he wouldn't have taken the license back if they'd offered it to him. He knew it was time; he just had to put on a show.

"But when people connived or lied or messed up other people's lives, that's what he couldn't tolerate, even if it was none of his damn business. He'd take himself off to the newspaper or city hall or anyone who'd listen. Confront the people himself. Remember when that old mayor, dead now, cheated on his wife? Finnegan let him know it'd be all over Mary Pisano's column if he didn't shape up.

"Oh, he nudged the best of them. Finnegan stuck his nose in everything, though you didn't always know it. Just the other day he saw someone—probably the same nut who tried to barge into his house a few weeks back—hanging around Canary Cove, so he started patrolling the streets over there. He was determined the guy was stealing from the artists."

Willow smiled, tracing a fancy pattern in the sand with a stick. "He checked my locks every night." She laughed. "And sometimes he even got personal. One night when Pete was at my place late, Finn got on him, told him to mind his p's and q's', treat me right and not go fooling around behind my back."

Nell laughed. "The last person on earth who would need such advice."

"I told him once he'd be a damn sight happier if he'd mind his own business and stop playing keeper of the commandments. It must be a difficult way to live, to think you're always right," Angus said.

A simple man—one who in death was becoming very complicated.

"So we don't have a clue who murdered him?" Izzy said.

"Wrong there, missy," Angus said. "There're lots of clues. They're probably right there staring us in the face."

"The police'll probably start with the vagrant Finn messed up," Willow said. "He'd be a likely suspect—"

"I suppose they will." Angus pushed himself off the wall and reached for his walking stick. "Time for my morning constitutional," he said with a nod to the path that ran above the rocky shore.

Izzy and Willow got up and brushed off their jeans. Nell gave Angus a hug.

"As for those likely suspects, sometimes *likely* isn't the key word," he said, looking off to sea as if there might be some kind of answer there. In the distance, Sunrise Island appeared, a curving piece of land on the sea's horizon. "Finnegan left us with a pile of pieces. Someone just needs to put them together."

They watched the old man walk slowly across the bumpy terrain. Nell hoped the walking stick would keep him safe. *A pile of pieces.* But when you worked a puzzle, the pieces were all laid out there in front of you, some with flat sides, some with irregular shapes. The pieces to Finnegan's puzzle seemed to be scattered all across the town—with little or no shape.

And she suspected Angus knew it was going to take careful eyesight to find the shapes that mattered.

"I think he knows more than he's saying," Izzy said, climbing into the car beside Nell.

"Maybe he's just trying to sort through things himself, things Finnegan said to him," Willow said from the backseat.

Nell drove down the winding park road and headed toward Canary Cove. "Maybe it was the vagrant seeking revenge. Finnegan worked him over badly."

"A vagrant who is probably halfway across the country by now.

Or Maine, where no one will ever find him." Izzy nibbled on her bottom lip.

"I'm sure the police have it under control," Nell said automatically. It was Ben talking through her, she realized with a start. And she wasn't at all sure she agreed with him. She drove slowly, the car moving automatically toward Canary Cove and Willow's gallery. Her thoughts were like raw fleece, unformed clumps and threads, drifting clouds across her mind—and they all carried images of Finnegan.

A sentimental Finnegan enjoying ice cream with a ten-year-old girl.

A sweet Finnegan watching the garden grow.

An angry Finnegan arguing with his daughter on the Palate's deck.

And a fiercely defensive Finnegan facing off with Nicholas Marietti . . .

"Nell, stop!"

Nell's foot went automatically to the brake.

Across Canary Cove Road, through the trees and brush and tangled weeds that guarded Finnegan's land, a light spun around and moved slowly toward the gate.

When it cleared the trees, they saw a patrol car with Tommy Porter behind the wheel. Sitting next to him was Father Lawrence Northcutt.

Behind them, bumping along the rutted path, was an ambulance.

Nell and Willow rolled down their windows as they stared at the procession of vehicles pulling out of the gate and turning onto the road.

Father Larry spotted them from the passenger's side of the car. He waved through the window but his expression didn't invite conversation, nor did Tommy's, his eyes on the road.

Instead, the young patrolman turned the car toward Harbor Road, not pausing long enough for their unspoken questions to find words—or to get answers.

But the ambulance drivers weren't as discreet. Or perhaps they didn't see the three women sitting inside the car idling on the easement.

The men brought the ambulance to a stop at the gate, checking for traffic.

And through the open windows, their careless words carried across the narrow road, loud and distinct.

"Can you believe it?" a beefy-looking man wearing a white shirt asked the driver. His voice was coated with incredulity, with a tinge of excitement.

"Who would've guessed the old coot had a body buried back there?"

$\mathcal{A}$ *body.*

The three women parted reluctantly at Willow's gallery, the disturbing thought that someone had been buried in Finnegan's yard hanging heavy over them. Someone, not just Finnegan, had died there.

How? When? Why?

And who?

They carried the questions away with them, loud, banging noises in their heads, as they tried to resume the day's ordinary responsibilities—a board meeting, a shop to manage, a gallery to run.

The old building in which the historical museum was housed always needed something: paint, a roof, new display cases. And Laura Danvers always managed to find the right people to donate at just the right time. She was the youngest board president they'd ever had, and, in Nell's opinion, one of the best. She ran meetings efficiently and always tried to keep things on topic.

Nell had left messages for Ben, even though she knew he would still be out sailing. But after the sail, she told him, they were meeting at Birdie's. *Cocktails and talk,* was all she said.

Talk to put some sense into what was going on in the quiet town they loved.

Laura was standing just inside the open front door, greeting people, when Nell walked up.

"Just the person I'm looking for," Laura said. She pulled Nell over to the side of the foyer. "My husband just called. Have you heard anything? Was there a body buried in Finnegan's yard?"

Before Nell could answer, Birdie walked through the door and hurried over.

"What's happening to this town?" she asked, and it was clear that the news was already rolling down Harbor Road. *A tidal wave,* Birdie said.

"But they just . . ." Nell began, but realized immediately that news like this—coupled with talkative ambulance drivers—would take a nanosecond to travel through town. Dozens of people would have seen the ambulance going in and out of Finnegan's gate. And Esther Gibson, though discreet when she needed to be, wouldn't hesitate to pass along something that would surely be in the morning paper.

"Do you think Finnegan knew a body was buried there?" Laura asked.

They fell silent, and the next question went unspoken. *Do you think Finnegan put it there?*

But Finnegan was dead. And perhaps he was the only one who knew the answers.

Laura checked her watch, then ushered Nell and Birdie into the boardroom. Buried bodies wouldn't deter the Sea Harbor Historical Museum board from beginning their meeting on time, not on Laura Danvers' watch.

But a man reported murdered one day, and the discovery of a body buried in his yard the next was too much even for Laura to control.

The room was a beehive, the buzzing so loud the words were ripped loose of sentences, colliding like fireworks in the heated air.

Body. Murder. Daughter. Land. Skeleton. Drifter.

With valiant effort and fierce pounding of her antique gavel, Laura finally brought quiet to the usually sedate group.

While talk then turned to housepainters and underwriters and fund-raisers, Nell sat back in her chair, pondering the ill-informed—but provocative—comments of well-intentioned women. They wanted what she wanted, what the whole town wanted: a return to the slow, easy summer that they had waited nine long months to enjoy.

After the meeting, Nell left another message for Ben, knowing it would sit in his voice mail until they had returned to shore, but somehow the connection seemed important—and comforting.

"Don't forget—cocktails at Birdie's when you bring Gabby home," she said to the machine as she and Birdie walked down the steps.

"*Home*," Birdie echoed as Nell hung up. "It's becoming that—Gabby's home. I see her everywhere—in the flowers she and Harold planted along the walkway, the orange hot pad she crocheted for Ella, scrunchies on the bathroom sink, and music everywhere."

"Do you think Nick will reconsider and stay a few more days?"

"I don't know. This murder business seems to have bothered him more than I'd have thought."

"He probably wants to get Gabby away from it."

"That's it, I'm sure. But somehow, I don't know, it seems more personal. The whole Finnegan thing. That land." Birdie stopped.

Nell was quiet.

"I know what you're thinking, Nell. We saw Nick arguing with Finnegan. But I asked him about it, and it was as we thought. He wanted to meet the man Gabby talked about and spent time with."

Maybe. They both wanted it to be true.

Nell took out her car keys and waved at Harold, patiently waiting at the curb in Birdie's Lincoln. "It makes perfect sense—we would have done the same if we didn't already know him. We'd have been staked out at his gate. But . . ."

Birdie waited.

"But Finn looked angry. Why? It doesn't fit. He was a stickler for propriety and doing the right thing. You'd think he'd have welcomed Nick's questions. Expected him to come calling."

"That's what you would have thought."

"Birdie, there's another thing. I think I saw Nick's car parked on that dirt road alongside Finnegan's property early yesterday morning."

Birdie took in a full breath and released it slowly, her chest moving in and out. Her eyes asked Nell to tell her more, but her face said she didn't want to hear.

"I didn't see him. Only the car. So it might not have been his. But it was the same make—and a rental."

"Monday morning . . ."

Mary's words came back to them. *He was an early riser. He had a key.*

"Finnegan was already dead on Monday. Why would Nick—"

Why? But neither of them even knew how to articulate the whole question. Why did Nick go to see Finnegan? And why would he have gone over there after Finn died? Did he know about the body buried on the land? And why had he lied about not knowing the old fisherman?

Harold honked lightly and pointed to the DO NOT PARK HERE sign near the car.

Birdie gave Nell a quick hug and walked toward the car, her head turned toward Nell. "We'll figure this out tonight over a glass of pinot gris, my friend," she said softly. "Tomorrow's supposed to be a sunny day. Let's make it so."

Cass was the first to arrive at Birdie's, her truck huffing and chugging around the drive.

"You need a new muffler," Harold hollered as Cass parked in the circle drive.

"I need a new life," she shot back, and headed for the door.

"Where's Danny?" Birdie asked, meeting her at the door. "We could use a good mystery writer."

"I think he had another book signing in Boston."

"You think? You don't know?"

"What, am I his keeper now?" Cass asked, then immediately pulled back her words. "I'm sorry, Birdie. You don't deserve that." Her dark eyes grew moist.

"No, I don't, dear. And Danny doesn't, either, but it's your worry talking, I expect, not my Catherine." She gave her a quick hug. "That nasty loan?"

"What's nasty is not paying it. I thought maybe Ben and I could talk for a minute."

"You know, sweetie, that I am—"

Cass shushed her with another hug. "I know exactly what you are. A dear, wonderful, generous, sweet friend." She pulled away and looked down the drive. "There's Nell. Ben might be close behind."

Birdie looked beyond her and waved as Nell pulled in beside Cass' truck.

Izzy was with her, and a minute later, the blue Altima drove up with Gabby sitting tall in the passenger's seat, her eyes filled with life. She jumped out before Nick had completely cut the engine and ran to Birdie and Cass. "I'm going to be sailor. We had a fab-u-lous time. The most fun I've ever had in my whole life. Sam taught me *everything*. I can heel and tack and . . ."

Laughing, Birdie hugged her granddaughter.

"Uncle Ben says I was born with seaweed in my blood."

"Gabby has a new passion," Nick said. "We may never get her back on a skateboard."

"And look." She held up a cloth sack, her eyes filling her face. "Sea glass!"

Nick explained. "Sam took us over to Sunrise Island for a walk on that little stretch of beach, and Gabby here spots sea glass like a pro."

"That's wonderful, Gabby. And where are the other two sailors?" Nell asked Nick.

"They'll be along. Jerry Thompson was at the club, and Ben cornered him with some questions." Chief Thompson. Good. Ben would find out what he could, and maybe be able to answer some of their questions.

Nick rested a hand on Gabby's shoulder, listening to her spin her day in glorious detail for her nonna. He had gotten some sun himself, and his dark skin glowed with health. His knit shirt was open at the neck and his tan shorts comfortable, informal. For the first time since his return from Italy, he seemed more relaxed. And friendlier, as if some burden had been lifted from his shoulders, leaving him free to concentrate on the people around him. Nell watched as he listened to his niece, his feelings filling clear blue eyes.

Nick Marietti didn't look guilty of anything. Except maybe being overly protective of someone he loved, a crime of which they were all guilty as sin.

It was thirty minutes before Sam and Ben appeared.

Birdie began peppering them with questions as soon as they appeared in the doorway. "How could there be a body buried out there? Wouldn't Finnegan have known about it? Who is it, Ben?"

They'd gathered on the stone patio that fanned out from the harbor side of the house, high above the water. Soft gaslights cast early-evening shadows across the granite floor. Cass and Izzy had claimed their favorite seats—two original ocean-liner chairs, refurbished and polished until the teak arms were slippery beneath their touch. The others moved to cushioned teak couches and chairs, while Gabby rushed off to the kitchen to talk to Ella.

"You'd think he'd have known, sure," Ben said quietly, accepting the glass of Scotch Nick handed him. He sat down near Nell.

The thought hung there for a moment. In the distance, the sounds of boats coming in for the night and cars pulling into restaurants and bars along Harbor Road were all that reminded them they were close to civilization—and to a crime so close to home.

"You can almost see Finnegan's place from here," Sam said, looking across the water. It jutted out, the rocky shore that ended up at Canary Cove. Beyond it, as the shoreline roped around and moved farther out into the ocean, was Anja Angelina Park. And Sunrise Island a dot in the distance.

"What do they know about the body?" Nell asked.

"Not much. The coroner said it'd take a while. It was buried in an old wooden box and had been there for years."

"How did they find it? I never saw signs of a grave," Cass said.

"You wouldn't have. The grave was well hidden in a far corner of the property, Jerry said. Close to the shore. There were lots of bushes around it, a tangle of weeds. No headstone. No one, not even Finnegan, would have any reason to go back there. The police were searching for some sign of the drifter who'd been giving Finnegan trouble when they found the grave."

"So Finnegan may not have known it was there?" Birdie asked.

"It's possible, but not likely. Birdie, you have acres of woods around your house, but I'd bet you'd know if someone buried a body on them."

Of course. And Finnegan wandered around his place all the time. He would have known.

"Well, Finnegan could be a grouch, but never a killer," Izzy said.

"Of course he didn't kill anyone," Birdie said softly.

"We know that because we liked the guy," Sam said. "The police will work from facts and theories."

"What's the theory?" Nell asked.

"That Finnegan could have killed someone years ago. And last weekend someone came back for revenge and killed him," Ben said. "Simple as that. Revenge."

"But all these years later?" Cass said.

"That's a problem, sure. And when you're dealing with something that happened so long ago, it's difficult to find enough facts to verify or prove anything. Once they find out how long the body's been there, they'll look for a disappearance, a crime, something that happened back then."

"So it adds a new suspect to the list—someone completely unknown," Sam added. "But it's something they'll have to investigate."

"In the meantime, the possibility of Finnegan being a murderer is out there and talked about?" Cass' words came out angry and defensive.

"It doesn't seem fair, does it?" Birdie said. "First the poor man is murdered. And then his memory is sullied with accusations. Let the poor man rest."

There were murmurs of agreement around the patio.

"Are there any other leads?" Nell asked.

"They found an old shoe or boot, not Finnegan's size, near the house. Finn lived in the apartment upstairs. The downstairs area—the part that he used to rent out, was still filled with junk. It looked as though the tenants were evicted all those years ago and Finnegan didn't let them back in. There were metal boxes full of things, a dental chair in one. Filing cabinets. Pretty much untouched. Finn's apartment, on the other hand, was ransacked. His wallet was gone, a television taken. It was hard to tell what else, Jerry said, because no one knew what Finnegan had up there.

"The rain made a mess of things, too, but as best they can figure out, the only tracks going from the gate inward are yours, Cass. But there're signs of tracks going the other way."

"Toward the water?" Cass leaned forward, her elbows on her knees. "That's odd."

"Well, there's that path back there, the one that goes all around Canary Cove," Sam reminded her.

"And the water," Izzy said.

"So it looks like revenge?" Nell asked. "Or a robbery gone bad . . . ?"

But no one answered because they were all thinking the same thing. A thief could have picked a much better target to rob than Francis Finnegan.

The patter of flip-flops announced Gabby's entrance, followed by Ella's quiet step. A quick shower had left Gabby's hair damp and even more voluminous. It flew around her head in a dark, curly swirl, the fading light creating a fuzzy halo behind her. She carried a giant tray filled with lobster rolls, Chinese cabbage salad, and baskets of warmed rosemary bread and pita triangles. A bowl of Ella's homemade hummus sat in the center.

"I tasted every single thing. Ella is amazing." She looked up at the thin woman standing behind her, then added dramatically, "*Magnifico.*"

Ella blushed, set another tray down on a wrought-iron table, and relieved Gabby of hers, placing it on a sideboard.

"You are *both magnifico,*" Birdie corrected.

"I was so starving that we ate in the kitchen. I stuffed myself. Three lobster rolls! I ate so much, Harold thinks I'll be woozy and he'll beat me at chess." Gabby's laughter at such a thing happening floated behind her as she plucked an olive from the patio bar and followed Ella into the house.

Without waiting on ceremony, they all dug in, piling their plates full, and, for a time, allowing the food, the wine, and the hazy moon to block out the matters pressing heavily on their minds. Talk turned to gardening, sailing, and a new restaurant opening up near the Gloucester Harbor.

Ella reappeared a while later with lemon bars, coffee, a tray of cordials, and a report on the chess game.

"Harold's queen is about to have a stroke," the tall, thin woman said, smiling. She collected the empty plates and disappeared.

"I think she was humming," Izzy said.

Birdie laughed.

Across the table, Ben was filling brandy snifters and Cass was suggesting they talk turkey.

"Unfortunately, there's not much more to tell. Jerry said the body is throwing a wrench in things. But they're still focusing on the drifter Finn caught stealing from him a few weeks ago. The fact that things were stolen this time adds some credibility to that theory, along with the fact that Finnegan broke the guy's nose. Maybe he didn't mean to kill Finn. Maybe he came back to steal something, and they fought. But like Jerry said, they'll look deeper, examine other motives, talk to people who've had recent altercations with Finn. The Delaneys. Council members. Beatrice Scaglia was incensed at first, but then I think she rather enjoyed the attention."

They laughed at the thought of the councilwoman submitting to questioning. Beatrice was usually the one doing that. And no matter how assertive she could be, the idea of Beatrice killing anyone was hard to imagine—voters wouldn't stand for it, and Beatrice stood for voters.

"Who else?" Nell asked.

"He didn't say. But he did say finding the will is important."

"I guess it would be," Izzy said. "Inheriting that land would be a prime motive for murder. Somehow, taking Finnegan's wallet and an old television doesn't make as much sense."

Ben nodded.

"So Beverly could be a primary suspect." Nell thought of the quiet woman sitting on the dock with Finnegan's boat moored nearby. She didn't like her father—and inheriting his property would make her wealthy. But murder?

"They'll be looking at anyone who had a grudge against the man or something to gain. Anyone who'd been in his face."

In Finn's face. She might not have described it quite that way, but that's where Nick Marietti had been the day before Finn died. Was he on the list? Nell glanced over at him. He sat comfortably beside Birdie, an interested expression on his face. Calm, relaxed.

"So, your trip with Gabby," Birdie said, as if reading Nell's glance. "Next stop, Maine?"

Nick nodded. "I suggested to Gabby that she wind things down tomorrow and then we should get on the road in the next day or two."

They all fell silent, waiting for Birdie to take the lead.

But she simply smiled sadly. Her thoughts about Gabby staying longer had probably come full circle. She was thinking of the best place for Gabby to be right now. As a grandmother would do. And no matter what she herself wanted, that place was probably not here, where she was gallivanting around a town involved in a murder investigation.

Birdie could use some time alone with Nick, Nell suspected. Time to work it all out. She stood and held her keys out to Ben. "It's time," she said.

A shuffling of bodies followed, and soon everyone was reaching for keys, sweaters, purses, reluctant to leave but feeling the weariness of the night press down on them.

A ringing cell phone caused several hands to reach into pockets.

"Mine," Ben said, and looked down at the name.

He stepped to the edge of the patio, the phone to one ear and a hand covering the other.

Nell watched from a distance. She could almost always discern the caller by Ben's tone and choice of words. But he wasn't saying much. Just listening attentively.

He hung up and walked back to the group slowly.

"Strangest thing," he said.

"Who was it?"

"Father Northcutt. They've found Finnegan's will. It seems the good padre is executor." Ben slipped the phone into his pocket.

"He wants to meet with me tomorrow to go over it together."

Nell looked at Ben as the light from the moon played across his face. She tried to read the expression that had settled in the lines and planes, the features she knew as well as her own heart.

Ben felt her concern and pushed a smile in place as he wrapped an arm around her and looked at the others.

They were all still there, waiting with keys in hand and sweaters looped over arms, wondering whether there was another shoe that would drop.

And there was, but it was a little plop instead of a thud.

Ben shrugged. "The will's a little surprising, Larry said. It's not what people might be expecting."

Chapter 18

en's parting comment the night before had been an understatement, one even he hadn't been fully prepared for.

Nell, Ben, and Father Larry sat in Ben's den, trying to get their arms around Finnegan's will and the mind of a man who had, even in death, shocked them.

Several copies of the will had been delivered to Father Larry from a law firm in Boston, one happy to pass along the documents and get on to more important clients. They promised to pull together the rest of the Finnegan file as soon as some assistant could get to it, but everything needed for the processing of the will was in this delivery.

Father Northcutt had dropped off a copy of it with Chief Thompson, at his request, and the other copies sat in front of them on Ben's desk.

Ben looked again at the piece of paper that topped the pile and read it out loud, as if the sound of his voice would make it more real.

> *Last Will & Testament of Francis Finnegan*
> *I, Francis Finnegan, declare that this is my last will and*
> *testament. . . .*

Ben skipped over the next bit of legalese about revoking all prior wills and codicils and other formalities. He began reading again when he came to the paragraph listing specific bequests.

I give my entire interest in my real properties,
possessions, bank accounts, and trusts
to my loyal friend . . .
Catherine Mary Elizabeth Halloran.

Ben looked up. "He even has all the names in the right order, spelled correctly—*Catherine Mary Elizabeth Halloran.*"

Nell sat on the leather love seat in stunned silence. Only her fingers moved, the stitches on Gabby's cardigan keeping her breathing even.

"Cass," she said finally. But the word came out in a whisper.

She looked up from the sweater, her mind still not grasping what they'd just learned. Finnegan had left his valuable land to Cass. She said it again inside her head, weighing each word.

It would be an amazing thing for the Halloran family. A savior for the family business. An answer to Mary Halloran's prayers. Next to finding Cass a husband and having grandchildren, ensuring that her children were financially solvent, without the worries Mary had grown up with, was near the top of her novena list.

But somehow the joy that should be filling the room was tentative and shaky.

Father Larry nodded, shuffling a pile of papers. "The whole estate, lock, stock, and barrel. His land, that boat he loved, the small house that Beverly lives in, all his possessions, bank accounts. It will take a while to get a complete list. There's a note here for Cass from Finn. Maybe he'll explain the questions Cass will surely have."

Ben sat behind the old desk that had once belonged to his father and his father before him. The wisdom of his forefathers. His fingers rubbed the leather inlays as if trying to absorb that wisdom through his skin. "Well, one thing is for certain: this inheritance will be the answer to Cass' financial problems."

They nodded solemnly. Nell thought back to the day they had found Finnegan's body. What was it Cass had said? Finnegan told her things would be all right—no, they'd be *better*—for her. *Cassoulet*, he'd called her that morning. Somehow, he had planned for Cass—for the Halloran company—to be taken care of.

"Father, is there something about Finnegan you're not telling us? He said something to Cass shortly before he died that sounded like he anticipated something might happen to him. But he couldn't possibly have known he'd be murdered. . . ."

Father Northcutt was silent, his balding head bent low for a moment, as if he were saying a prayer. Finally he looked up. "Yes, there is something else. He'd asked me to keep it private, but it will come out. It's not important to keep it a secret any longer. Here's the thing. Our dear Finn thought himself invincible—and he wanted everyone else to think of him that way, too. But he wasn't. Several months ago, he came to me and asked me to pray for him."

Father Larry chuckled, remembering. *You're talking prayer with me?* I said to him. *Well, that calls for a drink.* So I got out a pint of Irish whiskey, and the two of us sat on the rectory porch for a long time, talking about life, pulling up memories of his lovely Moira, things he held close to his heart. Not so much about prayer, though, so I was beginning to think it was the whiskey he wanted.

"But finally he came out with it, and he told me he had cancer. A bad kind. He'd decided not to fool around with the hospitals and mess of medicine they offered. *All poison,* he said. He'd joked that he'd just live his life, then go out in his boat one day when it was time, and that'd be it. *Like some Native Americans did,* he said. Only they went into the forest and found a good final resting bed of pine needles to cushion them. For a fisherman, though, didn't I agree that a boat would be best? Just to drift off into the great blue beyond?

"He had months to live, though, as best the doctors could figure out. Maybe a year. He made me promise to keep it between the two of us. He didn't want people looking at him different, he said, as if he had two heads. Or be coming around his place, looking sad."

Father Larry took a drink of water, put the glass down, and sat back in the leather chair, his plump fingers folded over the rise in his middle.

"He told me not to get any highfalutin ideas about him starting to go to church, but maybe we could meet now and then down at the water, have a Guinness. Talk a bit. So we started doing exactly that. Two old Irishmen sharing a pint. We'd go out to Angus' place sometimes. The old Scot would join us if he felt like it, sit out there on the rocks, watch the boats go by the island. We had good days. Even talked about the afterlife now and again, wondering how his Moira would welcome him."

Nell felt her eyes fill. Dear Finn. So he *did* know things would be okay for Cass. He knew that after he died—and that it would probably be soon—the Halloran Lobster Company would once again have what it needed to thrive. He'd made sure of it.

Father Larry and Ben fingered through the pile of documents, allowing Nell some time to process a dear man being murdered—a man who was dying before the knife was ever wielded. And now a tangle of details to sort out, like the mess Purl made of skeins of wool, creating so many loose ends, they didn't think they'd ever get it together again.

Nell started another row on Gabby's sweater. She fingered the ribbing at the end of the sweater sleeve and imagined Gabby in the loose, swingy cardigan. Racing across a dock or flying down Harbor Road on Birdie's bike. Climbing aboard the *Lady Lobster* or going out with Cass to see how real fishermen spent their day.

Her mind spun. *A lobster boat that can now get all the repairs it needs.* Or be replaced completely. A company that could repay its loans. Cass' problems solved in an instant with a death . . . and an inheritance.

She looked up at the two men. They had fallen silent, still leafing through the papers but not seeming to pay much attention to the words. Every now and then they exchanged looks of concern.

Nell frowned at them. "What are you thinking? Surely it's not that Cass had any idea this money would come her way when Finnegan died."

They looked over at her for a moment without answering, as if they hadn't heard the question. Ben picked up another stack of papers and leafed through them.

Nell answered her own question. "She didn't know about this. She had absolutely no idea." It was an answer that wouldn't tolerate contradictions.

She knew it was true, and Ben did. Probably Father Larry did, too. But it wouldn't matter when the police looked at Finnegan's will.

As they had all agreed the night before, the will was important. Money was a prime motive for murder. The will, they'd said, might change the whole investigation.

To make it worse, everyone knew Cass needed money desperately, probably more than any of the other money-hungry people waiting in the wings for the distribution of Finnegan's possessions.

Ben stared at the stack of papers. "Because of the murder, they wanted to get the will here as soon as possible, but perhaps we'll learn more when we go through the rest of Finnegan's papers. They'll be here in a few days."

"What could they be?"

"Nothing vital, the law clerk said. A few notes addressed to people. A couple of legal documents, but nothing to do with the will. That's all right here."

Notes to people. Nell tucked that aside. Cass' note was already here. But Finnegan had written someone else.

"But no matter how you look at it, we've our work cut out for us."

"Yes, there's work to be done," Father Larry said. "But before we do anything, we need to talk to our Irish lass and let her know her life is about to change."

"What's up?" Cass showed up a few hours later, dressed for work in rolled-up jeans and an old T-shirt. She stood in the middle of the family room. "Pete and I are dropping some traps out near the island today. He's got a crew of new kids working for him, and I said I'd help train them."

"Do they absolutely need you?" Ben asked.

Cass pulled her brows together, instantly on alert. "Why?"

"We have some things we need to talk about. It might take a while."

Father Northcutt appeared in the den doorway, and Cass' face went pale.

"Jeez," she said. "What is this? The last rites?"

They laughed, but nervously, and Cass fished her phone out of her jeans pocket to call Pete. "This better be good," she mumbled as she punched in her brother's number.

Hours later, Cass was still sitting next to Nell on the love seat, a sheet of white paper wobbling on her knees. The only difference in her position from two hours before was the glass of water Ben had put into her hand.

"Finnegan was sick?" Cass repeated once again, as if multiple repetitions would make it clearer. The soppy tissue in her hand did little to catch a fresh river of tears.

Nell felt the same sadness. It was a strange emotion, to be grieving over a friend's dire diagnosis days after that friend's murder.

"Somehow, if only I had known . . ." Cass said.

But there wasn't an end to that sentence. Finnegan didn't want any of them to know. And if they had, what could they have done?

"He told me things would be all right," Cass said. "I was miffed at him for being a Pollyanna and not the straight shooter he usually was. He had no idea if things would be all right for the Halloran company, I told him. But he did . . . he'd made sure of it . . ." Then she looked down at the tear-stained piece of paper again and said for the fiftieth time, "This doesn't make sense. Why would he do this?"

"It's all legal. We spent hours checking things out. The witnesses, the dates. The only things we haven't had a chance to establish are the monetary amounts in savings accounts and, of course, the value of the house and land. But we know it's worth a lot."

"But why me?" She took a long drink. And then her eyes watered up again and she wiped them with a fresh tissue Nell put in her hand. She rested her head back against the couch and looked up at the ceiling. "Oh, Finn. What were you thinking, you crazy old man, you?"

It wasn't clear to any of them exactly how Cass felt about the windfall. Her money problems, her father's business, her boat and truck problems could suddenly be a thing of the past, but as they all sensed in undefined ways, windfalls sometimes carried their own secret storms.

Cass was relieved. Profoundly worried. Happy. Sad. And puzzled by an old man for whom she had made a yellow fleece. "Do you suppose it was the fleece vest?" she asked now, trying to lighten things. "I know he really liked it, but this is some thank-you."

"Maybe he explained it in that note," Nell said, pointing to another piece of paper, this one a note card envelope with flowers embroidered across the top; something that must have belonged to Moira. It had been attached to the copies of the will and was addressed to Cass.

Cass tore it opened, and then, when her eyes grew watery, handed it to Nell.

Nell put on her glasses and began reading the list of things Finn had written to Cass in his distinctive scrawl: *"Here's why I'm doing this, kid. You are kind and just (and a little ornery like me—I like that), you know right from wrong, you will make sure the money and land are handled fairly, and you will not hurt people. Patrick and Mary Halloran raised you right, Cassoulet."*

Nell looked up. "Maybe the most important reason is what he says so clearly at the end of this—he loved your father, Patrick, he loved the Halloran Lobster Company, he loved your family. They became his family when he had none, and he trusted all of you. The Hallorans treated him right."

"That's it—he trusted you, Cass," Ben said. "Trust was important to Finn, and he knows you'll do the right thing with this inheritance."

"Does my mother know?" She looked over at Father Northcutt. He was packing up a briefcase, getting ready to leave.

Mary Halloran was at the church every day. If it wasn't to light vigil lights for her children, it was to work in the office, handling the programs Our Lady of Safe Seas sponsored, paying bills, and forcing good eating habits on the pastor. A part-time job she took as seriously as if she were president of the Sea Harbor bank.

"Sure and she doesn't, Catherine. This is your business. Yours to own, yours to tell." The kindly priest walked over to Cass and laid one hand on her shoulder. "As Francis Finnegan so wisely said, *You'll do what is right.* And you will."

Izzy and Sam showed up unexpectedly a short while after Father Northcutt left.

A whim, Izzy said.

Coupled with the fact that Nell hadn't answered her last three text messages, and Pete told Sam that Cass had deserted him earlier in the day.

"So what gives? Why are you three gathered here like this? You look funny—"

By then Ben, Nell, and Cass had moved out to the deck to watch dusk settle over the ocean—lacy strands of violet and purple and crimson floating across the sky, deepening into night. Ben had replaced the water goblets with thin-stemmed martini glasses and stood at the bar, carefully dropping an olive in each.

"What are we missing? What's going on? Where is everyone? Talk to me."

Cass looked away from the sky. The tears had dried up, but the shock was just beginning to ebb and surprise still filled her face.

"Cass, you look like you've seen a ghost," Sam said. "Are you okay?"

"I'm rich," she said softly.

Izzy looked at her and smiled. "Sure, you are. We all are. Look at that sky."

"No, Izzy. Rich as in paying off the Halloran company loan and still being able to eat. Rich as in buying a toaster . . . or a truck."

"We read Finnegan's will today." Ben handed Cass a glass and then returned to the bar to add more drink and ice to his shaker.

"He left everything to Cass," Nell finished.

Izzy's mouth fell open. She snapped it shut and walked over to Cass, prying the martini glass from her fingers. After a swallow, she returned it and sat down next to her friend. "I think you're serious."

"Deadly." Cass dropped her head in dismay at the bad choice of words.

"That's great. Amazing." Sam took a glass from Ben and handed it to Izzy. "You're gentry, Cass—a landowner."

While Ben filled them in on the details, Nell went inside and rummaged around in the refrigerator. She returned with a tray of manchego and Havarti cheese, a basket of toast rounds, and small chunks of marinated tuna with a small pot of mustard. A pitcher of ice water.

"There." She set it down with a pile of napkins on a low table near the chairs. None of them had eaten much all day, she suspected, and although Ben's martinis would take the edge off this surprising day, the drinks were best handled with something in the stomach.

Izzy was putting perspective to the news—the fact that not only would this make the Halloran company healthy, but Cass could finally help her mother get an air conditioner. And her dear friend might laugh more—like she used to.

"I can't really think about any of that yet," Cass said. "I can't. Not until this is all settled. Officially settled. It doesn't seem real, and we may wake up tomorrow and find out it was all a joke."

"It's not a joke, but you're right about taking it slow," Ben said. "Settling an estate takes a little time, though, as best I could tell, Finnegan's will was pretty cut-and-dried as to what he wanted. Things like that move faster here than in the big cities. Father Larry is executor, and though Finn never mentioned it to me, apparently I'm the Sea Harbor attorney on record to help see this through the court."

"So you're in the best of hands," Nell said.

"God and the martini maker," Cass said. Then she stood and wrapped her arms around Ben in a tight squeeze. "Thank you," she said in a husky voice.

They watched the wave of emotions sweep over Cass. To go from almost losing her father's business to owning a valued piece of land in minutes. But it wouldn't be without its bumpy road, not with a murder investigation in full swing, an unknown body buried on the land Cass had just inherited, and a relative waiting in the wings.

It gave Nell a headache to think of what the rumor mill might do with this.

Izzy speared a piece of tuna with a toothpick and dipped it in mustard. She plunged into the topic that had been lurking in the background, a part of the conversation without ever being spoken aloud. "What about Finn's daughter?"

Ben cleared his throat. "Well, that's a bit of a mystery," he said. He chose his words carefully, letting them know there was more to come, things they might be interested in. "Over the years, Finn actually made out three wills. One when he married Moira that left everything to his wife, as you'd expect. And then he finally got around to making a new one—a second one—last year. Old man Angus witnessed it."

He'd caught everyone's attention now and they moved closer. "The second will had several people in it. There was a sizable hunk for Cass and her family, a donation to the theater over in Rockport, another to Father Northcutt's soup kitchen and some others. But the land—that went to Beverly."

"Beverly," Nell murmured.

"I suppose that makes sense," Izzy said. "Even if they didn't get along, she was his daughter."

"But that's not the final will," Nell said.

"No. In fact, Finn took that second will and marked all over it, editing it like a madman, before he had the final will drawn up. It was almost as if he were taking his emotions out on a piece of paper. He crossed out every mention of Beverly—big black lines crossing out her name in a very definitive way. Angry strikes, Father Larry thought. A new one was drawn up, this one, which leaves everything to Cass."

They were silent.

Finally Sam asked, "What's the date on the final will?"

"A week before he died."

"So what do you suppose happened?" Izzy asked, then answered her own question. "Beverly Walden must have done something really awful to make Finnegan that mad."

"I'd guess you're right. He also knew that Cass needed money for the company. And he also knew the cancer was getting a little worse. So instead of fiddling around with charitable donations, he gave it all to you, Cass, figuring you'd do whatever was right."

"Does Beverly know?" Izzy asked.

"There's no way she could. Father Larry is the executor and this is the first look he's had of it. She may, however, have known she was in the second will. Angus wasn't sure, but he thought there might have been some communication back then. She definitely didn't know about him being sick."

They all thought about that. Knowing he was ill would give one patience. Thinking Finn might live for another twenty years would not.

"This won't sit well with her. She's counting on that money," Izzy said. "Making plans for it, in fact, according to Merry Jackson. She's already confiscated Finn's boat."

Ben frowned. "She did what?"

"It had her mother's name on it. Tommy Porter somehow got it off the property for her."

"Not a smart move on Tommy's part," Ben said.

"I think he felt sorry for her. And he probably thought, like the rest of us did, that she'd inherit whatever Finnegan owned. What would it hurt to let her have the boat early?"

Ben didn't seem convinced. He reached for a water pitcher and the martini shaker, refilling drinks, while Nell passed around little plates of tuna and cheese, encouraging people to eat.

"I have a favor to ask." Cass looked over at Ben, then around the group. "Do you suppose we could not talk about Finnegan's will with anyone—I mean, except for here? With just us? At least for right now?"

Ben nodded. "It's usually best to file wills as soon as you can," he said. "Sometimes there are taxes that need to be paid—that kind of thing. But once filed, they're public property and everyone will have access to it. We can hold off a bit, though, until things settle down. And for sure until we find out what other surprises Finnegan might—"

A vibration in Cass' pocket interrupted Ben. She pulled it out, read the name, and moved across the porch to take the call.

"It's Danny," Izzy said, reading her friend's face.

"Are those two okay?" Nell asked as Cass walked off to take the call.

"I don't know. Cass resents it when people want to help her. And Danny wants to help in the worst way. Her problems are eating him up. It's different when it's us, I think, though she doesn't let us help, either. But at least she doesn't resent us for it. Accepting help from Danny—in Cass' crazy mind, anyway—signifies some kind of dependence or commitment, or whatever it is. Her reaction doesn't always make sense, but I think it's because she knows how much he cares for her. And it scares her half to death."

Nell looked at her wise niece and agreed. But she'd go a step further. Deep down Cass cared deeply for Danny. And that scared her even more.

When Cass returned, she forced a smile to her face. "Danny's back from Boston. He's at my place, looking for me. Thinks I was swallowed by a lobster, I guess. I'm going to go fill him in. I owe him that. . . ."

"Owe him?" Izzy said with a frown. "That's an odd way to put it, Cass. The guy's crazy about you." Her voice held a hint of irritation.

They all loved Danny Brandley, the tawny-haired, laid-back mystery writer who had given up an award-winning journalism career to write a novel in Sea Harbor. It'd been Cass who had pursued him, flirted with him, and pulled him into their circle. So they'd gotten to know him, become fond of him, liked his stories and his easygoing ways. And they were definitely against abandoning him, whatever might be going on between him and Cass.

Cass was silent. She took a deep breath and straightened up her shoulders. "You're right. I *want* to see him, to tell him what's going on."

Nell walked her to the door and hugged her tight. "This is a good thing, Cass. Finn loved you. We all do. He wanted to make your life easier."

"Then why do I feel as if I've robbed someone's grave?"

"Because you have such a difficult time accepting things from people who love you. You haven't robbed anyone, dear. Other people don't factor into this right now. Accept that, and rejoice that Finn loved you."

Nell watched her walk toward the truck, her dark hair tangled in the wind. She'd pulled herself up, straightened her back, and climbed into the truck with resolve.

What Finnegan had done *was* a good thing. Deep down Cass must know that and be relieved at what it could mean to the Hallorans. A dream come true for most people. And it wasn't the old man's fault that the dream was coated with enough complications to make the wonderful part almost invisible. It was someone else's. Someone who had ended Finn's life tragically. Someone Nell felt desperate to find.

Chapter 19

*N*ell waited until a decent hour to call Birdie. She hadn't heard a thing from her the night before and realized, suddenly, that there was no update on when Nick and Gabby were leaving Sea Harbor. Surely Birdie would insist they have time to plan a suitable farewell. Nick wouldn't—couldn't—just disappear with her into the night.

When Birdie's voice mail clicked in, Nell left a message to call her back. "Soon, please," she added before hanging up. She checked her calendar for the day, scribbled some notes on a to-do pad, and then walked around the kitchen, undirected. Where was her focus?

There were too many uncertainties in their lives. Perhaps that accounted for the restless night and tangled sheets.

She moved to the kitchen table, a breakfast nook that jutted out on the back of the house with windows on three sides. The tree house, Ben called it, and a perfect spot to begin a day. It was a sunny day, just as predicted. Early-morning rays filtered through the trees, falling on the small guesthouse tucked in the far corner, partially hidden now by the thick hedge of rugosa roses they'd planted for Izzy's wedding the year before. The winding path through the woods was already trampled in place by neighborhood children taking a shortcut to the beach. The pathway to heaven, Izzy used to call it.

The beauty just outside the breakfast windows sometimes gripped Nell so tightly that she found it difficult to breathe. And it almost always helped her put things into perspective.

Today, the magic tonic eluded her. She felt discombobulated, muddled in thoughts that didn't link together easily.

At first she thought the noise was from the backyard, a new group of giggling swimmers off for a day at the beach.

But the rattling of the front door said differently.

"The door was stuck," Birdie said, walking across the family room. "For a minute I thought you had locked it, and then I would truly have worried." She took a mug from the shelf and poured herself coffee, then walked to the kitchen table, her step missing its usual bounce.

Nell frowned, sensing her slowness. Her heart sank. "Gabby and Nick have left, haven't they?"

"No. And they're not going anywhere. Not for a while, anyway."

"That makes you sad?" Nell got up and put two slices of bread in the toaster, then sat across from Birdie. "Tell me."

"The police have labeled Nick a person of interest in Finnegan's murder."

Nell was silent.

"They've picked up things here and there, enough connections between the two men to want to talk to him. Sal Scaglia—probably trying to take the spotlight off his wife—mentioned that Nick had been in his office, looking for information on Finnegan's land."

Nell frowned, then remembered. Although just a few days ago, it seemed somehow longer, something she had to dig out of the shadows of her memory. Nick had just come back from Italy. Birdie had thought he was working at the B and B that morning, but someone had seen him going up the courthouse steps. That must have been where he was going.

"So the police went to the courthouse, and sure enough, there was his name, signed in to look at deeds. And to make it worse, Nick had talked to people at Coffee's that day, asking about the land, questions about the owner, the building on the land, the offices people rented—those sorts of things."

"But that's not a crime."

"No. But there was more, some of which we'd seen ourselves.

We weren't the only ones who saw him arguing with Finn. It was broad daylight. There was traffic on Canary Cove Road and lots of people around. There's a reward out for information leading to Finn's murderer, and you know how that can bring people out of the woodwork. I don't think anyone in Canary Cove who's met Nick would think him guilty of anything other than gallantry and loving his niece, but when asked whom they saw going in and out of Finnegan's place, they would tell the truth. So would you or I. We would presume Nick had a good reason to be where he was, so in the long run it wouldn't make any difference."

"So did he? Have a good reason, I mean?"

Birdie paused for a moment. "He told the police what he told us. He wanted to meet the man who had taken his niece fishing."

"The arguing?"

"Finnegan was simply cantankerous that day, he told the police. The old man didn't want to be bothered with a stranger questioning what he did or didn't do. He wanted to see the property, to see where Gabby fished, and Finn refused."

Before Nell could say anything, Birdie answered her look. "No, I don't buy it, either. Finn was often grouchy, but the dear man always had a reason—maybe not one you or I would have, but in his mind he had a legitimate right to be angry. And he'd never be mad about a caring uncle doing his job."

"What about the looking up the deed?"

"Lots of people had done that and it didn't mean much. It was a flimsy way to tie someone to a murder. People wanted to buy Finn's valuable land, plain and simple. Nick said he was curious about it. That was all."

Nell got up and emptied her cold coffee into the sink. She poured a fresh one and brought it back with toast, butter, and a pot of fresh blueberry jam. "How is Nick handling all this?"

"He's remarkably calm. After spending a considerable amount of time at the police station, he came by the house and took Gabby for a walk, filling her in. Then he came inside and told me the whole story. He was clearly sorry to be dragging Gabby and me through this mess. But, as he said, there was definitely a bright side to the whole thing. The police had 'suggested' he not leave the area for a few days. So he and Gabby would be staying in Sea Harbor longer. And that news, he said, thrilled his niece far more than the fancy skateboard he'd sent her last Christmas."

"It's strange, maybe, but hearing his reaction somehow rids me of worry. Nick is innocent—I feel sure of it."

Nell's response drew a smile from Birdie. "Of course he is. He's lied to both of us—we can't forget that—but he didn't have anything to do with Finn's murder. And that's what matters now." Birdie slipped off the bench and walked around the table. She gave Nell a sudden hug.

"That's for being you, my dear Nell. And as for the lie, we'll certainly get to the bottom of that now, won't we?"

And then she was gone. Birdie's pain-free good-byes, they called them. No awkward time spent chatting at the door, no need for reasons; just a quick hug and the small woman with the white cap of hair was across the room and out the door, disappearing into her day.

But this one had been so quick, she hadn't had time to talk to her about yesterday's reading of Finn's will. She checked her watch. Not enough time to catch her, and she knew Birdie's Thursdays were full. But she'd see her tonight, and they would lay everything out on the table right along with their knitting needles and yarn. Things always made more sense with Purl on one's lap, knitting nearby, and a glass of Birdie's pinot gris in hand.

It seemed like a lifetime ago since they'd gathered in Izzy's shop for a Thursday-night knitting session. "The week that was," Birdie said, sitting next to Cass in the yarn studio's back room. She patted her on the knee.

Cass had given Birdie a ride to the shop, and used the drive time to fill her in on the latest events that had turned her life on its head.

"But it could be the best thing for this sweet head," Birdie had told her, tapping the top of Cass' Sox hat. "Finnegan was wiser than we knew. Money can destroy people or it can improve many lives. You will make sure it does the latter, and he knew that, my dear."

Then Birdie gave an abbreviated account of the Mariettis' day, although much of the story had already begun drifting down the windy roads and beaches of the town. "Nick can't leave town. He's telling Gabby everything—except, of course, what he hasn't told us."

"Meaning?" Izzy was puzzled.

"What he really argued with Finn about and what his interest is in that land. It didn't lead him to murder Finn, but he isn't telling the whole truth." The resolve in Birdie's voice was steely.

Izzy pulled open the casement windows and a cool evening breeze swept through the room. "Well, he's done one good thing that excuses a lot: he's brought Gabby into our lives."

"And given her an amazing grandmother," Cass added.

"Well, thank you, Catherine."

No matter that it wasn't a result of shared blood or genes, Gabby was Birdie's granddaughter, and the tie was already as tight as if she'd given birth to her herself.

"Gabby will handle this fine. It's the rest of us I'm worried about." Nell took the wrap off a basket of warm goat cheese croutons and set it beside the soup spoons, then began ladling a cool, summery squash soup into bowls.

"Mint," Cass said.

"Garlic," Izzy said.

"Fine wine."

Nell smiled at the weekly ritual of guessing ingredients. "Soupe au pistou. And you're all correct."

Nell spooned a dollop of the mint and garlic pistou on top of each serving, then swirled it into the soup. "Amazing, Aunt Nell." Izzy looped one arm around her aunt's waist and savored the smell. "Mint. It's perfect for tonight. Fresh and green. Something to clear our heads."

Next came a helping of sautéed shrimp atop each bowl. "It's ready to go, but don't touch this container," Nell warned, snapping a lid on a smaller bowl. She looked at Cass with a knowing smile. "Mae and her nieces are out front, stocking cubbies. This is for them."

Cass laughed. "Me, steal food from hungry teens? Never." She took a hunk of warm bread from a basket.

"I wonder how Nick will spend this time," Izzy said.

"His detainment?" Birdie laughed. "I don't think he'll have a problem. He loves Sea Harbor." She wiped the corner of her mouth.

"He met with Ben this afternoon," Nell said. "They were in the den when I got home."

"He needed to talk through this mess with someone, and Ben is a good listener. A good listener with a law degree is even better, considering the circumstances."

"What's the scuttlebutt in the shop?" Cass asked Izzy.

"People are obsessed with the idea that someone was buried on Finnegan's land. The younger kids—Jillian and Rose's friends—have dramatized it into an episode of *True Blood*, vampires and all. There're all sorts of guessing games going on about who it might be. Was it a guy who disappeared twenty years ago? Or the result of a lovers' quarrel? Kids trespassed on that land all the time. Was it some runaway teen who accidentally died there? Danny would have a field day following some of the story lines."

"But there's more serious talk, and that's what's awful. People wondering how someone ended up in a grave, dead," Cass said. "Did Finnegan kill the person?"

Nell confirmed she had heard the same rumor in the checkout line at Shaw's.

"As if that old man could kill anyone. He was so righteous, he drove people crazy," Izzy said.

"It's interesting that it's the grave—and not Finnegan's murder—that people are talking about," Nell said.

"People are connecting the two. Someone came back to seek revenge on what Finn did a long time ago. Maybe it was a guy he killed, and the wife has come back to get revenge. It's made-for-TV fare," Izzy said.

"I don't think most people believe it. It's flimsy," Nell said.

Birdie agreed.

"I heard some moms say they won't let their kids go over to Canary Cove until the person is caught," Izzy said. "People are frightened."

"That's not a good thing for Canary Cove business," Birdie said. "And not a logical reaction, really. Whoever killed him is probably not spending time around Canary Cove."

"Probably not, but I understand the fear. We know so little about what happened." Nell put her empty bowl on the tray, wiped her hands, and took out Gabby's sweater.

"Have you heard any names thrown out there of who might have done it?" Cass asked.

Izzy refilled wineglasses and collected the empty bowls. "In spite of the gossip, people are being cautious, I think. They don't want to be disrespectful. Finn hasn't even been buried yet. And even though there were a lot of people upset over his property—and many others wanting to get their hands on it—there are also people like us. People who liked Finnegan and liked what he added to our town. He's left a void. People are genuinely sad about his death."

"Murder," Cass corrected.

"Homicide." Izzy, the lawyer, shot back.

"Whatever. Someone cut him with a knife. Someone wanted to hurt him—badly."

"So who? Who would possibly dislike Finnegan enough to harm him?" Birdie asked.

Cass walked over for a second bowl of soup. "What would they gain from it?"

Did Cass really not discern what could be gained by killing Finnegan? For those who looked at facts and not emotions—people like the police investigating the case—what people could gain from killing Finnegan was simple. Money.

The most common motive in the world.

And right now, for all Finnegan's wonderful intentions, he had hoisted Cass Halloran to the top of that list.

The clunk of sandals on the steps announced Jillian and Rose Anderson. "Food? Aunt Mae said you were sharing, Mrs. Endicott." Jillian, the more talkative twin bounded over to the table with Rose close behind.

Nell laughed. The teenagers added a whole new population to the shop in summer months, and certainly increased the decibel level with their music, giggles, and friends who stopped in many times a day when their friends were working.

"You're, like, the best cook I know," Rose said. "Everyone says so."

"So can you guys believe all this stuff going on around town?" Jillian asked. "Our mom is freaked. She doesn't even want us to go out at night, but she does, because it would be pretty awful for her if we were at home all the time." She laughed. "She'd go, like, crazy."

"We're super careful, though," Rose assured them.

"Some of our friends got a look at the guy." Jillian peeled the top off the food bowl.

"What do you mean? What guy?" Cass asked.

"The murderer," Rose said solemnly, dipping a spoon into the soup. She bit into a piece of shrimp, closing her eyes. "This is incredible," she murmured.

"You know, Finnegan's murderer." Jillian stepped in, her eyes bright with excitement. "It was a few days ago, not the day it happened, but it must have been the same guy. Had to have been."

"What happened?" Izzy tried to pull the twins' talk into logical order. Or at least something they could understand. "Someone saw something—or someone—who might have murdered Finnegan? Where? And who?"

Rose pulled out a chair at the long table and was content to enjoy her soup, but Jillian jumped into the discussion fully.

"See, it was these guys we hang out with, friends from school. You know Oliver Porter—he's Officer Porter's cousin, and—"

Rose looked up. "Jason McClucken."

"Oh yeah, and Camden Gibson. Those three. They're always together."

"Where were they?"

"Down near the Canary Cove shore. They go fishing off the old docks down there sometimes."

"They're not supposed to," Rose said wisely, pausing with a spoonful of soup in midair. "Those docks are old and rickety, and besides that, it's private property."

Jillian's ponytail flew as she turned to look at her sister. "But lots of kids do it—you know they do, Rose."

"What did they see?" Suddenly the picture of three boys going fishing was playing out in front of Nell too clearly, with too much familiarity. Déjà vu in 3-D.

"They go down that old access road," Jillian said, "the one between the Arts Association office and Finnegan's. Once they're at the water's edge, they can scoot around the fence and along the shore—go all the way around Canary Cove, if they want to."

"But they don't go that far," Rose said. "And the other day they just went down to the end of the road, around the fence, and over to the dock."

"Finnegan's dock?"

Rose nodded. "They figured they could do it, you know, now that he wasn't there to chase them off with his BB gun."

"But while they were sitting out there"—Jillian was reaching the climax of the story now, and her words took on the tone of an actress on a stage—"they spotted a man going through the bushes. He hadn't seen them because he was farther in, behind a bunch of trees and shrubs. So they decided to spy on him. It was a great game, Oliver said. They watched him go into the house—that place Finnegan lived. They heard noises coming from inside and could see a flashlight every now and then, flashing in the windows. A while later the guy came back out. Oliver thought he was carrying something. Anyway, he went back through the bushes and around the end of the fence. I guess it was how he got in, just like the guys."

Nell took a deep breath. "Did they know who it was?"

"They didn't get a good look. They were afraid if they got too close he'd see them and shoot them or something." Rose helped herself to the last roll. She smothered it with butter, then licked her fingers clean.

"Was he young?"

"Oliver said old. Well, not old like Finnegan or the Old Man of the Sea, but old like . . ."

"Like me?" Nell said.

"Maybe. Maybe a little older," Jillian said with great seriousness. "He had gray hair. But he wasn't hunched over or anything."

"Then what happened?" Birdie asked, the words sticking uncomfortably in her throat.

"Well, then Jason—I think it was Jason; maybe Oliver—snuck over to the fence to see where he went. The guy was moving fast and was, like, almost to the end of the drive before Jason got around the fence."

"And that's it?"

"Yep. He got into a blue car and drove away. That's it. How's that for weird?"

Chapter 20

Ben hadn't heard about anyone who had gone onto Finn's property and into his house. No, it hadn't come up when he'd talked to Nick.

Nell sat back against a post on the floor of the yacht club dock that held Sam and Ben's still-unnamed sailboat. She bent her knees and wrapped her arms around them, the morning sun warm and soothing on her bare arms. The egg sandwiches she'd brought over to the two sailors had been most welcome, and the few remaining crumbs were welcomed by a pair of swooping gulls. The yacht club café wouldn't be open for another hour, and Nell's coffee had helped them all think more clearly.

Ben took a drink, but Nell knew from the deep furrows between his eyes that he found the story disturbing. If the trespasser was, in fact, Nick Marietti, then he hadn't been completely honest with Ben. If it wasn't true, there was a completely unknown person trespassing on Finnegan's property just two days after his death.

"Someone wanted something from Finnegan. But desperately enough to kill for it?"

"And you think that someone is Nicholas Marietti?" Sam reached for a bucket of water and a sponge.

"It's difficult for me to go there. I like him—but I don't like what Nell's saying."

"What the teenagers are saying," Nell corrected. "Maybe it wasn't Nick."

But it sounds like Nick.

Ben handed his mug to Nell, then picked up a hose, adjusted the spray, and began hosing down the side of the boat. He and Sam had taken it out early, before the world was awake, to test a new computer they'd just installed. And Sam, as always, brought his camera to record the beauty of the sea or a whale's nose or a gull doing ballet on a wave.

It's like a baby to them, Nell thought. This sleek, beautiful vessel, nurtured and lovingly cared for. Ben said being on the boat helped him think. Relax. Slow down. Be at one with the sea. And Nell knew it was a tonic that she'd never be able to find for him in the drugstore, so she embraced it, though she didn't completely understand it. All around them were other yachts and sailboats, equally loved and pampered. A neighborhood of boats.

She looked over at a sleek sailboat moored next to Ben and Sam's.

"Delaney's," Ben said, following her look. "She's a beauty."

"D.J.? I didn't know he was a sailor."

"No, the other family. D.J.'s son, Davey. The young kids are out here a lot, learning how to handle the sails, helping Davey's wife, Kristen, spruce it up."

The wind tossed her hair as she admired the sailing vessel, the small dinghy hugging its side. She tamed the hair back with her hand, her thoughts boomeranging from beautiful boats to more troubling scenarios.

"It's difficult to appreciate beauty with everything that's going on—this murder, the innuendos. Even teenagers are inventing their own versions of what might have happened."

"The trespassing story could be absolutely correct, and it still wouldn't mean the guy—whoever he was—killed Finnegan," Ben said.

Sam agreed. "But it's too closely connected to Finnegan to just dismiss it, I guess."

"According to Jillian and Rose, the boys went to the police yesterday. They didn't go right away because they didn't think too much of it at first. Some man sneaking into a dead man's house didn't seem like a terrible thing to them, I guess."

Sam squeezed the water from his sponge and dropped it into

the bucket. "That's because they were trespassing themselves." He picked up his camera and began fiddling with the lens, then aimed and snapped a shot of Nell.

Ben finished spraying the last section of the boat and turned off the hose. "I don't know if the police will tie the story to Nick. We don't even know for sure if it *was* Nick. But I'm going to tell him what the kids think they saw. And if there's a connection, he can get to the police before they get to him."

Nell listened, trying to squeeze the pieces together in a way that would take Nick out of the picture.

"I still can't see Nick Marietti doing anything unsavory," Ben said, helping Nell to her feet. "Maybe there's something he's not telling us, but I'd like to trust he has a good reason for it."

"How's Birdie doing with all this?" Sam asked. He picked up wrappers from their sandwiches and shoved them in a plastic bag.

"Birdie's a rock. And nobody's fool. But she feels just like Ben does—Nick is honorable—but might be holding something back."

"Not to change the subject, but I need to get showered and changed. Father Northcutt and I are meeting this morning to go over the documents again, and if the others have come, we'll look at those, too."

"What do you expect to find?"

"Not much. We'll see. Maybe it will clarify the will a little. There's more money there than we'd thought. We know that already."

"It's amazing to me that news of the will hasn't leaked out," Nell said. "I'm happy Cass is getting a reprieve—time to get used to it—before she's bombarded with looks and questions and offers."

"It won't be for long. It's hard to keep that kind of news quiet," Sam said. He lifted his camera again and focused on the well-tended sandy beach in the distance. Rotating his body, he spanned the club's pier with its offshoot slips, his lens capturing things Nell was sure she would never notice.

Sam lowered the camera and pointed over to the next row of slips. "Looks like there's another sea-loving soul up at this hour." He waved to Sal Scaglia, who was climbing off his blue yacht.

"We thought we were the only ones up this early," Ben called out to him. "Beatrice with you?"

Sal took off his sunglasses, replacing them with the dark-rimmed glasses he usually wore. He joined them on the pier. "No, not at this hour. In fact, not at any hour. Beatrice has a morning routine that's pretty steadfast. Ironclad, I guess you'd say. Hot yoga. Steam bath. Breakfast. Work." He pointed over to the yacht. "My boat is my yoga. Steam bath, too."

They laughed and looked over at his sleek sky blue boat, admiring the aft deck, the beautiful strip of chrome wrapping around it like a glove, the cabin tucked beneath, and the small matching dinghy at its side.

"We sure understand that, Sal. She's really a beauty. I noticed her the other night at your house."

"It's nice to be able to go back and forth. That dock's not really big enough, though, so I keep a slip here where I'll winter her."

Ben looked off down the coast toward the neighborhood Sal lived in. "You don't ever have to leave the water. A sailor's dream."

Sal nodded. "Right. Down the inlet and around the bend, and I'm here."

"And around another bend, you'd be at Canary Cove."

"And the harbor," Ben said.

Sal nodded. "It's nice. We can take the boat over to Gloucester for dinner, no car necessary."

"Good for you. I like that," Ben said.

Sam lifted his camera. "How about a couple shots?"

Sal looked back at the boat, then stepped aside, a look of pride on his face. "That'd be really nice. Thanks. I'd love a copy, if it's no trouble. I'll put it on my desk and pretend I'm out here all day."

"Living the life," Ben said with a laugh, and went off to get the car.

Sam angled his camera and began snapping while Nell and Sal stood by, watching.

"I hear things have been busy in your office lately," Nell said, an attempt at conversation. Sal was sweet, but not the easiest man in the world to talk with.

Sal adjusted his glasses, a wary look flickering behind the lenses. "The Finnegan land?"

"Well, I suppose that's what I mean. It's on people's minds."

She hadn't really planned to question the shy man. It almost seemed unfair to ask Sal job-related questions without allowing him the protection of his solitary office, his computers, his wall of musty-smelling books. *But,* she told herself, *deeds are public knowledge.*

"It's like any other land. If people want to buy it or find out who used to own it, who sold it to whom, the deed gives them useful information."

"A friend of ours has expressed some interest in it."

"One of the developers?"

"No. He doesn't live here."

Sal frowned.

"His name is Nicholas Marietti."

"Mr. Marietti is a friend of yours?" Sal was suddenly transformed into the man who managed the register of deeds annex— professional, serious.

"We've only recently met, but, yes, he's a friend."

Nell saw the hesitation on Sal's face, and realized too late what she'd done. Even though deeds were open to the public, Sal felt those looking up things in his office deserved confidentiality. Perhaps it added a mystique to his work, a layer of respect for a job that had come his way through his wife's connections. The Sea Harbor location was only an annex and Sal wasn't elected. But his office was his haven. He took the job very seriously. Asking him about someone who visited the department was like asking Father Northcutt what someone said in the confessional. Before she could apologize, Sam offered a halfhearted answer.

"Mr. Marietti was . . . yes, he was interested in the layout of that land. Some people are curious about those things. What buildings were there? Were they new? The original? The location. That sort of thing." Sal looked down at his boat shoes, then over at his yacht, as if he wished he were on it, rather than standing there talking to Nell.

Finally, he checked his watch.

"I . . . I'm sorry, Nell. I'm going to be late. I need to get home. Shower. Get to work . . ." He managed a smile, thanked Sam again for the photographs, and hurried off, disappearing around the corner of the club parking lot.

Chapter 21

The day had turned unexpectedly warm—warmer than usual for a June Sea Harbor day.

By the time Nell had walked down to Harbor Road, tiny beads of perspiration dampened her neck. She checked her watch, then headed across the street to Coffee's for a glass of iced passion fruit tea. The break would also give her time to answer a few text messages before meeting Birdie. The message from Birdie didn't say much, just that she had a dozen errands before the day ended on the Endicott deck, but a light salad with Nell might add some order to her life. Nick might join them. *The Ocean's Edge at eleven?*

Nell carried her iced tea out to Coffee's patio, hoping for a table or chair in the shade and wondering about Nick Marietti. *Has Birdie confronted him?* she wondered.

Mary Pisano was on the patio beneath her usual tree, staring at her computer screen. She was definitely in "do not disturb" mode, but when Nell started to walk by, Mary reached out and touched her arm.

"Just so you know, Nell, Nick Marietti is a gracious, lovely man, and no matter what rumors are swirling around, he's innocent. And I will be sure others know it, as well."

"I agree with you, Mary."

"I know you do; I just needed to say it out loud. I understand people's need to resolve this murder—each day seems like an eternity, like we're being robbed of living in the moment because all we're doing is wanting to race ahead and put someone in prison."

"And it's frightening for people, the idea that whoever did this could still be wandering around Sea Harbor."

"Or not. He could be long gone, Nell. He could have been mad at Finnegan for breaking his nose, retaliated, and taken off for Portugal."

"Portugal?"

"Or wherever." Mary waved her hand in the air dismissively.

Nell could see the earnest desire in Mary's eyes. It was always like this with her, even about small things. Mary couldn't—wouldn't—subscribe to anyone they knew being guilty of a crime. Even though she knew very well that people close to them could be—and had been—guilty of some horrible things. She clearly had Nick Marietti's back.

Nell wondered if Nick knew how fortunate he was. Mary was a force to be reckoned with. "Nick is an easy target because most people don't know him," she said. "I suppose that's at the root of this. But the thought of him killing anyone, much less someone he didn't know well, doesn't make sense. Did he ever mention anything to you about Finnegan?"

Mary paused and stared at her computer for a moment, then finally looked back at Nell. "Yes. He asked me how to get to his place. And then he wondered if I'd ever been beyond the gate."

"What did you tell him?"

"I told him where it was and that no one ever got beyond the gate, not for a long time. Except the Hallorans."

Nell sighed. She kept waiting for the story to be refuted, but it was seeming unlikely. Nick clearly had an interest in Finnegan. "Well, Nick knew Gabby was spending time with Finn. I'm sure that's why he wanted to know where he lived." She wasn't sure at all anymore, but saying it out loud might add weight to the shopworn premise.

Mary was silent.

"What? It makes sense. Nick loves Gabby and he's responsible for her right now."

Mary sighed. "Nick asked me about Finn's place the night he came back from Italy. Before he went over to your place."

And before he'd even seen Gabby.

Nick wouldn't have known anything about the old man who had befriended his niece. Birdie had wisely decided that mentioning Gabby's friendship with an old man Nick had never met while he was still over in Italy might have worried him.

"It doesn't matter," Mary said quickly. "He's still innocent."

"It does matter, but I still agree with you—Nick isn't the murderer. We just need to find out who did kill Finnegan before we ruin the lives of innocent people."

Mary thought about that for a moment, wrinkled her forehead, and rubbed her cheek with two fingers, the way she did when imagining an "About Town" column. Then, without another word, she buried her head behind the lid of her laptop and began working the keyboard with her small fingers, as if life itself depended on it.

She'd forgotten Nell was even there.

Nick and Birdie were waiting on the covered porch of the restaurant when Nell arrived. From a spot near the back railing, diners could see the whole span of the harbor—the working boats on one side, pleasure on another. And in between, excursion boats took vacationers out to spot the whales or to try their hand at deep-sea fishing. Today the crew of a large schooner was ushering people aboard to attend a wedding at sea. In the background a string trio played "Through the Eyes of Love."

Life in Sea Harbor . . . as it should be. Nell followed Birdie and Nick to a table.

At eleven in the morning they had the place almost to themselves. Nick seemed relaxed, and Birdie, too. Perhaps the confrontation was on the back burner.

"You have quite a fan in Mary Pisano," Nell said as Nick pulled back her chair.

"She's the consummate hostess," Nick said. "I don't know if you'll be able to pry me out of Ravenswood-by-the-Sea."

"Well, I, for one, am happy you'll be here awhile longer, even though the reason for it isn't exactly happy."

Nick turned serious. "Thank you, Nell. I don't mean to sound like I'm not taking this whole thing seriously. I am. I believe in the system, though, and I know I am not guilty of anything more serious than imposing on my new friends."

"But there's concern, Nick," Birdie said. "Police don't much believe in coincidences."

Nick listened with grave attention, his eyes on Birdie. His expression seemed to be one of regret. It was clear he didn't enjoy putting Birdie through any of this, but he still refused to explain his actions in a way that made sense to them. What kind of a friend did that?

"I understand, Birdie. All I ask is that you trust me—as difficult as that may be. They will find the person who did this horrible thing to Finnegan. And then it will all go away."

Nell's phone vibrated. Ben's name flashed on the screen. She frowned. Then excused herself and walked to the railing to take the call.

She listened carefully, her eyes wandering across the water to the fishing pier as Ben talked. From where she stood, she could see the boats lashed to the wharves and rolling with the waves. The work yard, brawny fishermen unloading pots and refilling bait bags. Pete's lanky form loomed tall, his sandy head towering over the traps and a bright yellow Fractured Fish band T-shirt singling him out. She squinted, looking for Cass, then spotted her bending over a pile of rope. Another dark head, with hair wilder than Cass', was leaning down next to her, the bright green beanie giving her away, as well.

"Yes, she's on the dock. Gabby's with her," she said into her phone.

Cass wasn't answering her cell, Ben said. Would Nell mind walking down there and giving her the news?

Out of batteries, Nell suspected. She walked back to the table.

"I'm sorry, but I need to run over to the fishing pier to give Cass a message. Anyone up for a short walk to stimulate your appetite?"

On the way over to the Hallorans' slip, Nell explained Ben's call. It wasn't an emergency, but he thought Cass should know what was going on. He'd been over at the police department, answering a few questions about Finnegan's will. Beverly Walden was there, too, being questioned about her father's death.

"So, this Beverly—was she close to her father?" Nick asked.

"No. Although shortly before he died she made an effort, I think. But she was pushing hard for the estate to be settled and the will read. She assumed she was the main beneficiary and hasn't been silent about it. Add that to their relationship—or lack of one—and there was good reason to question her. She was clearly upset that no one would discuss the will today, Ben said. Before she left, she tried to talk the officer at the desk into giving her a copy of it. I guess the young patrolman had reached the end of his rope, because he decided to quiet her."

Birdie guessed the outcome. "He told her she wasn't in it?"

"Exactly."

"Oh, dear."

"Yes, and then he told her who the sole beneficiary is."

Birdie sighed. "So soon everyone will know."

Nell nodded. "It was bound to happen. But Ben thought Cass should have a heads-up before the news started circling around her. Besides the fact that Beverly was so angry, she threw the officer's coffee mug against the wall."

"Not a good way to endear yourself to the police," Nick mused.

They walked across the grassy park area that hosted summer concerts and, in the winter, Santa Claus' arrival on a lobster boat. The fishing pier was just ahead, beyond the small parking lot where pots were piled as high as the roof of a nearby storage shed.

Nell took in the sounds and smells of the demanding, harsh work—engine oil, sounds of crashing traps, and the aching squeal of rope against wood. In the background was the constant slap of the ocean water against the side of vessels.

"Hey, what're you doing slumming down here with us working guys?" Pete was standing on the hull of the *Lady Lobster*, waving a dirty rag at them.

Gabby spotted the newcomers and jumped up, running over and wrapping her arms around Birdie, then Nick. She clutched a green striped buoy in her hand and a splatter of the same color competed with freckles across her nose. Nick ignored the green swipe left on his white knit shirt and kissed his niece soundly.

"So, what're you up to?" Cass asked. "Want to help?" She wiped the perspiration off her forehead with the back of her hand.

Before they could answer, Gabby grabbed Nick's hand and dragged him over to the line of Styrofoam buoys she was helping paint in Halloran colors—bright green Irish strips that progressed from a narrow band at the white-nubbed top to the broad one at the bottom. Nell looked at the dents and slashes in some of the older ones, thinking back to last spring. Cass had desperately needed a new supply of buoys and the expensive paint needed to cover them. But after purchasing new traps, there wasn't enough money left to buy the materials.

Knowing she wouldn't ask any of them for help, they'd thrown her a surprise birthday party at Birdie's. Everyone wore old clothes and brought along a new buoy. Birdie supplied the paint, and they'd gathered in the huge garage that years ago had housed Sonny Favazza's prized cars. Between chowder, crab cakes, and beer, they painted till dawn—and in a single evening, a new family of Halloran buoys was born.

She'd have no need for that anymore, Nell realized, looking around at the dented traps and frayed piles of rope. And while it would bring welcome relief to Cass, Nell felt a small twinge of regret, thinking of the good times they'd had.

"Are you here, Nell?" Cass asked. She pulled back her black hair and slipped it through the band of her Sox cap. "Whew. Warm day."

"Ben called," Nell began, pulling Cass a few feet away from the others, who, with Gabby in the lead, were now dragging Nick and Birdie onto the *Lady Lobster*.

"He asked me to stop by," she continued. "And, by the way, your phone is out of batteries."

Cass laughed. "Surprise, surprise."

"Just plug it in every night, Cass. You need a working phone, especially when you're down here on the dock."

Cass accepted Nell's motherly nudging without protest, though they both knew it would happen again, and probably soon. "So, you said Ben—"

Her sentence broke off and she took a sudden step to the side, looking around Nell and toward the parking lot. She pushed her sunglasses to the top of her head, squinting, a frown furrowing her brow.

"What's the matter?" Nell turned around, following her gaze.

Beverly Walden stood at the end of the dock, her arms crossed over her chest, her eyes boring into Cass.

She began walking toward them, her voice reaching out in front of her. "And what, exactly, did you have to do to steal my inheritance?" she called out.

"Beverly," Nell began, but Cass shushed her.

"My battle, Nell," she murmured, and she crossed the short distance remaining between them. "I'm sorry about this, Beverly. But apparently, it's what Finnegan wanted to do."

"Sorry? Right." Beverly's laugh was too high-pitched, and Nell could see she'd been crying. "He wouldn't have done this if he had been thinking right. What was in that soup you took him? The lemonade? What did you do to him, Cass Halloran?"

"I was his friend," Cass said quietly. "If it's any help, this doesn't make complete sense to me, either, but that's all I did. I was his friend."

Beverly's smile was filled with a tangle of emotions Nell would think back to later, trying in her mind to sort them out, one by one. *Anger. Disappointment. Fear.* And a terrible anguish that Nell didn't think had anything to do with losing a father.

She took a deep breath. "He owed me this. He had my mother. I had nothing. And I know he intended me to have it."

Cass started to speak, but Beverly quieted her, holding both palms forward, pushing back her words. "Just know this. I won't let you ruin my life. You will not steal my inheritance from me. I won't let you." She paused and took a breath, as if to gain courage to finish what she had to say. This time her voice had lost its hardness but her message was resolute. "It's mine, I need it, and I will have it, one way or another."

Beverly turned away slowly, as if departing quickly would bring harm to her, a bear at her back, ready to lunge.

Slowly, deliberately, she walked back to shore.

"I almost feel sorry for her," Cass said, watching her walk away. "There's something desperate in her voice."

Cass nodded. "She's a strange woman. There's no telling what she might do. I wonder . . ."

"What?"

"She's his daughter. If she contests the will, will she get it?"

"I don't know, Cass." Nell had the same thought. Beverly looked so determined.

"It sounds selfish, doesn't it, my worrying about that? But for some reason Finn didn't want her to have it. He was . . . I don't know. He thought things through. And he must have thought long and hard about changing a will."

Nell agreed. "He didn't do things haphazardly."

"I talked to my mother and Pete this morning. It will help us all, Nell—you know that. But it's all so messy. And now this—"

She pointed to the spot where Beverly had stood minutes before, then looked back at her friend. "I don't steal, Nell," she said softly.

"Of course not."

"How did Beverly know about the will?"

"The police called her in for questioning, and a policeman let it slip."

Cass frowned in thought. "Questioning about the murder?"

"Yes. They always talk to family. But especially in her case. She wasn't fond of him, and she thought she would inherit his money."

"Two strikes against her, I guess."

Nell nodded. They stood there for a moment, the silence cushioning thoughts playing out in both women's minds. Cass toyed with the end of a frayed rope.

"But I'm the one who inherited the money," she said finally. "And the whole town knows I need it. I was also one of the few people who had access to Finn's land."

Cass took a deep breath, then added sadly, "I was never very good at baseball, but is that three strikes?"

Nell was saved from commenting by Tommy Porter's shadow falling across the dock as he walked toward the two women. He was in full uniform, Tommy on duty.

"Cass," he said, his voice filled with regret. "Do you have a minute?"

Chapter 22

anny showed up at Nell's alone. He walked in, looking like he'd lost his best friend.

"Do you know where she is?"

Nell stood at the kitchen island with Izzy and Sam, tossing a salad. Her face mirrored Danny's concern. "She'll be here in a minute. Sit down."

Sam took a cold beer from the refrigerator and put it in Danny's hands, then clinked it to his own. "We'll have to rough it until Ben gets here."

"Cass is with Ben," Nell said. Birdie and Nick walked in next, with the Brewsters close behind. Nell paused while they bustled around, putting hunks of cheese on the island and flowers from Jane's garden in a vase. There was no reason to tell the same story twice.

When the movement slowed, Nell picked up a glass of water, took a long drink, and looked around the island. "I guess it's time to talk about the day," she said.

She began with the police calling Beverly Walden in, moved to her confrontation with Cass, and ended with Cass and Ben's absence.

"They're at the police station. They called Cass in for questioning. Purely routine, Ben said, but he thought it'd be easier if he went down, too," she said, trying to lighten the situation.

"What?" Danny was off his stool in an instant.

Sam put a hand on his arm. "Hey, it's okay, Danny. It's routine."

Sam didn't think it was okay. None of them did. But it was what it was and they needed to make the best of it. "They had to talk to her, Danny," Nell said.

The others took in the regrettable news, knowing it was, indeed, a logical thing for them to do—an utterly awful thing.

Danny refused to buy it.

"Think about it, Danny. Pretend you don't know her," Izzy said.

Or love her, Nell thought, but kept it to herself. The usually unflappable, laid-back Danny had genuine fear in his eyes.

Izzy went on. "She inherited everything that Finnegan owned."

Nell nodded. "And Ben is finding out that it's more than we thought. In addition to the land and that little house that Beverly is staying in, there's a large amount in a savings account and some bonds that have grown considerably. Finnegan didn't spend much money."

"Certainly not on food," Izzy said. "If it weren't for Mary Halloran, he'd have starved to death."

"The point is, it all goes to Cass, according to the will Finnegan wrote shortly before he died."

Jane Brewster settled on another stool, her skirt flowing down around her ankles. "But, *Cass,* Nell? We're talking about our Cass . . ."

"Of course. And it's ridiculous to think she'd have done anything like this. But as Izzy said, if this was a stranger we were talking about—and that's how the police will have to look at it—they're seeing a person who had been very nice to Finnegan. Taking him food, gaining access to his property and his emotions."

"Gaining his trust," Izzy added. She was back in the courtroom, pleading cases. Convincing jurors. Playing the system. Her hands moved with her words, her fingers miming quotation marks. "What if Finnegan had told this 'stranger' that he was going to leave her everything he owned? But there was a daughter in the picture, one who, let's just say, was trying to win back her father's favor? And our 'stranger' needed money badly, and if the daughter had enough time to ease back into favor, the stranger might not get anything. What if . . . ?"

"It's foolishness. Cass is no stranger. Cass is . . . Cass is one of the most amazing women I know." Danny's voice was hoarse.

The room was silent. Of course she was. Amazing, honest, funny, and all sorts of other things. They loved Cass.

But the people trying to track down Finnegan's killer could not be so moved. It was the facts they were looking at, not the character of a passionate, lovely lobsterwoman.

Danny's forehead wrinkled into a frown so deep it looked painful. "Saturday night? Is that when the old man was killed?" He spoke to himself, mumbling aloud as he thought back over a week that was now a lifetime long.

Izzy nodded and spoke his thoughts for him. "Sam and I took Cass home that night, Danny. You two had argued at the Scaglia party. You went to your place. Cass went home alone to hers."

So Cass' likely alibi had spent the night in a lonely apartment above his parents' garage. Clear across town from the woman he'd give his life to protect.

Danny's shoulders slumped.

The sound of Ben's car in the driveway turned all heads toward the front of the house. Cass walked in first, then stopped at the silent faces looking at her from across the family room.

"What?" She held out her hands. "You've never seen a 'person of interest' before?"

Her greeting turned the sound back on, people moving, talking, and Izzy hugging her friend in a squeeze that took Cass' breath away.

"What crap," Izzy whispered.

"I double that." Cass pulled away slightly and forced a smile to her face. "Can you believe it? From poor and distressed to rich and . . . and . . . Jeez, I don't even know what it is I am."

"Innocent," everyone in the room shouted in unison.

Ben was already taking the ice out of the freezer and moving like a man on a mission. "Don't even honor it with thought, Cass. It's nothing to worry about. It's what the police have to do. It's their job. They'll find the guy who did this soon and then this damned awful mess will be behind us. They're still looking for the man who robbed Finn's house that night."

Nell watched Ben as he talked, his hands moving automatically. Rote movements—pouring, lifting, shaking. But his thoughts were on Cass. And Nick Marietti. And how many other innocent people who might be pulled into this net of suspicion. She looked over at Nick. He had been quiet since he arrived, listening to the conversation, a thoughtful look on his face. This might ease things up for him, one more person for the police to look at. Spread the suspicion around. Is that what he was thinking?

As the group scattered about the kitchen, he walked over to Cass. He smiled in that confident way that he had, but this time it was colored with understanding, the kind that comes from walking in another's shoes. He placed one hand on the small of her back and said something, something that brought a smile to her face. And then, in an uncharacteristic move, Cass gave him a quick hug. In the next minute she disappeared out on the deck, following Danny and Ben and a tray of martinis.

Nell moved to his side and spoke quietly. "I don't always understand you, Nick Marietti. But anyone who can ease Cass' worry can't be all bad."

"Not all bad, Nell. That's probably the truth." He smiled again, then followed the others out to the deck.

Willow and Pete showed up with dinner—a cooler filled with crab, squid, and some small lobsters Pete knew they'd have trouble selling. If Nell would heat up plenty of lemon butter and slice a bunch of lemons, they'd throw everything on the grill and be in business, he said.

Nell had thanked them profusely when they'd called earlier with the offer. She'd had little time to go to the market or cook. A bag of baby potatoes was about all she could offer, along with cheese and fruit. And lemon butter, of course. A potful.

But nothing stopped Friday-night dinners at the Endicotts'. Rain or shine, snow or sleet . . . deaths or births. *Murders*.

Willow brought coleslaw; Jane a half dozen baguettes. And

Birdie managed to pick up an apricot crisp that would send every-one home happy.

By the time Izzy had turned on some upbeat music—a little Dave Matthews Band and some old Aerosmith—and Ben had re-freshed martini glasses, the mood had almost returned to a normal Friday night on the deck.

But not quite. Hanging heavy over them all was the sadness of the murder of an old man who didn't deserve such a violent death, and the knowledge that their lives were now intricately entangled in figuring out who would have—could have—done such a thing.

When the last of the apricot crisp—topped with a spoonful of Scoopers cinnamon ice cream—had disappeared, Birdie began col-lecting dishes and glasses, her way of suggesting everyone go home and get a good night's sleep.

Jane sidled up to Nell at the sink. She bumped her aside with her hip and dropped her hands in the soapy water, lifting a martini glass from the suds. "My job."

Nell picked up a towel and waited for the glass. Outside, the music still played and voices drifted through the open window.

"Beverly Walden isn't a bad person," Jane said. "This whole thing about Finnegan's will mystifies me."

"I suppose she thinks it's rightfully hers."

"She's been happier lately. She doesn't socialize much with any of the artists, but she seems to be trying to participate. I'm gathering art for an auction benefiting the community center, and I noticed Beverly's name on a canvas today that she'd donated to the cause."

"If she doesn't socialize, what does she do for enjoyment?"

"A mystery. Merry swears she has a boyfriend, as you've heard. It's hard to hide a romance in Canary Cove, though."

"Could she be worried that without Finnegan's money, she can't afford to stay here?"

"Ham mentioned that. So we checked into it, thinking we'd help her out—the Arts Association has some money for that kind of thing. But we found out that her paintings are selling fine, at least enough to support her. Which is great for a new artist in a new place."

Behind them, Sam and Izzy were wrapping up leftovers and piling them into the refrigerator, listening to the conversation at the sink.

"Something that seems to be forgotten in everything else going on is the body they found on Finn's property. What's up with that?" Sam asked.

Ben walked in, his arms full of napkins and silverware. "Jerry says they hope to know something soon. But it's old enough that it's difficult to know where to start. Dental records, but which dentist? Lots of folks around here go over to Gloucester, Danvers, even Boston. So it may take a while."

"Do they think . . ." Jane stopped and reshuffled her words. "Surely they don't think Finnegan killed anyone," she said. She dried her hands and looked around for her sweater and purse.

"I think they're more interested in who killed Finnegan right now."

The thought of Finnegan as a murderer was as difficult to fathom as Nick or Cass—or even the Delaneys—committing such a horrible crime.

A round of good-byes followed Birdie and Nick, Sam and Willow, and the Brewsters as they headed through the family room and out into the night.

As the dishwasher began to hum and lights dimmed, Nell looked around for Cass, hoping she hadn't snuck out without a good-bye. She looked through the family room doors to the deck, lit now by a hazy half-moon. At first she thought the deck was empty, but a movement at the far edge, beneath the hanging branches of the maple tree, caught her eye. Two silhouettes, slightly apart, moved into the moonlight.

Cass' voice rose out of the silence. It was an unusual sound, with none of the bravado, the humor, or irreverence that usually resided there. Instead a husky, pleading voice was carried on the breeze through the open door.

"How'd I get into this mess?" she asked, moving into Danny's arms.

He smoothed back her hair, her head tilted up toward his. "It's that damn Irish soda bread," he whispered.

"I didn't think I needed you, Brandley," Cass said. "I thought I could do it all alone, just like my pa did. I can't. I don't want to. Will you . . . will you help me out of this?"

Danny lowered his head until his lips touched hers, the shadow merging into one, his intentions clear.

Chapter 23

True to her word, the headline of Mary Pisano's Saturday column spoke her mind:

PROTECT THE INNOCENT IN OUR MIDST

It was a call to action, told with a flourish.

Our fine police force is doing an excellent job, she wrote, *just as we've come to expect from our men in blue. And now it's time for the rest of us to step up to the plate. We who feel the hum of our town as we walk through Canary Cove, who feel its heartbeat as we wander in and out of the Harbor Road shops, need to add our senses and our minds and our intuition to bringing the perpetrator of this crime to justice and to not cast suspicions at our innocent neighbors and friends and visiting relatives. Good deeds are not the sign of thieves and murderers. Good deeds, good neighbors are the fabric of which this town is made, and we can't ever forget that.*

And in the final sentence, after expressing deep sadness for Finnegan's demise, Mary managed to tell the whole town, in case they didn't already know it, about Cass Halloran's inheritance, along with her own bit of advice on what Cass might do with it. Nell read it aloud as Ben drained his coffee mug.

Even in death, our dear Finnegan has come to the rescue of Sea Harbor. In bequeathing his land and his worldly goods to Catherine Halloran, he has made certain Sea Harbor will benefit from his largesse. Be it a park with a carousel, a sweet little dance studio, or perhaps a small children's museum, the land will serve our city well once again."

Ben sighed. "At least it won't leak out in small pieces. This is probably easier on Cass. It's all out there now and by tomorrow it will be old news."

The ringing of the phone saved Nell from answering. *He's being generous,* she thought. It might not be old news quite so quickly, especially if Beverly Walden contested it.

It was the landline, which meant it was probably for Ben. He took it in the den while Nell emptied out their coffee mugs, then headed for her calendar.

"Well, that was news," Ben said, coming back into the kitchen.

Nell turned around. "Good news, I hope."

"Looks like they've caught the guy. The drifter that Finn fought with. Broken nose and all. And the boot found near Finn's house is a perfect fit."

By Monday everyone in Sea Harbor, even those who didn't live there year-round, felt the sense of relief that poured like a soothing rain over the houses and streets of the town. "A Cinderella ending," Mary Pisano called it in her "About Town" column the next day.

An attorney was appointed and Ned Smith—that's what the man said his name was—was forced to shower and then dress in gray cotton pants and a T-shirt and tell Jerry Thompson and his crew exactly what happened.

He was innocent, he swore—though a record of thefts and fights a mile long were baggage he couldn't deny. Ned Smith admitted to being on the property that night. All he'd meant to do was steal some cash and mess up the old man a bit. "He broke my nose, for chrissake," the man said. "But kill him? No way."

His story was recorded dutifully, and took over the front page of the *Sea Harbor Gazette* for two days.

He'd snuck onto the property by going down the dirt road and around the fence. He knew his way around and made his way into the unlocked building easily. Knew exactly what part of the rambling shack Finn lived in—upstairs above the two empty offices. But he couldn't find the old man anywhere. So he decided to mess things up a little, break a few things. He found Finn's wallet on a table and took it. A watch. Some other stuff that proved useless. Cheap.

It started to rain then, and the wind picked up. He heard noises. Voices, maybe. He could handle the old man easily, punch out his lights, but not two people, so he grabbed what he could and took off, back around the fence. And hightailed it out of town in the middle of a wicked storm.

Noises? The police asked. *Coming from the road?*

No, Ned Smith said. *Closer. Near the house.*

Then they'd returned him to his cell.

A fine story, for sure. But his fingerprints were all over Finnegan's place. He had motive. And he wasn't a very nice guy, to boot.

It created an uneasy truce. A lull before the storm is how Nell looked at it.

And the town knew it, she suspected, but was unable to let go of it. Though Ned Smith's ties to the murder might be weak, having a stranger to heap on the horror of Finnegan's death was a relief.

Nell sat in the back of the knitting shop, thinking of the twists and turns Finnegan's murder had taken. It felt like a sweater poorly knit and unraveling before their eyes. Suspicions were thick, answers were few, and now a derelict was being held with frayed strands of yarn connecting him to the murder.

She looked down at the comfort of the cotton yarn in her lap, a welcome diversion from the messiness of the week.

Gabby's purple sweater—a dahlia, that's what it reminded Nell of, one of the gorgeous purple dahlias they'd grown for Izzy's wedding last year. The scoop neck and soft drape would flow over her slender frame like a royal princess cape, not that Gabby would ever aspire to such a role.

Izzy sat right beside her on the window seat, Purl happily settled between them. The breeze off the water was cool on their necks. She reached over and fingered the deep sleeve rib. "Gabby'll love this," Izzy said. "No question."

Laura Danvers and her cousin came down the steps, waving hello and settling at the table, a pile of yarn in front of them. The Tuesday knitting group was a small one and didn't require much from Izzy—mostly her presence and a question here and there as a group of moms gathered to knit toddler sweaters and hats and warm hoodies for themselves. The Anderson twins provided child care in Izzy's magic room, filled with toys from her own childhood as well as donations grateful moms brought in—Cabbage Patch dolls, My Little Ponies, Legos, and *Star Wars* spaceships.

It was usually a quiet morning, and Nell came down solely to keep Izzy company. And to talk. To see how she was. To check on Cass, on Birdie.

In minutes the table across the room was full, and several others sat in the cozy sitting area around the fireplace. The room buzzed with chatter and laughter as an Adele CD played softly in the background. Nell was surprised to see Beatrice Scaglia join the group. She held her smile back when Beatrice produced two knitting needles and a ball of yarn. It was the same ball and the same empty knitting needles she had brought to the last knitting group she'd attended.

Izzy got up and moved to her side, patiently helping her cast on a row for the beginnings of a scarf and encouraging her to actually knit. Izzy suggested she might want to contribute it to the group making comfort scarves. "It's for women who've been abused. And this cashmere yarn you have would be perfect for it."

Nell listened with half an ear, watching the activity going on around her. They all knew why Beatrice was there and it wasn't to knit, though Nell thought her reason wasn't altogether foolish: she wanted to keep her finger on all segments of voters. The young-mom vote was important to her, and finding out what they cared about was crucial. Izzy nudged to make her visits altruistic, as well, with a worthwhile knitting project only added to it.

"I was at a tea yesterday with some of my constituents," Beatrice said to Izzy, then turned to include Nell. "There's concern the police aren't paying enough attention to the body they found on Finnegan's land. Was it murdered? Was the body diseased? Pollution is an issue. Are there more bodies back there? As I told the mayor, we need more information."

"I don't think they know yet," Nell said. "It happened years ago."

Beatrice's head was nodding, and by then several other knitters had leaned into the conversation, listening quietly, their needles clicking.

Esther Gibson's daughter-in-law said, "My mother thinks it's her old dentist. He used to have an office on that property—and he simply stopped practicing one day, she said."

A neighbor of Birdie's nodded. "My aunt went to him. Pulaski was his name. She thinks . . . she thinks Finnegan killed him."

"For heaven's sake, why?" Nell asked.

"Oh, there's always talk," Beatrice said.

"I heard that Finnegan's wife and the dentist may have been friendly . . ." one of Laura's friends said.

Nell watched the councilwoman sit back in her chair, letting the rumors swirl around her. She knew Beatrice was taking the conversation in, word for word, filing it away. Perhaps she thought she'd discover something in the discussion about Finn's death or the unidentified body that would make transitioning that land over to the city easier. She'd made promises to neighbors in the area, and pulling it off would make her queen for a day, or, at the least, a councilwoman who earned her keep, and one they'd certainly vote for again.

Laura Danvers walked over to the group, picking up on the topic. Her face registered displeasure. "That's all gossip, and all of you know it. I think we should let Finnegan rest in peace."

That broke up the talk, and soon a crying baby who wanted her mother was brought in, and talk went back to more neutral things—breast-feeding, going back to work, toilet training, and running the next marathon.

Nell got up to leave, with promises to call Izzy. She passed Laura Danvers on the way out and paused for a moment. Leaning down, she told her how proud her mother would be of her, the way she stood up to the group and shushed the gossip.

Laura fanned away the praise. "Finn was a decent man. And it's serious business, this murder."

"Which is why I wanted to ask you about something they said. I don't want to put you on the spot, but what is this crazy talk about Finnegan and the dentist? Is this something the police need to know about?"

Laura shook her head. "It's absolutely crazy talk. Almost as crazy as questioning Cass, in my opinion. My mother went to that dentist. And so did I when I was little. He was a lonely man, kind of depressed, my mom always thought. I think that's why she took us there—she felt sorry for him. He didn't have any family. My mother said Finnegan's wife, Moira, was nice to him. She gave him soup now and then—that kind of nice. And when he quit his practice suddenly, people talked. No one knew where he went. He just disappeared."

Nell was quiet, thinking about the innuendos in what Laura had said.

Laura nodded. "Yes, isn't that crazy? But back then, people didn't think much of his disappearance. He had told my mom he hated the winters up here and might move to Florida, so she assumed that's what he did."

"But now that there's a body . . ."

"Right. Now that there's a body, some who remember back to Moira's kindness to the man are saying, 'Aha!'" Laura's body language showed her lack of patience for the rumors. "A *body*. A missing dentist. Finnegan must have been jealous and killed the guy, then buried him in the yard." She looked at Nell sadly. "It's a crazy world."

"With some damn crazy people in it." Ben's feeling about the rumors matched Laura's exactly. "Don't people have better things to do?"

It was a brief moment together before Ben was off to Boston for a couple of days.

Nell watched him pack his suitcase, checking for reading glasses, his phone, something to read that night when the Endicott company board members finally called it a day. Ben didn't like hotels, and the long, into-the-night meetings were not his favorites. For a short time after they moved to Sea Harbor, he and Nell kept their Beacon Hill townhouse in Boston. Once they moved permanently to Cape Ann, it became a place to stay when they went into the city for musical performances, dinners, or board meetings for the Endicott family business.

But the upkeep and sporadic use finally convinced them to sell it, and now when family business called him into the city, Ben spent nights in a hotel. But he didn't like it, nor did Nell. The bed in the home on Sandswept Lane seemed to triple in size and was always cold without Ben's long body warming her own.

"Don't forget your phone charger," she said, picking it up and dropping it in the bag.

Ben leaned across the bed and kissed her. "I'll be back late tomorrow," he said. "Before you've even had a chance to miss me."

"We'll see about that." She folded a knit shirt and handed it to him. "By the way, did Father Northcutt ever get those remaining papers of Finnegan's?"

Ben tossed a paperback in his case. "I don't think so. I'd almost forgotten about it with everything else going on. Maybe I'll pick them up while I'm in the city. I don't suppose they say much, though there was supposed to be a note in there for Beverly. Maybe Finn explained why he'd cut her out of his will."

"Don't you suppose she knows?"

"Apparently not. She's quite serious about wrestling the inheritance away from Cass."

"More of a mess for Cass."

"That's right. She's got enough on her mind without having to go to court for a will." Ben lifted his bag onto the floor. "Speaking of that, what did the yarn-shop gossipers say about the guy being held?"

"Not much. People want him to be the murderer. What do the police think?"

"They want the same thing as everyone else: for him to be the guy. But right now there's not enough to pin it on him. There weren't any fingerprints on Finn, for starters, yet there were plenty in the house. So why would he protect himself performing one crime and then rummage through the house as if he were a guest?"

Nell thought about that. It didn't make sense. "But that doesn't really prove anything. He could have done it, even though it doesn't make sense."

"The guy also said he hitchhiked out of town that night. A local guy was headed to the airport in Boston. He saw the fellow's picture in the paper later and came into the station, verifying he'd picked the guy up, so that part of the story is true. He remembered him because the guy insisted on giving him a tip, not a common thing. It probably came from Finnegan's wallet. But the most important thing might be that the hitchhiker was muddy and wet and had lost a boot—climbing over a fence, he told the driver. But there wasn't a sign of blood on him anywhere, and the condition Finnegan was left in wouldn't have allowed anyone to get away clean."

"How can they hold him, then?" Izzy asked.

"They're holding him on another charge. He stole from Finnegan. And from some of the shopkeepers, too. Gus McClucken says he's the same guy who took off with a case of camcorders being delivered to the back of his store a couple weeks ago."

"So they're holding him because he's a thief. But they don't think he murdered Finnegan?" Izzy said.

"The chief won't say that. They're examining the guy with a fine-tooth comb—and in the meantime, his arrest has calmed down the town."

"But . . ." Nell said.

Ben checked his watch, then snapped the case closed. He looked at Nell, a sudden seriousness shadowing his face, as if leaving her was a dangerous thing. "Lots of *but*s—I know. Jerry's men will figure it all out, Nell. They're doing a good job."

But it was his eyes that spoke the loudest.

Don't get involved, they said.

Be safe.

I love you.

Chapter 24

A luncheon talk at the arts association kept Nell's musings in check, but a quick drive to the post office brought her thoughts back to Cass. She looked thinner. Losing a friend and then shouldering the awful suspicion of his death would make anyone shrink. Cass was healthier, just as they all were, when she could do something about the unwanted things that messed with her life.

They needed to put some order to things, to think logically about Finn's murder. Perhaps together they'd catch something seemingly insignificant. Little details, conversations overheard. What was it Angus had said? *There're lots of clues. They're right there staring us in the face."*

But by the time she reached the post office and parked the car, no answers stared her in the face, only a list of questions as long as Harbor Road.

Nell gathered the packages she was sending off to her sister and climbed the wide stone steps, her mind still cluttered but a new determination adding direction to her questions.

The serpentine line inside the post office was long but moving quickly. Nell spotted Mary Halloran at the front. Her silvery head of hair, pulled back in a neat bun, bobbed as she spoke with the postal worker and emptied a cloth bag filled with mail. Church business, Nell surmised. Bills, thank-yous, and notes to the sick. She was Father Northcutt's right-hand woman and, most parishioners thought, was the one who really ran things at Our Lady of Safe Seas. Father Northcutt agreed.

Mary turned, nodded to people in line as she headed toward the door, then spotted Nell.

"Nell, darlin'," she said, a look of relief flushing her round, pale face. She gave Nell a quick hug.

"Come, dear," she said, tugging Nell free of her coveted spot in line. "We need to talk." A small, kindhearted woman, Mary Halloran's size belied her determination and strength; requests were rarely protested.

Nell followed her into the post office foyer.

Her usual smiling eyes were clouded with worry. "It's Catherine. We need to help her," Mary said.

"She's strong, Mary. Just like her mother."

Mary brushed away the words with her hand. "There're the business worries—she takes those all on herself, just like Patrick did. But now Finnegan's murder on top of it. The suspicions, the police? Good lord."

"It's routine business with the police. No one thinks Cass could possibly have had anything to do with his death."

"Of course she didn't. She loved Finn. But it will never be better until we find the man who killed him. And if anything could make it worse, it has. Now they're saying our Finn killed someone and buried him back there in that mess of a yard. It's a double nightmare, Nell."

Nell's concern over Cass had blurred the added burden the rumors about Finn brought to those who loved him. Mary would be devastated by her friend's memory being sullied in so scurrilous a way.

"It's an awful sin to say those things about Finn," Mary said, her head nodding and her eyes demanding help. "He won't rest in peace until we stop the terrible talk."

Nell nodded, feeling suddenly helpless. Mary was right, at least about the stigma on Finn's memory. "Hopefully we'll find out who was buried back there soon—and that there's a logical reason for it—and the rumors will disappear in a flash."

Mary's attention seemed to flag, her eyes filling again with concern. She looked out the post office window at the cars going by, people walking by.

"Finnegan must have loved the Hallorans dearly to hand everything he owned over to Cass," Nell said softly. "He was giving it to all of you."

Mary's eyes filled. "Now, isn't that just like our dear Finn? That crazy man. He knew the troubles we had, that one. Always trying to help. Always, always, always."

"Some think it was your Irish stew," Nell said, trying to coax a smile from her friend's face.

Mary chuckled at that. "I don't understand him leaving that daughter of his out in the cold the way he did, but he must have had a reason. Finn didn't have a mean bone in his body. She did something that disturbed him greatly."

"Did he talk to you about Beverly?"

"Never. Nor did Moira. Not since the day Beverly ran away with a fistful of their money and broke her mother's heart right in half. Father Larry tells me she's contesting the will, wanting her fair share. Well, whatever the good lord wants."

She paused, then with the old sparkle returning to her eyes, added, "And I am fairly sure he wants the Halloran company to be healthy and strong again."

Mary reached into her purse and rummaged through it until she found what she was looking for: a folded roll of bills, secured with a rubber band. She pressed it into Nell's hand.

"What's this?" Nell stared at the money.

"It's to take Catherine out for an evening and make her forget about her worries, about Finn's death, the police questioning her, the inheritance, Beverly Walden—every single bit of it. She won't let me help, stubborn girl. She doesn't want anyone's help. Even pushes that sweet Danny boy away."

"Cass has an awful time accepting help. It seems to frighten her, as if it will make her weak or dependent, especially with Danny. But if there's anything good coming out of this mess, it might be with the two of them. I think she's letting Danny back in, at least a crack. Cass might be admitting she needs him."

Mary brightened. "He's a good boy and wants what's best for Cass. What's best is *him*, I told him."

Nell held the money up in the air. "Now, about this . . ."

Mary put one hand on Nell's arm and looked directly into her eyes, insisting Nell listen. "I know for a fact that Cass listens to you—and to the girls. She tells you things she thinks will worry her mother. She's not eating. A good meal, a glass of wine. Please . . . take care of my girl, Nell." She dropped her gaze and sighed. "They say that they cut the umbilical cord at birth, but they don't. Not really."

"You're absolutely right, Mary. Cass needs an evening out, away from lobsters, boats, and the rest of this mess." She hugged her tightly. "It will happen."

As Mary turned away, Nell slipped the money back into her friend's purse.

Chapter 25

It took Nell little time to make it happen—a few text messages, a call to Birdie. And calendars were immediately cleared for the next night.

"Ladies' night out—yes!" was Izzy's immediate response. They all needed it, not just Cass, and not just to relax. They needed to be together to put order into the chaos that was becoming their summer, and time to figure out what to do about it. So far, their efforts had yielded few results and way too many questions.

It was Birdie's idea to leave Sea Harbor, so they did, heading out in Nell's CRV, leaving drifters, gossip, and ominous graves behind them. Exploring them from a distance might help them think outside the box, they all agreed.

"It's getting more difficult to simply up and leave," Birdie remarked from the passenger's seat.

"Grandchildren will do that to you," Cass said.

"And husbands. I practically had to turn my passport over to Sam," Izzy said. "You'd think we were going to Sin City instead of Rockport."

They laughed. The sleepy town on the farthest tip of Cape Ann was not known for its wild night life. But it was not Sea Harbor, and that's what they needed. A big, wide deck where they could pull out their knitting, order dinner, and not run into their next-door neighbors. On a quiet weeknight, their chances were good of finding such a place.

And they did, at the end of Bearskin Neck, the rocky piece of land filled with tiny shops that jutted out into the water. White market umbrellas, roomy tables, and the feeling that they were floating out to sea suited their mood, and in minutes they were settled in with a plate of tiny lobster tacos in front of them, a pitcher of margaritas and iced tea nearby.

Nell filled them in quickly on Ned Smith—and Ben's opinion of his guilt.

"So he probably didn't do it," Birdie said. "But someone did."

"It's someone with a face. And, mostly likely, a face we know," Nell said.

Izzy pulled the soft pastel yarn out of her purse and, without looking, began knitting the ankle of her sock, the lacy ribbon pattern taking shape beneath her quick-moving fingers. Her thoughts seemed to parallel the rhythm of her needles. "So we think about faces, about people. Anyone who might have had suspicious connections to Finn." She looked over at Birdie. "This is hard, because I know you like Nick a lot. I do, too. But . . ."

Birdie nodded. "I like him very much. But he's not been honest; that much I know. I talked to him about it again today. He'd had another 'meeting,' as he called it, with the police. *They don't call people in for their entertainment,* I said. *No, they don't,* he said. And then there was that look, the one that told me not to worry." She sighed. "I hate the lie, but I trust the man. *Don't worry,* he said. *It's fine.*"

"Yet it isn't fine, not until he can explain it. He argued with Finn. He was on his property. And he refuses to tell you why," Nell said.

"Or the police. He's sticking to his story, saying his concern was for Gabby."

"Do you believe him?" Cass asked.

"No," Birdie said simply, but with a force that brought welcome laughter to the table. "He's lying, and I told him so. But it got me nowhere—except maybe the bouquet of flowers he had delivered later."

The laughter grew.

"When he came back here after being in Italy, something was

different with him. A worried look, and the secrets. There was something going on besides being here for Gabby."

And the reason had something to do with Finnegan, they felt sure. And Finnegan had been murdered.

"And then there's Beverly Walden," Izzy said. "Why did she really come back to Sea Harbor? Did it have anything to do with making sure she was first in line in Finn's will?"

"I don't trust her," Cass said. "I don't like her much, either."

"That's understandable. She's trying to rip your inheritance away from you."

"It's not even that, though that seems to be driving her kind of crazy. But there's something else, something sneaky going on there."

All of them knew Cass' feelings were colored by the circumstances. She was Finnegan's protector. And looked on Beverly as the enemy, even when Finn was alive.

"I ran into her in the cheese store shortly before Finn died. She seemed happy with life that day."

"Maybe that's it," Cass said. "One minute she's happy; the next, devious and angry. Dr. Jekyll and Mr. Hyde."

"She wanted Finnegan's money," Izzy said. "She's made that obvious. Not very smart if she doesn't want to appear as a suspect."

"That's the other thing about her. She doesn't seem to grasp the situation. Izzy's right—she's calling attention to herself, trying to get Finn's money. Could she be one of those amoral people who doesn't have a conscience? All that stealing when she was a kid; not coming back when her own mother was dying?" Cass asked.

"But money didn't seem to be such an issue when she first arrived," Birdie said. "Finnegan told me that originally she turned down his offer to stay in that house he owns. It was like she didn't want anything from him. And then she suddenly *did*."

"What changed for her?"

They all thought about that. The rumors were that she had a man in her life. But, as Nell wisely said, how would that have stirred up this sudden desperate need for money?

"Does she owe someone money?" Izzy wondered.

"A very curious part of this is that Finnegan originally had her in his will. Maybe it was in a small way, not what she expected. But it was something," Birdie said.

"Yes!" Izzy leaned forward. "And then he took her out of it. And Ben said it seemed Finn was angry when he did it."

Nell thought back to the incident on the Palate's deck. "Merry said Finn shouted at Beverly, accused her of hurting people."

"What Finn said to her was awful. Not like him at all. He said something about her killing her own mother," Cass said. "I don't like her much, but that seemed harsh."

"But he did mean that figuratively, of course," Birdie said. "She broke her mother's heart. But didn't Finn say she was ruining another person's life? Whose?"

"And is that why Finnegan took her out of his will?" Izzy asked. Her cheeks were flushed as if something finally made sense. Not completely, maybe, not in a way that explained murder, but it seemed to be a step in the right direction.

Cass spread honey butter on a freshly baked slice of herb bread. "All right, who could Beverly be hurting? Besides me, that is."

"She won't win that dispute, Cass." Nell said. But they all knew her assurance wasn't grounded in fact. Beverly very well might win. And the Halloran Lobster Company's troubles would once again be pressing painfully for resolution.

A sudden gust of wind whipped Cass' hair against her cheeks. She looked around the table. "You know what I hate most of all? I hate that you've all been pulled into this. I want to go back one short month. I want Finnegan to be hollering at me for forgetting to bring his soda bread and me hollering at him for spilling the buoy paint. I want to be happy for Danny that he's having a great book tour. I want to finish knitting that damn hat that's been sitting in my bag forever, and I want you three to be . . . to not be worried about me, to just be happy with me . . . to be . . ." Her voice broke off as Birdie silenced her with a gentle hug.

"We're happy with you, sad with you, whatever the moment calls for."

"We're thick-and-thin friends—no worry on that score," Izzy agreed. She took a drink of her margarita. "But as for that hat you were knitting? It's a mess, anyway. So don't bother finishing it."

Cass swatted at Izzy and then they clinked their glasses, knowing deep down what it was Cass wanted, what they all wanted, and what they'd get, by hook or by crook.

Their summer back. Peace. And friendships not burdened with the awfulness of murder.

The waitress removed the empty plates and returned in minutes with what they'd all agreed would suit them perfectly: a thin-crust pizza nearly as big as the table and piled high with sweetly marinated and grilled shrimp, scallops, and vegetables—red peppers, zucchini, strips of eggplant and asparagus, wild mushrooms—and topped with chopped tomatoes and creamy goat cheese.

"Things are looking better already," Cass said, sliding a huge slice onto her plate.

For a few minutes, the only sounds were sighs of pleasure, the soft crunch of pizza dough, and the lap of the waves against the rocks below.

Nell was the first to break the spell that the tangy, sweet shrimp had wrapped them in. "All right, so how far are we in sorting out this mess? Our thoughts are all over the place. We need focus."

"Maybe. Maybe Mary Pisano has the right idea and we should pay more attention to what we see and hear and feel. Cass, you asked why Finn was so upset with Beverly. Who could she have been hurting? That's question one. And then there's the flip side—who could possibly hate Finnegan enough to kill him?"

Cass shook her head. "You know, that's the hitch. Everyone complained about Finn, but I don't know anyone who hated him. What was there to hate? Grumpiness?"

"What about some of the fishermen? Could there have been some kind of feud?"

"The weapon was a knife they all own," Izzy added.

"We can rule the fishermen out. Those guys liked Finn and he liked them."

"Beverly may fall in the feud category," Birdie said quietly. A daughter hating a father was distasteful, difficult to talk about.

"So Beverly hated him, and she wanted his money," Izzy said.

"And she could have gotten on his land easily that night. She lived a short walk away; no one would have seen her walking along the shore side," Cass said. "She wouldn't have a knife, maybe, but . . ."

"Gus carries those in the hardware store. It'd be easy to get one from him."

"And as far as we know, she didn't know she had been taken out of his will."

"Okay, so Beverly is a likely suspect."

"Who else?"

"Nick, no matter how we feel about him."

Even Birdie agreed. Dishonesty wasn't the same as murder. But something about her brother-in-law was not quite right.

"And the police have me listed, so I should be on it," Cass said.

"No. Absolutely not," Izzy said sharply. "You are the reason we're doing this. So you can get on with your life."

"The Delaneys?" Birdie suggested.

"They were at the Scaglias' the night that Finn was killed," Nell said. "So we know they were in town. I talked to Maeve at the hair salon last week, and she told me that she came down with some awful bug that night. D.J. took her to the ER for fluids. So that rules him out."

"Davey?"

"He was at the party," Izzy said. "I think he single-handedly finished off the beer Beatrice served. He left about the same time we did. Sam asked him about that big boat they have docked at the club, and he made a big show about how powerful it was."

"Davey has tried to prove himself to his father his whole life. That's not a healthy way to live," Birdie said.

"Getting this land away from Finnegan would be a feather in his cap," Nell said.

"But how would killing Finnegan make sure he got the land?" Izzy said. "Unless . . ."

Nell nodded, thinking along with Izzy. "Unless he knew that Finn's daughter, once she got her inheritance, would sell it to him."

"Beverly and Davey knew each other—we know that."

"But how well, I wonder," Izzy said.

The uncomfortable thought hung in the air like a spiderweb.

Finally, Birdie said, "We can definitely eliminate D.J. and Maeve, not that Maeve could kill anything bigger than a bug. Davey . . . He needs to stay there, for now at least. "

"And there's the murky possibility that someone killed Finn out of revenge. Revenge for burying the unknown person in his back-yard."

"But that was so long ago that we have no idea who that person might be," Birdie said, clearly enjoying this piece of the puzzle. "If we can figure out the real reason that body's there—and I don't think it's because Finnegan killed anyone, for heaven's sake—we can squash that whole rumor. It will make this a bit cleaner. Elimi-nation is good." She sat back in her chair.

"But it's the squashing that might take some creativity," Nell said.

"And we have more than enough of that to go around," Birdie said happily.

Nell laughed. "All right, then. Is there anyone else we can think of whom Finn might have had problems with? You knew him bet-ter than anyone. What would he have done to make someone mad enough to kill him? Is there anyone else we haven't thought of who would have benefited from his death?"

Cass took a deep breath and let it out slowly. "Beatrice Scaglia was giving Finn fits about his land. She was somehow convinced if she could get the land away from him, turn it into a beautiful place, she'd be pleasing everyone—the mayor, the voters."

"It's hard to imagine anyone wanting political office that bad," Nell said.

"But, weirdly, she does," Cass said.

They agreed. They all knew Beatrice, knew her idiosyncrasies and her ambition. But like everyone else they knew, tagging those people as murderers was difficult.

Nell repeated the conversation from Izzy's earlier that day. "Beatrice wasn't contributing to the rumors, but she was enabling them. Letting people go on about the body they'd found in the grave and the possible connection to the dentist. Putting Finn in a terrible light."

"That's so silly," Birdie said. "I knew Dr. Pulaski, poor man. Not much personality, but he knew how to fill cavities adequately."

"I remember him vaguely," Cass said. "For a while he was the only dentist in Sea Harbor. Pete and I loved going to see him because he always gave us lollipops when we were through. Ma used to say it was to ensure repeat business."

"He was a character." Birdie chuckled. In the next breath, the smile faded and she straightened up in her chair. "The photos," she said. "Of course. I wonder if the police have thought of that."

"Photos?"

"The ones in the paper of Finn's poor house. There were a couple shots of the offices below—"

"The dental chair," Nell said, climbing into her thoughts. "Are you thinking that where there's a chair, there might be dental records?"

"And if the body they found is someone who lived around here, he might have gone to Dr. Pulaski."

But something else was nagging at Birdie; they could see it clearly on her face.

"Birdie?"

She shook her head. "There's something I'm forgetting about Dr. Pulaski. It's right here"—she pointed to the side of her head—"but I can't quite push it into focus."

"You don't think there was anything to the rumors about Moira and him?"

"No, no, no. Absolutely not. Moira and Finnegan were two of the most devoted people I've ever met. He adored his wife, and she him. And not to disparage the poor dentist, but he wasn't exactly a Casanova." Birdie wiped some sauce from her lips. "I remember Moira being nice to him, but Moira was sweet to everyone. No, this little itch up here in my head is something else. It will come to me. . . ."

Izzy cut the last giant piece of pizza into four parts and passed them around. She licked her fingers. "I think finding the body on Finn's land is important, but it's also a distraction."

"I agree," Cass said. "But we need to figure it out because I swear that man will come back and haunt me if people accuse him of something he didn't do. And rumors about Moira being unfaithful? That would absolutely kill Finn. In his mind, unfaithfulness was probably the absolute worst crime a person could commit. I don't know if it was something that happened in his early life or what, but he used to talk to me about it. Lecture me, I guess. He was so forceful about what he considered right and wrong. He won't ever find peace until we take care of this for him."

"So we will," Nell said. "But we'll also find out who ended his life so viciously. Between the four of us, we know nearly everyone in town—and Cass knows Finnegan better than anyone else. That's all we need to move ahead with this."

They paid their bill and walked into the evening air, the breeze ruffling hair and the waves sending salty spray up over the rocks.

"Invigorating," Birdie said. And they all agreed. *The breeze, the dinner, and the resolutions.*

They walked across the street toward the rocky bank and a view of the picture-perfect harbor. Dozens of sailboats rested like birds on the water, bobbing gently from side to side. The weather had brought out strollers and runners, families with children scampering up the rocks, young couples sitting at the very end of the road, bodies pressed together.

For a while they were quiet, the beauty of the scene sinking in around them while their private thoughts tugged at the images of Finnegan on the ground, a murderer fleeing. A stormy night. Picking it apart, pulling it into focus, each in her own way.

"The person who killed Finnegan had to have come in from the water side," Cass said. She climbed onto a rock, found a level plane, and sat back, hugging her knees to her chest.

Nell stood a couple of feet away, her eyes following several boats heading out beyond the breakwater for an evening sail. "So either he—"

"Or she," Izzy said.

Nell nodded. "Either he or she came down that side path and around the fence."

"A way familiar to Nick Marietti—" Cass said.

"Anyone who knows their way around Canary Cove would know that route," Nell said, feeling a sudden need to defend Gabby's uncle. And it was true. Anyone who took a boat along the shoreline knew which buildings were where—and the access path alongside Finnegan's property wasn't a secret to townsfolk.

"Who knows? They could have come in on water skis. But all we've proven is that it'd be easy to get onto the property without going through the gate," Izzy said. She leaned her elbows on a tall rock and waved at a seafaring couple coming in to moor their boat.

"Finnegan was so protective of his land," Cass said. "So private. Do you think he could have had something in there that someone wanted?"

It was a new thought and a worthwhile one. But pursuing it would lead easily to someone they were reluctant to point to: Nick Marietti. Nick wanted something from Finnegan; that was clear. And Finn didn't want him there.

"Merry said the newest restaurant rumor is that Finn was growing pot."

Cass laughed. "That's an old rumor. I asked Finn once if he had pot on his property. He said, *Sure,* and pointed to an old outhouse that sat down near the dock."

Maybe he wasn't growing anything illegal, but the idea of Finn hiding something made sense. Was it the grave that had been recently dug up, or something else?

Cass pulled herself up from the boulder and followed the others back down the narrow road toward their parking spot. They walked slowly, enjoying the sights and looking down the small alleys that led to the wharves and harbor, each filled with one or two more tiny shops. Everywhere colorful signs for ice cream and lobsters and T-shirts flapped in the breeze.

Suddenly Cass stopped. Next to her, Nell stopped, too. They

both stared down the street at a woman emerging from one of the shops. She wore a yellow sundress, her hair windblown around a face flushed from the sun, her smile bright. She looked lovely. And slightly tipsy.

"Beverly," Nell called out.

The woman stopped, turned toward them, her smile fading away. "Hi," she said, then turned away, walking toward the water.

"Are you enjoying the shops?" Nell asked, ignoring Beverly's attempt to flee.

Beverly turned back and managed to put a smile in place. "I was looking for . . . well, for a place to buy a bottle of champagne."

Birdie laughed lightly. "Rockport doesn't have liquor stores. But we just had a lovely margarita down the street in a restaurant—"

"Oh, no, no." Beverly said quickly. She looked nervously toward the harbor, then mumbled that she was in a little bit of a hurry. Would they please excuse her? And she rushed off in the direction of Tuna Wharf.

They watched her until she disappeared behind a building.

"What was that about?" Cass said.

Izzy shrugged. "We're here. I suppose Beverly can be, too. For dinner, maybe?"

"Maybe," Nell said, and they continued toward the parking lot, climbing back into the car.

Nell pulled out of the narrow spot and drove around the harbor bend and down Mt. Pleasant Street. At the entrance to the harbor, she paused at a stop sign and they all looked once more toward the water.

"There," Cass said. Heading out toward the breakwater was a familiar boat, the purple letters of Finnegan's wife's name catching the last rays of sunlight.

Beverly Walden was in a hurry.

And she wasn't alone.

Chapter 26

Ben had pulled into the drive just a short while before Nell got home. He met her at the door when her car pulled into the drive.

Suddenly Nell was inordinately happy to see him. She moved into his arms.

"I've missed you, Ben Endicott."

"Hmmm. I like this." He breathed in the salty scent of her hair. "I should go away more often."

Ben had already made a sandwich for himself, and the television evening news hummed in the background. A cold beer sat on the coffee table. He pointed to both. "M'lady?"

Nell shook her head. "Stuffed."

"Why do I think a lot has gone on while I was off in Boston, being bored?" He pulled her down beside him on the couch.

"Ladies' night out. Wild and raucous as always." She took a sip of his beer and launched into their trip to Rockport, complete with the Beverly Walden siting.

"Izzy and Cass said it was a man in the boat with her, though I don't know how they could tell. All I saw was a blur and the purple letters spelling out *Moira*." She slipped one leg up beneath her and leaned back against the couch. "But she was nervous when we ran into her. Definitely not happy to see us."

Ben finished up his sandwich and washed it down with beer.

"Well, if Merry's right, maybe that means nothing more than she wants to keep her friend a secret."

"Would being in a relationship affect her contesting this will in any way?"

"I don't think so. But that reminds me. I had a message from Father Northcutt. The papers to contest the will are being filed tomorrow."

"So Beverly wasn't issuing idle threats. How does Father Larry feel about it?"

"He thinks that as Finn's daughter, she probably has every right to do it. But he also knows that it's not what Finn wanted."

"Will that matter in court?"

"It depends on the judge. Beverly's best defense is to give some kind of proof that Finnegan's judgment was impaired when he made out the will. And there's that second will that clearly mentioned her—Beverly knew about that will. Finnegan could come off sounding fickle. And then there's the harsh way he crossed her name out of everything. Those of us who know him can easily imagine him doing it. But a lawyer could make it out to be erratic behavior. Being his daughter may influence the judge emotionally, since most people leave something to their children."

Nell remembered Beverly's shouts at Cass, asking if she'd put something in Finn's food. She thought Beverly was spouting nonsense because she was upset. Maybe she actually believed it, though Nell couldn't imagine anyone going along with it. Finnegan was as sane as she was. "I wonder if her recent romance has anything to do with her wanting so desperately to get her hands on Finnegan's property. People do desperate things for love."

Ben took a swig of his beer. "Could be. Maybe the guy is pushing her to do this. Maybe he wants the land for his own use." He rested one arm on the back of the couch.

"Will you be there tomorrow, representing the original will?"

"No. This is a simple filing. All Beverly has to do is sign a document identifying the case. She won't need a lawyer to do it, though Father Larry said she's contacted a guy in Boston who is very good at this sort of thing. And they're pushing the court to speed up the process."

Nell sighed. A murder to solve. A body to identify. And now a court case contesting a will.

"One thing I forgot to mention," Ben said, pulling his eyes away from the television. "I had a message from Jerry Thompson. Weirdest thing. First off, they didn't find any dental X-rays in Dr. Pulaski's office. Lots of unpaid bills and a few old patient files is all. But that's not the strangest thing." Ben took a drink of beer. "The really strange thing is that it wouldn't have mattered if they had found any records."

"Wrong dentist?"

"Nope. The corpse didn't have teeth."

Nell turned and stared at him. "No teeth?"

"That's right. None."

"How strange."

"Not unheard of, but strange. Sometimes people are buried with dentures if they had them, but it's completely up to the family."

Ben looked over at the television screen, where a weatherman was reporting sunny skies for the rest of the week. He looked back, his eyes sleepy.

"Nellie . . ." He began.

Nell's sigh turned into a smile, one that began with her lips but spread to her eyes. "I know that look," she said, shifting on the couch until they faced each other, her knees pressing against his thigh.

Ben tugged lightly on a strand of her hair. "Well, here's the thing. You had a ladies'-night-out night. I had a Ben-in-the car-alone night."

"So maybe we need another kind of night?" she asked. She brushed his cheek with the back of her fingers.

Ben picked up the remote and switched off the TV.

"Any ideas?" Nell's brows lifted.

"I have a few." He pulled her up from the couch and switched off the lights. With the moon guiding their way, they headed toward the back staircase and a promising Endicott night together, one that would prove to Ben exactly how much Nell missed him.

Just as the weatherman predicted, the day held abundant sunshine.

Ben was off for an early meeting at the bank. Then a call to Finn's

Boston firm to see where the rest of his files were. Father Northcutt was anxious to put it all to rest.

Nell watched him leave, his words lingering long after he'd pulled out of the drive and headed toward Harbor Road.

Put it all to rest. How nice that would be. It matched the day, certainly, with the waves rolling in, cleaning the beaches and rocky banks. The sun baking off grime and debris from piers and sidewalks. *If only weather could solve murders,* she thought as she slipped into a pair of capris and white T-shirt.

She checked the time, picked up her one garden glove without holes and her straw hat, and headed out to put time in at the community garden. A cup of coffee and a quick stop at McClucken's for new gloves and she'd be ready to weed.

Traffic was light as Nell drove through her neighborhood and toward the village shops, her mind flitting from wills to gardens, then back to a man murdered in his own backyard. She waved at a neighbor, then stopped to let a group of teenagers cross the street. Thick towels hung around their necks, and colorful bags swung from tan shoulders as they headed to the beach.

They didn't even notice I've stopped, Nell thought, watching the girls, arms swinging, heads held back to catch the sun's rays. The world was theirs to do their bidding. When did that confidence in the world's largesse disappear?

It disappeared when a friend was murdered. But it would be back. Soon.

When Nell walked into the hardware store, Gus was behind the counter, helping a customer. Nell waved to him and walked to the back corner of the store, where Gus kept his gardening supplies. A few aisles over, one could find televisions or watches or toys. And the whole north end of the store was devoted to small boat motors, sailing supplies, life vests, and other seagoing equipment. A full-service hardware store, Gus advertised. It was that and more.

Nell picked out several pairs of gloves, a couple of trowels, and a new spray head for the hose, then circled back around to the front desk. Next to the counter was a fancy display of new knives—

RIGGING KNIVES, the painted cardboard sign announced. They looked oddly elegant, packaged in bright orange-striped boxes.

A killing knife. Nell looked at the display model carefully, the curved back and microserrated blade, the wrapped handle grip. She shivered.

"In the market for a knife, Nell?" Gus asked, coming around the counter. He pointed to one of the knives. "These are the best—they'll cut through a synthetic rope in a flash. Skin a trout in a heartbeat. Got them in about a month ago and they're flying out of here like Annabelle's hotcakes."

He laughed, his belly shaking beneath a red knit shirt.

"These are good knives?"

"Best boating knife there is."

"You've sold a lot lately?"

"You betcha. Look at that display—not a whole lot left." He rubbed his chin. "My usual customers—the guys on fishing crews—they don't wait around so long. They get all their equipment and doodads in the spring before the amateurs—as Finn, rest his soul, used to call them—come and spend money on things they don't need."

Nell chuckled. She could hear Finn casting aspersions on the summer folk, as he called them. "So who's been depleting your supply? Vacationers going fishing for a day?"

He laughed as he walked back behind the counter and punched in the numbers for Nell's purchases. "Not so much. The tourist boats provide what they need. But Finn's daughter came in a few weeks back, bought one of these."

"Beverly?" *Beverly wouldn't have a rigging knife.* Cass' words echoed in Nell's head.

"Says she's learning about boats," Gus went on. "*More power to you,* I told her. *Your father was one of the best. You try throwing a line in, too. It'd make him wicked proud.*"

Clearly Gus avoided the gossip traveling around town. Good for him. And Beverly had a new boat in her possession, at least for the near future. It probably made sense that she was buying a boat knife.

"Anyone else?"

"Well, now that you ask, there was one customer that tickled the life out of me when she came in asking for one of these rigging knives. It was just as the weather was turning nice. She wanted the best, she insisted, and I teased her about it until she blushed, told her they could be dangerous.

"It doesn't quite fit your fine image, now, does it councilwoman? I said."

He handed Nell her credit card and bag.

A customer with a question about fishing lines came up, and Nell turned away, his words sinking in as she walked toward the door. Behind her, Gus' robust voice expounded on the unique qualities of superline, fluorocarbon, monofilament, and trawling lines. "All depending on what kind of fish you're after," he said.

Birdie was already at the garden, her floppy hat finished and shielding her face from the bright sunlight.

"Your hat looks great, Birdie."

"I look quite au courant. Don't you suppose?" She straightened up from the small kneeling pad and struck a pose.

Gabby ran over from parking her bike in the rack, her laughter preceding her. "You're très chic, Nonna."

"And you, sweet Gabby, have started a trend. I spotted a gal on the beach the other day with one of your beach beanies on. Soon they'll be everywhere," Nell said.

Gabby grinned. "Next step, NYC Fashion Week." Another laugh, bright and light. She plopped herself down between Birdie and Nell, her legs folding into a pretzel. "It's looking ugly," she said, pointing to a scattering of weeds peeping through the tomato plants and a row of arugula.

"Our work's cut out for us," Birdie agreed, tugging out a handful and piling them beside her.

"I miss Finnegan," Gabby said suddenly. She looked up at the two women. "It's like he's gone, but everyone goes on with their days, just like before."

"But it's not just like before. Is it?"

"Exactly. It's different." She looked over at the fence that held in the weeds and trash trees. "He's still there, but life is different."

"You should know something about Finnegan, Gabby. He didn't allow many people into his life in recent years. But he let you in. He liked you very much," Nell said.

Gabby forked her fingers through a tangle of hair, trying to force it into submission. "But he didn't hate anyone, no matter what people think. He just got crazy mad at things they did."

"Things like what?"

"Things like . . ." Gabby looked off in the direction of his land. She wrinkled her forehead. "You know. *Things*. He didn't like it when people lied or cheated or hurt other people. That's when he got goofy."

"Did you ever see him angry?" Nell asked. She pulled on her new gardening gloves and began pulling weeds from around a tomato plant. "Finn always seemed happy around you."

"I could see sometimes that he wanted to, but he'd hold back because I was there. Like once when we were eating ice cream, we saw a guy on a bike scratch the side of that councilwoman's fancy convertible. He looked around and then just took off. He didn't leave his number or anything, only a gash as long as a baseball bat. Finn got all red in the face and wanted to barrel down the street after him. But he didn't."

"Oh, and there was another time when he got mad right in front of me," Gabby said, picking up steam. "But I think he was sorry later. That time it was Beverly that set him off. I thought he was going to fling her right off into the water, clothes and all."

Nell looked at Birdie over the top of Gabby's beanie.

"But even her—he still liked her. But I think he hated that she wasn't like Moira, that she didn't act like her mother acted. Beverly's mother was quite a lady, Finn said. He talked about her a lot." Gabby stood up, a sudden springy movement that lifted her off the ground like a wind-tossed leaf.

Birdie watched her weightless rise and murmured, "You're going to have to teach me that move, dear."

Gabby giggled and stepped over Nell to grab a water bottle sitting on the ledge of the raised plot. She took a drink and looked back over the rows. "The Garden Celebration is just days away. Will we have anything by then?"

"For sure we'll have arugula and spinach and lots of herbs. The basil is up; the parsley and dill," Birdie said.

Nell could read the thought that coated Birdie's words. *We'll have herbs and vegetables, but will we still have you, sweet Gabrielle?* Would they be off in a heartbeat once Nick was given the word that he could leave the area?

"So we'll smell good, at least, right?" Gabby pulled off a long stem of rosemary, closed her eyes, and breathed in the smell. "Sophie says rosemary is for remembrance." She looked over at the rusty fence.

Nell cut off a sprig of lavender and handed it to Gabby for her growing herb bouquet. "When did Finnegan get angry with Beverly?"

"That day we were fishing, when I broke my skateboard and you came and found me. She came while I was there."

"To Finn's house?"

Gabby nodded. "She came in the back way—back there, behind the garden where that path goes along the shore. She came around the edge of the fence. She didn't see us sitting on the dock. Finn told me to shush up, so I did. Sat as still as I could, even though there was a fish tugging on my line."

"What did she want?"

"She started climbing up the steps as if she was going to sneak into his house, or maybe she was going to knock, but he yelled out her name and she stopped like she'd been struck dead. He scared her awful. Then he told her to come down where he was sitting on the dock.

"When she saw me, she looked at me funny, like, *What are you doing there?* But I didn't say anything."

"Did she talk to Finn?"

"She tried. She said she was thinking about her mother and just wanted to come over to see where she lived."

"She was sneaking into Finn's house. That doesn't sound wise, even if she was thinking about her mother."

Gabby nodded. "I know. *Dumb* was what I was thinking. And I'm not sure she was telling the truth, anyway."

"Why?"

Gabby shrugged. "I could just tell. Finn told her she was a little late to be thinking about her mother. And he looked really sad when he said it. He loved Moira sooo much."

"You're right about that, sweetie," Birdie said.

"He said that her mother would be ashamed of her. That if Moira hadn't already died, Beverly would be killing her right then. Then he got up and walked her over to the fence, the way she'd come in. He told me to stay on the dock or the fish would get away, but really he just didn't want me to hear. But I still could, a little, because Finn couldn't always hear so well—that sometimes happens when people get old—and he talked louder than he needed to. I know she said something about money, or about his land, because he said if she didn't act like a decent, honest person like her mother always did, he'd take her out of his will. And then where'd she be?"

Gabby took another drink of water and sighed. "He could get mad, that's for sure. He told me it was because he was Irish. I told him Italians didn't get so mad."

Birdie chuckled.

"So, I guess Beverly left then?"

"Almost. First she got mad right back at Finn. She must have forgotten I was there."

"Why?"

"Because she stood up on the path and glared at him like it was just the two of them alone in the whole world. And then she said that he should have died instead of Moira. She called her Moira, not Mom, and she didn't say the word very nicely. And then she started to leave. I was glad, but she turned around again, right on the edge of the path, and told Finn that she would get what was hers no matter what.

"And then she turned quickly to *really* leave, but she slipped on the rocky path and got her shoe all wet, which made her even madder still. But, finally, she was gone."

In the next moment, Gabby was off, an actress leaving a stage, her performance finished. She held a pair of clippers in one hand and headed for a bed of daylilies blooming along Finnegan's fence.

"I can't imagine how awful that must have been for Finn," Birdie said, watching her granddaughter bend over the flowers.

"For Beverly, too, I suppose," Nell said. But her words were hollow. It was Finnegan they cared about. And he was dead.

Nell stood up, brushed off her pants, and looked around at other gardeners a few rows down, doing the same thing. She'd been so engrossed in Gabby's story that she hadn't noticed they had company. The garden had come alive and active. Willow Adams, with her iPod, was working in the artists' garden along with Rebecca Early, and soon music filled the area as the soil was tended, more seeds planted, and weeds attacked to the singing of Katy Perry.

"It's a lively place—exactly what we'd hoped for." Nell turned on the hose and began spraying the tomato plants.

Birdie pulled herself up. "It's a community." She looked around, then frowned. "Where's Gabby?"

"She was over there a minute ago, cutting flowers."

"Her bike is still here; she can't be far," Birdie said. "I'm trying not to worry about her. Nick says she's street-smart. Living in Manhattan has made her savvy and wise beyond her years. I have orders not to hover."

Nell laughed. "For someone who didn't have nine months to prepare for being a grandmother, you're doing a great job. But I suspect Nick's right: Gabby doesn't need hovering. She'll be fine."

"But I won't be unless I have a cup of Polly's tea soon. I'm as dry as a cracker."

She brushed off her pants, picked up her bag, and in minutes she and Nell were headed down the road.

Polly Farrell's Tea Shoppe was on Canary Cove Road, two doors down from Rebecca Early's lampwork-bead gallery. And at this hour of the morning, they had a good chance of snagging a table.

A large stone teacup held the door open and allowed a light breeze to circulate air in the small space. Polly stood behind the counter, her smile as broad as her round face, waving them in. The tiny shop held but four tables, and today only one was taken.

Beverly Walden sat at the window table. She was dressed in a sundress, a lovely jade necklace circling her neck. Her hair was pulled back, held in place with a wide clip.

But more than the lovely dress, it was her face that held Nell's attention. She was looking out the window and smiling, her eyes bright, as if seeing something deep inside her head or heart and not the routine goings-on along Canary Cove Road. Her cheeks were flushed, as if from a heart pumping just beneath the surface. She was oblivious to Nell and Birdie's presence—and probably anyone else in the shop.

Nell watched her for a moment, wondering if the ride in the boat last night had given rise to the look about her. Or was it excitement over the documents she'd signed, the ones that could lead to considerable wealth from a father she didn't like?

No, it wasn't anything so pragmatic, Nell decided. At least not that alone.

She thought about the feud that Gabby had described between Beverly and her father, and tried to put that person with this one. Beverly looked soft, almost sensual today.

Polly appeared around the counter with a tray of iced tea and blueberry scones, and led them to a table next to the wall.

It was when Polly moved on to Beverly's table, refilling her glass, that Finn's daughter noticed the two women sitting a few feet away.

She murmured something to Polly. And then, unable to avoid Nell's and Birdie's eyes, she nodded a brief hello before pouring all her attention into a half-eaten bowl of fruit sitting on the table in front of her.

Finally Birdie leaned over. "Beverly, we didn't mean to make you uncomfortable last night. It was nice to see you enjoying yourself, that's all. Especially with the turmoil that's been filling all our days of late."

Beverly managed a small smile. "I was surprised to see you. We—I—hadn't planned to stop in Rockport. It was last-minute, so I was in a hurry. I apologize if I seemed rude."

"Not so," Birdie said. "We don't always allow people the privacy they rightly deserve. It's a trait of small-town folks, I suppose. But we also don't allow them to carry burdens alone—unless, of course, they want to."

Nell watched Beverly's expression, wondering if Birdie's message registered at all.

She speared a square of cantaloupe with her fork and moved it around the plate. The bag at her feet read CHEESE CLOSET in colorful letters.

Nell smiled and pointed to it. "I see you've been back. Ben says we're making sure they stay in business forever, but I see you're doing your part, too." The bag had pulled apart at the top and Nell could see a bottle of champagne, hunks of cheese, and a container of cashews. "The perfect ingredients for a happy time."

Beverly looked down at the bag as if it were revealing secrets. She closed the top flaps, then picked up the bag and slipped the rope handle over her arm. "A happy time," she murmured, more to herself than the two ladies sitting nearby.

She looked down at a large watch circling her wrist and pushed back her chair. "I've been daydreaming. Time flies . . ."

She stood and slipped a purse over her other shoulder. "Yes," Beverly said simply. "Perhaps a celebration. One never knows."

Nell and Birdie watched as she walked through the door and into the sunshine, her smile opening up, as if the happy day was beginning right then. She paused just a moment, then turned and walked past the tea-shop window with a lightness to her step, the kind that caused a passerby to pause and look at her twice—then smile as he continued on his way.

$\mathcal{N}$ ell and Birdie walked back down the street to Nell's car. On the way, Nell told her about her trip to the hardware store.

It was Beatrice's purchase more than Beverly's that caused a re-action in Birdie. Artists, after all, used plenty of odd tools in their galleries, she said. A knife was probably quite useful. But Beatrice . . .

"It's odd," she said.

"She wanted the best the store carried, according to Gus."

"Beatrice doesn't like fishing. She doesn't like boats. I've never even seen her near the beach. Sometimes I think she is biding her time here in Sea Harbor, until she can run for some district and move to the State House. I don't suppose that's an unusual thing to do, but . . ."

But you don't need knives to get ahead in politics.

Not a sharp carbon-blade knife, a perfect knife for gutting fish and cutting lines.

The kind of knife that had killed a fisherman they knew well.

Nell stopped at her car and rummaged in her purse for the keys.

"I'm glad they've taken that yellow tape down," Birdie said, looking over to Finnegan's property. She walked to the gate. It was closed, discouraging curiosity seekers, but when Birdie touched it lightly, it swung open.

She looked back at Nell and smiled. "I do believe it's inviting us in."

Nell dropped her keys back in her purse and followed Birdie

through the gate. They looked down the rutted drive that led to Finnegan's house.

Birdie looped her arm through Nell's as they walked. On both sides were overgrown trees reaching up for sunlight. "None of this even looks familiar. It's a jungle."

"A private jungle that didn't allow visitors. And yet he was so present in the town, down at the harbor, patrolling Canary Cove. Finnegan was not an antisocial person."

"His haven, I suppose. Perhaps we all need one."

"Though maybe not to this extreme." Nell looked off to the sides where a rusted lawn mower stood beside a few garbage cans tipped on their sides. At the end of the drive was the low-slung, two-story building, its shingles hanging loose from years of weather and neglect.

A weathered sign hung crookedly over a window: TIMOTHY PULASKI, DDS.

Birdie looked at the dentist's sign, then looked intently at the window behind it. Through the dirty glass, an old dental chair was visible. She took a few steps back and took in the rest of the building.

"Finnegan lived on the second floor?" Nell asked.

Birdie nodded. "He spared no expense when he fixed it up for Moira. She loved it there, Finn said." They looked up at the green patches of moss clinging to the roof, a chimney visible at one end.

Birdie walked the length of the building, then back to Nell's side.

"I'm remembering when Joseph had his office down here." She pointed west, beyond the rubbish and trees and fence, to the nicely kept property on the other side that now housed the Arts Association office. "That building matched this one. Twins. There was even a small path of green between them with picnic tables. I suppose the tenants all knew each other."

"Did you visit him down here?"

"Only a time or two. His office came furnished. We'd laugh about it, that if I aimed my telescope just right, I might be able to check up on him from across the water." She smiled at the old memory. "But, no, I wasn't the kind of wife who brought lunch to her husband in a nice little black box. Joseph would not have liked that—nor would I. That was how we handled our life together: he had his little office; I had my den. We came together in other places."

Birdie looked again at the dentist's sign. "Joseph mentioned Dr. Pulaski once or twice. He was a funny little man, quite odd-looking. He was . . ."

The crackling sound of dry wood startled away the rest of her sentence, and both women automatically took a step toward each other. Birdie clutched her chest.

Gabby Marietti appeared in the clearing, small twigs and leaves stuck to her green crocheted beanie. "Hi," she said.

"Gabby, sweetheart, you scared the life out of me."

Gabby skipped over the distance between them. "Don't you love it here? Look." She pointed to the water, where the rickety dock protruded like a bruised thumb. "It's so . . . so amazing here. So beautiful."

Gabby pointed at a small life vest hanging from a post.

"Finn got that at McClucken's for me. He made me wear it when we fished."

Nell watched the happiness in Gabby's eyes. She didn't see the rusty, broken-down appliances, the smashed cans and broken windows. Instead, she saw what Finn must have seen: the beauty of plants meeting the sea, and the happy memories that she and an old man had created in the middle of it.

A young reflection of Moira, thinking it was the most beautiful spot in the entire world.

No wonder Finn loved this child.

They walked around the house and looked down to the dock where Finnegan had kept his boat.

"That's where kids fish sometimes," Gabby said. "Finn didn't like it because he was afraid they'd fall off. It was okay for me to do it because he was with me."

Nell looked down at the dock, and in her mind's eye, she saw the three teenage boys huddled together, watching a stranger move through Finn's house, a flashlight moving from window to window, room to room. She looked up at the second-floor apartment that Finn had renovated for his wife. Skylights were still in place, though it was difficult to see if they were broken. A deck, leaning precariously to one side, fronted a wall of windows overlooking the water. It must have been a beautiful place.

The dock was similar to the one near the Artist's Palate, probably built around the same time and both in need of a good carpenter. She thought of Beverly coming around the fence and seeing her father on the dock with Gabby. Then arguing with him. Being chastised for something that went against Finn's moral code, whatever that might be. And adding insult to injury, her getaway thwarted by tripping on the path, thick and slippery with dead seaweed.

Beverly coming . . . Beverly fleeing. And in between the two, getting a lay of her father's land.

"Can't you just see why Finn loved it here?" Gabby tossed a stone down into the water. "And why he went ballistic when people tried to take it away from him?"

"I certainly can," Birdie said. "There's a kind of peace here. That must be what Finn found."

"Yes, he did," Gabby said, excited to have someone understand.

The realization that Gabby had been on the property before they arrived suddenly occurred to them. "But what were you doing back here, sweetie?" Birdie asked.

Gabby had appeared out of the brush like Puck. Their own mischievous woodland elf.

She seemed surprised at the question. "I brought flowers."

"Flowers?" Birdie looked back at the house.

"Not there. There." Gabby tossed her head, pointing toward some bushes, scrub trees, and a broken door leaning against a stump. "Finn used to do it, so now I do it for him."

"Where are the flowers?"

"Back there," Gabby said. She walked past the women and headed toward the broken door, then around two overgrown euonymus bushes. Though thick with weeds, there were signs of a pathway that led farther back into the brush.

Nell and Birdie followed the quickly moving child.

In a small clearing, barely identifiable as such, Gabby had put a handful of daylilies in an old bottle and leaned it up against a tree. Beyond the tree was a hole, carelessly filled in with dirt and debris.

A hole from which a casket had been recently removed.

Chapter 28

It wasn't yet lunchtime, but the day felt full, with chunks of a puzzle falling onto the ground, waiting for order.

Gabby said she was off to Willow's to work on some things for the Garden Celebration.

She hadn't offered more information about the flowers, just that she'd seen Finn take flowers into the woods and come back without them. He never let her come along, she said. "Maybe he talks to the woodland nymphs. I do that sometimes."

But Nell and Birdie suspected it was more than woodland nymphs that lured Finnegan into the woods.

They made their way back up the drive and climbed into Nell's car. "Where do we start?" Nell asked, pulling back into traffic. "It's as if a storm has tossed pieces of people's lives—and deaths—up in the air. Now all we need to do is put them into an order that makes sense."

"How about we talk to Father Northcutt? He's wise—and old. He's seen a lot."

Nell nodded. Father Northcutt knew as much about Finn as anyone. Perhaps he knew some secrets about Moira, as well.

Birdie checked her watch. "We'll lure him with the promise of food."

She took out her phone and punched in Father Larry's number. Mary Halloran answered, as she usually did, her sweet Irish lilt a pleasure to hear. "The good father is with a parishioner," she said, "but he has no luncheon plans." She assured Birdie there was nothing he'd like better than having lunch with her and Nell. She would see to it that he was at the Ocean's Edge in thirty minutes.

"That gives us time for a stop," Nell said. "I've been curious about the people checking out the deed to Finn's property. We already know Nick visited the deed office. But Sal was hesitant to tell me much more. He should have been a priest, the way he holds confidences so close."

"Even when he doesn't have to," Birdie said. "I think Beatrice trains him to keep everything in their life confidential so she'll never have to worry about little things leaking out and surprising her during some campaign."

Nell laughed. "A wise woman, perhaps."

Parking karma, Birdie called it, when a parking spot magically appeared right in front of the city office building.

And the karma walked inside with them, for when they opened the door to the register of deeds annex, a young woman sat in Sal's place, her head buried in an open chemistry book. There'd be no need to finesse their way around Sal Scaglia.

The college student looked up and a smile instantly lit her pretty face. "Yay! Nell and Birdie, two of my favorite people in the whole wide world." She jumped up, nearly toppling the chair.

Birdie hugged her. "Dear Janie. Now, what in heaven's name are you doing here?"

Janie Levin held up the textbook. "Studying organic chem. Next-to-last semester of nursing school," she said proudly. Then she looked around and pointed to the desk. "Oh, but you mean *here*. I'm a substitute gal Friday. That's what my boyfriend calls me." She laughed. "This office needed some major computer upgrades, so I'm doing that, bringing them up to the twenty-first century. Or at least trying to. And I do pretty much anything else they need me to do around the offices. Great summer job, especially on days like this when I get to study."

Nell hugged her warmly. "We're very proud of you, you know. Tommy tells me—and everyone he sees—how well you're doing in school."

Janie blushed. She and policeman Tommy Porter had been dating for a while now, and Nell suspected that a diamond would arrive before nursing school graduation, but an engagement wouldn't alter Janie's plans one iota. She was the first in her family to go to college, and sweet Tommy was as proud of her as if he'd single-handedly made it happen.

"What brings you two into this musty old office? I told Sal that it was unhealthy in here, and I made him open every single window. Years ago, before people knew any better, someone used to smoke in here. I can still smell it. I can. It's in the books and that carpet around the computers and those old upholstered chairs. It's dreadful."

If Janie's enthusiasm for disease, health, and diagnosis of her friends and neighbors matches her grades, she will graduate with the highest honors, Nell thought. "So, Sal's not here?" she asked.

"Sal? Nope. He just left. So for today, I'm him. Sitting in his chair, anyway." She looked sheepish, then laughed. "And studying my organic chem. But enough about me. How are you two, and what brings you in here? Would you like to look at some deeds? A little local history? A . . ."

Nell laughed at Janie's antics, swinging her arms theatrically toward the computers and the wall of dusty books.

"Actually, it's simpler than that. We'd like to see the sign-in book that Sal keeps."

"That's it? Easy as pie. Here." She picked up a lined tablet from the desk and handed it over to them. "But don't sit in those upholstered chairs. Try the wooden chairs at the table. Less germs."

They thanked her and moved to the library table, sitting down and opening the book, leafing back over the past few weeks. There was Nicholas Marietti, signing in with his distinctive scrawl. Sal made people indicate what they were looking for in another column, along with time in and time out. Nick was looking up the deed to the Francis Finnegan property, it said, and he stayed exactly one hour. As far as they could tell, that was his only visit.

Birdie ran her finger over the columns, backing up to a couple of weeks before Finnegan died and taking it up to the most recent entries. Lots of developers' names checking out Finnegan's place—Davey Delaney, some Boston companies, some investment bankers.

Birdie's finger stopped: *Beverly Walden* was written clearly on several different dates. They checked across the rows to see what she was interested in: Canary Cove deeds one day, Francis Finnegan land another, some random places. All in all, they came across ten entries for Beverly Walden, even including the property on which she lived, and a couple of refurbished homes in the most expensive neighborhood in Sea Harbor.

Birdie looked at Nell. "How strange."

"Indeed." Nell slipped her glasses back into her purse and scribbled a few notes on the tiny notepad she kept in the bag, and they quietly exited the office, careful not to disturb Janie, her head once again buried in organic chemistry.

"We need to keep our thoughts going in a straight line," Birdie said as they drove the few blocks to the Ocean's Edge. "I feel we're going in too many directions."

"But there's overlap in all of this. The body in Finn's yard. His murder. His changing his will. Nick's interest in the land."

"I hope not too much overlap," Birdie said.

Nell knew what Birdie was thinking. Not enough to implicate Nicholas Marietti in anything more serious than . . . More serious than what?

A boatload of questions—and not even a tugboat of answers.

Father Northcutt had already arrived and was seated in his favorite booth when they walked into the restaurant.

Jeffrey Meara, who had tended bar for at least thirty years at the Ocean's Edge and probably knew as many secrets as Father Larry, said the priest had already ordered his favorite stout and they should go right on back.

The priest greeted them effusively, his broad hands grasping theirs. "To what do I owe this extraordinary pleasure, my darlin's?"

A waitress appeared before they could answer. Birdie and Nell ordered the salmon salad special with glasses of iced tea. Father Larry would have his usual, he said, and the waitress beamed.

Nell frowned at him. "Father . . ." she began.

"I know, I know, dear Nellie. It's that nasty cholesterol beast you fear. But I promise you that Mary Halloran, bless her sweet soul, insists on stuffing my refrigerator with lettuce and uncooked vegetables most days, so this is a treat I save to complement the pleasure of dining with two such beautiful women."

"Father," Birdie said sweetly, "you're full of it."

The waitress laughed at Birdie's choice of words, then went off to place their order: two salad specials and a grilled filet mignon, rare as a bottle of Midleton's, with just a hint of béarnaise sauce drizzled on top.

They talked about the weather, the influx of vacationers, and the upcoming Garden Celebration before settling into their steak and salmon and the real reason they were there.

"A question for you," Nell began. "Did you officiate at Moira Finnegan's funeral?"

"Oh, sure, and I did. Moira was a wonderful lady. So generous to the church and she never missed a Sunday."

"Where was she buried?" Birdie asked. "I vaguely remember the funeral. But I can't remember much of what followed."

"Old St. Mary's Cemetery, out near the quarries. A beautiful place to put someone to rest. Lots of trees. I visit her grave now and again. It's on a rise in the land beneath a huge hawthorn tree, a wee bit of ocean visible in the distance."

Birdie agreed that Moira would love an ocean-view resting place. She dearly loved the water.

"Finn wasn't as attentive as others," Father Larry went on. "Some people aren't, you know; the grave is simply a place to bury a body. Sure, and that's fine, as long as they hold the loved one in their heart, I say. But no matter what, I like a well-tended grave, so I take fresh flowers out to Moira now and again."

Although the gentle priest's comments were not exactly what she and Birdie were expecting, they filed them away in their heads to pull apart later. They'd come in expecting one answer, but would leave with another.

The chunks of rare salmon were flavored with a lemon tarragon dressing, and Nell tried to pick out the ingredients. It would make a perfect dish for the knitting group some night. She mentally recorded: lemon, wine, tarragon, and a tiny bit of good mayonnaise.

Father Larry was devouring his steak bite by bite, with obvious enjoyment. Nell waited until he'd finished a bite, then slipped in another question.

"Have you heard the rumors surrounding that body on Finn's land? You don't think he killed anyone, do you, Father?"

"Did our Finnegan have anything to do with that grave? It's a mighty perplexing question." Father Larry took another bite of steak and chewed it thoughtfully.

"I can imagine that an accident might have occurred back there," Nell said. "A drifter, maybe, trespassing through unfamiliar land, and for whatever reason, he accidentally died. Maybe Finn left a rake in a bad spot, or a piece of rusty something-or-other. But what doesn't fit into anything I know about Finnegan is covering it up by burying the man back there."

Father Larry was nodding as Nell talked. He sliced off another bite of steak while listening carefully and thoughtfully.

"He couldn't have lived with that kind of deception," Birdie added. "And that's the truth. He couldn't have. And you know that, too, Father." Her fork stabbed the air as she talked.

"So the question is this: who, in heaven's name, was buried in that grave?" Nell's words hung over the leather booth.

The theory that someone was seeking revenge on Finnegan for a long-ago crime was weak, Father Northcutt admitted. "I don't think the police buy it, either, though nothing's been ruled out. Why would someone come back all these years later? That body had been there for years. Doesn't quite make good sense, now, does it?"

The waitress cleared their plates and returned with a dessert tray filled with sugary delights. Much to Nell's surprise, Father Northcutt demurred, but his look of longing following the disappearing tray was so intense, Birdie and Nell half expected the tray to be pulled back by sheer desire.

"Enough is enough. Right, Nell?" he said, his eyes still lusting after a piece of banana cream pie. "Of course, the fact that I have a meeting with your fine husband in ten minutes might have something to do with my sudden restraint." Laughter filled the booth, offering a nice sorbet ending to the discussion—a gentle cleansing of the palate, washing away the unpleasant things they'd touched upon.

But as they walked past the bar, waved to the bartender, and walked into the sunshine, Birdie brought them back on topic once more.

"Just one more question. Something that's been bothering me. Did Moira Finnegan have any health problems that you remember? Before she got cancer, I mean."

Father Northcutt gave the question some thought, his white brows pulling together and his head leaning slightly to one side. "None that I can remember," he said. "She was as sweet and pretty and delicate as an Irish rose. A blooming healthy lady, I believe she was.

"Except for the teeth, of course."

Chapter 29

It was Father Northcutt's final comment that triggered Birdie's memory.

"It was like turning the lights on. There it was, all of a sudden, a perfect memory of that funny little dentist. "Suddenly I can see him as clearly as if he were right in front of me," she told Nell as they drove through the streets of Sea Harbor. "And I can imagine him and Moira, too."

Lunch was followed by a trip to the post office to mail some letters and a stop at the library to return a stack of books before heading over to M.J.'s salon. While they drove, Birdie shared her suspicions about the dentist.

"But they're only suspicions," she reminded Nell, after going through her parade of memories of Dr. Pulaski. "They need a day or two to percolate."

"But I think we're on to something." Nell made a mental note to ask Ben that evening about the body that had been exhumed. Perhaps he would have the key that would turn the lock. It would be nice to be able to excuse one more person from the lineup.

They pulled up in front of the hair salon and parked. Nell picked up some shampoo, and Birdie had a scheduled appointment with M.J.'s new masseuse.

Cass and Izzy had teased her about it, but Birdie insisted the woman was marvelous and her gentle manipulations were lowering her blood pressure. "And she says I have good bone structure," Birdie added proudly.

The door of the salon opened as they approached, and Beverly Walden walked out, squinting as she adjusted to the bright sunlight.

At first Nell and Birdie weren't absolutely sure who it was.

Beverly's hair was lightened considerably, with dramatic highlights woven in. Her shoulder-length style had been cut in a layered, feathery way, with a loose fringe of bangs swinging across her forehead. It was a dramatic departure from the simple, more conservative hairdo that had been hers since she moved to Sea Harbor.

"Goodness," Birdie said. "Imagine running into you twice today. You look lovely, Beverly."

"I needed a change."

"Well, it's quite a nice one. M.J. does a wonderful job."

Beverly touched her hair lightly, as if making sure it was still there. She started to walk away when Nell touched her arm, stopping her.

"I meant to ask Father Northcutt about your father's funeral, but perhaps you would have the details. Are there any plans?"

Beverly paused, as if trying to recollect who her father was. But her answer was cordial. "Yes, actually. I think it will be soon. Things are finally moving to closure, thank God. I just received a call, in fact. Apparently, the priest received the final packet of Finnegan's papers this afternoon and wants to go over them with me immediately. I have plans, but he was insistent and said it wouldn't take long. My lawyer is coming, too. Actually, it's perfect timing. It will be good for everyone to have this mess over with. It's time." Her parting words were unemotional—and definite.

They watched her walk down the street, a new confidence in her stride.

"I must say, I don't like her calling Father Larry *the priest*," Birdie said. "She can be . . . rather unlikable."

"I think she only lets us see a tiny bit of who she is." Nell watched Beverly cross the street. "I wonder what the meeting she mentioned is really about."

"She could be right. Maybe something's happened that will put the ball—and Finn's property—in her court."

Nell looked down and read a message from Ben. "Could be. Ben is going to be there, too, he says. Perhaps Beverly's right and the additional documents have changed everything. Poor Cass. This has been such a roller-coaster ride for her."

Birdie was worried, too. Beverly was so confident. Too confident. "I don't mean to be unkind, but she unnerves me," she said to Nell. "She doesn't make it terribly easy to be around her."

An understatement, Nell thought. Both she and Birdie knew exactly why she unnerved them and why it was uneasy to be around her.

A father dead. A child alive. And very greedy.

Birdie insisted on bringing Ella's prized empanadas to knitting that night. The recipe was from her Argentine friend, Sophia Santos. "Ella loves making them, and we will love eating them—and you have no time today to cook, dear friend."

Nell was grateful for the offer and didn't put up a fuss. She had plenty of vegetables in her home garden to make a salad. Arugula and escarole, red pepper, cucumber, and mushrooms, a handful of chopped-up hearts of palm and some sugared pecans. A little lemon basil dressing to bind it all together. Someone would bring dessert. And if they didn't, it would serve all their waistlines well.

She left Ben a note in case he forgot what day it was, and headed to Izzy's shop. Her head felt too full, as if she'd eaten too much and was having trouble digesting it all. Perhaps that was their problem. They were all too full, too close to a hundred things running through their minds.

Izzy and Cass had put out plates and glasses, opened the windows, and had an old Martin Taylor piece humming in the background when she walked in.

Birdie was close behind, carrying a heavy glass dish.

In the front of the store, Jillian and Rose busied themselves stocking a new shipment of cotton fleece that had come in. Over the music, a male voice joined the teenage laughter.

"Rose's new boyfriend," Izzy explained. "At least for today. Oliver Porter, Tommy's cousin."

"Oliver? Wasn't he with the group that watched the intruder going through Finn's house?" Birdie asked. "The intruder who was probably one Nicholas Marietti?"

Without waiting for an answer, she climbed the steps and disappeared into the front of the store. Her voice trailed back as she questioned the embarrassed teenager about fishing off Finn's dock.

The words came back down the stairs in pieces. "Flashlight. Yah, Miss Birdie. Nah, he wasn't upstairs. The light was coming through the windows downstairs. We thought about telling him Finn's place was on top, but then, you know, that woulda been so dumb. We'd a been caught." He laughed nervously.

Minutes later, after assuring Oliver he wasn't in trouble and had been a big help, Birdie reappeared in the back room. "So," she said, her eyebrows lifting quizzically, "was Nick lost? Did he think Finn lived on the first floor?"

"Or not," Nell said, reading Birdie's thoughts and recording the new information in her head. Perhaps Nick knew exactly where he was. Perhaps he wasn't interested in Finnegan's apartment at all.

"We'll just have to see, now, won't we?" Birdie said, determination backing up her words. She looked at Izzy. "And, by the way, Rose and Jillian have emptied all the boxes."

"Those teenyboppers are a step ahead of me. Pretty soon I'm not going to be needed around here."

Cass dropped her backpack next to a chair. "Want to come to work on a lobster boat? One with leaky nets, a scratched hull, and numerous mysterious ailments?"

Nell set down the salad bowl and started shaking the dressing jar. She waited a moment, gauging Cass' mood. *Frustrated* seemed to fit it best.

"Have you heard anything about the will?" Nell asked.

Cass nodded. "From the horse's mouth. Though I think I'd use another animal if the twins weren't listening to everything we're saying." She peeked up the stairs just as Jillian scurried out of sight.

"Beverly informed me earlier today that her lawyer is speeding things up for all sorts of reasons. One, there was an earlier will in which she got the land; two, because she is Finn's daughter; and three, because I am, basically, nothing. And for all those reasons she will make sure she wins the dispute. Soon. Any minute. She was on her way to meet with him."

She pulled the foil off the heavy glass baking dish Birdie had brought. It was filled with empanadas. "So you told Ella we were having the whole fishing fleet for dinner?"

"You know how Ella is. It's important to her that Gabby becomes an expert at making empanadas before she has to leave. It's as if without that recipe, she'll forget us. She's even reluctantly agreed to let Gabby make some with spinach and cheese to suit her vegetarian tastes. So, as best I can tell, we have a little of everything here." The tantalizing odors of garlic and parsley, sautéed onions and butter surrounded neat rows of crisp pastry pockets, perfectly browned. "We have potato and beef, shrimp and hearts of palm, spicy chicken and cheese. Marinated beef with caramelized onion. Shall I go on?"

Cass opened two bowls of sauces and closed her eyes. "Chimichurri and one of unknown origin."

"Brilliant, Professor Halloran."

In minutes they were sitting around the coffee table, plates filled with salad and empanadas, a bottle of chilled white wine and water glasses nearby.

"We do know how to live, don't we?" Izzy said, piercing an empanada with her fork and releasing a river of white oozing cheese.

A moment of bliss. Friendship and food. And the rest of the world faded away for brief, blessed moments.

Then Birdie broke the spell. "I have something to say," she said, deciding on the spot that there wouldn't be time for eating, quiet time, wine, knitting, solving Finn's murder, and small talk. The small talk and quiet time would have to go.

Forks paused in midair.

She waited for Cass to take a drink of her wine and settle back in her chair, then continued. "I'm worried about you, Cass, and about all of us." Her arms lifted to circle them all. "It's as if an insidious layer of air is blanketing us, getting into the nooks and crannies of our gentle town—and we're having trouble stopping it."

"We have dozens of little pieces of the puzzle," Nell said. "I know we do. And we're getting close—I can feel it."

"Sure, we have all these tiny pieces, but we still don't have a murderer," Cass said.

"But we will. We'll let all the things in our head fall out on this table like strands of yarn," Birdie said. "And then we'll knit them into a magnificent . . . well, into something that makes sense and has no loose ends. I believe that glass of wine is wreaking havoc with my analogies."

They all laughed.

"Okay. For what it's worth, this is in my head. I'm about to lose my never-been-touched inheritance," Cass began. "Which isn't the end of the world, but the person going after it frightens me. I don't trust Beverly Walden, and I think she had something to do with her father's death."

Birdie finished her first empanada—spicy chicken and cheese—declared it magnificent, and said, "I agree with you, Cass. I think she has an agenda that we know nothing about. She's doing something behind our backs, and I think Finnegan knew it, too. There was a reason he cut her out of the will entirely."

"According to Gabby, Finn was upset because she was doing something dishonest or unethical—or something that was terribly offensive to him." Birdie repeated the conversation they'd had with Gabby earlier in the day. "That sweet young girl doesn't miss a thing."

"They caught Beverly sneaking onto his land?"

"Yes," Nell said. "And she ended up threatening him. I guess that's what bothers me the most. How far would Beverly take a threat?"

"Here's something else to weave in. We know that the Delaneys, several investors, Beatrice Scaglia, and my dear Nick weren't the only ones in the public records' office. Beverly spent a fair amount of time there, too. Thanks to dear Sal's attention to detail, we know each time she was there and what she was looking at."

"Doing what?" Izzy asked. "If she was so sure she was inheriting everything, why look up the deed?"

"Maybe trying to assess the value?" Cass said.

"Could be," Izzy said, "But there'd be more efficient ways to do that. Check with a Realtor, for one. The deed wouldn't necessarily indicate today's value, only what Finn bought it for a thousand years ago."

"It wasn't just Finn's property. She looked up a lot of deeds, some that seemed frivolous, almost like excuses to be using the computers."

"What do you think that was about?" Izzy asked.

Nell shrugged. "It doesn't make a lot of sense."

Cass slid several more empanadas onto her plate. "Jane said Beverly was active in the artist community when she first arrived, but seemed to have lost interest recently. They think it's because she's seeing some guy, but when Jane asked her about it, she was defensive and did everything but tell Jane to mind her own business. Some things should be private, she said, like what went on in one's bedroom, and she would certainly never ask Jane about her life behind closed doors."

"She said that?" Izzy asked.

Cass nodded. "Her main interest now, Jane says, is getting her hands on her father's money, even to the neglect of her art."

"All right, then. Why? She's certainly defensive about her life. Why does she care if people know she's in a relationship?" Izzy asked.

"Maybe she isn't sure of the relationship and doesn't want to be embarrassed if it doesn't work out," Nell offered.

"Or the guy is married," Cass said.

They all paused. A possibility. And a reason for keeping it under wraps.

"But what would all of that have to do with Finn's murder?" Cass asked.

"People do crazy things for love," Izzy said. "If Beverly thought money would make the relationship work . . ."

She might murder to get it?

It seemed far-fetched, but it was possible. People killed for love. The thought hovered over them as they ate the empanadas and passed around the bottle of wine.

Nell set down her glass. "Here's another loose thread: the body in Finn's yard."

"The rumors are awful and ridiculous," Birdie added. "As if Finn would kill someone, bury him on his own land, and then live there, right next to someone he'd killed."

It was silly, but as Ben said, the police weren't concerned about the emotional element. And the fact was he *could* have killed someone, and he *could* have kept everyone off his land so they wouldn't find out.

"So we need to figure out who was buried there and why. If it doesn't reveal who killed Finnegan, at the very least we will clear Finnegan's name," Izzy said.

Nell explained about the futility of using dental records to identify the long-buried body. "The whole thing is strange, but Birdie and I have a theory—"

Everyone leaned in while Birdie and Nell spread their thoughts on the table, including the role of Timothy Pulaski, DDS.

When they were through, Izzy clapped her hands. "Yes!" she said. "Sherlock Holmes has nothing on you two."

"The police would say we're hopeless romantics, out chasing rainbows," Nell said. "But sometimes that's where the gold is. So let's start with burials. Do any of you know someone we can talk to at St. Mary's Cemetery?"

"There're lots of Hallorans over there, but it's hard to get a word out of them."

"*Living* people, sweetie," Birdie said.

"I can provide living, too, because I love this idea. I think you are onto something. The grandpa of a friend of Pete's has been the caretaker over there for a zillion years. I forget his name—Henry something. Pete and his buddies used to spend a lot of time over there, riding bikes and hanging out. The grandpa loved the company and even put up a rope swing for the guys."

Nell scribbled the name on a pad of paper and switched the topic to knives. "Both Beatrice and Beverly purchased rigging knives recently from McClucken's. And they both insisted on buying the best he carried."

"Beatrice Scaglia with a boat knife?" Cass laughed. "Imagine her in that spotless white suit, gutting a trout."

The thought made them laugh. But there were other uses for a knife than gutting fish, Birdie reminded them.

"Surely no one wanting to kill Finnegan would walk into the only hardware store in Sea Harbor and buy the murder weapon," Izzy said.

"Unless that's the best way to do it. What did Angus say? It's those things in plain sight that we don't see. It's when you're hiding something that you get the attention."

"Like the secretive Beverly," Cass said.

"Who also bought a knife," Birdie said. "But she also confiscated a boat. Perhaps the two went together."

Nell pulled out Gabby's sweater and smoothed it on her lap, listening to the conversation spinning around her. *Beverly bought a knife, too.* She replayed the conversation with Gus in her head. She'd been so taken with the image of Beatrice and a rigging knife that she hadn't processed carefully what he had said about Beverly. It came back to her now, and, in hindsight, she realized something she'd almost missed.

She looked up. "No, I don't think the knife went with the boat, unless she was making plans to buy a boat of her own. According to Gus, Beverly bought the knife a few weeks ago, before her father died, so she wouldn't have been buying a knife for her father's boat."

Unless.

The unspoken word hung heavy in the air. Unless she had a different use entirely in mind.

It was a gruesome thought, and the jingling of the front door was a welcome relief.

They could hear male voices, deeper this time, joking in the outer rooms, the twins bantering back. Minutes later Ben and Sam appeared in the archway. With hellos all around, they headed for the table and peeled back the cover from the Pyrex dish.

"We're in luck," Sam said.

"Weren't you two headed to the Gull to watch the baseball game?" Izzy said.

"Plans change," Ben said. "My fault." He looked hungrily at a dozen remaining empanadas. "Besides, these top Jake Risso's greasy burgers any day."

"Hey," Cass said. "That's my week of dinners you're about to inhale."

Birdie laughed and patted her knee. "Cass, dear, there are dozens more where those came from. Gabby can stock your freezer. Ours is already overflowing."

The two men filled their plates and pulled out two old library chairs, turning them to face the women.

"Okay, so why are you really here?" Izzy asked, handing them each a cold Modela. "It's a Yankees-Sox game you're missing. It takes more than empanadas and our amazing company to do that."

Sam grabbed her hand and pulled her down for a kiss. "Can't a guy miss his woman?"

"*Woman*? You've been reading too much Dashiell Hammett, Perry." Izzy kissed him soundly and returned to her almost-finished pink socks.

Ben made it through three pastries and a pile of salad quickly. He put down his fork, wiped his mouth, and took a long swig of the cold Modelo. "It's been a long day," he said finally.

The women were silent. Their needles clicked as their heads turned in Ben's direction.

"But a good one," he added. "At least for some. Not so much for others." He looked over at Cass.

"So, what's the deal?"

"Beverly's case contesting the will is being thrown out. Or, to be more accurate, her own lawyer is telling her to let it go."

Cass moved to the edge of her chair. "Why?'

"For starters, there was some question about whether Beverly was in a position to judge Finn's mental capacity. The two rarely saw each other. And if she wanted to recruit allies, no one in this town—even those eager to grab his property—would argue that he wasn't mentally competent."

No one moved. It was clear from the look on Ben's face that he wasn't finished.

"There's something else," Nell said quietly.

"All right," Cass said. "Let's hear it."

Nell's thoughts ran the gamut, and she knew from Cass' expression that she, too, was expecting the worst. The land was being foreclosed upon. There was another relative, another will uncovered. Or, perish the thought, another dead body.

But Ben's words were simple and unexpected.

"Beverly Walden isn't Finnegan's daughter," he said.

Chapter 30

The news landed like a grenade right in the middle of the knitting room.

And then came the explosion, with voices colliding.

"What?

"Are you sure?"

"How do you know?"

Finally, Birdie quieted everyone, walking around the group pouring wine and replacing empty beer bottles with full ones. "All right, now," she said, sitting back down and pulling her knitting into her lap. "Please explain, Ben."

Ben smiled. He nodded to Birdie. "That, I will. The rest of Finn's documents came today. Although it had seemed rather perfunctory stuff to the Boston firm, they don't live here in Sea Harbor and didn't know that an adoption application, particularly one that had been denied, would be of interest.

"Finn had agreed to adopt Beverly, apparently because Moira wanted him to. Father Larry remembered that part of their story. What he didn't know was what the application and accompanying letter revealed. Beverly's biological father refused to sign over his rights."

"Her father?" Izzy asked.

"A marine Moira had met in California. He and Moira never married, and he didn't seem to have much interest in having a baby. So Moira moved back East and had the baby. But years later, after she and Finnegan married and he petitioned to adopt Beverly—she was around ten when the application was filed—the guy refused. Wouldn't sign the papers. No one's sure why. A power thing, maybe."

"Did Beverly know that?"

"No. And we had to put Angus McPherran in the hot seat to find out why. Angus knew about the failed adoption, but the man is as closemouthed as they come. He said Moira had sworn Finnegan within an inch of his life never to tell Beverly. She wanted her to think she was Finnegan's adopted daughter."

Wanted her to feel wanted, Nell supposed.

"I don't suppose Beverly had an easy life," Izzy admitted.

"Probably not. But it wasn't for want of trying. Finnegan and Moira did everything they could to give her a decent life, Father Larry said. She was a troubled kid. She probably blamed it on the two of them, but sometimes it runs deeper than that."

Bad blood, perhaps, from a father she never knew.

"She started getting in trouble early, if memory serves me right," Birdie said.

Ben nodded. "Moira thought Finn could straighten her out if he was legally her father. She probably thought Beverly might listen to a parent figure."

Beverly had been so optimistic about meeting with the priest to-day. It would all be over, she'd have her money and. . . . run? No, not that, if she was looking at property around town. Nell looked at Ben. "Does Beverly know this? She said she was meeting with you today. Did you tell her?" But it was rhetorical. She knew from the weary look on his face that he had, and that it had been difficult.

"Her lawyer was there, too, to offer advice. We thought it was better that she hear the news from Father Larry and me, rather than in a court as she tried to lay claim to her father's money. There was also a letter Finnegan had written to her, to be given to her when he died. She looked at it, but not really, then threw it on the table when she left."

"What did it say?" Cass asked.

"It was formal, but kind. He explained about the failed adoption, about wanting her to have a good life, and regretted that it hadn't been the kind of life her mother wanted for her. He also mentioned the will, and that she would understand why she wasn't in it."

"How did she react?"

"She's a tough lady. It's hard to know what she feels. She seems to have many different faces, but we saw a mean one today. She was determined there was a loophole somewhere. She didn't care at all that she wasn't Finn's daughter, but she cared a hell of a lot about his money. I think when she left, she was still plotting a way to turn this around. She seems to think this money will get her something she desperately wants. She's one determined lady. Frankly, I think she might be dangerous."

The room was absolutely still, with thoughts of Beverly Walden sucking out the air.

"I've seen a soft side to her," Nell finally ventured.

The others agreed. "Soft. Hard. Even sensual at times, like the night we saw her in Rockport," Izzy said.

"I think above all her craziness, Beverly Walden is a very needy woman," Birdie added.

Ben concurred with Birdie. "*Desperately* needy, I think. And to the point of doing almost anything she deems necessary to fill that need."

The group that locked up the yarn shop and headed out into the June night a while later was a sober one, filled with emotions that ran the gamut.

Ben had called Danny Brandley and suggested he meet them at the yarn studio to give Cass a lift home.

Home, Nell knew, from the look of concern on Ben's face, meant wherever the two of them landed together—his place or the little house Cass was renting from Izzy. Just not somewhere alone.

Danny agreed in a heartbeat.

Cass gave Ben a quick hug and whispered, "I'm learning. And he's patient."

The others pretended not to hear.

Nell and Ben had gone directly home from the shop, relishing the quiet embrace of the big old house on Sandswept Lane.

"Who knows if Beverly would actually hurt anyone?" Ben said to Nell. "But she wasn't thinking clearly when she left, and Cass would be a good target for her anger. She said some things that didn't make a lot of sense, muttering about some kind of celebration she planned. Said she'd have to switch gears now."

"Do the police know about this?" Nell sat on the edge of the bed, watching Ben move back and forth from his closet to the bathroom to the dresser, dropping his keys and wallet beside his cell phone. A routine as old as their marriage, and one that brought great comfort to the night.

"Yes. Father Larry went by after we met today. Frankly, I don't know what it all means, but I know Jerry will want to look into it further. He'll probably want to talk to Beverly again. I suspect there's a huge part of this picture that hasn't come into focus yet, but maybe this will bring us a step closer."

Nell nodded. She sat back against the white pillows and looked out into the darkness. The breeze lifted the filmy curtains, turning them into dancing shadows against the moonlight.

Somewhere out there, Beverly Walden was facing another bitter disappointment in her life. Altering her plans. She tried to imagine her as a ten-year-old child. But the image that pushed the young Beverly to the edges of her imagining was Gabrielle Marietti, a ten-year-old who grasped life, embraced it. It was difficult to imagine Beverly at that age, already wanting to take what was hers—even when it wasn't. Had she changed in all these years?

Ben turned out the light and slipped in beside her. He pulled Nell to him, fitting her perfectly into the curve of his body, his arms wrapped around her, holding her safe.

"It's going to be all right," he whispered into her ear. "Soon . . ."

Nell nodded and closed her eyes, blocking out the night. *Soon . . .*

But lives could be altered in a heartbeat.

Soon needed to be now.

Chapter 31

$\mathcal{M}$orning came too early, and the tangled sheets gave testimony to a restless night. Nell pulled on a pair of capris and a T-shirt, her thoughts tumbling on top of one another.

And that is the problem, she thought. They were tumbled thoughts, difficult to pull apart. A messy pile of yarn. And the only way to straighten it was to find one end at a time and trace it back, around and over and around again.

One strand at a time.

"I have a meeting with the mayor this morning," Ben called up from the kitchen. "We're getting some great PR on the community garden. Sam is going to provide some photos of it for a magazine article."

A part of his Sea Harbor summer series. Then a second thought came to Nell, and she made a mental note to ask Sam for a preview of his summer project. One never knew what might be lurking in a photograph.

Perhaps one of those loose threads.

She headed down to the kitchen and a cup of coffee. Up with the sun, Ben eased Nell into her day with the smell of his robust brew dripping away in the pot. Her mind was moving ahead to a day filled with ordinary things: a morning meeting at the library, a stop at the market, finishing an article on fund-raising for the local paper.

But it was the in-between things that were filling her mind. She picked up the phone to call Birdie—maybe Gabby would like a trip to the fish market. But before she had a chance to dial, her cell phone buzzed.

Cass. Nell picked up the phone, but before she could say a word, Cass assured her that she was fine. Not to worry.

"Is my worry that obvious?" Nell said, slightly embarrassed.

"Absolutely. But I'd be offended if you didn't worry about me. I'm fine, though. And Danny, too." She paused and let her words sink in.

Nell laughed.

"And I'm not afraid of Beverly Walden. She's not a foolish person, and doing anything to me would be foolish. It's not like she's next in line."

Both those things were true. But it was Beverly's *mind* that was beginning to worry Nell. How it worked, her sense of right and wrong. A mind that could lead to actions that didn't always make sense. She'd been capable of doing things outside the norm since Archie Brandley caught her stealing from his bookstore when she was ten. What did that kind of a conscience mature into when one was nearly forty?

"Just be careful, Cass," she said aloud.

"I'm always careful." Then she added, "But if the truth be known, the only person who frightens me right now is Finnegan. If we don't clear him of those rumors surrounding that grave, he'll be rattling chains in my bedroom for the rest of my life. He's starting to invade my dreams."

It was true. Finnegan didn't have relatives left to worry about his legacy. But he had friends. Friends who cared—and who wouldn't rest until Finn's life was free of innuendo and rumor. "We will," she said softly into the phone. Silently she added to the vow, *Nor will we rest until our dear friend Cass is free of the same.*

"We will," Cass repeated. "But for right this minute, I'm off to the sea. At least you can rest easy—Beverly can't get me out there."

It was past noon before Nell had another free moment. The library board meeting had gone longer than expected, and she was starving.

She walked out of the library, down the hill, and across Harbor Road to Harry Garozzo's deli, hoping to catch a quiet moment, a glass of tea, and one of Harry's famous prosciutto and pesto sandwiches. Time to sit in the quiet back booth at Harry's and sort through her thoughts about Beverly Walden.

As she reached for the big silver handle on the deli door, it opened on its own and Beatrice Scaglia walked out, deep in thought. Oblivious to Nell's presence, she stumbled on the doorstep, then jerked her head up.

Nell put out her hands to steady the councilwoman.

Beatrice's hand shot to her mouth, embarrassed. "What a klutz I am. I wasn't looking. I'm sorry, Nell."

Nell looked at the frown that creased Beatrice's usually smooth forehead. "You seem a million miles away. Is everything all right?"

"All right?" With one hand, Beatrice smoothed an imaginary wrinkle from her pencil-thin skirt and forced a smile to her face. "Of course. Things are busy. You know how that can be."

"Especially with this ongoing investigation," Nell added. "I'm sure it affects city business. People are worried—"

Beatrice nodded in a vague way that made Nell wonder if she'd heard a single word she'd said.

The buzz of Beatrice's phone seemed to pull her to attention. She reached into her purse, removing it quickly. With a small, apologetic wave, she pressed the cell phone to her ear and walked quickly across the street. Nell watched her straight, determined back and wondered what was going on with the usually talkative politician. As she started to turn away, she noticed the small, crumpled piece of paper that fluttered in Beatrice's wake, landing in the curb.

Nell picked it up and headed for a nearby trash can, then looked absently down at the words written on the paper scrap. She frowned. Smoothing it out on the top of the trash can, she read the words *B. W. 22 Coastal Road.*

"Cleaning up trash now, are we?" Harry Garozzo stepped outside his door, his white apron stretched tightly over his abundant middle. "Such a fine citizen. I've a mind to tell Mary Pisano about this—it would give her material for a column."

Nell laughed. Mary had been known to applaud her neighbors in print for doing good deeds; not the kind of attention Nell coveted. She slipped the piece of paper into her purse. "Well, all this cleaning has made me very hungry, Harry. And I'm quite sure that nothing but a Garozzo prosciutto sandwich will satisfy it. Do you have any left to feed a hungry friend?"

"Make that four hungry friends." Birdie walked up behind Nell. She gave her a quick hug, then looked at Harry. "And please make those to go, dear, along with a jug of your spectacular iced tea and some lovely lemon cakes."

"Your wish is my command, fair Bernadette. Now, what's this fine gossip I hear about the good-looking Italian?"

"Believe it, Harry. It's all true. Every lascivious word of it."

Harry's hearty guffaw caused heads to turn, and Birdie shooed him on inside to prepare their lunch. Then she walked to the curb where Harold waited in the Lincoln Town Car, and shooed him off, as well.

"All right, now. That leaves you, me, and four pesto prosciutto sandwiches. Where are we going?" Nell waved to Harold as he disappeared down Harbor Road.

"A picnic," she said. "In the cemetery."

Nell drove while Birdie gave directions.

"I was hoping I'd find you," Birdie said. "Harold drove them out here, but I thought it might be productive for you and me to pick them up."

"Them?" Nell drove down Harbor Road, then north toward the outskirts of town.

"Gabby and Ella. It's part of Gabby's quest for family, I think." She pointed to a narrow road that wound up a wooded hillside. "Apparently she and her father's cook watched a show on grave rubbings and Gabby found it fascinating. She has visited nearly every cemetery within twenty miles of her home—Manhattan outlawed them in the mid–eighteen hundreds, Gabby informed me, so she and Sophie took field trips once they'd covered Manhattan. She was looking for the Marietti clan, but finally resorted to any marker that intrigued her."

"There's something quite touching about that."

Birdie nodded. "Yes, there is. She wants what we all want: to belong. She's a remarkable child." Birdie sat up straight and watched for signposts. "Sometimes I get the feeling that child knows every single thing that's going on around her. She quietly takes it all in, files it away."

Birdie pointed to the next curve in the road. "The entrance Harold used is just around that bend. Some of the cemeteries around here prohibit rubbings, but I think we're safe here at St. Mary's. If not, we'll call Father Larry to get us out of jail."

"St. Mary's. Good choice."

"My suggestion," Birdie said.

"Of course it was. Killing two birds with one stone. And in a cemetery, most appropriately."

Nell parked near the cemetery office, a small stone building near the entrance. It was surrounded by flowering bushes and a small stand of pine trees. In the distance, over the tops of trees and houses, was the ocean, and everywhere else, up and down the gently rolling slopes of the grounds, were headstones and mounds, trees and flowering dogwoods, magnolias and small groves of pine and hawthorn trees. Bouquets of flower arrangements were planted in urns or simply laid gently on top of gentle rises in the earth.

"I think when the time comes, I could lay down here beneath one of these trees and be happy."

Birdie agreed, though she said that her own plan was to have her ashes scattered into the ocean just beyond her and Sonny Favazza's home. It's where he was, and where she should be, too. "Frolicking in the deep blue," she said, a twinkle lighting her eyes.

Birdie pointed to an area just beyond a granite bench positioned in a small sitting area, a stone angel protecting it from behind. "There they are."

Gabby Marietti and Ella knelt on the grass beside a flat gray headstone. Their bodies held great enthusiasm for the task at hand. Beside them, spilling from a cloth bag, were the tools of their trade: scissors, masking tape, paper, lumberman's chalk that they'd picked up at McClucken's, and a small spray bottle and brush for cleaning off dust before getting down to serious rubbing.

"We brought sandwiches," Birdie said, walking slowly so as not to frighten them, though Gabby looked like cemeteries were the least likely place in which to be frightened.

And perhaps, Nell thought, she was right. The feeling that covered St. Mary's Cemetery, its grass and flowers and grave markers, was one of total peace.

"Food!" Gabby sat back on her heels. "Cool. Ella and I are starving."

Ella wiped beads of perspiration from her forehead. "She speaks the truth. But we are getting quite good at this rubbing business."

"Show me," Nell said, and leaned over the stone Gabby was working on. She had taped a thin sheet of paper over the surface, and was gently rubbing with a fat piece of chalk. Miraculously, words and a subtle design of an angel entwined with flowers rose to the surface.

"Grace was her name. She was only three," Gabby said. She touched the paper with her finger. "They must have had a bad disease that year, because we found lots of kids' graves. I think it was polio. There are amazing stories all over these stones. You just have to look for them." She nodded to a stack of papers that already had rubbings on them. "Ella and I are giving them to the historical museum. Maybe I'll write down the stories so people will remember."

Birdie leafed through the rubbings while Nell unpacked the sandwiches.

"Wow," Gabby said, moving from tombstone to bench in an instant. She looked hungrily at the baguettes stuffed with prosciutto, tomatoes, mozzarella, and Harry's special walnut pesto sauce.

"Why don't you two get started?" Birdie said. "Nell and I are going to stop by the office for a minute."

Gabby's mouth was already full of sandwich as they turned away, and her words came out muffled.

"We found Moira's grave, Nonna," she said.

Birdie and Nell stopped and turned around.

"It's up there." She pointed to the top of the hill.

"Do you have a rubbing of it?" Nell looked over at the stack.

She shook her head. "I wanted it to be my very first rubbing. I wanted to do it for Finn. But there's no stone."

Birdie frowned. "No stone?"

Gabby's hair flew around her face as she shook her head. "Nothing. Only some flowers that needed water, so Ella cleaned and filled the vase. It was a lonely grave. Not like some of the others here, because . . ." She pulled her brows together, thinking. Then decided that was the end of her sentence, and she lowered her head, giving her full attention to the prosciutto.

A lonely grave. Certainly not what Finnegan would have wanted for the love of his life.

They turned and walked on over to the stone house. Before they could knock, the door was opened by a short elderly man. He looked at them silently, scanning their faces with small, beady eyes. In the next instant, a smile spread across his lined face and he threw his arms around Birdie, grabbing her in a tight hug.

For a moment, Nell wondered if Birdie could breathe, but before she could intervene, the man pulled away. He looked with pleasure from one woman to the other.

Birdie took a quick breath to regain her equilibrium. Then she focused on the man and began to laugh. "Oh my goodness, Henry Staab. I didn't know you were still with us." She laughed harder, and the hunched-over, gnomelike man did the same. Tiny wisps of white hair, scattered willy-nilly across a nearly bald head, flew in the breeze of his bobbing head.

"Birdie Favazza. My darlin' Birdie."

Nell looked from one to the other. Finally Birdie wiped the laughter from her eyes and introduced Henry to Nell.

"Ah, the Endicotts. I know of you, but don't get into town much anymore. I kinda like it here with my friends." He spread his short arms wide, encompassing the graves. "They listen. Good folks, the lot of them. Well, most, anyway."

He laughed again while Birdie explained to Nell that she and Henry had known each other a half-century ago.

Henry looked at Nell. "I once proposed to this fine lady when she was out here visiting some grave site or another. Turned me down, she did." The man's laughter was loud and gravelly.

Birdie laughed. "I'd forgotten all about you working out here."

"So it's an accident, our meeting like this? Then what brings you here, if not my charming self?"

"Moira Finnegan."

His smile faded.

"We wanted to visit her grave," Birdie said.

"Why's that?"

"You know that Finn died, don't you?"

"Course I do. He was murdered," Henry said. "Finn was a good man—used to bring me fish sometimes. Especially cod. He didn't deserve to end his days on earth like that. Now, lots of these folks here were ready to come out and call it a day, and that's as it should be. But no one has a right to send someone here. When it's your time, that's when you come."

"Like Moira," Nell said.

"Sure, like that, though it was too soon for her in my opinion. The old fisherman loved that lady like there was no tomorrow. Too bad she got that awful cancer."

"Do you remember when she died?"

"Course I do."

"May we see where she's buried?" Birdie asked. "With Finn gone, we thought it would be nice to pay our respects to her memory. It'd be nice if you'd go with us."

Henry looked up the hill, then back to Birdie and made a harrumphing sound, as if he suddenly had a million other things to do. But finally he pulled the door closed and shuffled his way up the hill.

The women followed silently, their eyes focused on the old man's bent back.

At the top of the hill, beneath a tree, was the vase of flowers Ella had refilled. A small sign, enclosed in plastic and affixed to the ground with a stake, read MOIRA FINNEGAN, and below, the dates that spanned her short, fifty-year-old life.

"That's it? Where is her tombstone? A monument?"

"Isn't one." Henry shoved his hands in the pockets of his baggy jeans. He took a step back and his back grew rigid. "Some folks don't, you know."

"The flowers?" Nell asked.

"Father Larry comes by to say hello once in a while. He was here to bury her, you know—sprinkled the water on the grave while Finn and I stood by. He said some prayers. Now he brings flowers. Probably does some praying, too."

"But Finnegan didn't?"

"Finn didn't like graveyards. Too many strangers here, he told me once."

Birdie chuckled and the sound relaxed Henry's stance, his shoulders slumping back into a curve.

"It's odd, though," Birdie said gently.

"Odd, schmod." Henry started to walk away, toward the safety of his office.

Birdie held back her words, and she and Nell quietly followed.

By the time they reached the door, Henry's expression had altered. He looked suddenly weary—and relieved. He turned around and looked at his old friend.

"Okay, so now you know. With Finn gone, things all a-shambles like they are with this murder hanging over our heads, I s'pose it's okay that you know." He looked intently at the two women, his shoulders seeming to square back with his words.

"She's not up there, is she?" Birdie said gently.

"Nope. She's not here. I did it for the old man. It was what he wanted. Didn't hurt no one, and sure as hell made the fisherman happy."

Chapter 32

They dropped Ella and Gabby at the house with their treasures, and while Birdie got them settled inside, Nell called Cass on her cell. She could barely hold in her excitement.

She had just gotten off the *Lady Lobster*, Cass said, but if Birdie could handle the fact that she hadn't had time to shower, she'd meet them in ten minutes.

"It's a date," Nell said, then turned the car toward Canary Cove. "Cass will meet us there with her keys in case we need them."

"When did she get keys?" Birdie asked as Nell drove around a mob of tourists spilling off a bus and into Harbor Road.

"Ben talked to Jerry Thompson about getting her a set. Even though the estate isn't settled, there didn't seem to be any reason why she couldn't go in and look around if she wanted to. They haven't arrested her for anything, at least not yet."

"Not ever. Rubbish. Foolish thought."

Nell turned onto the road that led to Canary Cove and Finnegan's land. "Have you had a chance to talk to Nick?" she asked. The teenager's revelation that the intruder's flashlight had only appeared on the first floor was puzzling. Even the drifter knew Finn lived upstairs. It wouldn't have been difficult for Nick to find out.

"No. But I'm going to." Her voice was steady, but tinged with anger, something Birdie rarely succumbed to. "It's time to stop the deception. I'm tired of it, Nell."

Nell nodded. Lies between friends could simmer until they became toxic. And Nick, in spite of everything, was a friend.

Cass was waiting at the gate. She had parked her truck in the parking area near the garden. "I felt uncomfortable," she said, "driving straight on in. Like it was mine or something."

"It is yours, sweetie," Nell said. "But if walking is more comfortable, we'll walk."

Nell parked next to Cass and she and Birdie piled out of the car. Arms linked, they walked down the drive toward Finnegan's house.

"It looks like we have company," Birdie said.

Parked in the gravel clearing ahead was an empty patrol car.

They looked around, then down toward the dock, but there didn't seem to be a soul in sight. They called out, but the only answer was from some hungry gulls dipping into the water at the end of the dock.

Cass shrugged and looked at the house. "This place looks like it could use a cleaning."

"Or perhaps a complete gutting." Birdie glanced at the dangling sign on the window. TIMOTHY PULASKI, DDS. "It's a mess. Poor Finn."

Cass walked up to the dental-office door and tried a key, then another. The handle turned and she pushed the door open, then looked back at Nell and Birdie. "Now, exactly why are we going in here?" she asked.

"The police said there were some old dental records left behind," Birdie said.

"And the body they dug up didn't have any teeth, remember?" Nell prompted, walking past Cass and into the dusty rooms. She stepped around a pile of mice droppings.

"I remember that they said the dental records wouldn't help them out for that very reason," Cass said, looking eye to eye at a spider hanging down in front of her.

"Right," Nell said.

"So why are we here?"

"Dental records tell you more than the placement of a person's teeth." Birdie walked over to a filing cabinet and pulled out a drawer. She reminded Cass of the ugly rumors that Moira and the dentist might have been overly friendly.

"Which was crazy," Cass said.

"Absolutely, at least in the twisted way they were presented. But I think Moira *was* grateful to Dr. Pulaski. And here's why. . . ."

Cass listened while Nell laid out their hunches, complete with Father Northcutt's comment about Moira's health and what they'd discovered at St. Mary's cemetery.

Cass grinned. "It makes good sense . . . if you're right."

"Voila," Birdie said, and pulled out a yellowed folder with a typewritten label reading MOIRA FINNEGAN.

They took it outside, spread it open on the hood of the police car, and with the help of sunlight highlighting Dr. Pulaski's precise notes, learned why Moira Finnegan—and Finnegan himself—were grateful to Dr. Timothy Pulaski. And it didn't have anything to do with romance.

Father Northcutt suspected.

And Finn, of course, knew.

But probably no one else on earth.

Moira Finnegan had no teeth.

And Timothy Pulaski saved her from a lifetime of embarrassment by building her dentures, which he repaired and replaced as needed.

Moira Finnegan, for her part, made sure he was well fed.

Nell tucked the file in her purse.

Birdie pointed across the drive to the spot where the rotting door leaned against a tree. "Come, Cass. Look at this."

Stepping over the debris, they walked single file around the bushes and scrub trees to the spot where Gabby had left her flowers and the newly dug earth formed a mound of dirt.

Cass stared at the spot where a body had been.

They walked around the loose earth gingerly, as if the body were still there, noticing the things no one would have paid attention to: the rosebushes planted in between the brush and lovingly pruned, the bushes cut back and the tiny birdhouse swinging from a low-hanging maple branch.

It was a tended gravesite. A loving place.

Moira Finnegan's grave wasn't lonely at all.

"It's an amazing love story," Nell said a short while later. They stood in the driveway, looking around at the house, the bushes that hid Moira's special spot.

"All these years he kept everyone out to protect her." Cass shook her head.

They felt like cheering. A happy story. A glorious ending.

"And he won't be haunting me anymore," Cass said. "She looked up at the sky. "We did it, Finn. We're halfway there. . . ."

They all felt giddy. Teenagers who had come upon a lovely secret.

Birdie looked again at the Timothy Pulaski sign. "That dear old man. He was just as we thought: sweet and good at cavities." Her eyes traveled from the office door to the next office. "Is there a key on that ring to the other office?"

Cass shrugged. "We can see."

It took three tries, but finally Cass found one that turned. "This door had probably not been locked for years until the police put these new dead bolts on."

They walked in tentatively, invisible webs brushing their faces. Every surface—the old leather chair, a desk, a clothes tree—was covered with dust. It was a ghostly space, eerie in its coat of disuse.

Nell knew where Birdie's thoughts had drifted. If the flashlight intruder, Nick, hadn't gone upstairs that day, he had been searching these two offices. A dental office and this space. *What was he looking for?*

Birdie ran her fingers along the back of the gray chair, and a line of dark green leather peeked through.

"I'm not a great housekeeper, but this is something else," Cass said. She coughed and sent a flurry of dust flying across the room.

"We're leaving our mark." Nell pointed to their footprints on the floor—Birdie's sneakers, her sandals, Cass' flip-flops were clean outlines on the dirty floor.

Nell frowned. "But it looks like we're not alone."

She pointed to another set of prints, bold and clear, circling the room, as if a ghost were there with them.

Cass knelt down. "Weird," she said. They looked down, their eyes tracing the prints from the door to a small file cabinet. The drawer was still open. Inside was nothing but a dusty outline of once-stored files.

"It's been cleaned out," Cass said.

"But recently. These are fresh tracks."

"The police?" Cass wondered.

But it didn't look like a police search. It was more focused, as if someone were looking for something specific.

And found it.

"I wonder who rented this space," Nell said. She walked over to a desk pushed up against the back wall in front of the window. Pushing aside a decaying curtain, she looked out at the dock, toward a few boats coming into the harbor.

The wooden desk was covered in gray like the rest of the room, a pencil jar to one side, an old desk mat. She opened the drawer and found yellow pads, more pencils. "There aren't any business cards," she said.

"What's that?" Birdie pointed to an object on the floor beside the desk.

Nell picked it up and blew away the dust. It was a leather picture frame, green and gold. She held it close to the window, her finger tracing the broken glass.

She gasped. "Oh, my lord," she whispered.

Birdie and Cass were at her side in an instant. Nell handed Birdie the frame.

The photo was yellowed from sunlight and distorted by the broken glass, but there was no mistaking who smiled out from the frame. Birdie Favazza, dressed in a soft blue dress, standing beside a handsome man who wore a flower in his lapel. His arm was wrapped around the woman at his side.

It was Birdie's turn to gasp. She stared at the photograph. Then she looked around the office more carefully, stripping it of the dust and dirt, focusing, remembering. She looked at the photo again. "It was our wedding day."

She rubbed the glass with a corner of her shirt, wiping it clean.

"Hello, Joseph," she said, a soft smile filling her face.

Her eyes settled on the open filing cabinet and the footprints on the floor. "These two buildings, this one and the one across the drive, were identical. I'd simply imagined Joseph a few yards to the west. I suppose because as the years passed, it was the more respectable of the two. But this one . . . This one must have been his office. Of course—that's why he knew Dr. Pulaski. Oh, my . . ."

Her eyes returned to the picture frame, then over to the empty cabinet drawer.

"Nicholas, Nicholas," she murmured to herself. "What have you been up to?"

Daylight was fading when they walked back down Finn's drive to Canary Cove Road, feeling a lightness that came with rediscovering the past. Finn's Moira. And Joseph Marietti. More than they had bargained for.

"Have we been here an hour? A week? A day?" Birdie said. "When one is unburying the dead, time escapes. Does it not?"

Nell smiled. A day of revelations—and couched in the middle of them, one thing was becoming clear: Nicholas Marietti's habit of harboring secrets was about to end.

They stopped at the end of the drive just as Tommy Porter appeared around the bend, his jacket tossed over one shoulder, his eyes tired.

Instinctively, Nell pushed the edge of the dental file farther down in her purse. She wanted to talk to Ben about the transfer of Moira's casket before handing it over to the police. There were a few promises that needed to be made before the story of Finnegan's grave was told to the police.

"Tommy, you look like something the cat dragged in," Birdie said. Perspiration dotted his forehead and spotted the front of his uniform shirt.

"Feel that way, too. What're you guys doing here?"

"I'm just checking to see if these keys work," Cass said.

Tommy looked at the key chain. "So . . . so, what'll you do with this place, Cass?"

"It's not really mine yet."

"Sure, it is. It's all paperwork now, but it will be yours free and clear soon." He paused, then looked at Cass again. "I know this is a bad time for you, Cass. It isn't fair. None of us think you'd do anything like what happened to old man Finnegan. No way. It's just the process. We gotta find the guy who did this. Then everyone can breathe clean air again and be about their business."

"You're a good guy, Tommy," she said. "Thanks."

"Are you here on official business?" Nell asked.

"Sort of." He looked at Cass again. "I s'pose you heard I let Beverly Walden take Finn's boat."

"I heard that."

"Stupid thing to do. I know. But she was his daughter—or I thought she was, anyway—and I figured it'd all be hers. I found her back here, looking around. She wanted the boat in the worst way. She looked at me, her eyes all big and sad."

Birdie smiled. "Tommy, I'm surprised at you, falling for such wiles."

Tommy shrugged, a blush spreading above the collar of his uniform. He stuck a finger into the collar of his shirt, tugging at it. "I . . . I felt sorry for her, I guess." And then his voice changed, his words edged with anger. "But no more feeling sorry for her, for sure. No more of that."

"You sound mad," Cass said. "What gives?"

"The chief told me to go get that boat back. He thought she might feel threatened or something and said to take someone along if I needed backup, but I didn't think I'd need it. So I called her yesterday, said I was coming by today for the boat. Told her exactly what time."

"She was okay with giving it up?"

"No. She hung up on me. But I called again later and left a message so she wouldn't forget."

He looked over at the patrol car. "I figured I'd leave my car here, walk over to her place and drive the boat back. It's yours, Cass, not hers."

"Doesn't matter, Tommy. If it means that much to her—"

Tommy interrupted. "Don't go there, Cass. Hell, who knows what that woman may have done?"

They stared at him.

"I mean . . . she sure had motive—or thought she did, anyway. She wanted Finn's money in the worst way. So don't go giving away boats, Cass. At least not to her."

Cass looked back toward the dock. "So, where is it?"

"Gone."

"The boat or Beverly?" Birdie asked.

"Both. She wasn't there at the house, and the boat was gone. A neighbor said she'd gone out early last night carrying a picnic basket and a couple bottles of wine, and she hasn't seen her since."

Nell remembered the Cheese Closet sack that Beverly had with her in the tea shop. She had plans, she'd said. A celebration? But that was when she thought she had an inheritance to celebrate.

"She was dressed in a sexy outfit, the neighbor said. All dolled up, was how she put it. She said something about Jimmy Choos, whoever he is. Maybe the guy she was meeting."

Nell smiled. "She was alone?"

He nodded. "She told the neighbor she was meeting a friend."

"Strange," Birdie said.

Tommy nodded. "I went by the galleries to see if anyone knew where she was, but no one had seen her since yesterday. So I walked back here to pick up my car."

Tommy shuffled his feet, his polished shoes gathering gravel dust. "Chief'll kill me," he said.

"Why? Because maybe Beverly Walden had plans for a romantic evening? Spent the night with someone? It's been done before," Cass said.

Tommy looked at her blankly. Then he kicked a stone so hard it flew all the way over to the rotting door and bounced off into the brush.

"No. Because I may have let a murderer get away."

Chapter 33

It was late afternoon by the time Nell dropped Birdie off and drove up her own driveway, crackers, milk, and fruit in a bag at her side. Ben's car wasn't in the drive, and she silently cheered his absence, knowing she desperately needed a shower—not only to wash away the stress and fatigue of the day, but to think. A few moments to put her thoughts in order. If, in fact, there was any order.

She put away the groceries and headed upstairs. Suddenly things were happening quickly, and with each new revelation, Finn's murderer seemed to be walking closer to them, heralding his presence.

And he wasn't coming out of the past, seeking revenge for a long-buried relative. The grave nestled in Finn's circle of rosebushes was dug with tenderness, a testimony to an old fisherman's love.

Nor, she felt sure, was the murderer a gracious Italian. The secrets he harbored were still there, still lurking like a blemish on a lovely painting. But she suspected they wouldn't be hidden for long.

Leaving her clothes in a heap on the bedroom floor, she stepped into the shower and lifted her face to the spray. Slowly she began to relax, the water massaging her body, loosening her muscles. Clearing her mind.

She smiled into the heated shower, her thoughts moving back to the circle of rosebushes hidden in the forest that was Finnegan's land. There, protected by his overgrown bushes, discarded debris, and no-trespassing signs, he kept his memories safe and his Moira close, settling her in her favorite spot. *Did he spread rose petals down first,* she wondered, *a blanket of them to cushion her bed?* Nell's smile lingered on the thought as the scent of ginger soap filled the shower and bubbles ran down her body in rivulets.

Finally, reluctantly, she stepped from the shower and into the steamy room, out of the fairy-tale story of Moira and Finn.

And into real life, where a murderer walked free in their midst.

Ben was in the kitchen when Nell came down, her hair still damp and curling around her cheeks. He was laying thick swordfish steaks on a baking sheet and coating them with spicy chipotle sauce.

"Compliments of our friends." He nodded toward the deck, where Danny and Cass stood, side by side, talking.

"They're doing a lot of that these days," Ben said.

"Talking?"

Ben nodded. "Cass even seems to listen . . . sometimes, anyway. I had a long talk with Danny earlier today over a couple of beers. He understands Cass, I think—maybe even better than we do. He knows her life's been a maelstrom these past months and that she needs her space. He gets it. So he's there when she wants to talk. Disappears when he thinks she needs space. And she seems to be coming back for more. Leaning on him some. And learning that she doesn't crumble in a million pieces when someone holds her up."

Nell wrapped her arms around him, listening to his words and watching through the window as Danny teased smiles from Cass, and vice versa. It was a lovely dance—moving away, then back together, staying in step.

Ben breathed in the soapy smell of his wife. "I was tempted to join you up there, but something about the clothes on the floor and the somber silence in the bathroom made me think differently."

"I wasn't singing, you mean?" Nell kissed him.

"I mean that the vibe you left in your trail made me think you'd had a busy day, one you needed to pull apart quietly and alone."

She kissed him again, letting the warmth of his body push away the uncertainty of her thoughts.

"Are you two at it again?" Izzy came across the family room. She spread her arms around Nell and Ben and nuzzled her head into the space between.

Sam was behind her, carrying a large bowl of salad. He put it on the counter and laughed at the group hug. "Am I failing on the hug front? What am I—chopped liver?"

Izzy broke away and tilted her head back to Sam, encouraging involvement. He complied with a kiss.

"It seems that kind of day, doesn't it? Hugs. Touches," Nell said.

Ben already had the martini mixings going and moved back to it, the sound of his shaker greeting the next surge of friends.

Birdie set a blueberry crisp on the counter and gave Ben a tight squeeze. "Sounds like we're just in time. And how intuitive of you, dear Ben, to know we might need a bit of your magic. It's been what Gabby aptly calls an arduous day, although hers resulted in some lovely grave rubbings. Mine had a few lovely answers, but those were accompanied by a head full of troubling questions."

"I think the questions hurt more the closer they come to resolution," Nell said. "Where're Nick and Gabby?" She looked at Birdie, wondering if they'd talked.

"They're out cruising on the Scaglia boat," Sam said. "Gabby was helping me scrub the trim when she spotted Sal's boat. It seems she has an eye for expensive ones."

"She asked Sal to take her out?" Nell frowned.

Sam laughed. "No. She told him. But in a very gracious way."

"Did Beatrice go?" Jane Brewster asked. She walked over to the island, her arms filled with flowers from the community garden. Ham was close behind, a bottle of wine in hand.

"No. Gabby suggested it, but Sal explained that Beatrice gets seasick sitting on their dock. She's not a big boat lover."

"It'd be hard to wear Jimmy Choos on a boat, anyway," Izzy said as Cass and Danny walked in the room, Danny's hand on Cass' back.

Jimmy Choos and boats. Twice in one day, Nell thought, though Beatrice's apparently would never be touched by salt water. Beverly, on the other hand . . .

Ben was watching her, reading her thoughts. He poured a

round of drinks. "I stopped by the station on my way home to ask if things were squared away with Beverly Walden. If she'd calmed down or caused any problems." He looked at Nell, then Birdie and Cass.

"Tommy was there and mentioned seeing you three. He explained about the boat. It seems she's gone off with it. No one knows where she is."

"She's missing, Tommy said." Birdie took a glass from Ben.

"Missing?" Izzy asked. "What does that mean?"

They explained what Tommy had discovered, complete with a description of Beverly's outfit.

"Jeez. Jimmy Choos?" Izzy's brows shot up. "She must have been trying to impress someone in a big way."

"Kind of a crazy thing to do," Sam, the practical boatman, said. "So she was meeting someone? Picking someone up?"

"So it seems," Ben said.

"It must have been important to her. She was supposed to give a report at our Arts Association meeting today but never showed up, and that's not like her," Jane said.

"The police think she may have taken off."

"Why?" several voices asked at once.

"Maybe she felt the police were going to look at her more carefully—and she would have been right," Ben said. "The money she thought she was getting when Finn died is a sound motive for murder. They need more—fingerprints, the murder weapon. Something. But the pressure is on, and Beverly is a prime suspect."

"But why would she take off in a boat, wearing a fancy dress and taking along wine and cheese? Do you know how much those shoes cost?" Izzy said.

Ben resumed his ritual, shaking the container. "That's the question of the hour," he finally said.

Without an answer to the question, it faded away, and people began to move about, filling small plates with cheese, admiring a new painting Jane had brought to Nell, shaking off the uncertainty of Beverly Walden's innocence or guilt, presence or absence.

Ben looked at Nell. "I have a feeling other things happened today." There was concern in his voice.

"Yes, they did. But I need a promise from you before we talk about it. A solemn one."

"A promise," he repeated.

"I need you to talk to Jerry Thompson to make sure Henry Staab doesn't get in one iota of trouble for something he did years ago to help a dear friend."

Ben looked at her curiously. "Henry Staab? That old man from the cemetery? I didn't know he was still around."

Nell shook her head. *Poor Henry. Buried before his time twice in one day.* "He's very much alive. He was a friend of Finn's. He showed us Moira's grave over at St. Mary's, complete with flowers Father Larry religiously puts there in her memory." She paused. "So . . . the promise?"

Jane looked up from slicing bread. "A promise?"

"Intrigue," Izzy said, moving to Nell's side.

"Sure, if you think it's important, I promise," Ben said, "So, Moira is at St. Mary's. That makes sense," he prompted.

"Except she isn't. There's a grave there. But Moira's not in it. I suspect no one is."

Ben frowned. Then, slowly, the realization of Nell's message sunk in and a slow smile spread across his face. "Well, I'll be—"

Nell nodded. "Finn talked Henry Staab into pretending to bury Moira at St. Mary's. He even had Father Northcutt do a graveside ceremony after the mass, saying a couple of prayers and blessing the casket. But after Father Larry left, instead of lowering it into the ground, Henry Staab and Finn lifted the casket into the back of Finn's old pickup and moved her to the spot she loved more than any other place on earth."

Izzy's mouth fell open. Sam came up behind her, wrapping an arm around her, a smile on his face.

"Wow. That explains everything, doesn't it?" Jane said. She smiled, too, then sniffed and pulled a tissue from her pocket. "What a loving man. It's why he didn't want people trampling around over there."

"And why he let the place turn into a jungle pit." Ham was smiling, too.

It was a love story that would be retold for a long time to come when memories of the old fisherman were brought up and passed around dinner tables. A story, Nell hoped, that would replace the more tragic one of Finn's death.

"He couldn't handle the thought of Moira being all the way across town, in a place filled with 'strangers,'" Birdie said. "But the authorities and powers that be wouldn't have taken kindly to a grave on private land, right next to the water, so it remained his secret, and he did what he had to do to keep it private and to keep his Moira close."

Cass and Danny stood at the edge of the group, listening quietly.

Then Danny said, "Finn talked to me once about Moira, how much he loved her. His love was as real that day as if she were right there beside him. Finn loved. That's what he did." He looked at Cass. "He loved. Fiercely."

And that said it all—except for what it didn't say. The man who loved with a giant heart was dead. Murdered.

Hours later, they settled on the deck chairs, stomachs filled with grilled swordfish and brown butter sauce, and Norah Jones' husky voice and nimble fingers playing in the background. It was almost normal.

Nell looked over at Birdie.

She was checking her phone. When she got up and headed inside, Nell followed.

"Nick just sent me a text message," Birdie explained as they walked into the kitchen. "He's coming over."

"Now?"

"Yes. There's been some news, he said."

"About Gabby?"

"No. She's home with Ella and Harold, safe and sound."

Nell opened the oven door and Birdie pulled out the blueberry crisp, lifting it to the island.

"Is everything all right?"

"I don't know. It was cryptic, short. But odd that he'd want to come at this hour. I was actually hoping to talk to him when I got home tonight about what we discovered this afternoon. Confront him about the office, I guess I mean, and demand he tell me why he was in that building." She looked around for a spoon. "But Gabby's fine, and that's the important thing."

Nell held the plates while Birdie spooned out the dessert, topping each helping with a scoop of ice cream.

"I don't have a good feeling about this, Nell."

Nell pushed away her own uneasiness. She pulled out a tray and began filling it with plates. "He probably just wants a piece of the dessert."

But they both knew that it wasn't Ella's blueberry crisp bringing Nick out at this hour.

Birdie carried the tray outside while Nell waited at the front door.

She looked up at the moon, nearly full, its light casting shadows across the street and lawns of the neighborhood. In the distance, an animal's howl broke the stillness. A plaintive cry.

Headlights pierced through the moonlight, and seconds later the blue Altima pulled up behind Izzy and Sam's car.

She waited, holding open the screen door.

"Am I turning into a bad penny?" he said with a worried half smile, kissing Nell on each cheek.

"I hope not," Nell said. "Come. Everyone's out back."

Ben had already poured Nick a drink.

He took it gratefully, then sat in the chair Sam had pulled over from the dining table.

"It's not good news," he began.

The deck grew quiet and the moon seemed to grow in size while they waited. Its bright white light fell through the trees and across the deck. Nick's face was lit, as if he were on stage.

Birdie was watching Nick with the same apprehension that rattled around inside Nell. *Nick's lie,* whatever he was hiding. Was it yet another disruption to their summer? She closed her eyes briefly, her words a whisper inside her head. *Do not be guilty of anything more than surprising Birdie with a grandchild, of bringing Gabby into our lives, Nick Marietti. Do not . . .*

But Nick's news had nothing to do with Nick. He leaned forward and began to talk, his distinctive accent filling the deck. "Gabby and I went out on the Scaglia boat today. On our way back in, we saw a couple patrol boats circling around, lights flashing. They were towing a boat back to shore. It looked like trouble, so Sal turned his yacht around and headed in the other direction to get us away from whatever was going on. That boat is fast, let me tell you, and quiet. He was protecting Gabby. But it's hard to get anything past her. She spotted the boat, pointed to it. Even from a distance, she knew whose it was."

He looked over at Cass.

"It was Finnegan's boat," he said.

The *Moira*, the boat that Beverly Walden had taken out to sea in a pair of Jimmy Choo shoes.

Nick took a deep breath. "Well, we went on around, circled a few coves. Sal assured us the boat probably just ran out of fuel. Happens more than you'd think, he said.

"But when we got back to the club, the police were there. Some reporters were lurking around. There wasn't any way to avoid the confusion, though Sal tried his best. Before we could stop her, Gabby climbed out and ran over to where they'd towed the boat. It was as if she wanted to claim the boat, protect it somehow."

"Was Beverly there?" Cass asked.

"No," Nick answered. "There was nothing there but the boat, picnic things—cheese, glasses, some beach towels, an empty, broken bottle of wine—and a piece of torn dress caught on a bolt on the side of the boat.

"They're looking for a body," he finished.

Chapter 34

It took the police until dawn to find Beverly Walden's body, although the body actually found them, was how Tommy Porter put it. It washed up on shore right near the yacht club, as if looking for the boat it had lost.

And it took only a few hours more to piece together what had happened.

Beverly Walden had been poisoned.

"The wine was laced with enough phenobarbital to kill a horse," Tommy told Izzy as they waited in line together at Coffee's. "The chief said it was an amateur job, if someone was trying to make it look like a suicide. As if we wouldn't find the poison. And it gets worse," Tommy said. "They found things over on the island indicating someone else had climbed onto the boat when it was anchored. The body itself had bruises, probably from getting pushed over the edge—and a weight was tied to one ankle.

"It looked desperate, the chief said. Definitely not done by a pro."

"I suppose there's some relief in that," Nell said. They were in their favorite back booth at Harry Garozzo's deli, hoping Harry would be too busy on a Saturday to join in the conversation. He was a veritable font of rumor, and they had had their fill of that.

"Tommy was pretty sure Beverly had killed Finn," Izzy added. "This sets them back."

"I knew it wasn't suicide," Cass said. "Beverly wanted something desperately, but it wasn't death."

"Two murders . . ." Birdie said. "They have to be related, of course."

"The police think so."

"It's difficult to put them together," Cass said. "I'm not proud of this, but I think I wanted Beverly to be responsible for Finn's death, maybe to justify the way I felt about her," Cass said.

"You don't need her to be a murderer to justify your feelings, Cass. You didn't like Beverly because of the way she treated the man she thought was her father, a man you loved and respected. The way she acted was shameful," Birdie said.

They all agreed. And the fact that anyone would cast even an iota of suspicion on Cass, who truly loved Finnegan, made it all the worse. But those suspicions were out there. And they would stay out there until the real murderer was behind bars.

"I don't think any of us thought Beverly killed him. Not really," Izzy said.

Nell agreed. "Finnegan was killed because he knew something that someone didn't want him to know. It's simple. Revealing what he knew—whatever it was—would hurt that person. So he or she killed Finnegan."

"Beverly must have known the same thing that Finnegan knew," Izzy said.

"Or caused it, perhaps? Been involved in it? Remember, he was furious with her," Birdie said.

"That's right," Nell added. "So Finnegan knew whatever it was and was going to do something about it. He was murdered to stop him. For some reason, Beverly wasn't a threat to the murderer at first. Then maybe . . . maybe when it became known she didn't have any money, she wasn't needed, either?"

"But to kill someone because they lost an inheritance? There has to be more to it," Cass said.

They fell silent, sipping iced tea and trying to capture random thoughts, forcing order or sense into them, while the background din of Harry's deli offered a comforting, familiar grounding.

"Let's go back to Finn again," Izzy said. "We know Finn was

upset with Beverly, something she was doing. But she wasn't afraid of Finn. And his threats didn't seem to deter her."

Izzy's analysis seemed to fit the conversation Merry overheard. And also the one Gabby heard between Finn and Beverly. "So if Beverly wasn't threatened by Finn, who would be?" Nell asked. "Who was threatened enough by Finn to kill him?"

Margaret Garozzo appeared with four grilled tomato and mozzarella paninis, each with a cup of cold cucumber soup on the side. The smell of fresh grilled tomatoes and basil filled the small booth.

"You're keeping Harry away, aren't you?" Birdie smiled.

Margaret just chuckled and walked away to refill iced-tea glasses at a nearby table.

Izzy picked up the conversation. "Okay. Beverly and Finn argued. What was it Merry heard him say? She was ruining someone's life?"

"But she was such a loner. Whose life could she possibly have been ruining?"

"And why? I didn't like her, but I didn't think she was malicious. If she were, she would have done more to me. Don't you think?"

Birdie nodded agreement.

"Willow said Finn was their self-appointed night watchman," Nell said. "When he couldn't sleep, he patrolled Canary Cove."

"He also went out in the *Moira* when he couldn't sleep. He told me once he'd cruise around the cove and look up at the stars, and Moira would talk to him. His midnight love, he called her. So he could have picked up on any late-night trysts. I bet he knew plenty that was going on."

"And since Beverly was Moira's daughter, he would have latched on to her behavior aggressively, wanting to be sure it honored her mother, not disgraced her," Izzy said. "Her indiscretions would have been way more personal than those of the old mayor he threatened." She took a bite and chewed thoughtfully. Tiny flecks of basil floated onto her plate.

"Even if it was none of his business," Birdie added.

"That's right," Nell said. "Angus said it was a horrible habit Finn had, minding other people's business."

"Infidelity, in Finn's religion, was one of the deadly sins."

"Do you suppose anyone else around Canary Cove noticed anything? Ham and Jane haven't said much, but what about the neighbor, the one who saw Beverly leave in the boat?"

Cass put her sandwich down. "That's Jake Risso's aunt June. Pete and Andy used to mow her lawn. She's kind of a shut-in, Andy says."

"Shut-ins need visitors." Izzy's brows lifted with suggestion.

Cass looked around the table. "Okay. I'll go talk to her if one of you comes with me. Sometimes I can be . . . how should I say . . . *indelicate*?"

They all laughed, and Cass laughed, too.

Then Nell grew serious. "I sound like Ben, but we need to remember that we're talking about a murderer. Someone who took two people's lives. No one should go anywhere alone."

The thought that two of them could defend themselves when one couldn't wasn't entirely reasonable, and they all knew it, but it didn't matter. There was comfort and security, if not real safety, in one another's company.

Nell took another bite out of her sandwich and looked around the restaurant. It was rare to have this kind of privacy during lunch—especially with the news buzz blanketing Sea Harbor like a nor'easter. She was sure that in quiet corners and not-so-quiet patios, all talk focused on the artist from Canary Cove who had been swept onto the shore last night. Finn's almost-adopted daughter. Murdered.

Somehow the relationship between the two would bring a certain comfort to people, Nell suspected. It was a family affair. Those outside the family were safe. Not many people knew Beverly Walden, and although everyone knew Finnegan, few called him a close friend. So the crime could be removed, set apart, and talked about from a comfortable distance.

"Look," Cass said, chewing a mouthful of sandwich and pointing across the restaurant to a table near the window.

Beatrice and Sal Scaglia were deep in conversation. Beatrice talking; Sal listening.

"I ran into Beatrice here yesterday," Nell said. "Outside. She was tense about something. When her cell rang, she jumped on it as if it were a lifeline, or a line to pull her away from me, anyway."

She looked over at the table again. "She left in a hurry and dropped a piece of paper in the street. I'd forgotten about it until this minute." She searched in her purse and pulled out the crumpled scrap of paper, then smoothed it out on the table.

B. W. 22 Coastal Road.

"That's Beverly Walden's address. Why would Beatrice have that?" Izzy asked.

Cass looked at the paper scrap. "It kind of makes sense," she said, lowering her voice. "She's always had her own set of plans for Finn's land. When she thought Beverly was going to inherit it, she probably paid her a visit, getting her name in early."

Nell shook her head. "She did that the day after Finn died. But she visited her at the gallery, not her house."

"A follow-up visit? Beatrice is persistent," Izzy suggested.

They looked at the paper scrap again. Nell slipped it back into her purse. "It could be anything or nothing, I suppose. A name to add to her campaign list, maybe."

"You don't sound convinced," Cass said.

"I don't know. It's logical, but . . ." Nell took another bite of the warm panini and looked over at Beatrice and Sal. "No, you're right. It must be that," she said finally.

"Do you suppose Beatrice will come after me for the property now?" Cass asked, wiping a trace of sauce from her mouth.

"No doubt," Izzy said. "And for all your talk, Cass Halloran, you'll listen. And you'll probably end up doing something nice for the city, and Beatrice will be your new best friend."

With all the turmoil, no one had talked about Finn's land or Cass' inheritance. But there was no doubt in anyone's mind that

Cass would honor Finn and do exactly, as he had wisely said, what was right.

"Hello, ladies." A familiar voice filled the booth. Harry pressed his palms flat on the table and leaned in, bringing the smell of basil and garlic with him. He cast a quick look over his shoulder, then focused back on his captive audience. "What are you hearing about that girl? Dead. Murdered, they tell me."

"That's right, Harry. It's not a good thing," Birdie said.

"Folks are talking. Said she was out to get Finn's money to buy her a husband."

Izzy smiled sweetly. "Harry, did you say that about me before I got married?"

Harry guffawed. "But here's the thing: she came in here lots these past few weeks, but always alone. Like she didn't have any friends. But she was a nice-looking gal—I told her so myself. And these past couple weeks, a sexy one, too."

"Harry, Harry," Cass said.

"It's the gospel truth. Low-cut dresses. Streaks in her hair and falling all loose like they do. Makeup. Not trashy, but out to please someone, for sure. She was feeling it, believe me. You can tell those things when you've been around the block a few times, like I have."

So even Harry thought Beverly was in love, or wanting to be in love. Or needed by someone in a way that brought joy to her life.

"But like I said," Harry continued, "she was always alone. Never with a guy—or girl. Whatever. She'd buy sandwiches and antipasto, eggplant parmigiana, and she loved my pasta primavera something fierce. I teased her the other day about how often she got takeout, but she told me she never had anyone to teach her to cook and she didn't know diddly-squat about turning on a stove. So it'd be our little secret that she hadn't made the food herself."

"So you think she was entertaining someone?"

"Oh, I'm sure of it. And passing off Harry's fine food as her own, that's what she was doing. Hell, I was flattered. It was fine with me as long as she paid for it."

Margaret walked over and touched Harry on the arm, whispering that his pot was boiling over. "Come, my dear," she said sweetly. "Let the ladies talk." And Harry, looking back over his shoulder with eyes rolling, followed her.

Izzy looked at her watch, shoved a handful of bills beneath her bowl, and slid out of the booth. "Gabby and I have a class this afternoon." She looked at Birdie. "Can you believe she's filled our town with crocheted beanies? It's the in thing. One of the Rockport boutiques wants to sell them."

"Imagine that," Birdie said, her smile dripping with pride. "You be off, Izzy dear."

She looked at Cass and Nell as they pulled bills from purses and gathered their things. "And the three of us?" she asked expectantly.

"I believe it's a perfect day to visit a shut-in," Nell replied.

Nell drove toward Canary Cove, then up the hill to Coastal Road, a dead-end street that anchored a block of small houses backing up to the sea. Modest homes with million-dollar views.

Number 22 was at the end of the street. Cass pointed to the house next door. "Aunt June," she said.

A gray-haired lady with glasses was standing on tiptoe, picking weeds out of a window box.

JUNE RISSO was printed on the mailbox.

Aunt June was delighted to have company. In minutes she had settled her visitors on the back patio and insisted they try her lemon cake and mint tea. And then she proceeded to tell them everything she knew about the house next door.

"I loved it when Moira and Finn lived there, but the house became sad when they moved out. So I was happy to have Beverly move in. Noise, laughter—that's what I was wanting."

"So you became friends?" Nell asked.

"Well, no. Not like I'd hoped. She was very busy with her painting and all. She kept to herself until recently."

"Recently?" Cass helped herself to another lemon cake.

June beamed, then continued. "She started going out at night, later than the usual date. My bedroom's right there." She pointed to the back windows next to the patio. "I go to bed early these days. One gets tired, you know."

"You could hear things from the street all the way back here?" Cass asked.

"Oh, no, no, dear." June's round face smiled at Cass. "Beverly came and went this way, back here." She pointed to the steps that led down to the water. "By boat. Most of us along Coastal Road have little boats that can take us into the harbor in no time at all, or to the club, to the beach. It's lovely. Like living in Venice, I suppose, although I've never traveled abroad."

"But she didn't have a boat until a few days ago."

June frowned. "Well, now, that's true, dear." She pushed her index finger into her cheek to help her remember. "That's it, of course. She was picked up—that's what happened. I would hear the motor go putt, putt, putt, the way they do. The dinghy would slow down at the dock. And off they'd go, into the night. It was quite romantic."

"Did you ever see the boat?"

June blushed, as if ashamed to be watching her neighbor's comings and goings with such diligence. "To be truthful, yes, I got up once or twice, wanting to be sure no one was breaking in. I'm single, you know. And there she'd be, usually carrying a bottle of wine and a picnic basket, walking down the hill to the dock, trying not to disturb me. I was happy she was having a good time."

"Did she ever have friends come to the house?"

June thought about that while she sipped her tea. "No, I don't believe so. She must have loved boats. That's the way she liked to travel. Lots of people do. Of course, you can't take a boat to the malls."

"But they're good for getting around Cape Ann," Nell agreed.

June nodded, brushing flakes of cake off her lap. "The girl wasn't one to invite conversation. She never talked to me about her work or her beau, just a quick hello or good-bye. And as for the back-door gentleman—that's the name I gave him—I never got a good look at him. Sunglasses can change a whole face, and the distance, the light—they all play havoc with this vision of mine." She touched the rim of the thick glasses that magnified her brown eyes.

When the cakes were finished, their glasses emptied, and June began talking about a nap, they took their leave.

"You have quite a green thumb," Nell said, looking at the crimson-colored geraniums filling the flower box just outside the front door. "What gorgeous flowers."

June looked at Nell as if she had said something extraordinary. "Flowers, of course! How could I forget?" June laughed at herself. "Someone sent flowers to Beverly—more than once. Gorgeous bouquets. One time Beverly wasn't home, and the delivery boy left them with me. They filled my whole house with the loveliest fragrance."

"Do you know who they were from?"

June frowned at Cass. "Of course I don't. How would I know that?"

"Cass meant which *florist*," Nell said quickly. It wasn't what Cass meant at all, but Nell knew June would never confess to reading someone else's card.

"The florist. Oh, of course." The smile came back. "I walk down there myself sometimes. It's that lovely little shop on Canary Cove Road. Such beautiful arrangements—and all with a touch of art."

"She was seeing someone who owned a boat," Nell said, driving slowly down the curvy Coastal Road.

"So that's everyone we know," Cass said, "or just about. Danny doesn't have one yet, so we can drop him from the list."

That was true. Everyone had a boat. But not everyone who had a boat sent flowers to Beverly Walden.

The flower shop was nearly empty when they walked in, and Birdie immediately spotted a small Christmas cactus and held it up, admiring it.

Nell and Cass walked over to examine a display of ceramic vases, and gave Birdie space to work her magic with the shop clerk.

It took little time, and they soon left the shop with three Christmas cacti, a bouquet of roses for Ella, and a slip of paper.

Nell stared at the name Birdie scribbled on the paper.

Birdie sighed.

"Well, he has a boat," Cass said.

Chapter 35

"*W*hat's wrong, Nell?"

It was Sam, not Ben, who sat in Nell's kitchen, a beer in his hand and his laptop open on the island.

Nell dropped her purse on the side table and walked over to the island. "Nothing. Everything. I need a distraction to clear my head, Sam."

"How about some Sea Harbor portraits? My little love affair with this town." The project had occupied Sam for a month, while he captured with his camera the magnificent faces of fishermen and sunbathers, the flowers and clouds and beaches of the town he'd adopted as his own.

Izzy and Ben came in from the deck. Izzy wrapped her arms around Nell and looked intently at her face. "Aunt Nell, what's that look?"

"A long day. I'll tell you about it. What are you up to?"

"Just spending time with my favorite uncle while my favorite husband borrows your laptop before we head out to meet friends for dinner. Sam's computer is in the geek shop."

Nell checked her watch. Dinnertime already? After dropping off Cass and Birdie, she had gone over to the community garden again. It brought a kind of peace to her, the neat rows, the fresh green plants. She had walked down to the shore and looked over at Finnegan's old pier, imagining his boat tied to the side. Finnegan teaching Gabby to fish. Teenagers casting their lines.

She looked up, startled at a sudden thought. "Someone could have accessed Finn's land by boat, couldn't they? Come up quietly without being seen by anyone."

"Possible. Sure," Izzy said.

"All day today, boats kept coming into the picture. But as Cass said, nearly everyone around here owns a boat."

"But not everyone uses them for daily transportation."

"Or to sneak onto someone's land and kill them," Sam added.

"So maybe . . . maybe the person who killed Finnegan planned it and got there by boat," Izzy said. She leaned against a stool.

"Coming in from the waterside, they were assured of cover. No patrol cars or late-night revelers would have seen them," Ben said. "No car tracks."

Nell told them about the visit to June Risso. "A sweet lady who minds her neighbors' business quite nicely. The person Beverly was seeing was coming to her by boat—then later, after Tommy gave her the *Moira*, she was going out to meet him by boat."

"Boats. Everywhere," Izzy said. "And boat knives."

Ben took out a bottle of wine. "It seems clear that if we could find the person Beverly was meeting, we'd be closer to finding out the truth about Finnegan's death. And maybe Beverly's, as well. He had to know something of what was going on."

And then Nell dropped her bombshell news and told them about the flowers.

"Davey Delaney!" Izzy's voice filled the room.

"Yes," Nell said. *Davey Delaney was sending Beverly flowers.*

The name hung above the island, a dark cloud.

"Davey . . ." Izzy repeated. "But . . ."

Nell knew what she was thinking. *But his wife is my friend. I know his kids. I'd know if their father could do something so awful.* It was one thing to sit in the back room of the yarn shop and add people's name to a list of possible suspects, but a different one entirely to think they actually murdered someone. Davey Delaney could be rude, but a murderer?

Finally, Ben said, "Sending someone flowers doesn't mean he killed someone." He handed Nell a glass of wine.

"Flowers from that shop cost a fortune," Izzy said. "Why would he do that if he didn't care about her?"

"They've been together. We saw them at the dock that day—"

"And Davey looked guilty as sin," Izzy added. "He couldn't wait to get away from us."

"He has a bruiser of a boat," Sam said.

They tried to force the image. Davey . . . Beverly Walden . . .

But the puzzle pieces didn't move smoothly.

"His wife was out of town the night of Finn's murder. He could have taken a dinghy and gone over there after the party. No one would have missed him at home."

"But Davey," Sam said, shaking his head. "He's a strange guy, but I can't see him romancing Beverly Walden."

"But think about it, Sam," Izzy said. "He wanted that land, and Beverly would have been a sure way to get it. . . . until she wasn't."

"So you think he'd give up Kristen and the kids for that land?" Sam argued. "I think he wanted the land to please his dad. But getting it by having an affair would certainly not be the way to please D. J. and Maeve Delaney."

Izzy glared at Sam. "I hate it when you make so much sense, Perry."

Sam swallowed the last of his beer and grinned.

But Nell wasn't so easily convinced. "Still, the flowers, the fact that we saw them together, that he had opportunity the night Finn died . . ." Nell looked off, listening to her own words as they circled back to her.

But where was the proof?

She rubbed her arms and reached for her wineglass.

Sam had gone back to fiddling with the computer and announced that the show was ready to start. The conversation needed a pause, he said, but more important, he needed some critical feedback.

He pressed a slide show into action while they crowded behind him to watch.

They watched in rapt attention as the images moved from dribbles

281 · A Fatal Fleece

of ice cream sliding down little boys' faces to fisherman sitting along the pier, dominoes lined up and with legs hanging over the edge and brown, weathered faces lifted to the breeze. And there were plenty of Gabby, her hair flying as she stooped down toward the sand, her fingers finding a piece of smooth sea glass, or as she sat playing chess with Harold, the two heads leaning forward, eyeing the small ivory pieces on the board as if life itself depended on the next move. Sam had been everywhere—the harbor, the beaches, the backyards filled with kids, and the raised garden beds where artists planted seeds.

The next photo took them to the yacht club and a shot of Nell leaning against a post, her arms wrapped around her legs. He'd pulled the lens in close and captured her intelligent eyes—slightly perplexed, thoughtful. High cheekbones, brush stroked by sun and wind. A fan of tiny lines spreading out from her eyes like a silky spiderweb. Her shoulder-length hair mussed, a streak of gray here, a dark column there.

"Next photo," Nell insisted, embarrassed at how intimately Sam had caught her thoughts.

The new series was of boats and piers and the yacht club sand raked clean of debris and patterned by the early morning tide.

"There," Ben said.

Sam paused on the photo.

"That's the Delaneys' boat."

Sam clicked through a few more that showed off the clean lines of the boat.

"These next ones I took of Sal's boat. I promised to blow one up for him."

It was a portrait in luxury, the icy blue streak along the yacht's side catching sunlight and glowing like a comet, the cushioned deck benches soft and inviting, wineglasses ready on the teak table.

Another group of photos took them to the Artist's Palate's deck, with the Fractured Fish in high gear. The crowd was animated, the faces, one after another, reflecting the joy of the evening.

And then a close-up of a face not hearing the music but filled with its own joy.

Beverly Walden, standing off to the side, away from the band and the crowd, behind the shadow of the bar, where back steps led down to the water. Her hair was loose, her cheeks flushed, and a silky dress caressed her body. Sam had taken it from a stool at the bar, a quick shot without thought or planning—or Beverly's knowledge. She wore the elegant, wide-brimmed hat that Nell had seen before. The whole ensemble was elegant—and very sensual.

Beverly's eyes were focused on something the camera couldn't see, something in the darkness on the other side of the rail. Only a man's hand was visible, and in the unfocused part of the photo, it seemed to touch Beverly's where it lay on the wood. An intimate gesture.

"Can you bring it in closer?" Nell asked.

Sam focused on the two hands, just barely touching. One, a woman's hand, resting on the rail. And the other, a shadowy outline of blunt fingers. And the glint of a plain gold wedding ring.

Chapter 36

After Sam and Izzy left, Ben told Nell that Birdie had called earlier.

"They're coming over. She—or maybe Nick—needs to talk to us. It seemed urgent."

Nell frowned. She told Ben about their visit to Finn's place and discovering Joseph Marietti's office and the photo of Birdie on the desk.

And the open file cabinet.

They arrived in Nick's car. The bright blue Altima that Nell wanted to drive off the end of Pelican Pier.

Birdie handed Ben a bottle of wine and suggested he open it immediately.

Nell encouraged everyone to sit. Something told her they'd be there a while.

As soon as she was settled on the couch, Birdie began. "I'm not sure why Nick is bringing you two into this, but he seems to think he can bare his soul better to me in your company. So here we are, and here's what I know." She cleared her throat, her face filled with worry.

"As Nell may have told you, Ben, we discovered today that someone had recently taken files from Joseph's old office—files, I must admit, I didn't know were there. I never gave his office a second thought after he died—his last attack was sudden. And even if I had thought of closing his office, I probably would have gone to the wrong place." She took a sip of the wine. "It was a month-to-month rental and Joseph kept little there."

Nick sat next to her, his expression unreadable.

"Some teenagers saw a man go into Finn's house—they saw the flashlight through the windows." She looked at Nick. "It was you, Nick." Her voice was tender and angry and sad, all at once.

Nick nodded, leaning forward, his elbows on his knees.

"All right then," Birdie said, regaining her composure. "We assumed you were going through Finn's things. Until we found out the light they saw was behind the first-floor windows. Not Finn's place at all."

They were all looking at Nick now.

"That was a relief to me. I didn't want you messed up with Finnegan's murder in any way." She managed a slight smile. "But you're still lying to me. To my dear friends." She looked at Ben and Nell. "And we need to know why. What are you hiding from me, Nick? And why did you require an audience to tell me?"

Nick was quiet for a few moments. Finally, he began, and soon the Marietti story was lying naked on the coffee table.

"My mother is a dictator of sorts and not the honest, upstanding woman one would hope for in a mother. Once we grew up, Joseph was the only one of us who still deferred to her, afraid to say no. So when she started the antique-import business, it was Joe she turned to. Sweet, smart, never-say-no Joseph. Except the business she pulled Joseph into was—how shall I say it?—an illegal one."

Birdie listened carefully as the story of her husband's involvement in managing his mother's antiques—stolen, imported, and sold—was detailed by a brother who didn't give a hoot about saving the family name.

"I would have walked out of her bedroom that day and never looked back," he said. He looked at Birdie. "But I didn't want innocent people hurt.

"My mother had only recently learned that Joseph's records had never been returned—or destroyed. She'd long ago settled things with the Italian police. Paid them off, closed the business. But the files would stir things up, and she wanted it all cleaned up so she could die in peace. So I was sent to do it. And I only agreed because I thought I could protect you, Birdie, and perhaps Gabby and her father, from the embarrassment of a Marietti family crime."

"So, you went to his office—"

"And I found them, every last one, in that old file cabinet."

"And you destroyed them?"

Nick paused, looked down at his hands, then went on.

"That was the plan, but, no, I didn't. I didn't want the police here to know about it—I was afraid it would be embarrassing for you. But I met with the proper authorities last week in New York and turned everything over. There's no one left to prosecute. Joseph is dead. And my mother won't live much longer. But I thought maybe some of the antiques could be found and returned."

He looked at Ben and Nell. "I didn't intend for Birdie to ever know about it. I wanted to keep Joseph's memory intact. But stubborn as she is, she forced the issue. So I wanted you two to hear, too. Just in case . . . well, in case there's any backlash at all. It can never hurt to have good friends—and a lawyer besides—at your side."

He sat back and looked at Birdie. "Maybe it was foolish not to tell you. But I was ashamed of my family, and I didn't want you to carry that same shame. Why should you?"

Birdie was silent for so long that not even Nell could read what was going on behind her clear blue eyes. And then she began to laugh, a lovely, lilting sound that blew away the tension in the room.

"My Joseph was a crook?" she said, and her laughter grew more and more robust, until Nell couldn't help herself and began laughing, too.

Nick and Ben watched the two women quizzically. And finally, though they weren't sure why, they began to laugh.

"Oh, my dear Nick," Birdie said, her laughter refusing to stop. She grabbed a tissue and wiped the tears from her cheeks. "A lovely skeleton to tuck away in my family closet. Our first crook, I do believe."

She leaned over and hugged him tight. "You are a dear, sweet man. And don't you ever, ever lie to me again."

Chapter 37

It was Izzy's idea to go out to the park. Gabby had never seen it, and it was a beautiful Sunday.

A girl's outing, Gabby had called it.

So they'd left the men behind, enjoying coffee on Annabelle's Sweet Petunia deck, boxed up a spinach and sausage frittata for Angus, and headed out to the rocky tip of land and Anja Angelina Park.

Cass was unusually quiet on the way out, and Izzy nudged her as they neared the visitors' parking lot. "What's up, girlfriend?" she said quietly.

"Nothing."

"Something."

"Okay. Something. It was just weird, out checking the traps today."

"Weird how?" Nell asked as she pulled into a parking spot. Gabby tumbled out of the car and ran around to the other side, waiting for Birdie.

"I'm more thin-skinned than I used to be, that's all. The guys on the boats can be rough kidders. We care about each other. But the kidding is hard to take sometimes."

Izzy and Nell knew that was not only true, but also an understatement. How Cass put up with it was a mystery. "It goes with the territory," was her standard reason.

"About the inheritance?"

Cass unlatched her seat belt and got out of the car. Izzy followed, waiting for her friend's answer.

"No. About how I *got* the inheritance."

"Oh, Cass. They don't think you had anything to do with his d—"

"No, they don't. But the money is more than any of them will make in two lifetimes. So they handle their envy by teasing that I hastened it up a bit. If I . . . if I hadn't cared about the old guy so much, I suppose the jokes would be easier to take."

Nell had seen Cass cry only once. And she wasn't crying today, but her eyes held enormous sadness.

Izzy wrapped her arms around Cass, and the three of them followed Birdie and Gabby over to Angus' cottage.

Nell looked at Izzy, who was looking at her. Their eyes sealed their resolution. Finding Finn's murderer as soon as possible wasn't just something the law required. It was something their lives required.

They walked around the cottage to the side that faced the sea and found Angus sitting in a rocking chair on a small porch.

He welcomed them with a smile, as if he'd been expecting them.

"You can see forever from here," Gabby said, then fit her small hand into Angus'. "I'm Gabby. And this is a great place."

Angus tilted his head to one side as he scrutinized the newcomer. "Birdie's granddaughter, I suspect."

"Yes," Gabby answered. "I call her Nonna. It's Italian."

"Humph," Angus said. "Italians."

Birdie had gone inside and helped herself to a fork and plate. She put the frittata down in front of Angus. "Annabelle sends her love."

"How did she know I was waiting for breakfast?" Angus laughed and stuffed a napkin in the neck of his T-shirt. He balanced the plate on his legs and dug into the creamy egg dish. "Want some?" he asked Gabby.

She shook her head. "Stuffed to the gills. But did you know I sailed out there with Ben and Sam?" She pointed to the island. "It looks different from here."

Angus looked out at the island as if Gabby had said something of great import. "That's a popular place to go these days, wee one," he said. "What did you find there?"

"Sea glass. Tons of it. Huge." Her arms shot out in a half circle.

"Sea glass," Angus said, mulling it over. "What kind?"

She dug in the pocket of her white shorts and brought out a flat, smooth piece of kelly green glass. "I found this one. Look."

She put it in Angus' large, wrinkled hand.

"Feel it. This is a common color for sea glass—but I think it's beautiful. Just like my beanie." She took off her hat and held it next to the stone.

Angus looked at it carefully. "Common can be beautiful."

"Sure," Gabby agreed. "See how the water tumbled all the sharp edges away?"

"Like life. Washing away the sharp edges."

Gabby looked at the stone, then the old man. "Yes."

"Maybe your sea glass will tell you a story," he said. "You might find some pieces that aren't the real McCoy. But even those can tell a story. Don't miss anything, darlin'."

"I won't," Gabby answered, their eyes meeting as if sharing a secret code. She looked at his eggs. "You better eat. They're getting cold."

Gabby scampered down the incline toward a bank of boulders begging to be climbed.

"You done good, getting that one, Birdie," he said.

Birdie smiled.

"Have you heard about Beverly Walden?" Nell asked.

Angus nodded. "Sad story, all sides of it." He watched Gabby climbing up a large boulder.

"Did you know her?"

He shook his head. "Only what Finn told me about her. Like I said, it was sad."

"Do you have any idea who killed her, Angus? And Finn?"

He looked out toward the island, his forehead pulling together. "I knew Finn as well as anyone could. He had a great capacity for love. But he also had an unerring sense of fairness and couldn't tolerate deceit. He told me once he wished he wasn't that way, but it's how he was made so he did the best with who he was.

"Long story short, I don't know who murdered him. But I know why. It was because Finn was going to reveal their sins, as he called them." Angus snorted. "The padre and I used to laugh about it. For a nonchurchgoing man, Finn was filled with commandments."

"And Beverly?"

"She must have known the same thing that got Finnegan killed. Maybe she even knew it up-front and personal." Angus stroked his beard, choosing his words carefully.

"Desperation and fear can drive a truly bad deed. And once you've done it, a smaller threat could tip the cart, precipitate another bad act. Like a bad habit. Lie once; the second time is easier."

And the third easier than that?

Gabby had gone down to a narrow stretch of beach, and they watched her bend low, her hands on her knees, searching for glints of glass.

Angus looked at Birdie. "Look at how carefully she searches the beach and picks up the pieces that look like sea glass. Some will end up being plain old glass with sharp edges."

"Throwaways," Izzy said.

"Not always," he answered. Then he sat back and scraped up bits of egg with a piece of biscuit.

"You said there's been traffic on the island recently. There's not much over there to see, is there?" Birdie asked.

"Nope, not much, but it's a good place to find privacy, at least at night. Except for the little stretch of beach where people picnic and look for sea glass, it's rocky and a good place to get out of the limelight. Finn's boat has made a few visits."

"Recently?" Nell asked.

He nodded.

"So, that's where she goes," Birdie murmured.

He nodded again.

"What about the night she died?" Izzy asked.

"Yep. But never saw her leave, not that I would have. Like I told the police, sleeping's more important to me these days than keeping track of wayward sailors. But it was Finn's boat I saw—I was sure of that. The purple *Moira*."

"Did you see another boat?"

"Nope. But if a boat came in from the other side, I wouldn't have seen it."

They looked at the island for a long time and thought of the righteous Finn, wanting to right the wrongs of the world.

By the time Gabby came back up the hill, her hands and pockets full of new treasures, the motive for murder seemed more real, as polished as a piece of sea glass.

But Angus' message echoed clear. *Watch out for the throwaways.*

Chapter 38

Cass sometimes took Mondays off, a habit started a long time ago when she realized other people didn't and she could plan her day around herself. But when she met Nell at Izzy's shop that morning, she wanted to plan it around finding a murderer.

Birdie had brought a coffee cake to the back room, while Mae handled customers in the main shop—shoppers mesmerized by the display of luscious garden-colored yarn, who wandered in the store wanting some of everything. Izzy had given an excited Jillian and Rose bonuses because of all the business their display had generated.

The back of the shop was quiet, with no classes scheduled that morning. Cass sliced the cake into pieces and slid them onto small plates.

At the other end of the table, Nell pulled out Gabby's sweater and spread it out. "Once I get these loose threads woven in, I will have a sweater. Or, rather, Gabby will."

They stood around the table, looking at it. In the beginning it had been a nice gesture for a new granddaughter; now it was a lovely purple sweater, perfect for a young girl who had woven her way tightly into their lives and hearts.

"She'll love it," Birdie said, her words slightly choked.

Izzy tugged on a thread to smooth out a loose stitch. "And with her green beanie, she'll certainly make a fashion statement. I'm going to have to stock up on the pattern and the yarn to meet the demand."

They didn't mention Gabby leaving. It hadn't come up in recent days and no one asked, as if without a reminder, it wouldn't happen. Nick was no longer a person of interest. He had simply been cleaning out his brother's files in the old office, he told the local police, and Birdie confirmed that it was Joseph's place. "Better late than never," she had said to Jerry Thompson, her smile discouraging further questions.

But though he was free to leave Sea Harbor, he didn't.

"Davey Delaney was at the Gull last night when we went in to watch the end of the Sox game," Izzy said, pulling their thoughts back to the matter at hand. She swallowed a bite of crumbly cake.

"Was he alone?" Nell asked.

"Yes and no. Davey comes alone but flirts his way into any group that'll take him."

"And Kristen?" Birdie asked.

"No. She doesn't like noisy bars—or baseball. She says it works out great, though. They are fine with separate interests."

"Did you talk to him?"

"Yes. I asked straight out if he knew Beverly Walden, and he said no. That kind of ended the conversation."

"Those were expensive flowers to send to someone you don't know," Cass said. "He's lying."

Birdie frowned. "This isn't stacking up well for Davey. We know he sent her flowers. And you saw them together in what looked like a romantic way—something Finn might have seen, too, and thought Beverly was breaking up a family."

"Add to that that Kristen was out of town the night Finn died. He could have taken their dinghy around to the dock and come up on land that way," Nell said.

"And maybe it wasn't the inheritance he was after. He wanted the land—and thought if he romanced her, she'd sell it to him."

"But when it wasn't going to be hers, she became a handicap," Cass said. "And, worse, maybe she started making demands on him or threatened to tell Kristen."

"There's one thing that doesn't fit, though," Izzy said. She looked at Nell.

"Remember Sam's photo of Beverly at the Fish concert? Remember the man's hand?"

Nell nodded.

"Well, Davey wasn't wearing a wedding ring last night. I checked. I don't think he ever has."

They looked down at the soft sea of purple cotton on Nell's lap. In the distance, the sound of customers grew louder.

The wedding ring wasn't a deal breaker, they decided. Maybe the glint was something else.

Mae Anderson stuck her head into the room. "There's a group that wants to knit and gossip. Is that okay?"

"Of course," Izzy said, and began cleaning up the crumbs from the table. She looked up to greet a chatty group of women who frequented the shop and loved the comfortable knitting space in the back. "A home away from home," was the way one woman put it. "With the added benefit of not having husbands or teenagers underfoot."

The athletic group bounded down the steps in tennis shorts and exercise pants, tan and fit. "Izzy, you're our haven," a woman named Louise said. "Don't ever leave us."

Kristen Delaney was next, followed by an acquaintance of Nell's from the museum board, and Elliot Danvers' older sister, Sharon.

Kristen walked over and gushed over Nell's sweater as she began to fold it. "That's absolutely beautiful, Nell. My ten-year-old, Sasha, would love it. It would match her room. All purple, even the ceiling."

They laughed.

"I still have a few skeins left," Izzy said. "The yarn is heavenly. You'll want to sleep with it."

"Izzy says you spend a lot of time in here," Nell said to Kristen as the others settled themselves in the comfortable chairs around the fireplace.

"A lot of money, for sure. Izzy hooked me. It's like an addiction. But I have three kids and they actually love the fishermen-knit sweaters I make. They keep them toasty on the boat."

Kristen laughed easily, and Nell wondered briefly how she put up with Davey. But maybe it was the difference of interests—Davey spending time in Jake Risso's bar or on his boat, and Kristen having weekends away with friends. People had different ways of making marriages work. And for all the unpleasant thoughts Nell had heard about Davey Delaney, she found herself hoping that he wasn't guilty of this horrific crime that would surely devastate this nice woman wanting to knit a purple sweater for her daughter.

"I hear you had a weekend away," Izzy said from across the table. "We missed you at the Scaglias' party."

"We had a great time," Sharon called over from her chair.

"And we have the tans to show it," Louise added. "It was a bit of heaven. No kids. No husbands. Plenty of sun and wine and music."

"Where was this magical place?" Cass asked.

"The sea," Kristen said, laughing. "I am turning all my friends into sailors so we can escape. We sailed down the coast, stopping wherever we felt like it. Taking the dinghy in to shore for great meals."

"So, Davey's not the only boat lover in the family," Nell said.

The group in the background burst into laughter.

Kristen put out a hand to calm down her friends. "What they're saying, in their raucous way, has to be a class-A secret. It cannot leave this room."

"Of course," Izzy said. "Mum's the word."

"The truth is, my macho husband, Davey, doesn't sail. In fact, a short ride in the dinghy makes him seasick. His dad bought that gorgeous boat for us when Davey landed some big job, but he's never been out on it. I'm the one who loves it. Me and the kids—"

"And your friends," Sharon said.

"Yes, and my friends. But Davey won't sail with us, though he'd never in a million years tell anyone. He thinks it'd make him look wimpy."

"Well, that was a surprise," Birdie said when they left the shop a short while later. They walked down the street to Nell's car.

"Without a boat, how would Beverly's affair have happened, assuming it was with Davey, anyway? It adds a new twist to things."

"I don't think we can eliminate him completely, though. Maybe . . . maybe he says he is seasick to throw Kristen off?" Cass said.

"Frankly, I can't imagine Davey falling for someone like Beverly Walden when he has a wife like Kristen," Izzy said. "I like her a lot, and I think the two of them actually have a decent relationship. They give each other a lot of room."

"But what about the flowers? And the lunches people saw them having?"

Izzy walked with them as far as the car. "I'm leaving work early today. How about we meet at your house, Aunt Nell? Sam and Ben are sailing with Jerry Thompson. Maybe they'll bring back something to throw into this messy stew."

They agreed, and waved her off to a noontime class on finishing details.

"I need to run a photo over to Sal. Are you two game? Maybe we can look at that list of deeds Beverly was so interested in during her visits. When we were there the first time, she was still alive, and we were looking for different things."

They left the car parked at the curb and walked the few short blocks to the three-story stone building. Mondays were busy at the courthouse, but Sal Scaglia's office would probably be quiet. And most likely empty.

As they walked down the short hall, Beatrice walked out, a surprised look on her face as she came face-to-face with Nell, Birdie, and Cass.

"Hello," she managed. "I don't often see you over here." Her voice was slightly accusatory.

"We need to check a few things in the deed's office," Birdie said. "That's all."

Beatrice's hand was still on the doorknob. For a moment she looked as though she wasn't going to let them go in.

"Oh?" she asked. "Is it something I could help you with?"

"I am sure you have better things to do, Beatrice, but it's a kind offer. I think we'll be fine. Is Sal in?"

"Sal?" she asked, as if she wasn't quite sure who they were talking about. She looked back at the closed door, the frosted glass with REGISTER OF DEEDS ANNEX printed across it.

"Oh. He'll be back in a minute. He must have gone to the restroom."

Beatrice managed a smile, checked her watch, and then excused herself quickly for a meeting, her heels clicking on the hardwood floor as she disappeared around the corner.

They turned at the sound of a door swinging shut at the other end of the hall. Sal Scaglia stepped into view. He stopped short, seeing the women collected at his office door. Then, with a puzzled look, he walked toward his office.

"Greetings, ladies. This is unexpected," he said. He held the door open for them, then walked around the desk and sat down. A pharmacy lamp cast a yellow light across the sign-in notebook. He looked up, then pushed his glasses up his nose and smiled. "What can I do for you?"

His glasses slipped again. He apologized and took them off.

"Mine do the same thing," Nell said. "Are they new? You have a different look today."

"These?" He shook his head. "No, it's an old pair. I can't find the other ones. The curse of bad eyesight, I guess. So, how can I help you? I have only two computers working today, but I suppose you could share one. You'll need to sign in here." He pointed to the notebook.

"Actually, we don't need the computers today," Nell said.

Sal sat back. He tented his fingers. "If you . . . if you are wanting more information about Nicholas Marietti, I don't feel I . . ."

Nell smiled. "No, Sal. I appreciate your respect for people's privacy. I promise not to ask you about Nick. But I do have a question about someone else. It's about Beverly Walden."

Sal frowned. "The woman who was killed?"

"Yes. We know that she was in here looking some things up and—"

"In here?" Sal's frown deepened. "I saw the photo in the paper, but I don't remember seeing her before. Are you sure you saw her here?"

"We didn't actually see her," Birdie explained. "But she signed the book. In fact, it seems she was in here several times."

"In here?" Sal sat back, thinking. "I suppose it's possible, but I think I'd have remembered, at least once her name was in the paper."

"Well, it will be in the book, so maybe that will trigger a memory," Cass said.

"Of course. That's right. Do you know when she was here? What day or week?" He reached for the notebook.

"She was here several times over the last month or two," Nell said. "As many as ten, I think."

Sal's frown deepened. "Odd," he murmured. He put his glasses back on and opened the book. Carefully, he turned page after page, slowly running his finger down each line. After covering two weeks, he looked up and shook his head. "I don't see her name. Could she have signed in with a different one?"

Nell looked at Birdie. "That's crazy. We saw her name . . . Maybe earlier?" she suggested.

Sal dutifully turned several more pages, and again, line by line, searched for Beverly's name. Finally, he looked up. "I'm sorry. I don't see it anywhere." He rubbed his forehead.

"So, you don't remember her ever being in the office?"

"No. Maybe if I looked at the newspaper photo again," he offered. "I've had some help this summer so I could take a day off every now and then. Let me ask Janie and get back to you."

"May I?" Nell took the book out of Sal's hands before he could protest. She flipped through it, frowned, then looked again more carefully. Finally, she closed the book and handed it back to him. "Maybe we were mistaken. We're sorry for wasting your time, Sal."

"It's always a pleasure to have you come in," he said. "It's usually quiet in here."

They turned to go, and then Nell remembered the photograph. She pulled the photo envelope from her purse. "I almost forgot. Sam Perry asked me to give you this."

Sal took the envelope and pulled out the photograph of his boat. His face brightened as he looked at the photo, his usual quiet demeanor melting into one of pure pride. Sam had mounted the photo on foam core, ready to be matted and framed.

"May I see?" Cass asked.

Sal handed it to her, a proud parent showing off a snapshot of a newborn.

"What a beauty," Cass said.

Sam had captured in crisp detail the polished teak trim of the deck, the leather seats and shiny chrome accents, its deep blue sheen. Cass looked at it closely, then handed it back. "I'd love to go out on her sometime."

"Just name the day," Sal said, taking the photo back and looking at it again. "Sam's good. He captures everything." He held it closer, pushing his glasses up his nose. A puzzled look shadowed his face. Then quickly he slipped the photo back into the envelope and looked up. "Thanks, Nell. And thank Sam for me. Now I guess I'd better get back to work."

He looked down at his desk, empty except for a book on sailing in one corner and the sign-in notebook on the other.

"All right, Nell. What did you see when you looked at that sign-in notebook?" Birdie asked as they walked outside and down the steps, three abreast.

"Someone tore the original pages out, the ones with Beverly's name on them."

"Are you sure? It looked legit to me," Cass said.

"You were looking at it upside down. I could see a few rough edges where the original pages had been. It was picked clean, but not entirely."

"That's odd. Anyone, even Beverly Walden, has a right to look at deeds." They turned the corner onto Harbor Road.

"Beatrice . . ." Birdie murmured.

"She looked guilty of something. Or concerned, maybe?" Nell said.

"Why wouldn't she want us to know Beverly was in the office? Or was it the deeds she was looking at that someone didn't want noticed?" Birdie said.

"But we saw those. And they were almost silly. It looked like she jotted down anything, just because it was required. We've all done that, I suppose, when we have to sign in or out somewhere, just to make it go fast."

"Sure, I've done that. Especially if the request for information seems foolish. Like, who cares what deeds I want to look at? Deeds are public information. I think it's Sal Scaglia's quest for control and perfection, covering every little thing. But it's actually kind of silly."

Nell looked at Cass. "You have a point. Sal's mostly there to be sure people know how to use the computers. He must get terribly bored."

"Yet it's good that he takes pride in his job, no matter if it's just signing people in and out," Birdie said.

"I suppose." Cass frowned. "But something's not right. I feel it. Beatrice . . . She looked strange."

"It's because you need caffeine, Catherine. Next stop, Coffee's."

It wasn't just a lack of caffeine, and they all knew it. But a double latte would certainly help.

The·line in the coffee shop was short at that late hour of the morning, and in minutes they were headed back outside with Coffee's signature blue and green cups in hand.

"Ahh," Cass said, breathing in the smell. "I'll soon be human again."

They walked through the patio, headed toward Nell's car, when a hand on Cass' shoulder caused her to jump. Her cup tumbled to the ground, a river of brown liquid flowing under a nearby table.

She stared up at Davey Delaney.

"What are you trying to do, Delaney? You scared the bejeezus out of me." She looked down at the now-empty cup. "And I needed that coffee. Desperately!"

Davey's face fell, chagrined. "Hey, I'm sorry. I didn't mean to scare you. You're awfully jumpy, though. I barely touched you. Maybe you've had too much caffeine."

He stopped a young man clearing tables and asked him to bring another cup. "My tab," he added, and turned an unexpectedly apologetic face back to the three women.

"So, what do you want?" Cass asked, her tone softening, but only a little.

Davey apologized again. Then tried to explain. "I just wanted to tell you I'm glad old man Finnegan picked you."

"Picked me?" Cass said.

"You know. To have his money. Handle his property. It'll be done right now."

Birdie moved closer to Davey, her eyes kind but her voice with the serious "listen to me" tone that no one in Sea Harbor ignored. Even Davey Delaney.

"Davey, what are you trying to say?"

"Just that, Miss Birdie." His face was less bold when he looked at her. Like a child before the principal. *Respectful with just a twinge of fear*, Nell thought.

"I think Cass'll do what Beverly Walden would never have done. No disrespect for the dead intended."

"Didn't you tell Izzy you didn't know Beverly Walden?" Nell asked.

Davey shifted from one foot to the other, clearly uncomfortable. "I didn't know her. Not really. That was the truth. And I sure as hell didn't want to be connected to her now that she's dead."

Then he looked at Nell. "You're still upset with me from the other night. I know I wasn't exactly nice to you at the Scaglias'. In fact, my dad said I was a jerk. A forty-five-year-old jerk who'd had too many beers, was how he put it. I was in a bad mood. My wife was away; one of my kids was sick. I didn't want to be at that party watching Beatrice Scaglia be a peacock, trying to get everyone to do exactly what she wants, when she wants it, how she wants it. If you think I was hard on Finnegan, look into that lady's behavior."

Birdie brought the conversation back to Finn's will. "What did you mean about Beverly Walden?"

"I just meant that if she'd been Finnegan's heir, it would have been a damn shame."

Birdie frowned. "Why? How can you say that about someone you don't know?"

"Okay, so I met her. But didn't really know her. I tried to. I tried to be nice to her. My wife told me to. Kristen said if I didn't start acting gracious to people, I'd never get anywhere with the new projects I was trying to land. So I followed her advice and tried to be nice to Beverly because I thought she was going to get Finn's land. And I wanted it. There. I said it. That's the honest truth."

He looked at Cass. "You're different. You'll think about it and do what makes sense. If I have a piece of that, it'd be great." His lips lifted in a half smile. "But no matter what, you'll figure it out. But Beverly was a different kettle of fish. She didn't know the town, didn't care about it, didn't know us. I took her to dinner once, tried to get on her good side. Even had Kristen send her flowers. Sort of an investment, I guess. Kristen said I could write it off."

"What was her response?" Cass asked.

"She liked the flowers. But the fact is, she didn't care what happened to the land. I finally figured that out. She would have taken the highest offer she got, even if it meant someone was going to build a nuclear power plant on that land. There was something sad about her. I think she thought Finn's money would help her turn her life around. Maybe run off with some guy."

"Some guy?" Nell said.

"Whoever it was she was having an affair with. She was crazy about the guy. She talked about him as if he were some kind of Adonis, and from what she said, he felt the same." Davey shrugged. "Some guys like to be needed. And that lady was definitely needy—that much I know about her."

They left Davey on Coffee's patio and walked across the street in silence. An uncomfortable feeling was closing in on them, like a vise.

"Do you believe him?" Cass finally asked.

"I don't know," Nell said.

"Not to disparage poor Davey, but I'm not sure he could make that up," Birdie said. "It would be a very creative lie. Though he's great with a hammer, he's not terribly clever, I don't think."

"He knew she was having an affair. It sounds like she was becoming more open about it," Cass said.

"Which might not have been comfortable to the other person involved," Nell said, picking up on Cass' thought.

"But . . ." Nell began. The end of her thought hung there in the air, unspoken.

Uncomfortable enough to kill?

Chapter 39

After a quick lunch at the Artist's Palate, they went their separate ways—Birdie to meet Nick and Gabby for a whale-watching tour, and Cass to meet with her mother. "Our weekly catch-up time," she explained, which meant Mary Halloran would take notes on everything going on in her daughter and son's lives, sprinkling the list bountifully with advice.

Nell went to a monthly meeting of grant writers over in Gloucester, and finally returned to an empty house, drained.

The quiet settled in all around her, comforting her, muting the suspicions and thoughts that had permeated the hours before.

Davey Delaney had seemed sincere today, but the day she'd seen him across from the garden, watching Finnegan, he'd looked fierce. And then there was the barely controlled anger he'd exhibited at the city council meeting. The thoughts tumbled on top of one another, the events mixing up in her mind.

She made herself a cup of tea, pushing the thoughts away, and climbed up on a stool at the kitchen island. She pulled the laptop over and turned it on to check e-mails. *Normalcy.*

But it was Sam's photos that popped up first. He had taken the CD but left the photos on the screen, presenting in their very ordinariness the grandeur of a seaside town. Nell rested her elbows on the butcher block and flipped through the photos, smiling at the beauty Sam had seen in his lens and preserved with a click.

The faces of the fishermen, the men and women who braved the sea, who read the water, communed with it, held her captive. People who wanted no other life. *Like Finnegan,* she thought, wishing she'd known him and his wife in their younger years. A gentle, soft man with a crusty outside, like a loaf of perfectly baked Irish peasant bread.

She continued clicking through, pausing now and then, so immersed in the photos that at first she was unaware that Izzy had come in. She came up beside her aunt, watching the images slide by.

A new set of photos showed a contrast to fishermen and beachgoers. Around a council table sat city leaders, their faces reflecting the onus of keeping a town healthy and whole. A close-up of Beatrice Scaglia was a portrait of concern and compassion. But a clenched fist on the table showed something else.

Gabby had come in with Birdie and made herself comfortable at the other end of the island, pouring out her bag of sea glass and sorting through the pink and green and blue pieces.

"These photos are lovely," Birdie said, standing next to Izzy. She pointed to one. "Can you pause that one, Nell?"

They were back at the yacht club dock and a close-up of a beautiful, sleek boat with the Delaney name written across the side. "Now, what kind of a name is that for a boat?" Cass asked, coming up behind Izzy. "Shouldn't it be something fanciful, like the *Lady Lobster*?"

"D.J. probably had it painted on before he gave them the boat. Good marketing. I can't imagine Kristen picking it." They pulled the photo in close and saw the signs of fun—inner tubes and sun hats, boogie boards and coolers on the deck. "Family life," Nell said.

"Speaking of which," Cass said, and filled Izzy in on the talk they'd had with Davey Delaney. "He didn't lie, he said. He didn't *really* know Beverly Warden. I suppose not. Not in the biblical sense anyway."

"Do you believe him?" Izzy asked.

Birdie sighed. "It's hard to say." She pointed to the monitor as another boat came into view. "There. Look at that one."

"Can you get in closer on that one?" Cass asked.

Nell enlarged the shot until the aft deck filled the screen.

As the image enlarged, the photo grew grainy and hard to see.

But in all its fuzzy definition, Nell could see one thing clearly: the pieces falling into place so loudly she could hear them.

Behind her, even before she heard Izzy's gasp, she knew Birdie, Cass, and Izzy felt the same.

"We need an expert," Cass said in a quiet voice.

"I have one you can borrow." Izzy turned to see Sam and Ben coming across the room.

The men were full of the excitement of the sail. Sam carried two flat boxes smelling of basil, garlic and tomatoes.

Gabby jumped up, scattering her sea glass. "Pizza!"

Nell glanced at the computer, then moved it, still open, to Ben's den. *To be continued*, she thought, preferably without a coating of cheese. *And soon.*

"Great day for a sail," Ben was telling anyone who would listen. He headed to the refrigerator and pulled out some beers, while Izzy unwrapped the pizza and took plates from the cupboard.

Nell examined Gabby's neat row of sea glass, the smooth pieces creating a rainbow across the butcher-block top. "They're so beautiful," she said. "Are they all from Sunrise Island?"

Gabby nodded. "Angus says to look at them carefully. Every single one. And they'll tell us things." She picked one up and frowned. "But this is just a piece of plain glass. I picked it up by mistake. See?" She showed Nell the curved piece of clear glass. "It hasn't been tumbled by the water like the others."

Nell looked at it carefully, then held it up and looked through it. On the other side, a letter on the pizza box loomed large. Nell looked through it again. Again, the letter was magnified.

"May I have this one, Gabby?" she asked.

Gabby laughed. "You need a beautiful one, not that one." She handed Nell a smooth pink oval.

"Thank you, sweetie. Angus would be proud of you." Nell carried the oval, along with the piece of clear glass, to the safety of a jar on her windowsill.

Once again, the Old Man of the Sea's wisdom spoke to them.

Look at each piece carefully, and they'll tell us things.
And they did.

Gabby was yawning by the time they'd finished hot-fudge sundaes. Birdie suggested making it an early night. At least for the three whale watchers. "The rest of you can do what you want," she said, and she told Nell she'd talk to her first thing in the morning.

They hadn't wanted to discuss the day's happenings with Gabby there, but the instant the door closed, Cass and Nell spilled their day out on the table. Sometimes saying things aloud uncovered hidden details.

"Jerry Thompson was with us on the boat today," Ben said. "He was discreet, like he is, but said a few things. Did you know that Beverly had promised Beatrice Scaglia she'd work with her on plans for the land she was to inherit? There was an e-mail on the city system saying as much."

"I suppose that doesn't surprise me," Nell said. "Did Jerry say what their focus is now that Beverly is dead?"

"Her life," he said.

"Life?" Izzy asked.

"Affair," Sam said. "Some of the holes are plugged, but there are missing pieces. Important ones."

"Like proof," Ben said. "They can come up with everything but that."

"I can't . . . I just can't get my arms around this," Nell said. "And we could all be dead wrong."

"Sure," Ben said. "We could."

Nell got the computer and brought it to the kitchen island. Sam's slide show came into focus. They explained what they thought and what they needed: a close-up that wasn't fuzzy. Using his magic, Sam made it happen.

As they all stared at the photos, silence filled the room so loudly Nell wanted to cover her ears. They looked at one picture, then another, squinting, then tilting their heads. It was clear but not clear.

"Are we reading into it?" Izzy asked.

But there was no easy answer, and they turned off the computer. "Maybe we'll see things more clearly tomorrow," Ben said.

"Maybe tomorrow will tell us we're climbing up the wrong tree," Izzy said. "I want that to be what we hear. And yet I can't bear for it to be what we hear. This needs to be over."

Nell walked over to the kitchen window and returned with the piece of glass that Gabby had found on the beach. She explained where it came from—Sunrise Island—then passed it around.

When it came back to Ben, he took it into his den and put it into the small safe beneath his desk. "Till tomorrow," he said. "We'll see. It could be just a piece of broken glass, you know."

The next day was cool and rainy—a needed rain, the weatherman said. And somehow Nell felt it appropriate. It matched her spirits. And the garden certainly needed it.

She dressed in stretchy slacks and a light knit sweater, grabbed her rain jacket, and headed down to Izzy's. Gabby's sweater was blocked and ready for buttons. *Buttons. Yarn. Izzy's shop. Perfect escapes from thoughts of murder.*

Cass was already there, along with a cardboard carafe of Colombian blend that she'd picked up at Coffee's. "Couldn't sleep," she said to Nell. "How about you?"

Before she could answer, they saw the Lincoln Town Car pull up. Birdie got out, hurrying in between raindrops as Harold drove away.

She shook the rain from her head, her white hair fluffing out. "I don't think we need phones any longer. It seems all we have to do is think, and voilà—here we all are."

"Confused and desperate—"

Nell's cell phone rang before Cass had poured the fourth coffee. It was Jane Brewster.

"Nell, meet me at the Arts Association office. There's something here I need someone else to look at." Her voice was loud and urgent, and they all heard the message, standing feet away.

Nell drove, and they reached the arts office just as the heavens broke loose. Jane had left the door unlocked, and they rushed in, stomping water from their shoes on the rubber mat.

"In here," Jane called from the boardroom in the back. All along the walls were paintings of different sizes, some still wrapped in brown paper, others leaning against the wall, their landscapes or waterscapes or abstract art muted today in the low light.

"This is the artwork donated to the public auction that the community center is holding later this summer. We've been stacking them in here, but Willow, Ham, and I finally got around to organizing them last night. I had almost forgotten that Beverly had donated a painting. She left it here shortly before she died, and in the confusion, we forgot about it. I unwrapped it this morning."

She pointed toward a painting directly behind Izzy. It was a large oil filled with brilliant colors. Greens and blues and a bright white-yellow that looked like light pouring through the canvas from behind. It was a joyful painting, without some of the heaviness they'd seen in Beverly's earlier works.

And then they saw what Jane had seen. There it was, tucked away in the blues and greens and golden sunlight. They saw what Beverly Warden had painted, and what everyone would see when the paintings were displayed, what Beverly wanted everyone to see.

Jane wrapped the painting up in heavy plastic and taped it back together, then helped them put it in the back of Nell's car. Nell called Ben and told him what was happening.

The trip back to Harbor Road was anxious, but beneath the anxiety was hope. Hope that soon, very soon, the nightmare would be over.

"Ben will meet us at the police station," Nell said.

They drove into the visitors' parking lot between the police station and city offices just as Janie Levin pulled in beside them. She jumped out of the car, her yellow umbrella springing into action.

"Are you coming to visit me again?" she yelled through Birdie's window. "I hope so. That's the loneliest office known to man."

Birdie rolled down the window. "You're working for Sal today?"

Janie looked around to see if anyone was close by, then stuck her head through the window and whispered, "It's a huge secret. I'm not supposed to tell."

But Janie told.

They were out of the parking lot and headed toward the yacht club before Birdie got the window back up. She wiped the rain from her face and dialed the necessary numbers. *Hurry* was the message she left.

Nell pulled up in the yacht club parking lot and they piled out into the rain, pulling their slickers tight and rushing down to the dock. She pointed to a red Saab. "Beatrice," she shouted over the rain.

With Nell in the lead, they rushed to the dock, pointing to where she remembered the boat being moored. Peering through the sheets of rain, they finally saw and heard it: lights and the purr of an engine, idling in preparation. Standing on the dock, dressed in soaking-wet exercise gear, was Beatrice Scaglia.

Screaming.

Sal stood on the boat, tugging at the stern lines. Trying to ignore the pounding of the waves and the screaming of the woman he knew he couldn't live without. "Come with me, Bea," he pleaded.

Birdie and Cass reached Beatrice and held her tight.

"He's crazy. He'll kill himself," she said. She broke free and ran to the end of the dock with Nell close behind. She reached over and grabbed the edge of the boat railing, holding tight. "I can't swim, Sal. I hate water. If you try to move this boat, I will fall in the water and drown. I swear I will. Is that what you want? Now get off this damn boat."

In the distance, heavy footsteps made their way to the dock.

Sal looked startled at the lights shining from flashlights, the heavy footsteps.

And in the time it took for Nell and Cass to pull Beatrice back on dry land, Tommy Porter had jumped on the boat and read Sal Scaglia his rights.

For killing his mistress, Beverly Walden.

And Francis Finnegan.

"Beatrice's sister is with her," Nell said. "And Father Northcutt. She's a strong lady. She'll be fine. It's Sal who won't be. I don't know if he can exist without her, a fact that Beverly Walden never understood."

It was early evening and the rain had left the town soaked in the wonderful freshness of summer. The doors to the deck were open, bringing in the smell of roses and evergreens, of new grass and ocean breezes. The coffee was on; martinis were mixed.

"It's intoxicating," Nick Marietti said, looking out over the yard. "It's like the color has come back."

Beside him, Birdie nodded.

The weight of sadness that settled on the town was lightened by the knowledge that it was over. At last.

The siege on their summer was no more.

Jane Brewster looked over at the painting, still leaning against the wall. "The painting was like Beverly's coming-out announcement. Her way of telling the world that she and Sal loved each other."

"An announcement Sal could never have let her make," Nell said.

They turned toward the bright, happy painting of the sea. And riding the waves like a chariot was a magnificent yacht, sharply angled with strong, broad strokes, but as recognizable as the photos they'd seen the night before. A brilliant boat with a deep metallic blue sheen, and painted on the side was its new name: BEVERLY.

"Do you think Sal loved her?" Nell wondered out loud. She'd been grappling with it for hours. Such complicated relationships. Beatrice was Sal's anchor. He would never have left the one stronghold in his life that kept him safe.

"I think Beverly loved him desperately, and needed him in a way Beatrice didn't," Birdie said. "Her love was total and adoring, and it made him feel vigorous and important and manly. So, in a way, I think he did. Certainly he loved being needed. He never had that role before. It's not uncommon. But he'd never have left Beatrice. He couldn't. He was too dependent on her."

"And he truly loved her, I think," Nell said. "Maybe not in the normal husband-and-wife way. But he did love her."

"I feel sorry for Beverly," Cass said. "I didn't think I'd ever say that, but the woman had rotten breaks."

"She also had a temper," Ben said. "Kind of a Jekyll and Hyde. And my guess is that after she lost the inheritance, she was desperate. She knew Sal and Beatrice were wealthy, and thought that having her own would equal the playing field. But once that was gone, she was frantic. All she had left were threats to tell Beatrice. Sal couldn't stand for that, and it pushed him right over the edge. Just like Finnegan pushed him when he said he was going to tell Beatrice about the affair. For Finn, Sal's infidelity was the worst sin of all."

"Davey Delaney had me fooled," Ham said. "That guy is scary sometimes. I thought he did it."

Izzy nodded. "Scary, but I'm beginning to think he's a teddy bear underneath."

"We've Gabby to thank for steering us away from Davey. It was the broken lens she found with her sea glass," Nell said. "Her throwaway piece."

"Sal's broken glasses," Birdie said. "He told us he'd lost them, but he didn't say it was on the island where he and Beverly would meet each night."

"Do you think Beatrice knew . . . maybe suspected?" Izzy asked.

Birdie sipped the martini Ben handed her. "I don't think she'll ever tell us—and I don't think we need to know."

But Nell remembered the scrap of paper, something Beatrice probably found in Sal's pocket early on. She was no one's fool. Maybe she knew and the affair was all right with her. As long as it was quiet and discreet. Maybe she'd torn the sheets out of the sign-in book—or insisted Sal did it.

"And Sam is a hero, too," Izzy said proudly. "No wonder that Sal turned white when he saw your great photographs."

"I didn't think anything of that big, white sisal hat, except that it made an interesting object in the photo," Sam said. "Just like the two wineglasses. It was the four of you who put it all together."

"Beatrice never set foot on the boat, so the hat couldn't have been hers," Birdie said.

"Beverly wore it several times in Canary Cove. She must have forgotten it on the boat the morning that we ran into Sal at the club."

"And the rigging knives—Beverly and Beatrice both probably bought them as gifts for Sal—never dreaming one would be used to kill Finnegan," Nell said.

"We've answered lots of questions," Jane said. "But not all . . ."

"Right. The big one." Ben's eyes were laughing.

They all looked at Cass.

Cass looked like a new person. Her eyes were bright, her cheeks flushed. The weeks had taken a toll on her. But tonight, in the midst of all the sadness that the murders had wrought, there was new life in her eyes.

"Me?" she said innocently. "What's the question?" And then she laughed. "Ah, the land—Finnegan's wonderful land . . ." She looked over at Danny, whose eyes hadn't left her face. "Danny is helping me sort through it all. Sort of my sounding board."

"Meaning Cass talks and I listen," Danny said, his eyes still locked on hers, a look of pure pleasure on his face.

"But it takes a lot of trust to bare your soul to a writer," Cass said. "A lot. Trust, Brandley."

"Trust," Danny repeated. He nodded and moved closer, his hand reaching out and capturing hers.

"The land?" Izzy prompted,

Plans were taking shape. Ideas coming in. It would make Finnegan proud, Cass promised.

First, a cleanup. And then a memorial for Moira and Finn—with statues made by the Canary Cove artists and surrounded by yellow rosebushes. The statues would look out over the harbor, in the very spot where Finn had visited his wife's grave every single day.

Moira's favorite place on earth.

Laura Danvers was researching a small park for kids. Maybe

even a hot dog stand, like in the old days. A couple of new galleries—one of children's art? A beginning, for sure.

The trust fund was more than enough to put the Halloran Lobster business back on its feet, and Pete was already hiring help to take some of the work off Cass.

She'd also turned in her rental notice to Izzy. She wouldn't need her friend's house any longer.

Finnegan's old house on the hill was being renovated and brought back to its original glory with lots of big windows framing the sea.

Cass' mother was in charge. Mary Halloran had insisted on making the corner room on the second floor into an office for Danny Brandley—"Just in case," she said, without explaining herself further. It had four large windows that looked out over the water, the perfect spot for a writer, she'd said. If a writer should be in need of such a spot.

"Just in case, Ma?" Cass had asked. "In case of what?"

But she offered no objections.

And Mary Halloran was overjoyed.

Chapter 40

The Garden Celebration was set for Sunday morning, one that dawned with promises of a glorious day. Even the carrots and kale and beans were cooperating, poking up through the moist soil.

Much to Ben's delight, Annabelle Palazola had promised to have a booth down at the garden site so his Sunday morning would be complete—quiche and frittatas to go, she promised. Along with carafes of dark-roast coffee from Coffee's.

But as they came around the bend in Canary Cove Road and passed the entrance to Finnegan's place—already mowed and with the rusty fence removed—the biggest surprise was not Annabelle's booth or the green beans and spinach, or the music coming from Pete's Fractured Fish band.

It was Willow Adams' and Gabrielle Marietti's transformation of the community garden site.

"We bombed it!" Gabby yelled with great glee.

People were clapping and cheering. Oohs and aahs were everywhere.

"Indeed, you have," Birdie said. She looked around, her smile widening with each new discovery.

Yarn graffiti surrounded the area, dressing up the garden posts, the streetlights, the garden benches. Rakes and shovels—even the solar lights dotting the raised plots—had bright knit coverings. They were all decked out in every color of the rainbow. Stripes, polka dots, fancy knit neckties. At the entrance to the garden sat a lovely mermaid, completely covered in blue, green, and pink yarn, with neat ribbing outlining her form. A bright green crocheted beanie with an orange flower in front sat on her head.

"Aidan's mermaid," Nell said, emotion coating her words. It was Willow's father's wood sculpture, dressed completely in yarn, winsomely guarding the tomatoes and spinach.

"I've never seen anything like this," Ben said.

"And it explains where all my leftover yarn has gone," Izzy said in awe.

"And my often-missing granddaughter," Birdie added. Nick stood right behind her, his eyes on his niece. They were leaving the next day, a short trip to Maine. But at Gabby's insistence, they'd stop back on their way to New York. After all, she needed to check her garden. Her friends.

Her nonna.

And they'd be back often, both of them, Nick promised, every chance he got. Gabby needed Birdie, and the feeling was more than mutual.

Nick was considering a part-time position at Dana-Farber in Boston. That way he'd be halfway between the two most important women in his life. Not a bad place to be, he thought.

The graffiti artists, Willow and Gabby, stood side by side, collecting the comments and laughter and surprised exclamations happily. Willow looked at Gabby as the garden family gathered around the entrance, their mouths dropping open at each new graffiti discovery, their eyes as big as Gabby's.

"Should we confess everything?" Willow whispered.

Gabby's head bobbed, and they climbed up on the concrete garden bench, now festooned in lovely knit garters and leggings. They looked over to the edge of the crowd where Danny Brandley stood quietly next to Mary Halloran, watching the happy crowd. Gabby held both of her hands out to him.

"Our assistant!" she cried.

All eyes turned toward Danny, who laughed, then took a short bow, his face coloring.

"Danny was our chief helper," Willow told the crowd. "He can only knit, not purl, but he did a great job with the light post's garter and the fire hydrant's orange cape."

"Not to mention seven neckties," Gabby added.

Cass came up behind Danny. She pressed into his side, one arm looping around his waist. "I want one of those," she said, and pointed to the garter.

He kissed the top of her head.

Father Northcutt sobered the crowd, acknowledging the fruits of the garden with a short blessing. And then reminded the small group near him that the *Moira* would leave at noon.

And at noon, it did. The *Moira*—complete with its flagpole wrapped in Gabby's handiwork and filled from port to starboard with Francis Finnegan's friends.

Cass and Gabby stood at the bow as Pete propelled them out into the open waters, a blinding white path of sunlight guiding them.

Gabby climbed up on the step where the railings came together and threw her arms wide, miming the famous scene from *Titanic*, and those behind her laughed in relief as Cass pulled her back.

Their faces lifted to the sky, the puffs of cloud moving along with them, as if Finnegan were up there, leading the way.

It was Finnegan and Moira's grand hurrah, their ashes joined in a ceramic container that Ham Brewster fired for the occasion.

Pete, with Willow as first mate, took the boat out to a quiet spot beyond the breakwater, and Nick helped lower the anchor. The *Moira* rocked gently to lilting Irish lyrics spilling from Izzy's iPod.

Angus McPherran, standing with Sam, Ben, and Danny, stood up, thrusting a thick stein into the air. "Frolic in the deep, my friend," he said.

"To the Finnegans." The response rose in the air as glasses of iced tea and beer caught the sunlight and cast a kaleidoscope of white light across the deck.

Nell, Izzy, and Birdie stood behind Cass and Gabby at the railing, listening to the toasts behind them.

Gabby looked up at the sky. "To my best friend, Finn," she whispered.

Father Northcutt came over and handed her the brightly colored urn.

With Cass' arm steadying her, Gabby tossed the ashes into the sea.

"God be with you, dear friends," Father Northcutt whispered behind them. "Go in peace."

"In peace," Cass and Izzy, Nell and Birdie repeated, their eyes blurred and their hearts full.

In peace.

At last.

Gabby's Purple Cardigan

Designed for Gabby Marietti by Cheryl Erlandson

24" size 7 needles
40" size 7 to magic loop sleeves, or 7 DPN's
(5)(6) skeins of Aslan Trends Pima Classico (111 yds worsted weight
   cotton)
Stitch Markers
Button(s); sweater can be made with two small or one large button
Gauge: 4.5 stitches to 1"

Size
8–10, 10–12

Cast on 122 (128) stitches

Row 1:   K2 P1 rib to end, ending with K2.
Row 2:   P2 K1 rib to end, ending with P2.

Repeat for two more rows if you are using the larger button.

For **two small buttons**, work rows 1 and 2, and on row 3 knit to last
4 sts, K2 tog YO K2

Work three rows, and on next right-side row, repeat buttonhole again.

The next two rows are the set up for the **large buttonhole**.

Row 5:   Work K2 P1 rib to last 7 sts, and bind off 4 stitches for buttonhole and finish in rib pattern.

Row 6:   Continue in established rib pattern, and cast on 4 stitches over buttonhole and pattern to the end.

Repeat rows 1 and 2 for 2" from cast on edge, ending on WS.

Next row: Work in rib pattern to last 12 stitches, and bind off 11 stitches.

Next row: Bind off 11 stitches and continue in rib to end.
100 (122) stitches

Separation for body and sleeves worked in stockinette stitch.

Knit 20 (21)   stitches and place marker, knit 10 (12) stitches, place marker, knit 40 (40) stitches, place marker, knit 10 (12) stitches, place marker, knit 20 (21) stitches.

Next row: (Increase row) knit to one stitch before marker and KFB, slip marker, KFB, and continue increasing one stitch before and after each marker in this manner.

Next row: Purl all stitches.

Next row: Repeat increase row.

Repeat these two rows until you have 15 (16) increases

{35 (37) sts for the fronts, 40 (44) sts for both sleeves, 70 (72) sts for the back}

Next RS row: Knit to first marker, remove marker, place sleeve stitches on waste yarn, cast on 3 (4) stitches with backward loop cast on method, remove marker, and knit across back. Remove marker, place sleeve stitches on waste yarn, cast on 3 (4) stitches in same manner as before, knit to end. (146,152) stitches

Continue in stockinette stitch until piece measures 17" or desired length, from cast-on edge and bind off on knit row.

Remove first sleeve from waste yarn; join yarn and knit to end, pick up and knit 2 (4) stitches from cast-on stitches, omitting the center stitch, and join in round.

Continue in stockinette stitch for 5", and work 2X1 ribbing for 16 rows, and bind off loosely in pattern on the next row. (Use a needle one size up if you tend to bind off too tightly.)
Work second sleeve the same as the first.

Right front band: Pick up stitches along front edge with right sides facing, approximately stitch for stitch, making sure that the number of stitches are easily divisible by 3, and work 2x1 ribbing for 10 rows. Next row bind off loosely in pattern. Attach bound-off neck edge to band.

Repeat for left front band.

Weave in ends. Block and sew on button(s).

Add one adorable little girl, and enjoy.

Author's note: For more designs, visit
http://keepyourneedleshappy.com/shop/.

And for more about the Seaside Knitters, go to sallygoldenbaum .com and visit Sally on Facebook and Twitter.